-Not Him, Us

Tatum Dire

Crimson Pages, LLC

Second Edition 2024 Tatum Dire

Printed in the United States of America

Published by Crimson Pages, LLC

Edited by Morgan Waddle

Cover Design by Artista Gráfico

ISBN: 979-8-89372-036-5

Content Warnings

-Not Him, Us is a mature college/new adult dark romance that contains mature and graphic content. This is a reverse harem/why choose novel, meaning the main character has more than one love interest.

This book is not recommended for readers under the age of 18 and may not be suitable for all audiences.

Be advised; there is a high chance that this book will rip your heart out.

Please put your mental health first and read all content warnings before continuing.

Content Warnings:

Choking/Breath play

Sadomasochism

Knife play

Voyeurism/exhibitionism

Bondage

MM for FMC enjoyment

Blood/Pain kink

Domestic Abuse

Murder

Stalking

Self-harm

Suicidal ideation

Sexual Assault/ Non-con

Dub-con

Cheating (ex-boyfriend)

Drug use

Drugging without consent

Death

Vibes and Links

Check out my reader groups to connect and get exclusives!

Linktree

https://linktr.ee/tatumdireauthor

Playlist

Spotify @ Tatum Dire Author

"-Not Him, Us Vibes"

Mood Board

Pinterest

@tatumdireauthor

Dedication

To the love of my life,
you will always be my favorite anti-hero

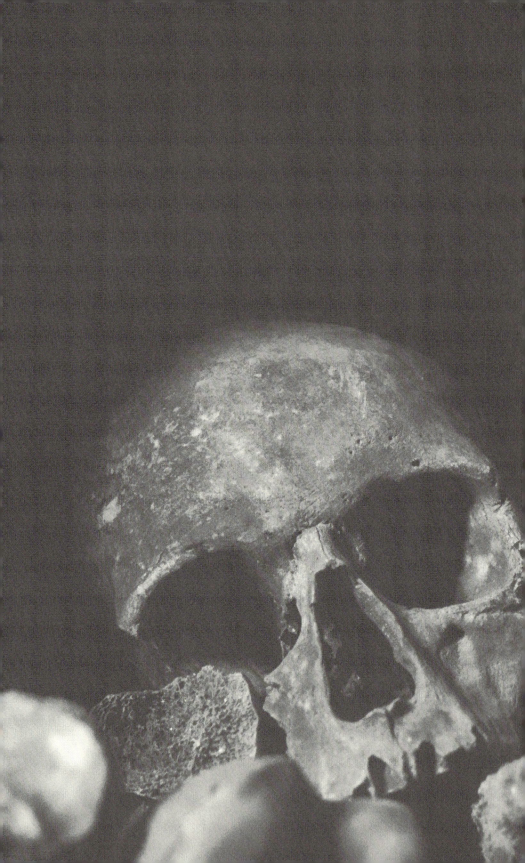

Not Him

My fisted hands shake and my stomach knots as I watch the news broadcast the crime that single-handedly ruined everything.

"A hit and run, in Acadia Creek earlier this week, killing our towns very own, Damian Mason, Lawyer at Davis Due Process. His funeral date is to be announced and at this time, the family has had no comments."

I was so close.

I crumple the letter I was going to leave for her that night. Now, a letter she will never read.

Meet me at 419 Reverence Rd.
-Not Him

I was finally going to show her who I was.

I had it all planned out. I was going to save her, and she was going to be happy with me.

Now, I will never have more of her than I do now. Letters, secrets, and stolen moments in the middle of the night.

I rip out another piece of paper and start over.

Shout at death like death can hear you. Be angry, ask why, and demand answers from the silence. Never go quietly. Set the world on fire, baby...

I do my best to soothe the pain I know will haunt her for years. A pain we will share, because for me, it will only ever be her.

And for her, I will only ever be...

Not Him.

Meet me at 419 Reverence Rd.

—Not Him

Shout at death like death can
hear you. Be angry, ask
why, and demand answers
from the silence. Never go
quietly.
Set the world on fire baby...

-Not Him

Amelia

Feeling my way through the nothingness, my arms stretch, reaching for anything to steady me. My chest feels hollow and heavy, like my body wants to rip in two, but something wills it to stay whole. Nothing but the sound of my own steps echo as I venture further, searching for any sign of life. Goosebumps prickle my skin- an intangible clue that someone is here.

I spin around, fear creeping in, overshadowing any hope. The weight on my skin grows heavier, like the presence is inching closer, stalking me like prey.

A whisper beckons me, and I turn again, my heart pounding. The faintest glow of a light in the distance greets me, sending its warmth.

I put everything I have into my sprint toward this unknown escape.

I run and run, but the light never gets any closer.

My chest heaves as I stumble, falling to my knees, and a sinister laugh echoes around me. I shut my eyes, refusing to look into the face of my murderer, welcoming death to take me.

Light flashes around me, my body warms, and another voice rumbles softly.

"Shh," it soothes. "Open your eyes."

But I can't. I try to force my eyes open, wanting to see, but the same thing that wills my body whole binds my eyes closed.

Please. I beg. Let me see him.

"Come with me," the voice whispers, the warmth around me slowly dissipating.

I try to stand from my cowering position but find myself stuck.

Please. Wait.

My skin grows colder.

Don't leave me.

Wait...

But the darkness looms again.

I jerk awake, finding myself in bed, sweat coating my skin. My heart still in a knot, tears soaking my cheeks. I miss the dreams that left me feeling hopeful in the mornings. These days all I get are night terrors and endless reminders of the hell that is my life.

My pain never goes away - it lingers. It creeps in as I fall asleep, then again when I wake up, and my brain grasps reality. It comes for me when one of my senses picks up something that inevitably returns a painful memory.

When I'm lying in bed, and the voice in my head gets louder and louder, chanting all of my faults, until it's screaming at me. When people surround me, and everyone wears a smile, everyone but me. Pain demands to be heard, and at some point, I can no longer shut it out.

My growing reality has amplified the pain digging its dagger-like claws into my heart. The man lying in my bed, the man I've been dating for years, does not love me. He may even be a stranger now.

I turn over, looking at the man I once loved, wondering how the hell we got here, and if I'll ever find the strength to get out.

The reality is I don't want to be alone, and honestly, I think I would die without someone next to me.

During my first year of high school, his charisma swept me off my feet. I fell hard and fast, letting my entire world revolve around him. After that first year, the truth crept in, month by month, and I tried so hard to ignore what he was proving to me.

It started small. He stopped wanting to hold my hand all the time and was *busy* more often than not. Then came the ignored calls, belittling my concerns, and embarrassing me in front of his friends. Eventually, it reached the point that he was blatantly ignoring my declining mental health, forcing me to have sex, and leaving me in unfamiliar places stoned out of my mind.

Anything would send him over. Speaking to another man while wearing shorts a little too short for Lance's liking had me labeled a whore. When I wore baggy clothes and stuck to the background, it made him want to prove he could find someone so much better than me.

I lost a little more of myself every time I accepted the shame he put on me and ignored the signs of abuse. Every night spent clinging to his side, knowing I was no longer the only woman in his life, my hold on him slipped. He pushed me further away with every lie, with every woman that laid in my spot in his arms. And every time I found a piece of myself and tried to leave, he made me feel crazy for thinking I could live without him.

No matter what I did, I lost.

And still, I beg him to choose and love me with every unwarranted apology I give.

And unlike every other college kid searching for their new identity, I've spent these years slowly losing who I am. These last days of junior year, I don't even recognize the person in the mirror staring back at me.

I am a shell - a shadow.

Day in and day I beg to be loved, but my pleas fall on deaf ears. With no love from others and no love for myself, I'm left with nothing but unkept promises, false hopes, and the desire to be anywhere but where I am.

Careful not to wake Lance, I turn back, then quietly pull out my journal from under the mattress and write another desperate letter to someone I have never met. To someone who has seen every piece of my soul.

I slowly rip the letter out and fold it before slipping it into the drawer of my bedside table, making a mental note to leave it outside for *him* tomorrow.

He is my escape.

Maybe I'm wrong for finding love and comfort in another man. But part of me is so irrevocably in love with what we have that I silently beg for the freedom and willpower to chase *him*. While the other part holds on to Lance, filling the void he leaves with *our* written words so I can still pretend he is everything I've ever wanted.

But I'm only lying to myself.

Coward, the voice deep inside me whispers.

I tilt my head to look back at Lance, still sound asleep before exchanging my journal for my most recently returned letter. Unfolding the paper, I look over the familiar writing again.

The secret words bring me a sliver of comfort; quite frankly, it's the only thing that makes me smile these days.

My finger brushes over the ink, and I try to imagine the hand that made the strokes. The hand that tells me even if breathing was the only thing I accomplished some days, it was something worth celebrating because I'm still here. I made the choice to stay, regardless of everything around me telling me to leave. And if I could only make one choice for myself each day, then there was hope.

But my anonymous writer would never physically be here for me. Never be more than words, slipped to me in the shadows to soothe my heart just enough to keep me hanging by a thread.

For a short time, I was convinced it was a sick prank. *His* words were too soft, *his* truths were too real. I thought there was no way a man would spill his heart onto paper in such a raw way and follow them with the heart-wrenching fact that he would never save me. I envisioned some preppy bitch pulling my letters out of her pink Dooney and Bourke purse, laughing as she slipped letter after letter into my locker, under the stalls, and in my window.

He didn't like that. His cologne wafted through my window that night. His presence warmed me, but I was too scared to open my eyes; not sure I wasn't dreaming. But I woke up the following morning to his letter. *His* words were fierce and angry because I was so lost that I had given up all hope that night.

I spiraled. I burned, and I bled. I drugged myself, and for the first time, I wanted to die.

He wrote more that night than any other. He saw my thoughts for what they were and shined a light on them when I couldn't. I was only trying to dig the knife deeper - trying to convince myself I had nothing to live for. *He* told me to focus on my surroundings and feel for him when I needed to feel his strength.

So, I did.

From then on, no matter where I was, I always searched for proof that *he* was near, as he promised. I felt his eyes tracking me through the halls of Acadia High. Sometimes the smell of his cologne blew through the wind, but no matter how hard I searched, I could never find proof of the person it belonged to.

Even if my dreams of one day being with *him* turn out to be wishful thinking, I can take everything he has taught me, look back, and say *I didn't give up on life*.

This world and the shitty people that walk in it will not consume me. It may splinter and agonizingly tear me apart, but it will not defeat me. It couldn't because there is someone on my side, silently watching, demanding I keep breathing.

Keep breathing.

A heat wave climbs my spine the way it does when I feel someone's eyes on me.

Fearing that I have woken Lance, I turn abruptly, finding him still asleep, and a sigh leaves my chest. My eyes drift through the window next to my bed, to the quiet night sky, and my mind drifts to the many nights in my old house when I felt that same warmth, knowing that the eyes I felt watching me in the dark belonged to someone who never wanted to be seen but would always be watching. Protecting.

Maybe he is near.

My heart is heavy but hopeful, and I squeeze my eyes closed as the voice chants in my head.

Alone. Coward.

I fight back. *Keep breathing. Just keep breathing.*

His letters have become less frequent, but he still writes and sees; still never coming close enough to be seen. He is broken like me. He understands and has always promised to be there, somewhere, but has made it clear that he would never be found.

There is a man in my bed, and I have never felt more alone.

***

As I drift deeper into sleep with the help of my usual poison of benzos, I hear a *ding*.

Then another... and another.

I sit up while rubbing my eyes, pause for a minute, training my ears to listen for it again. As the fog of sleep clears, the sound registers.

A message tone.

Who's blowing up my phone at this hour?

It's surely close to two a.m. now. I roll over to turn on my lamp, then check my phone. I wince as light temporarily blinds me, causing my eyes to sting. Once they adjust, I see that I don't have any notifications.

Not my phone then.

My roommate, and best friend, Jean's phone whistles that annoying bird ringtone, so most likely not hers either. That leaves one other phone.

Lance's.

My heart sinks, and bile rises to my throat. Should I check it? I try to convince myself going through his phone won't end well, but knowing this may be the only time I can get his phone in my hand is too alluring. Another one of the many red flags Lance has given me over the years.

Flags I force down in my little box of trauma that I try to ignore so I can pretend everything will be okay.

My anxiety is off the charts as I dig around for his phone, tangled in the blankets. Once I find it, my heart stops beating as I stare at the black screen. I begin second-guessing my decision to snoop.

Do I really want to see what I already know?

Looking will give me enough ammunition to end the relationship, leaving me utterly alone. If I choose to stay oblivious, my relationship remains, but so does the fact that I am not seen, heard, or loved. Either way, I feel pain, but if I choose to do this, there is no going back.

One shaky breath of cool air, in, then out.

One... Two... Three.

I click the side button, and disappointment hits my gut like a brick.

Shit.

Of course, he has his message previews turned off.

Wait!

Most iPhones are Face ID locked now. I don't need his code when I have his face right next to me, relaxed by an unbothered slumber.

He's a heavy sleeper, not even budging as I readjust myself to scan his face.

Click. My heart drops again, fear and anxiety swimming through my veins like fire. I flip it over to face me again and click messages. My eyes go to the first one I see, and I swear to God, the room starts spinning and closing in. My heart rate picks up, and I begin to sweat. Involuntary tears stream down my face and burn against my skin.

My stomach twists into a knot, and I think I'll throw up. I need to choose my next moves carefully. Do I read everything I can? Do I scream and throw shit or stay calm and collected? I'm unsure how to react, but I know I can't do this alone. I need someone to keep me from falling into a full-blown panic attack or possibly beating the shit out of him. I have never stood up for myself, so I'm unsure how my anger and pain will manifest.

I slide out of bed, walk eight feet to Jean's, and sit beneath the wooden "JJ" decor hanging on the wall. She stirs a bit and then sits up, her eyes wide as she sees my tears and shaky limbs. When she goes to speak, I hold a finger to my lips, silently instructing her to keep her voice down. I turn the phone towards her, brightness turned down, so she doesn't get blinded as I did, and I just stare at her while she reads the text message that shredded my heart and liberated my aching soul.

Rubie:
Did you wear a condom??

Amelia

The feeling of JJ reading over my shoulder makes my hair stand on end. Her breathing isn't as shallow as mine, but I can feel the anticipation rolling off of her.

Lance:
I miss ur pussy :P

Rubie:
Im late

Despite the vomit that threatens to spill out, I reread them repeatedly until it sinks in enough for me to continue. My eyes lift to my bed, where Lance still lies unconscious, and I fill with the urge to make sure he never wakes up.

"That sick fuck," JJ mutters quietly.

I say nothing. No words will come out, so I keep scrolling. I read over their plans to meet up at a party. Then it's the embarrassment that gets caught in my throat. I hate that JJ is reading this.

Lance:
Dont worry abt her. Shes so fuckn desprate I can fuck who I want

JJ drops her chin on my shoulder in a gesture of comfort.

Hot tears of hurt and anger stream down my face. I do my best to stay quiet, but clamp my hand over my mouth and cry into it. I scroll back to the bottom of the messages and my fingers rest over the keyboard. I watch the cursor blink as I debate whether or not to text her back.

"If you don't, I will," JJ says before opening her palm beside the phone.

I exhale a shaky breath in an attempt to get my bearings. I nod solemnly and begin typing.

> **Lance:**
> I dont remembr Itll be fine... What I do remembr is how good u felt :P

> **Lance:**
> What was ur fav part

I'm torturing myself. All the proof I need is right in front of me, but some masochistic part of me wants to see her respond live.

I look at JJ, and she nods. I switch the vibrate button on and hit send.

Rubie reads it in seconds, taking another minute to respond. The second the message comes in, my breathing catches, and JJ audibly sighs behind me.

> **Rubie:**
> I def <3 you bending me over the couch where anyone could walk in on us

> **Rubie:**
> I need $$ for a test just to be sure tho

So many emotions tangle inside of me.

He was so confident that he didn't even try to hide what he was doing. He didn't delete the messages. He wasn't even responsible enough to buy her a Plan B pill.

Disgust is the strongest emotion. I have spent years next to him as a laughingstock. I'm disgusted with him, myself, and everyone who has seen the truth with their own eyes.

I keep scrolling through the years of messages he kept on his phone. I find message after message to women I know and some I don't.

None of them turned him down. None of them said anything to me. All of them willing to sleep with a man in a relationship just because they could.

There are messages surrounding the time that my stepdad died. His police case was messy and drawn out, causing the grieving process to become prolonged and distorted. And not one person involved in all of this was concerned about me. Not even Lance.

For a short time, he attempted to show that he felt sorry for me, but when that time passed, he left me to get plastered with his friends constantly. All while getting laid because I was selfishly too tied up in grief to spread my legs.

I stop at a message from an unsaved number two months after my stepdad's death telling Lance to meet at the lake. He went. It was the night he walked in on me, cutting in the bathtub. The water was tinged pink, and I was slouched against the back of the tub. He came in to style his hair and never once looked at me as he informed me of necessary plans that he couldn't miss. I didn't try to stop him.

I spent so long convincing myself that our few good times were worth the lies, yelling, betrayal. The bruises. In my head, those few moments meant that some part of him still loved me, and I couldn't let that go. I had to hold on. If I followed him, he would see how devoted I was to him and would eventually fear losing me as much as I feared losing him.

I was wrong.

Lance doesn't nurture. He smiles and charms as he sneaks his cold hands inside of me, ripping my heart right out of my chest, muscle by muscle. Leaving it a bloody heap on the floor.

His lies in my head as I stare at another naked woman on his phone. I try to force my feet to move, but my head is spinning too much to allow it. As if my body knows I would fall flat on my face.

JJ sits there silently, her eyes watching me and her hands twitching as if waiting to catch me as she has so many times before.

There is no denying it now; no way he could spin it, and some fucked-up part of me wishes there was. My heart begging for me to lock his phone and pretend I saw nothing

But I did.

No matter how much my heart begs, there is no more future for us.

I have nothing left to lose and so much to gain.

Lance's voice echoes in my mind again. *Alone.*

Maybe there is peace in starting over.

He always told me to fight.

Well, here I fucking am. One step at a time, I will fight for what he has spent so long trying to convince me of.

I think about all the girls, fights, lies, and time lost. Anger boils through my veins, turning my blood hot and my cheeks red.

I am so over this shit. I do not deserve this!

My sorrow threatens to turn into the blinding rage that always scratched at the surface. I fight to shove it back down, digging my nails into the palm of my hand over and over, leaving blood-bruised crescents there.

It's time, I whisper to my battered heart, begging it to agree with my head. Its cracks and scars cry out to me, begging not to be ripped apart again.

I can't do this anymore; I silently try to rationalize with it.

"*You will survive. Not for anyone else, but because you will it.*" My voice recites the words of a voice from my dreams.

Heart pounding, I cross the eight feet back to my bed, where Lance sleeps soundly. With his phone gripped tightly in one hand, I slap him on the chest with the other.

"Wake up, you piece of shit." I spit at him, my voice shaking, the hint of rage resurfacing.

He jerks awake, popping up to a sitting position, and I cringe, instantly regretting my actions.

"What the fuck, Amelia?! What is your problem?!" He yells back.

I instinctively shrink, ready to apologize again, but JJ scoff steadies me. I take a deep breath, regaining my courage.

"My problem is that you've been fucking other girls for two years. You fucked *Rubie* two nights ago, and then come sleep in my bed." I say, bringing the phone inches from his face, distorting my own in disgust as I picture her wrapped around his dick hours before he buried himself inside of me.

I think I'm going to be sick.

"Why were you snooping through my shit while I'm sleeping?" He challenges, his face expressionless other than the squint from the light.

"I woke up to whoever the hell Rubie is, blowing up your phone, asking if you wore a condom when y'all had sex the other night because her period is late. For her sake, I hope you didn't get her pregnant. I would hate myself if I had to be tied to you for the rest of my life." I say blandly, hoping that it strikes home. "I prayed to God I was wrong, like you insisted I was. I looked past all the ways you hurt me because I loved you, but not anymore." Tears stinging my eyes, I swallow a lump in my throat, knowing this is the end.

There is no pride in the way I feel right now. Only an aching where my heart used to be.

He stares at me silently as he, no doubt, tries to think of a way out of this like he has many times before.

"I have seen everything with my own eyes, Lance," I cut in before he gets a chance to spew some bullshit to make me waiver. "There's no making me think I'm crazy this time. Get your shit and get out before I call campus security and tarnish your precious linebacker reputation."

His face reddens and I can't help the smirk. He'd be gone if they knew he was rigging those drug tests. He'd lose the only thing he really cares about in this world.

Standing quickly, he tries to take my face in his hands, but I shove them away before they can make contact.

Bile riles up, the disgust growing stronger.

I never once sat down and thought about all the places his hands and dick had been before coming back to my bed.

"Baby, please, can we talk about this? Privately," he asks quietly, his eyes jumping to JJ.

"I've already seen it all, you sack of shit," she says, crossing her arms. "Looks like I'm the only one who stuck by Amelia's side, and that's not changing now unless she requests it. Unlike you, I respect her," she says with a bite in her tone.

I look over my shoulder and give her a grateful smile before turning back to Lance, trying to hide the nervousness riddling my body.

"Okay, fine..." he starts. "I- I think I have a problem, baby. I think I'm a sex addict."

I let out a loud scoff. "Lance, do you hear yourself? I'm not doing this anymore!" I scream, frustration overriding any calmness I had left.

I'm surprised at my gall. I have never raised my voice to get my point across. My tears always take over and become a panic attack. So I choked my emotions down, letting the other person win. This time, something finally snapped.

"Do not fucking yell at me!" He shouts back, shoving his finger into my sternum and forcing me to take a step back, dropping his phone. "We are not breaking up! You love me. And I love you. We can fix this," he pleads pathetically, anger whispering across his face as if he is unable to hide his true motives this time.

I let myself see that. Focusing on the anger that should be guilt or even sorrow. He doesn't look like he is asking for forgiveness, just demanding something from me once more.

I stop the thoughts before my pathetic mind can form them. I cannot continue to surrender my self-worth for the feeling of familiarity.

I deserve to be loved. *Truly* loved.

"No. I may have loved you once, but I'm no longer in love with you. Whatever excuses you have, you can shove them up your ass and let Rubie, or one of those other girls you've screwed, eat it out." I throw back at him and turn to walk towards the door, intending to show him out immediately.

He snatches me by the hair and throws me into the bathroom door.

Fear strikes me as he grabs me around the throat tightly, cutting off my airway and staring into my eyes with nothing but blackness looking back at me.

JJ hurries to the front door and yanks it open, yelling for security.

"You are such a BITCH!" Lance booms, his face an inch away from mine. "I bet the reason you don't want to try to fix this is because you can't wait to fuck another guy like the trash that you are!"

I can see the sweat beading on his forehead, and I wonder if it is from his adrenaline or the hard drugs leaving his system.

Laughter tickles the back of my throat in hysteria.

I am so sick of it. I am so sick of being the punching bag for everyone.

Him. My mom. My thoughts.

He raises a hand and strikes me across the face, forcing my head to turn in his grip. Letting out a snide laugh, his entire demeanor changes.

"You know..." he says, his voice dropping low and his eyes darkening like I have never seen before, as if he is finally dropping his act. "I chose to stay with you all this time because I was having fun playing house, but now it's just to prove that I always get what I want. This is not over until I say it is."

He reaches between us and pushes his hand between my thighs, licking up the side of my face.

I still my features, not letting him get a reaction from me as he grabs his phone off the floor and storms out before security can get here.

The second he's out the door, JJ runs to me and wraps her arms around me.

I can't believe I let him be my everything when I was almost nothing to him.

I lean into her, letting her bear my weight. I feel lighter than before, like some of it has left with him.

"Oh, my God. I have never seen him act like that before," she breathes into the side of my head.

"I have," I murmur, making her step back. "He's never hit me before, just punched something next to my head. But he's grabbed me so hard it left bruises."

She gives me a sad look. "Why wouldn't you leave after that, Amelia? You are not stupid. Those are the first signs of domestic abuse."

I look down at the floor. I know she's right. He has scared me sometimes when it has gotten bad, but I chose to overlook it, like many other things. My mom got physical with me after the accident, blaming me for the death because of my choices that night and losing her shit mentally. So, some part of my head just told me it was just something I had to endure.

Now, I realize deep down I knew if I had tried to leave, he would've reacted exactly like he just did.

JJ doesn't wait for an answer. She already knows what I would say. "We will handle this day by day, and I won't pry, but you know I am not going anywhere."

God, I love her.

Security shows up and JJ handles it, giving them Lance's description and sending them away.

She walks me to the shower, knowing I will need some time to wind down before climbing back into bed. I will not be getting any more sleep tonight, or any time soon, for that matter.

The look in Lance's eyes rocked me to my core. I wonder how well he learned to read me and if he had seen that. I have a bad feeling Lance has more sides to him than he has shown me, and this time, it would be smart to trust my gut.

I needed to stay the fuck away from him at all costs until this blows over.

Fuck him. This is over.

He doesn't get to decide shit. Not anymore.

I climb into the shower and turn the water as hot as it will go, hissing as it hits my skin but forcing myself to endure it.

"I'll be in the room if you need me, okay?" JJ soothes, and just like that, I am left in peace.

Well, with all my thoughts. So not peace.

Alone. Burn. The voice taunts me, and I sink into my mind's familiar darkness, letting myself spiral.

Alone. So utterly alone.

Amelia

The next week passes by in a blur. I wrote another letter telling *him* about what had happened and where I am mentally. Leaving it in our new usual spot, under my car's windshield wipers.

But it's still there. Some days I take a peek out the window to see if he came, others I stare at it for hours.

He hasn't come to retrieve it, and the thought of losing *him* too makes me want to die.

I need *him* more than I ever have. So where is he?

I know he's gotten the news by now. Wouldn't that make *him* want to be a part of my life more? I always thought maybe he was waiting for things to end with Lance, like the respectable man he is, but now I'm not so sure.

Maybe it was just a fun little game of chase for *him*.

Maybe I have failed him.

Weeks blend together, and I'm just floating through the motions. Sure, I'm alive, but I don't feel like it.

Maybe I don't want to be.

I have more pain than happiness in my life. And the only thing I have for myself is my college classes.

I enjoy some of them, the art and the literature, but my degree was something I started pursuing to make my mother happy, so I guess in the end, that isn't mine either.

JJ hasn't left my side, skipping class with me. It's probably less to do with cuddles and more to do with her worrying I might take things a little too far if she's not here. I haven't hit rock bottom this hard since junior year, and the parallel of having someone leave my life has her freaked out. Worrying she might find me passed out on the bathroom floor, barely breathing again.

For the best part of the week, I've stayed high as a kite in my bed, watching "Shameless" on my laptop, eating my weight in pizza and chips, and barely speaking.

My grades were slipping there for a while, but JJ convinced one of her boy toys to turn in our work for us. That was the only way I was going to be able to keep my grant.

Thank all things Holy for pussy-whipped men.

I'm sure my mom has more than enough money to pay the expenses out of pocket if she hasn't blown it on God-knows-what, but that is one nuthouse I do not enjoy venturing into. Asking her for money that was rightfully mine would only result in a knock-down-drag-out that eventually had her passed out somewhere from her inability to stay sober after such a mental exertion.

JJ demanded I head outside for some fresh air this morning, thinking it would help.

It didn't.

My letter was still there.

I had a panic attack after another, crying so hard my eyes were raw and puffy, begging for the ground to swallow me whole.

Deciding that was enough reality for today, I smoked a bowl and took a few Xanax, hoping sleep would take me so deep I wouldn't remember my life or the nightmares that haunt me.

It mostly worked, the combo put me on my ass. My thoughts have quieted, and I can just be, but sleep evades me. Eyes closed, earbuds in, blaring on a 90s slow jams station, I lay curled in a ball.

I feel lighter now that I finally stuck to my guns and proved I was done being treated as less than I am. Even if the void Lance left burns like an open wound, and not in the way that I like. Yet the pain of *him* being absent hurts worse than any betrayal Lance had ever dished out.

And I can't even talk to JJ about it. I was always careful, keeping my letters a secret from everyone. An agreement between us to ensure whatever we had stayed untainted from outside thoughts.

JJ takes my right earbud out, and I look up to see her wrapped in a towel, fresh out of the shower. "I need to go to the store for some more snacks and stuff. Do you want to go, or are you okay here?" There's no pity in her tone.

She coddled me the first day, then decided tough love was what I needed to get out of my slump faster, and I was grateful for it.

I sit up. "I'll be okay, JJ," I reassure her. "And I'm feeling much better. Plus, I don't think dirty dick is stalking the dorm room."

She snorts a laugh at my nickname for Lance and smiles softly, seeing through my facade. I was doing better, but *okay* was not the word for it.

"Alright then, I'll be back in thirty." She throws on some clothes and heads out, locking the door behind her just in case.

I sit there staring at the wall, second-guessing my next decision. With my head in my hands, I play with my hair, telling myself this has to end. So why do I love the pain of it so much?

I finally get up and walk to our little kitchen, not wanting to dwell any longer. Our dorm is more like a tiny apartment.

My side sports more of a neutral color pallet, full of pin boards with Polaroids and notes, a desk that holds my schoolwork and laptop, and a bookshelf crammed with my favorite books. Those worthy enough to buy paperbacks of, even after reading them on my Kindle.

JJ's is vibrant and full of life. Perfectly expressing who she is as a person. A neon sign reading "Hello, Gorgeous" hangs above her bed and various colors of flower pillows accent it. The perfect ray of sunshine to my cloudy day.

Rummaging around in our junk drawer, I look for my lighter. I flick it once and stare at the flame, my eyes glazing over. I've always had a strange fascination with fire.

My mother was always preaching the old wives' tale that if you played with fire as a kid, you would wet the bed. But I think it was just something she made up to keep me from getting burned.

She never could have imagined I would grow to love the bitter bite on my skin.

Moving into our hardwood floored bathroom, I shut and lock the door in case JJ returns before I'm done. I pull my shorts off and sit on the floor with my legs in a butterfly position - feet together, knees falling to either side, exposing my scarred thighs.

It started as a way to cope with the stress of being the perfect child. It was a way to do something I wanted. I was in control of the pain I felt. Twelve-year-old me couldn't control anything else in her life but she could control this. Make herself less perfect in some way. In any way her mother couldn't control.

I've never felt the unconditional love that's supposed to come from a mother. She pushed me so hard to be perfect. Too hard.

To please her academically, I had to keep straight A's, play sports, and maintain hobbies. Socially, I was expected always to dress nicely, have any flaws covered by makeup, and always have popular friends and boyfriends.

Once I reached high school, she started grounding me if I began slipping in any of her sacred categories. It was like her love was waiting to be yanked away by a simple mistake or natural flaw that I couldn't control. She demanded perfection and punished me if she felt I had failed her. Never wiping my tears away when I did. It was figure out how to do it right or lose her love.

So I wore shorts long enough to cover my scars, even in a bikini, and only burned myself where I knew I could hide it or tell a believable lie about how it happened.

Lance never asked about them. He pretended they weren't there to avoid any conversation deeper than surface shit. Maybe that should have been a red flag, too.

But secretly I appreciated that he didn't ask. I was embarrassed by my actions. Why would someone who had it all need to self-harm, right? Any explanation would just sound like a spoiled brat throwing a tantrum to get attention.

Succumbing to my thoughts, I bring the lighter down to my thigh, trailing a line ever so slowly. Riding my high, the nerves are numbed just enough so all I feel is a delicious burn.

I pull it back, ignoring the smell of burning flesh, and lean my head back against the door. The visions of my past flash in my mind and disappear into the flames I conjure. Feeling sated, I take a couple of deep breaths before standing up to wet a cold rag and press it to my thigh, a soothing contrast to my aching skin.

I pull my shorts back on, light a candle on the counter to hide the smell, and return my trusty lighter to its rightful place. Just as I get situated back on my bed, I hear the door unlock, and try to calm my erratic heartbeat.

That was too close.

JJ comes prancing in, heading right toward me with a shit-eating grin. She jumps on my bed, straddling me and wrapping her arms around my back. Her weight on my lap causes my fresh burn to rub against my other thigh painfully. I force the discomfort into submission.

"Soooo," she says dramatically, and I roll my eyes letting let a small grin creep up my face, knowing she is up to no good.

She giggles and continues, "Tyler invited us to a party tonight. Wanna finally get out and have some fun?" Her eyebrows wag suggestively. "Hmmmmm?"

I want to say I'm not feeling up to it, but I stop myself, knowing I need to get out at some point. And I don't want to ruin the joy all over her sweet face.

She's talking about getting laid, and the thought of having sex with someone else for the first time in years makes me nervous.

Maybe a good party is what I need.

To get out, socialize, laugh, and dance.

It'll be good...not horrible at all...

"Sure," I say with a timid smile still trying to convince myself that this is not a horrible idea.

"There's my girl! Oh, how I've missed you!" she says dramatically, kissing me about a hundred times on the cheek. "Let's go party it up in honor of the last week of our junior year being over!" She cheers as she climbs off me and heads to her closet.

Shit. It's almost the end of the semester?!?

I had lost track of time in my wallowing. We had finished our finals the week before my shit hit the fan, so I know I passed with a solid C.

But I only have a few days to pack my room and move out for summer break now. Luckily, when I moved out of my mom's house, JJ and her parents offered to let me stay with them whenever needed.

Fuck Kinesiology, and thank Jesus for whoever JJ has been fucking good enough that he was willing to complete the last week of bullshit work for both of us.

I need to figure out who he is and thank him.

I might kiss him on the mouth now that I am a free woman, or maybe I should be praising JJ. Fuck it. I'll do both.

I inhale slowly, seeing all the possibilities of being single for the first time since I was fifteen.

Cheers to senior year, bitches!

Amelia

I dress in my favorite black leather skirt that cups my ass perfectly, and pair it with a black bodysuit, solid cotton in the front with sheer lace down the sides, allowing my dragon tattoo to peek through. I add my black thigh-high boots and gold dangly earrings. Smokey eyeshadow and deep purple lips stand out against my raven-black hair that falls to the middle of my back.

JJ comes out of the bathroom, having just finished with her makeup, as I shove my weed into my boot. Her favorite pair of black leather pants and a pink spaghetti strap bodysuit show off her breasts well. She has me beat by a whole cup size. Her pink lipstick matches perfectly, and her lightly curled caramel brown hair is only a few inches shorter than mine.

We take each other in and simultaneously catcall each other with a loud, "daaamn."

She takes my hand in hers and excitedly leads me out of our dorm, locking the door behind us. Her keys and phone get shoved into her back pocket as we approach her car.

We arrive close to 10 P.M., the street and front yard already flooded with cars.

The cool night air teases my bare skin as I try to soak in the good vibes around me, willing myself to have a good time. To forget everything that makes me want to curl up in my bed with sad songs and ice cream.

The music and chatter gets louder as we make our way up the driveway, and my skin buzzes with excitement that I welcome.

I take in the large three-story house that sits on the north side of Acadia. The soft lights wrapped around white pillars illuminate the white brick, and the huge windows give a clear view of the beautiful interior. A beautiful fountain sits in the middle of the lawn.

My ears strain, wanting to hear my favorite sound of water falling, but find it nearly impossible due to the commotion.

Tyler walks out through the floor-to-ceiling door, instantly spotting us. He closes the gap between us and wraps his arms around JJ, lifting her off the ground, causing her little feet to hover above the rocks.

She giggles as he sets her down with a peck on the cheek, followed by a few whispered words I'm sure I didn't want to hear.

He looks us over, eyes sparkling with delight, then runs a hand through his hair and down his face as he sighs.

"You two are going to get into trouble tonight, huh?"

"That's the plan," JJ says with a saucy wink, bumping her hip into mine playfully.

"Oh, by the way, slacker, you're welcome for the help with your homework and covering for your asses with the dean," he says, pointing a look at me.

Ah, the pussy-whipped friend.

JJ isn't the girl who sleeps with a never-ending list of men. She usually has a select 2 or 3 that she rotates, and they always know about the situation. They are more casual hookups, none of them looking for something serious.

Or, they weren't the last time I checked.

It looks like JJ and Tyler might have something more going on. Which might explain why she is looking at him like magical wishes come out of his dick when you suck.

Maybe kissing him in thanks isn't the best idea.

"Ha, thank you, Tyler," I snort, feeling a little pitiful, but ever so grateful.

He shrugs and turns back to JJ.

My boots click on the wide steps as we walk into the house. As soon as we reach the threshold, Tyler steps in front of us, cupping his hands to his mouth.

"The party's here!" he yells.

Nearly every head turns our way, and I want to shrink into myself. I don't do crowds.

"Jesus, Ty," JJ teases, but instead of matching my pink cheeks, she smiles huge. Loving the attention despite her protest.

He turns and winks at her. "Just giving my favorite girl some deserved attention. I'm gonna go grab some drinks."

I turn to JJ as soon as he is out of ears reach. "You and Tyler, huh?" I ask, nodding towards the man in question.

At five foot nine with blonde hair with a medium fade, always freshly cut. He's not bad looking by any means.

Her cheeks turn a shade of pink, and her eyes dip to the floor. "Uh, yeah. I didn't want to mention it because we only started talking more a few days after-" A nervous look takes over her face.

Ah, I see.

"JJ, come on, you know you can always talk to me, no matter what I'm going through," I reassure her, sending a soft smile, meeting her eyes so she knows how serious I am.

I don't like when people walk on eggshells around me.

Yeah, I have a lot of shit to deal with, but I'm not made of glass. She knows almost every secret I've ever had and has told me every truth I needed to hear. Even if it pissed me off, and vice versa. Our bond is unbreakable.

She nods nervously. "We aren't serious, but I like spending time with him. He makes me laugh and accepts me for me. We aren't insecure about whatever *we* are and just kinda vibe together," she explains unnecessarily, as if she is still not convinced I am okay with her being in a relationship just because mine ended.

"I'm happy for you, JJ. Really, I am. He seems like a cool guy, and from what I can see, whatever y'all have going on works for y'all."

I take her hand, and we walk around the crowded house. Tyler finds us with our first drink, and we wander off again. Talking to people we know, making new friends, and dancing our ass off.

JJ manages to keep me busy. Parties have never been my scene, but I can't lie and say I'm not enjoying this more and more every hour.

The smell of spilled beer, body sweat, and weed waft around me. I inhale deeply standing in the corner, talking to a group of girls I vaguely remember. JJ talks freely, it coming naturally to her, as I stand idly beside her, half listening to the gossip and half people watching.

My social battery drained, I begin to let myself mentally fade into the background. But I'm not ready to go home and fight with myself, so I politely pull JJ to the dance floor with the determination to grasp onto what's left of my manic behavior.

I light the pre-rolled joint from my boot, and put it out on the heel of my boot after taking a few hits. Then, I let the music take me even higher.

My hands roam up my body seductively. The feeling becoming more intense as I feel someone's eyes on me, as if they are peeling my clothes off with the motions of my hands. I glance around, and for a split second, my eyes connect with dark irises somewhere in the back. But once someone passes in front of them, they are gone. The heat on my skin lessens at the loss, and now I want to seek that warmth out.

Before I can move, JJ bends over in front of me, grinding her ass on my crotch. I grip her hips and cheer her on as she uses me like a pole.

A few guys near us turn to watch. One approaches, trying to take my place, and I swiftly palm his forehead in rejection. He tries again, this time getting JJ's attention with the hope of a different reaction.

The second she feels his hands on her, she stands up straight. Side by side, we stand, unmoving with blank expressions.

Finally taking the hint, he scoffs and moves on with a bruised ego.

We laugh hysterically as we mock him, utterly enjoying knocking a grossly entitled man down a few pegs, and then we continue dancing.

"Hot In Herre" by Nelly ends, and we are sweating, out of breath, and tipsy. The flip cup table opens up, and I take the opportunity to cool off. We claim the next round against two guys.

The one with shaggy blonde hair glances up at us, then, just as fast, looks back down to where he resets the cups. I swear I saw him roll his eyes, and I narrow my own at him. The side of his lips tip up in a small smile, and I wonder if he can feel my eyes boring a hole into his forehead. He tongues his silver lip ring, drawing my attention to his small pink lips. Then his partner speaks, pulling my attention to him.

"You two ladies looking to get your asses beat?"

He has dark brown hair, maybe even black, and a narrow face with a defined jawline. A fucking walking orgasm, but that may just be my under-met sexual needs about to burst at the seams. Standing a few inches shy of six feet, he peers down at me from across the table, and I realize I have been ogling him instead of answering his question.

Fucking hell, Amelia.

"Is that a threat or a promise? Because it doesn't sound like a bad time," I quip, meeting his intense stare. Letting my desire take the lead and immediately hating myself as a filthy grin spreads across his beautiful features, nearly making me drop my panties right there.

What the fuck are you doing?

"Alright, dirty girl. You're going against me."

I flash a mischievous smile right back at him, lining up at the front of the table while the blonde refills the cups on both sides. I toss my long hair behind me and ready myself.

It's just a little fun, right? I deserve that much, at least.

"What do I get if I whoop your ass instead?" I ask before we start.

Mr. Walking Orgasm leans across the narrow table, a few inches from my ear. His warm breath tease my neck as he answers, "Oh baby, I'll give you anything you want from me."

A delicious tingle spreads over my body, settling right between my thighs, making me slick with desire.

"Challenge accepted," I say, shaking his hand to confirm our deal.

Tyler comes up behind JJ just in time to watch the bet take place and volunteers himself to be our official referee.

"We got a challenge on the tables over here," he howls, and we're instantly crowded by a few dozen people wanting to see how it plays out.

I look around the crowd nervously, making eye contact with a mountain of a man.

His jaw is clenched, his hands fists by his side. A strange inkling that I know him lingers, but I'm unable to place how. He doesn't look like anyone I know. Short brown hair, a sharp square jawline, piercing honey eyes. He looks like he could snap me in half over his knee.

His mouth parts like he is going to speak, but another guy bumps into him, drawing his attention.

I use that to refocus on the game and on the man dripping with sex across the table.

"I must warn you, we are a lethal team," he says, his eyes begging me to stay for the challenge.

"Don't underestimate people you haven't met." I say, bracing my hands on the table. Using my liquid courage and lack of give-a-fuck to take it one step further, I wink across the table at him.

"Easy now." He places his hand on his chest, clutching his heart. But I don't miss the way his eyes slightly darken.

I hear someone shout off to my left. "Motherfucker!" The huge man from earlier booms, shoving people out of his way and grabbing a girl on his exit in a testosterone tornado.

I have to physically hold back the scoff daring to rip through my throat at how familiar that looked, only now I'm on the outside. I'm free.

I look back across the table once more finding our opponents staring in the same direction I was. Green eyes turn back to me with a smile so intense I have to break the contact before I blush.

Then with no warning, Tyler yells, "Go!"

JJ and the blond finish at the same time. Then it's me and Mr. Walking Orgasm.

He holds my pace for the first few cups but fumbles the next after watching me chug my cup so fast, beer trails down my jaw and onto my chest, his eyes following. My nipples harden at the cold contrast to my sweaty skin, and my chest rises and falls with labored breathing from the rush of the game. His movements are still for a split second, but that's all I need.

He's still chugging his last while I try to land my last cup. The crowd is going nuts, everyone chanting for their victor. Just as he goes to attempt his first flip, mine lands and everyone screams at the top of their lungs.

Tyler grabs me by the hips and throws me up on his shoulders, jumping up and down, yelling with the rest of the crowd. He sets me down, and everyone praises me with high-fives or exaggerated bows with their arms stretched out in my direction. I giggle and take it in, loving the unfamiliar feeling.

What's the big deal?

Regardless, I am so glad we came out. I'm having a blast and can physically feel my stress dissipating.

Heartbreak who?

The crowd eventually leaves, going on about whatever they were doing prior. Tyler is hanging off of JJ, and looks at the man I just wiped the floor with. "Damn it, Finn, you are no longer the reigning champ. Mel kicked your ass!"

So, Mr. Walking Orgasm has a name.

Reigning champ?

That's why everyone freaked out. I can't deny the feeling of pride it gives me.

Finn walks around the table and looks me up and down. "She sure did. Great game, Mel," he says, stretching out his hand. His eyes shimmering with all promises of filthy things in the most respectful way.

Hearing my name on his lips makes my knees weak and my throat dry.

"Amelia," I counter. "And thanks." I stretch my hand out for a handshake, but he flips it over to kiss my knuckles.

Fucking swoon.

"I like Mel better."

I quirk a brow at him, but he holds my stare. I'm unable to break my gaze away and acknowledge that there are other people in the room. A lot of people.

"Oookay, Ty and I are going to go dance," JJ says and slaps me on the ass, walking away as if to encourage me further.

"So," Finn says, leaning against a wall. "Fair is fair. What do you want for your epic win, dirty girl?"

Amelia

I have never been one for one-night stands, but right now—*Why the fuck not?*

He has got to be one of the sexiest men I have ever seen in my life. He looks a few years older than me, and almost every part of me wants to see what he has to offer.

I tap my chin playfully as if pondering what I could want. "I believe I recall a promise of whipping my ass."

His eyes darken with a touch of humor. "I see. Well, in that case..." he trails off, throwing me over his shoulder, his hand resting firmly below my ass, holding my skirt down.

I squeal as he takes off, running up the wooden stairs to the second floor. My head bobs above his tight ass, and for a second, I think about calling this off. But the smell of amber, soap, and musk have my mind swirling with anticipation.

Turning into the first open bedroom, he spins to lock the door, then walks over to the bed slowly, with me still over his shoulder. The moonlight pours through the window lightly illuminating the room.

Hopefully it's dark enough that he can't see everything. I take a deep breath, steading myself. The room smells like him.

Is this his house?

He slides me back over his shoulder but stops when our eyes are level, gripping my ass, and I wrap my legs around his waist.

"God, you are gorgeous," he says softly, trailing kisses down the side of my neck, the smell of liquor on his breath. His deep voice and wet kisses make my body ache with need.

Knees against the bed, he lowers me down, never taking his mouth from my skin.

I sigh, realizing just how badly I have been wanting this - playfulness. The excitement and butterflies, things I haven't felt in a long time.

He pushes me further on the bed and crawls up to straddle my waist. Leaning over to cup my face, stopping just short of a kiss.

Ummm... Why are we stopping?

"Wait... you're gonna call me after this, right?" he teases.

"Oh, I don't know. I just got out of a pretty brutal relationship. I don't know if I'm ready for that kind of commitment," I play back with a half-fake look of nervousness.

"Oh, so you're just using me?" he says, giving me a sad look.

"Is that not acceptable?" I ask, raising a brow and chewing on the side of my lip.

He leans to my ear, whispering. "Baby, I told you I would give you whatever you wanted from me."

My smile quickly turns into a slack jaw as he slips between my legs, pushing my skirt over my ass, lifting my hips. A chill rushes to the freshly exposed skin, and a small gasp escapes. It may not be dark enough in here to conceal my scars.

He pulls my panties down, bends my knees, and plants a trail of wet kisses, nibbling down my thigh.

I squirm and wiggle as he teases me, my hips searching for friction. My heart racing at how close his lips are to the rough skin of my scars. Even if he can't see them, he's about to feel them.

His lips brush over the raised skin of one of my larger burns, pausing, and my heart sinks.

Laying as still as possible, I wait for his reaction.

Moving again, he tentatively runs his thumb over the skin he just kissed, before kissing a few more scars and trailing to hover at my center.

The warmth of his breath has me throbbing with anticipation, adrenaline causing my heart to beat painfully in my chest.

He tilts his head up to look at me giving me a chance to stop this before I do something I regret.

But no matter how hard I search, I can't find even an ounce to care. There is nothing in me saying this man cannot be trusted with my life.

"Tell me what you need, baby," he purrs, then drops his head, taking the tip of his tongue through the center of my lips before separating me with his hands. He flattens his tongue, slowly rubbing over my clit again and again.

Lifting his head slightly he smirks, giving off some big dick energy.

"You like that?" he asks in a voice so deep and sexy I moan a sound of approval, halfway to an orgasm already.

He smiles against me. "You taste so fucking good."

My heart stalls at the dirty praise. I have never been talked to like that, but shit, I want him to say more.

He flattens his tongue again, licking me from bottom to top, before taking my clit in his mouth, giving it a gentle suck. He lets it free with an audible pop, and I jerk, gasping as he goes right back. Providing gentle circles that feel so fucking good. I can't keep the soft groans from filling the air.

My back arches, my body begging for more, and he slips two fingers inside me, curling them just right.

Jesus Christ, have mercy. It's never felt this good.

I reach for his dark hair, pushing his face further between my legs, and he gives me exactly what I want.

He licks the wetness dripping down my ass and moves back up painfully slow. His tongue works me over furiously, like making me come is his mission in life. Such a contrast to any sexual experience I have had before.

"Oh God, Finn!" I yell, not caring if anyone hears me, but it's unlikely anyone will.

He squeezes my breast firmly, and my thighs clamp around his head, as he pulls his fingers out of me. With both hands, he pushes my thighs back open.

"I can't give you what you need if you don't give me room to work, baby girl."

Fuck! I would call this man daddy on any given day.

My legs go slack, and he goes back to work. Licking me so intensely that my hips ride his face and fingers. That warm tingle starts to build in my stomach, toes curling and I grip on his head tightening.

"Right there," I whine, "Don't stop."

He obeys, keeping his pace, allowing me to take what I need.

"Fuck! I'm gonna come!"

"Come for me, baby," he encourages, and that's all I need.

A vigorous orgasm tears through my body, and I dig my nails into his skin, dragging them over his shoulders.

He groans, not stopping until I relax into the soft sheets.

He moves up, wiping his mouth while I'm panting. I stop his hand, pulling him in for a kiss, pushing my tongue into his mouth, wanting to taste myself on his lips. Breaking our kiss, he begins trailing more sloppy kisses down my throat, rubbing his hard cock against my bare and sensitive skin.

"You really are a dirty girl," he says between kisses. "Is that all you wanted from me, or do you demand more from such a devastating win?"

As if this is still solely about our bet, we both know it's not.

I sit up and lean into his ear, my lips brushing the shell. "Baby, I'll give you anything you want from me." I mimic his words playfully, but there is no lie or joke within them right now.

He lets out a little laugh as he frantically takes off the rest of my clothes followed by his own.

"Oh, I'm sure I can come up with something," he teases, rolling us over and pulling me on top of him.

Grinding back and forth, I spread my cum along the shaft of his dick.

He tilts his head back, hands grabbing my hips raising me up, before letting go to line his cock up. His hands move to my hips and slowly guide me down.

We moan simultaneously, and hearing his gives me a feral urge.

"I need you to come all over my cock."

Your wish is my fucking command.

I move my hips back and forth, pushing as far back as our bodies will allow so I can feel the burn of him being as deep as possible.

His eyes stay glued on mine as if he can see into my soul, and I slightly cower.

Don't look too close.

His grip gets tighter, and I move faster. Leaning back, I grab his thighs, eyes closed, taking in the beautiful sounds of his pants and grunts.

That familiar warmth begins to build again as I lean forward, my face in the crook of his neck as my hips rock. The position rubs my clit perfectly.

My breathing grows short and labored. "Fuck. I'm going to come again already."

A slap across my ass shakes my focus

"Not yet, you're not," He demands sharply flipping us, so I'm on my stomach.

He pulls up on my waist, lifting me to my knees, and pushes in with a groan. Fingers trail the snake tattoo down my sweaty spine, making me light-headed. They grip my hips, finding the crease between my thigh and my ass.

"I'm almost there. You ready?"

I nod, my voice not working while he's balls deep. Smacking my ass every few thrusts, then rubbing firmly to soothe the burn.

He pounds into me unyieldingly while I rub my clit slowly, careful not to come before he's ready. I'm not sure why I care, but he has my devotion. Enjoying the drawn-out ecstasy for a few more seconds, I let little whimpers slip into the air around.

He gives my ass a punishing smack and grunts.

"Now."

I rub myself furiously a few times before he pulses in me, sending my world spinning.

"Ah, fuck," he grunts, the low tenor of his voice making me tighten around him even more.

My vision darkens, and I fall apart as my orgasm rips through my body again, this one even stronger than the first. I swear I feel it in my toes.

He rolls off of me, laughing and panting. I roll to my back, feeling like a bowl of Jello, watching him discard the condom I didn't see him put on.

You dumbass! You didn't even make sure he had a condom.

I don't feel ashamed but, some illogical part of my heart aches with betrayal.

Finn smiles like the cat who got the cream, and pulls me over to him. And for the slightest moment, I hesitate, then cave, unable to prevent myself from succumbing to the warmth and comfort surrounding us.

Why are we cuddling? Is this something one-night stands do?

"I like you," he says into the dark, and it takes me a minute to register that he is talking to me.

"Oh yeah?" I ask, keeping my eyes low, but curious.

"Yeah," he chimes, and I swear I can hear the smile on his face without looking.

"I'm going to be real with you," I say, "I've never had sex like that, and it was probably the best I've ever had."

He chuckles. "Top three for me, for sure."

I drop my mouth open at his joke, then slap him on the chest. At least, I think it's a joke. Maybe he is being honest.

He laughs even harder.

"So that ex-boyfriend wasn't any good, huh?" he teases, and my skin goes cold, making me tense, leaving his playful question unanswered.

"Hey, I'm sorry," he says pulling my chin to look at him. "I didn't know you were serious about the *just got out of a relationship* thing. We don't have to talk about anything personal if you don't want to, but this is a judgment-free zone."

"Do you ask all of your sexual partners to spill their trauma?" I laugh softly, trying to lighten the mood, unable to pull myself out of the darkness clouding my head.

I take a minute to think, not hearing his response.

Deciding I'm still a little drunk and could use a new ear, I leap. "It ended about a week ago, and it... *was* brutal."

"Brutal, how?" he asks, and I think I hear a touch of concern riding his inquiry, and it feels good. So good.

"Well... long story short, our relationship started going south years ago, but I kept brushing it off. I should have trusted my gut because I found proof that he had been cheating on me the past two years, making me feel crazy whenever I questioned him. When I finally had undeniable proof, it got physical, and he refused to accept that I was done. Hearing it all out loud, I sound like an idiot for not seeing him for what he was long ago."

"That doesn't make you an idiot," he cuts in before I can give anymore. "It makes you hopeful and full of love. Sometimes love can be blinding in the worst ways."

"Yeah, I guess." My fingers draw circles on his chest idly. "I did love him, but I don't think I've been in love with him for a long time. Now I'm just pissed and don't know if it's at me or him. I hate that I let him add to the shit I was still dealing with."

"You want to share that?"

I hesitate, but when I look up into his brown eyes, all I see is affection and sincerity.

How could someone I just met convince me that they feel more concern for me than most people I have had in my life?

So I cave.

I cover all bases, probably more than I should, given that I don't know a fucking thing about him. I explain my childhood with my mother, never knowing my real dad, my self-harm, and then move into my stepdad's death.

"He died three years ago in a car wreck, hit by a drunk driver on the way to come get me from a party when I was seventeen. Damian married my mom when I was eight." I shrug, "He's the only father figure I've ever had, but he was more than that to me. He was my best friend before I met JJ when I was twelve. Even then, he was a close second."

"Anyway." I shake my head. "That night, my DD ended up drinking, and it wasn't safe to walk, so I called him. He never minded - always happy that I made the responsible choice... His death was hard on me, and I stayed holed up in my room for months. A few weeks after his funeral, my mother began to dope up on drugs and booze, so I wasn't really able to grieve properly. In her frequently intoxicated state, she constantly told me that he wouldn't have died if I hadn't called him that night."

Finn pulls me in tighter, stroking my hair, holding me as I continue to word vomit.

"She wished I would move away, so she didn't have to look at me anymore. She's pushing me away, relentlessly pounding me with words that cut like knives. I know it wasn't my fault directly, but after years of drunken phone calls, hearing that it was... the voice in my head began to side with my her."

Your fault. Your fault. Your fault.

"I'm just a big mess right now, but I'm trying to keep my head above water, you know?"

He's still stroking my hair, a comforting touch that keeps me calm, but a little strange.

"You may be a little bit of a mess up here," he taps my temple, "and understandably so, but I think you still have a lot to give in here," He says touching my chest above where my heart should be.

"You don't seem like the type of person that wants someone's pity, so I'll just say everyone has baggage and handles it differently." He pulls my face to his, making sure our eyes lock. "Don't ever feel embarrassed about how you chose to cope with what this world has done to you. However, moving forward is something that you have to do. Harming yourself doesn't need to be done when you find someone willing to help you carry the weight. While also giving you hot sex, of course." He smirks.

I don't reply to his comment about my scars because there is nothing I can think to say. It's not something I am ready to give up.

But I think about what he's said, what he's done.

How in just a couple of hours, he already seems to read me like a book. How he has shown me more kindness than Lance ever did.

Lance never wanted to sit and listen to how I felt.

We never had a true heart-to-heart conversation about anything. Maybe it was always about sex, and I just didn't see it until he made it impossible not to.

So why didn't he just leave if he wasn't happy?

My thoughts cut like razors, opening all the wounds I have tried to close for the past two weeks.

Do we live a destined life, every minute written in the stars? Or do we make our own happiness and cause our own dismay?

For the first time I am honest with myself.

Change is what I feared.

Being forced into the unknown. Being somewhere new with no safe space to hide when I got scared.

I am scared.

I fear Lance and his words laced with a promise.

I fear my thoughts, never allowing me to search for happiness, consuming me with darkness and screams.

I fear everyone around me, not knowing who will hurt me but unable to stop myself from diving into them the first opportunity they give.

I fear my mother's actions and words, praying to God that my mind doesn't grasp one of the grief-riddled insults she stabs me with and decides that it is the last that my heart and soul can withstand.

I close my eyes as I try to push out the thought sneaking up. I don't want to die, but this isn't living.

You will survive because you will it.

I take a breath and force myself to focus on the present. Focus on the steady hands holding me, the warmth and love I feel in them already.

"So, do you usually cuddle your one-night stands?" I tease, wondering what the hell is going on but not wanting it to end. I move my head to rest on his chest to look at him.

He looks at me like he knows what I want his answer to be.

No, only with you.

"I have had a few one-timers, but it's usually more of what Tyler and your friend have, and no, I don't usually cuddle." He laughs like what we are doing is ridiculous, but somehow it feels right.

"Ah, I see. And what if I say all I wanted from our bet was a one-night stand?"

He hums. "Well, I guess I would have to honor the terms of a deal. However, I sincerely hope that's not all you want from me. I'm not sure I could stay away if you asked me to." He states matter-of-factly, taking me by surprise and causing my stomach to flip.

I by no means want another relationship right now, but I'd be down to hanging out with good sex on the side to keep me distracted.

"Well then, it wouldn't be fair of me to ask." I smile. "I also just spilled my whole life story to you, so I gotta keep you around now to make sure you don't use me as the butt of your jokes," I say, teasing him. "I'm sure we could be good friends."

"With benefits, right?" he asks, pulling me on top of him.

"Why, of course. Just don't catch feels for me." I wink at him, but the reality is I'd be the one to fall.

He lets out a playful growl, pulling me in and biting my neck.

I most definitely can work with this.

We lay there a little longer, talking more about him.

"Okay, quick rundown version of me," he says stroking my arm. "Twenty-four. Going to college for psychology. Living here with my friends by choice, but my uncle gave me a place in the city when he left to travel."

"He just gave you a house?" I ask lifting my head.

"Yeah," he says pushing my head back to his shoulder. "He's my legal guardian."

I want to ask more, but he didn't push me so I return the favor.

We sit in comfortable silence until about 2am then decide to get dressed and rejoin the party, which should be thinning out. I do my best to fix my smeared makeup and tousled clothes.

"Don't worry," Finn says, coming up behind me and gripping my hips. "You look beautiful."

I blush and follow him out of the room, eyeing the red scratches I left just before he pulls his shirt down over them.

JJ spots me on the stairs, through the ten or so people left. She's matching my 'just had sex' look, and we both grin at each other.

We grab our things and head to the door. With great sex, a heart-to-heart, and a lack of alcohol the past few hours, I am definitely sober. So reluctantly, I will be the one to drive us home.

Tyler pulls JJ to the side to tell her goodbye, and Finn grabs my hand and pulls me in for a soft kiss, gently resting his hands on my ass.

"Call me if you have trouble sitting down tomorrow, and I'll come and kiss it better," he whispers in my ear. His dirty promises give me tingles all over my body again, so I push away from him before I climb him in the middle of this room.

"Well, in that case, I need your number, friend." I smirk, purposely pushing his buttons.

He takes my phone out of my skirt pocket with a tug and types it in after I unlock it.

"With benefits, don't forget that part, dirty girl."

Why do I feel like that nickname is gonna stick?

As I put my phone back in my pocket, JJ is perfectly in sync, meeting me at the door, and we turn to leave. We are about halfway down the driveway when I see Finn standing in the doorway.

"Goodnight, Mel," he semi-yells.

I press my lips together to hide my smile, "Goodnight, Finn."

Amelia

I tap my phone idly against the windowsill staring at the piece of paper still tucked beneath my windshield wipers. It's been three days since the party, and besides the fact that *he* hasn't come for my letter, all I have been able to think about is Finn. Already becoming more attached than what we agreed on. Unlocking my phone, I stare at his name and contemplate texting him for the hundredth time.

"Get up, bitch," JJ says busting into the room. "We have a double date at Dixie's."

Without hesitation, I jump up from my bed and attempt to throw together an acceptable outfit. I stop with a shirt halfway over my head and scowl at my best friend. "We are not dating."

She smiles mischievously. "Sure," she purrs dramatically.

I roll my eyes, but can't help but wonder if Finn thinks this is a date. The last thing I need is get my hopes up on a man that only wants to fuck.

But here I am, doing exactly that.

I would rather burn than not feel everything he has to offer.

I pair my ripped shorts with an oversized tee, high tops, and hoop earrings. My hair goes into the kind of messy bun that takes ten minutes to perfect before coating my lips with a light pink gloss.

JJ is dolled up a bit more than I am, but I don't want to look like I prepared for an actual date.

We hop in her car and I ignore the letter on mine, thankful JJ never brings it up.

Walking through the diner's door, I spot Finn in a booth near the back corner. He's wadding the paper to a straw as he talks with Tyler, like he's nervous. I wonder if it's from the none-date that is about to happen or the small talk he's making with Tyler, whom he knows just about as well as I do.

Tyler doesn't exactly hang with one particular crowd, but has no problem inserting himself wherever he wants.

Finn's eyes find mine as we approach the booth and his demeanor changes. His expressions become more familiar, and my nerves settle ever so slightly as I take the seat across from him.

Tyler leans across the table and kisses JJ.

I blush nervously, not knowing the appropriate behavior for whatever this is.

Finn opens my knotted fists on top of the table and takes ,my left hand in his. He kisses my knuckles, and my stomach erupts with butterflies; always a sucker for the cheesy old-school moves.

"You look beautiful, as always," he compliments.

I thank him with a smile I can't hold back.

The waitress comes to the table to take our order, and I am so captivated by Finn that it takes me a moment to realize that he orders for me. I open my mouth to speak on it, but the brow he raises has me pressing my lips back together.

When the woman returns, a bacon cheeseburger and caramel milkshake is placed in front of me. Finn stares at me, waiting for my approval.

"I wanted to test my skills, learning about someone without them telling me. How did I do?"

I look down at the food again, thoroughly inspecting it while making a variety of facial expressions. His brow furrows, and it feels like I'm harming a puppy.

"A plus on the milkshake. However, I usually order my burgers with extra cheese. But I'll make an exception this time."

He stares at me momentarily. Then pulls the top bun off his burger, grabs the cheese, and places it on mine.

He sucks on the tips of his fingers while giving me a wink.

Fuck, I wish he would keep touching my food so I can watch that over and over again.

Despite the playfulness, I'm actually very impressed with his choices.

Small talk rounds the table as we eat, and at some point, Finn places his feet on either side of my own, our legs touching.

"So, how about a movie night tomorrow?" he asks us, his foot moving to push my legs apart suggests he is more specifically asking for a night together.

"I would love to, but we have to clean our dorm room out and move everything back to JJ's parents' house."

Her parents look at me like another child of theirs, but they are rarely home in the summer. I am extra thankful for that this year. There won't be any awkwardness with explaining who Finn is to me if he comes by.

"I don't mind helping. That way, we can get it done faster and still have time afterward," Finn says.

Seriously? He would help just to spend time with me?

Not wanting to make things sweet and weird, I outstretch my hands in my lap and place them on his thigh as I thank him and agree.

His throat bobs, and then he turns to Tyler. "Why don't you and JJ take the corner booth for a minute?"

Tyler tilts his head. "Uh, why-"

"Fuck off for five minutes," Finn says shoving him from the seat.

JJ laughs and takes a stumbling Tyler with her a few booths over.

Finn turns back to me, his expression is sad. Disappointed.

"You didn't call," he says flatly.

"I didn't-"

"Maybe next time I fuck you, I'll just make sure you can't sit properly before you leave." He levels me with his stare. "Better yet, I'll make sure you can't leave at all."

"Call me if you have trouble sitting down tomorrow, and I'll come kiss it better."

I squeeze my thighs together tightly, hugging his leg in the process, showing him exactly what that thought is doing to me.

His tongue darts out, and he sucks down some of his chocolate shake. I watch every second of it, he has my undivided attention. He licks the remnant from the inside of his lips and grins.

"Am I the only one you are seeing?" I ask before my stupid brain can stop it.

"Are you hoping for a specific answer?" He slowly pushes a fry into his mouth, and I have to use every ounce of strength to focus on his question.

I know what answer I want to hear, but hearing him say no would make this easier. I nod, trying to be as transparent as possible.

"If I were fucking someone else, I would have the decency to tell you."

"Good." I say, referring to the fact that he's not.

He motions for the waitress to bring the checks. She brings one to JJ's table and one to ours. Finn immediately hands her his card, and she walks away.

"A gentleman always pays for the first date."

Date.

***

I quickly tuck all my letters in the bottom of a box and cover it with books before Finn comes back up to the dorm room. He's on his tenth load down with Tyler. The room is nearly empty now, except for the few things I have left to pack and the furniture that belongs to the university.

I have loved my time here with JJ, but as I look around the room, the thought of summer excites me.

It's the only time of the year I have no obligations. Sure, I could get a summer job, but paying to finish school is not what I want to do.

College was always the path I saw myself taking, but it was never one I truly wanted to take. Not that I know what I would want to do instead. Being spoiled by a rich man isn't practical, but I miss the time in women's history when having no job was our job. Who wouldn't want the freedom to do whatever they wanted every day?

"Are you sad we only have one more year living together?" JJ asks shoving her clothes into trash bags.

"Yeah," I answer truthfully.

Neither of us is moving far, but she's moving into a studio apartment once we graduate. I don't doubt that she would make room for me if I needed it, but it's time I figure out what the hell I am going to do with my life.

I don't tell her I am considering dropping out until I can get on my feet. She would lecture me about how there is always a way to make things work and that I shouldn't give up since I have come so far.

But I'm broke. What good is it to have a degree in physical therapy when you don't have a place to live, food, or work attire?

"Have you already packed up the rest of your lingerie, or do you need help with that?" Finn asks, and I spin towards the door to find him holding a pair of JJ's lacy panties against his hips.

JJ grins, and I snort a laugh. "I'm all good. However, I don't think JJ would mind if you'd like to try those on."

His hips stop wiggling seductively. He eyes the dresser that he grabbed them from, and as realization dawns on him, JJ snatches the garment.

"I absolutely would mind. His ass is bigger than mine, and I would like to *not* stretch them out," she protests, shoving the panties deep into the bag.

I purse my lips together at the look of mortification on Finn's face. He contorts his body to stare at his own ass, which is, indeed, bigger than hers. Then moves next to her for comparison.

Tyler walks back into the room, just as Finn smacks his ass with pride then walks closer to me.

Tyler looks at me with amusement but says nothing.

Finn takes the box once I have taped it shut. He lifts it with ease and leans in as close as he can. "I better get to see you in something lacy soon."

I scrunch my nose. I have lingerie but only wore it to take pictures. He would be the first I've worn them for. I have a feeling he will be my first for many things. Which doesn't make it easy to keep strings from getting attached.

As I pack the final box, I roll that thought over in my head.

Tyler hauls the last of JJ's bags out.

Carrying my box, I follow him and give our room one last look. JJ locks it up and goes to return the keys to the office while I follow the guys to the cars.

I slide the box into the backseat next to the one labeled 'books' - the box that holds my letters.

I spin and round the front of my car, hoping to snatch my letter before Finn sees it.

It's gone.

"Hey, uh- did you happen to grab a piece of paper from my windshield?" I ask Finn while he helps shove the bags into JJ's trunk.

"No, babe. Did you get a ticket?"

I swallow hard. If Finn didn't grab it... *he* did.

"Uh, no. Just a school flyer. No worries."

Finn stands straight and stretches his back before wrapping me in his arms. "Let's drop this off and get started on that movie."

We spent a few more hours unloading everything into JJ's house, deciding to save the unpacking for another day.

We piled up on the two queen-sized beds in JJ's large bedroom and watched movie after movie.

Finn stayed cuddled up next to me, always touching me in some way, and the longer he stayed like that, the more the line of our relationship blurred in my mind.

***

I lay on my bed frustrated, phone gripped in my hand.

What are we?!?!?

Friends with benefits don't go on dinner dates or actually watch the movies when they hang out. They don't call frequently or meet up to play board games. Yet, we did all of those things, and I loved every minute.

I want more of it. I want more of him.

But Lance sneaks his way into my brain. And how I wish he would have done any of those things with me.

As if I manifested it, my phone rings the distinct sound set for him, and my heart nearly falls out of my ass. I pick it up, my finger trembling as it slides across the glass screen, still warm from me constantly clutching it like a lifeline.

"Hello?" I answer, trembling as my stomach clenches so tight that I might actually throw up.

"Hey, baby. I was hoping I could see you," Lance coos on the other end, and my internal battle begins. His voice tempting me back.

"Yeah, I- I think that would be okay," I mutter, trying to restrain the expected excitement in my voice and convince both of us that I am in control of this situation.

"Meet you at our spot in thirty?" he beams. I can just imagine him winking at all his douchebag friends, silently bragging that he is about to get some pussy from his pathetic girlfriend yet again because I have no fucking morals or strength.

Fuck him. *I do have those qualities.*

I try to convince myself.

I agree and hang up before he can tell me he loves me because I just cannot fucking hear that right now.

I am going just to see him for closure. Nothing more.

The dumbest thing I could do right now is let him get his claws in me deeper. It's always the same. I cave, and he soothes. We have sex, get back together, and for about a week, everything is perfect.

Then...it's not. But for a short time, he is almost everything I need.

Almost.

***

"I've got to go run some errands. I'll be back," I say grabbing my car keys.

JJ gives me a curious look.

Since Damian's death I rarely drive. PTSD manifests in odd ways, and for me, I am terrified of killing someone with my car.

"I'll be ok. I just need to get some things and clear my head."

"Ok. Call if you need anything," she says, and turns back to her book.

Unlocking my car, I get in and drive to the old abandoned train yard on the outskirts of town.

Our usual train car is littered with empty crates and spray paint can. Lance is propped up in the corner, admiring the art.

"Do you remember the night we did this?" he asks, rubbing his hand over the two yellow stick figures with their middle fingers out and our initials sprawled across them in orange.

"Yeah. That was the night my mom told me she was sending me away to camp all summer before sophomore year of high school. We were so pissed."

My heart aches at how he looks at me like he did all those years ago. As if I was the only thing keeping him from falling off the edge of a cliff.

"Without you, I would be lost." Lance's carefully chosen words echo in my head. He knew my heart was too big to leave someone who said they would end up dead on the side of the streets without them.

I was the one that picked him up off the floor when he got so fucked-up he couldn't stand. I was the one that cleaned him up after he made a mess of himself. Because I cared, and he knew that. Without me, he would have no one to keep him from going too far.

"We were only kids and knew that life would give us hell, but it didn't matter because we loved each other." His soft voice brings me out of my thoughts. I nod, feeling the weight of the world on my shoulders. He motions me to him, and my feet obey, bringing me right into his arms.

"Hey. We are not perfect, but we have seen each other through some very low lows and the best fucking highs. We can make it, Mel."

I sink into him, just as I have done before, wanting moments like this to never to end. I hug him so tight my muscles ache and tears fall without so much as a warning.

Don't break us. I don't know who I am begging or what I want to change; all I know is that this hurts.

He takes a step back and slides my spandex shorts down my legs. I swallow the lump in my throat, watching his eyes as he undresses me. He lifts me up and my bare skin itches against his clothes. I wrap my legs around him instinctively as he backs me up towards the train car wall.

I bury my face into the crook of his neck and inhale his scent. The smell of body odor covered by Abercrombie cologne turns my stomach sour.

How did I never notice that he smelled so horrifically trashy?

In a flash, my body turns cold, and I long for the scent of amber and musk that has tainted my senses forever. Lance will forever own the brokenness inside of me, but he is no longer the person I want to run to.

I need to leave. I feel dirty and filled with betrayal from my actions. Finn does not deserve this. I do not deserve this.

Lance forces me to look at him, but the smile I find is completely different from the one minutes ago. Like he knows he has won.

Is that the same look I have always perceived as remorse and healing? Was I always that blind, or has something shifted in more than just me?

My heart cracks again, finding a small piece not yet shattered into dust.

I knew in my heart this time wouldn't be different. I will never be more than a place for him to put his dick; that truth shows now more than ever. My tears spill over, gliding down my warm cheeks.

With you, I am lost.

I have spent so long trying to mold myself to Lance and his ideation of the perfect woman. I would never be what he wants, and I will not make myself smaller.

"No." I whisper, trying to find the voice lodged in my throat.

His motions slow, and his eyes narrow in fury. "What do you mean, no?"

The skin of my back scrapes against the wall, and I use it as leverage to push his body from mine as I drop my legs to the floor. Liberated, my palms harshly collide with his chest, pushing him back.

His anger rises, and I prepare for the lashing I know will come.

I battle with myself, forcing my feet to stay planted, fighting against my instinct to retreat. "I can't trust you, Lance. You abused my trust, always wanting someone else. I deserve better than that." I keep my tone low, wrapping my arms around my chest, feeling the lowest I have ever felt. I feel exposed and broken. Used-up.

"I just told you I was sorry," he thunders.

"You're *sorry*?"

"What else could I say? Why do you have to make everything so fucking difficult?" His tone turns annoyed, no doubt frustrated that his dick and soft looks didn't fix everything this time.

A throaty laugh leaves my throat, and my eyes roll so fucking hard they nearly get stuck. Suddenly, this seems even easier.

"It's not about what you say; it's about what you do. You haven't changed, I doubt you ever will, and I don't want to stay around any longer to find out if I am right. You don't care about me."

He groans, clearly irritated that he isn't getting his way.

"Why do you even want me if you continue to sleep with other people?" My hurt mixes with pure rage, and I wonder if he will ever reveal a hint that my pain hurts him too.

His face turns cold and stiff right before he spins on his heel, throwing his fist into the metal wall of the train car, making me jump and my eyes clamp shut on instinct.

I open them again, finding an amused and wicked grin curling his lips.

"Because I fucking want to." He steps closer to me, and I step back, fearing the look in his eyes. "You want to be a stubborn cunt, fine. But pissing me off will not earn you any points. You are becoming more of a pain than it's worth." He jumps out of the train and treks through the gravel back to his car.

"Then leave me the fuck alone! That's all I want!" I yell, begging he would make this easier for me.

He stops dead in his tracks, spinning back around and wrapping me in utter fear as he storms back. Before my body can catch up to my brain's warning, he is gripping my face with a snarl. The pressure of his fingers causes my teeth to dig into my cheeks.

"I will... when I fucking feel like it," he spits in a deadly tone, and an alarm sounds in my brain telling me to shut my goddamn mouth. My eyes flicker back and forth between his nervously. His grip loosens slightly, then he leans in, his heavy breathing assaulting my ear. "Don't forget the power I hold over you. Look at yourself. You are mine until I say otherwise."

Moments pass as I stand frozen inside my own body, guilt and self-loathing holding me hostage as I stare down at my own bare feet, overly aware of the dirt coating them.

The sound of his Camaro roaring and skidding out of the rocky drive is the only indication that he is finally gone.

For good.

Amelia

F riday morning comes around, and my phone chimes with a reminder for my 10 A.M. appointment with my ob-gyn. I've been on the pill since middle school, but my mental health is not in the best shape. But I am not trying to have a baby any time soon, so I decided to switch to an IUD. More effective and no maintenance for three years.

Confirmation of Lance's dick having an open invitation for whoever it wanted was enough motivation to make the appointment and ensure I didn't have an STD or the fucker's child growing inside me.

I have left Lance's messages unanswered and have declined every phone call. Fuck him and the hold he may or may not have on me. It is time to close that chapter of my life, no matter how much it fucking hurts. It's been excruciating, but hearing him voice my dependency and obsession, as if it's easily spotted by anyone, has me beyond embarrassed and ashamed of who I am.

Getting dressed in some comfortable clothes, I tell JJ where I'm going.

"Twice in one week?" She looks suspicious.

"I'm fine," I reassure her, telling myself that I need to try harder. It's time to drop the weight tied around my ankle, preventing me from taking any steps forward.

She gives a nod and a soft smile. "Watch out for Lance."

Absentmindedly, I rub my neck where his hand wrapped around it the night he was here before rubbing my thumb over the fresh wound on my bottom lip.

"I will."

My stomach sinks as I walk to my car.

The fifteen minutes to my doctor's office go by in a blur as I replay Lance's hands on me.

The sanitary smell of a hospital wafts by my face as I open the heavy doors, and I hold back a cringe. Trying not to breathe, I push through another set of doors leading to the check-in desk, and I feel like passing out when I try to speak.

She hands me some paperwork to fill out, and I sit, tapping the pen as my eyes stare blankly at the overly-personal questions about my vagina.

I fill out most information, embarrassment lighting my nerves as I inform the staff that I need to be checked for infections, have had multiple sexual partners recently, do not consistently use condoms, and may be pregnant.

For fucks sake. I am a damn mess.

I return the packet to the receptionist with a forced smile that does nothing to hide my state of unease. Which increases as she informs me I need to get a copy of my insurance card faxed over to them so that they can bill it. Some bullshit about changes in their system and needing to re-scan everyone into the new software. They accept cash payments, so I could avoid the unpleasantness if I had money.

The deal with Damian said I got a generous direct deposit every month as long as I was a full-time student. But they stopped a year and a half ago when my mother realized it was another way to punish me for his death. I think she likes watching me stretch the little I have left while she blows all of Damian's life work away.

I get the fax number from her, along with the app name she recommended sending it with, and return to my seat. I swallow hard, trying not to have a full-blown panic attack in the middle of this office. After nearly a full year, I have to go see my mother.

Fucking insurance card.

"Amelia?"

When my eyes refocus, a young nurse in scrubs is waiting at an open door with a small smile. I gather my things and avoid eye contact as I follow her into my exam room, nervously wringing my hands.

I answer her questions about my situation and needs as vaguely as possible. Surprisingly, she doesn't push for more than is medically necessary and it doesn't seem like she thinks I am a horrible person. I'm sure she's seen worse situations, but being in front of a medical professional has a way of making me feel filthy for having any kind of sex life.

She eyes my nervous ticks a few times before asking me if I have been harmed or am scared for my life. I politely respond *no* but silently snort to myself. How the fuck do I answer that?

The rest goes smoothly. Until she tells me I can't have sex for a week to avoid bleeding. With Lance that wouldn't have been an issue, but Finn is another story.

I dress, trying to ignore the ache in my belly that may be from either the implantation or the fear of my test results coming later.

***

I sit in the car, staring at the brick, two-story house that hosted so many good memories for seventeen years of my life. It wasn't perfect, but I had it better than most. But now there is nothing but pain as I stare at my mother's house.

Breathe. My anxiety builds as I step out of my car, rubbing my palms up and down the sides of my thighs.

Not wasting any more time, I unlock the front door and waltz right in. Honestly, I'm surprised she hasn't changed the locks.

"Mom?" I call out, the name sounding weird on my tongue after months of not speaking.

She comes out of the kitchen with a glass of wine, looking like she just rolled out of bed. As I get closer, I can see her bloodshot eyes, accented by blackened circles under them. I let out a sigh and drop my head.

Your fault. You're responsible for this. You're the reason you're alone.

No matter how much I tell myself otherwise, there are times when that voice is so loud that I can't do anything other than accept what it's telling me. Every emptiness in my life is in fact my fault.

"Hey, uh, I just need my insurance card. I just scan it on my phone, and you can keep the physical copy here," I say, getting right to the point.

She stares at me with empty eyes for a minute before waving her hand in the air and walking away, dismissing me. Not wanting to waste any of her precious breaths on pathetic little me.

"Mom.. at some point, we have to move past this," I whisper slowly, careful not to poke the bear but needing to try just one more time. Always, one more time.

My heart aches. I miss my mother. She may have been hard on me, but I know she loved me. Maybe it was something I mistook for love. But whatever it was, it's gone.

My mother hates me.

She looks at me like I'm her biggest regret. A waste of space or some rancid dog shit she stepped in.

She snaps her head around to look at me. "Move past this, Amelia?! The love of my life died, because of your actions," she spits at me. "You think any amount of time is enough time to grieve all the love he gave? All the memories? All the time lost?" ...

She stumbles as she walks closer to me, gripping a door frame to steady herself.

"You don't get to tell me when it's time." She moves closer with every verbal punch.

"You don't get to do anything but revel in the guilt that I hope will plague you for the rest of your life."

Her words encourage the darkness.

'Revel in it. Burn.'

My fingers itch to feel the flame of a lighter as my next words come, and I don't know who I try to convince more with them. "You know that's not true! He picked me up many times before. It was just a freak accident. Dami-"

"Don't you dare say his name!" she shrieks, grabbing the closest thing to her and chucking it at my head.

I turn my body in a flinching motion just in time to avoid getting hit in the head. "Are you insane?!" I protest as she continues my way with swift, staggering steps.

Snatching me by the front of my shirt, she shoves me into the full body mirror on the wall to the left. I close my eyes as it shatters around me, cutting my left shoulder.

I wince in pain as she screams in my face.

"Get what you need and get out! I don't want you here!" She walks off, slamming her bedroom door behind her. Soft sobs leak from the room and I stand there in shock, holding my bleeding arm.

It's not the first time she has gotten rough with me, but it's the first time she has made me bleed. Was that intentional?

I understand she needs someone to blame, since the true person responsible was never caught. But I shouldn't be her punching bag.

Please, I need you, I beg silently as hot tears stream down my face.

'Burn.'

I grab my insurance card from her office and immediately send it so I don't forget. On my way out, I stop by my mom's door.

Noting that the sobs have stopped, I crack the door to see her passed out on the bed, his picture in one hand and a pill bottle in the other.

Fuck, Mom.

I walk in and gently check her pulse to make sure she's still breathing and let out a relieved sigh. I brush the hair off of her sweaty forehead and leave without so much as a look back. She doesn't want me here, and neither of us needs this.

Just as I start my car, my phone rings. I answer, chewing on my lip.

"Hi, Ms. Mason. This is Jenny from Women's Health. I just wanted to inform you that we rushed your test due to the lack of your family's medical history and the risks you had. I have the results. Do you have a minute?"

I exhale sharply as I pick at my jeans. "Yes, ma'am."

"Wonderful. All tests were negative except for one. You have tested positive for Chlamydia. This STI is the most common and easily treated, so we've called in a prescription to your pharmacy. It's also recommended that you inform any sexual partners you've had and have them tested as well."

My brain short circuits. What the *fuck*.

Swallowing hard, I thank her and end the call, trying not to throw up. I zone out, thinking about any symptoms I may have been having while on the drive back home. I come up with nothing, and although I know it isn't my fault, I am ultimately disgusted and embarrassed with myself.

As I'm getting out of my car to walk back into JJ's house, my phone dings. A smile spreads across my face before I am immediately met with guilt.

Finn:
Wanna go to the lake?
Small party. Some people
I want you to meet

Finn:
Tyler is going too

Me:
Absolutely

Finn:
I'll meet you there in an
hour

Finn:
Wear something sexy

I snort a laugh and jog to the room JJ and I share. My steps slow to a hesitant walk, realizing I have to tell Finn. I temporarily force the thought to the back of my mind and focus on the excitement of seeing him. In the meantime, I can pretend that he won't be repulsed.

Busting through the door, I scare the shit out of JJ.

She screams, holding her chest. "What the *fuck* Mel?!"

"Sorry!" I laugh. "Get your ass up. We're going to Tipsy's lake to see the guys."

She scrambles to her feet with hoots of excitement and throws on her blue string bikini that barely covers her boobs and throws a t-shirt over it before she even stops to notice the dried blood on my arm.

"Fuck, what happened?!" she almost yells, pulling my arm closer to inspect it.

"It's nothing," I say pulling it away softly. "I had to see my mom, and she was high off something. Safe to say she wasn't thrilled to see me."

JJ sighs. "She needs help."

"Clearly, but what am I supposed to do? Drag her to rehab? I'll never get her calm enough to go anywhere with me."

JJ gives me a look. "Just wait until she passes out from the high and then involuntarily bring her. It would be easy to get her in because anyone can see she's not okay."

I wonder if I could make that happen. Not that I want to lock my mother up, but she is becoming a danger to herself and anyone near her. And it only takes one time to take a high too far and never wake up, and God knows she doesn't care enough to be cautious about it.

JJ grabs some towels, allowing the conversation to end there while I get dressed and contemplate telling her my test results.

I slip on my black bikini top with the matching shorts to cover my burns. It always hurts to have material rubbing them while they heal, but hurts so good. Once it subsides, I make new ones and repeat the process. I throw a shirt over me, grab our phones and sunscreen, and pop a Xanax, deciding that I am not in a sharing mood and need to chill the fuck out.

We blast the radio with the windows down the entire forty-five minute drive to the lake. The warm wind blowing my hair every which way while I sing my heart out.

Amelia

I throw my messy hair into a bun on top of my head, and we strip off our t-shirts, throwing them in JJ's back seat. Walking down to meet them. I smell the dirtiness of the water, the yeast of beer, and the delicious aroma of good weed.

Finn runs toward me through the crowd of about fifty people. He lifts me off the ground, propping his crossed arms under my ass, and licks the warm skin of my stomach slowly.

"Mmmm, delicious," he says setting me down.

I roll my eyes and he gives my cheek a soft kiss.

He loops his arms through mine and JJ's and escorts us to the tent with tables covered in food, drinks, and a Bluetooth speaker blaring music.

"How have you sexy ladies been?" he purrs, looking down at me and then at JJ.

"Watch yourself, pretty boy," Tyler says, walking up and smacking JJ on her ass.

Finn grins playfully before his eyes spot the cut on my arm. I cleaned it up, and the bleeding stopped, but it's still very noticeable. He takes my hand and leads us further down to the water before he holds my arm up in question.

"Long story," I say shortly, trying to brush it off.

He lets it go but gives me a wary smile that says he's there to listen when I'm ready to talk, but there's something resembling fury in his gaze.

I give a thankful smile that doesn't meet my eyes as the voice starts back up in my head, begging for release.

"I really am happy to see you," I say with a true smile. "Resorting back to old company... has proven to be...problematic."

He raises a brow and gives me a punishing look only a dad could get away with. "I don't like the sound of that."

"I don't know..." I breathe out, no words seeming to justify my lack of rationality. "I guess old habits die hard. And apparently go out with a bang."

He brushes the hair out of my face with gentle fingers. "If you need a booty call, you have my number. No more old habits."

I bite my lower lip and nod, realizing this is my opportunity. "I uh-I actually needed to talk to you about something."

He looks at me curiously, and my eyes sink to our bare feet in the sand. Gently, he tilts my chin back up. "What is it, baby?"

My heart sinks.

"I- I went to the gyno today, and they..." I stop, unable to force the words out, fearing what his response will be. I can already hear him laughing with his friends, calling me all the names in the book.

My eyes drift around before meeting his again, and kindness shines back. It's as if he has already read me like a book and knows where this is going, but is allowing me the time I need to say it for myself.

"I... tested positive for chlamydia. I'm pretty sure I got it from Lance and not you. I haven't slept with anyone else since you," I ramble nervously, unsure why I want him to know he's the only guy I'm sleeping with.

He takes my hand in his, stroking the back of it. "I get tested after new partners to be safe, so I know I'm clean, baby, but I can test again to give you peace of mind."

Fuck, he's more responsible than I am.

I nod, still unable to fully read how he feels about it.

"It's not a big deal, love. We will treat it and be back at it like nothing happened." He kisses me on the cheek and my heart skips a beat.

It can't be that easy, can it?

"However, I find out that you go back to him, we might have a serious problem."

My cheeks warm as I take his hand and he leads us back to our crowd.

I stand there for a few minutes, pretending to listen to Tyler and Finn talk, and my chest feels tighter by the second.

"Is Lyle coming today?" Tyler asks.

The ringing in my ears grows louder, drowning out the rest of the conversation as I try to clear it and my nerves.

Finn glances my way and reaches for my hand intertwining his fingers with mine. I stare down at them, trying to use his touch to ground me, but the overwhelming feeling of what is growing between us has my heart rate jumping even higher.

"I need a minute," I say when there is an opening.

Finn looks at me curiously, but the crease in his brow instantly smooths, and his face lights up.

"Oh, hey. I got this for you." He passes me a tightly wrapped blunt.

I take it from him and dig my lighter out of my bag, thanking him with a kiss on the cheek.

He returns one, then whispers low so no one else can hear. "I'm not going anywhere if you need a minute to yourself."

"You're the best. I'll be back in a few."

I grab my towel before walking away.

Finn doesn't judge me or push me to open up. And he's learning my triggers and body language fast. He may not be able to relate, but he understands why I am this way and gives me my space when I need it.

Even making excuses for me when he see's that I'm having a hard time.

We were playing games the other night, and my energy quickly dropped, and I slid into the background. Finn didn't hesitate to take the blame, telling everyone he was ready for bed before taking me away with him. He didn't comment on it afterward either, but I felt what he did somewhere deep inside my chest. Something so small was so incredibly personal. It felt more intimate than sex.

Yeah. I'm catching feelings fast.

I make my way into the woods and plop down on the ground to light my blunt. Taking a deep hit, I sigh on the exhale. Leaning against the tree, I close my eyes and take in the sounds.

The laughter and chatter down by the water, the music. The water splashing, the wind whipping through the trees. I let myself soak in the present and let the THC numb everything else.

I open my eyes and flick the lighter, staring at the flame like always. Contemplating while I take a few more hits with my other hand. I look around to see if anyone is around before I drop my thighs down and pull my swim shorts up. I bring the flame down to my thigh and close my eyes.

One.. Two...

Rustling leaves and the lighter being slapped out of my hand, snap me out of the painful bliss.

My heart pounds with embarrassment as I look up to see Finn crouched in front of me, wearing a t-shirt over his previously bare chest.

"What the hell are you doing?" he asks, his voice tinged with anger and hurt. Gripping my wrists he pulls me to my feet.

I pull out of his grip and turn my head in embarrassment.

"I told you that I do this sometimes, Finn. It's been a hard day. I'll be back down there in a minute."

He stares at me blankly, then his lips curl in a snarl. "No, I'm not going to sit by and let you hurt yourself like others do."

He stares at me for a long moment, his jaw grinding. "You need something more than weed to take the pain away? Fine. Let's go." He grabs my towel off the ground and takes my hand, pulling us further into the woods.

"What are we doing?".

"I'm going to fuck you so hard. All you'll think about is how good my dick feels inside you."

I almost laugh. *What?*

Everything blurs around me, the high hits me hard, and I feel a wetness form between my thighs.

Finn's never been so firm with his words - demanding. He's usually all about what I want to give or ask for and nothing more. I could get used to this side of him too. Taking control and forcing me to let go. But I know if I said no, he would stop.

Far enough away so we won't be seen or heard, he lays the towel down in front of a tree and yanks me onto it, pushing me back against it.

Anticipation swirls inside of me, and I shake with need.

He drops to his knees before me and rips my shorts down my legs. I gasp at the abrupt motion, and he looks up at me, his gaze softening as he smirks. He lifts my right leg wrapping it around his shoulder, then shoves his mouth into my pussy.

"Oh, God," I murmur.

He pulls back just a little and I whimper at the loss.

"Don't be afraid to yell, baby girl. Let it out while I eat you like my fucking life depends on it."

He continues to work me over with his tongue, stopping now and then to focus on my clit, and I don't try to hold back the sounds he forces out of me.

"Yes, that feels so fucking good."

He groans, pleased, and looks up at me. Our eyes lock as he pushes his tongue into me, tasting what he is doing to me. His eyes have a green tint today, and I wonder if his true eye color is hazel, changing daily or with his mood.

I force his head back, and tears pool in my eyes for no reason, emotions I can't read flooding me.

"I need you inside me," I desperately beg, and my voice trembles as I try to drown myself in my desire for him and everything he does to me.

A devilish smile flashes across his face. He pulls me down to the towel and leans me back. The leaves and sticks poke through, but I quickly dismiss the discomfort when Finn pulls his swim trunks down, revealing his impressive length. He runs his hand down my pussy and pushes his fingers in, raising an eyebrow. "You are already so wet for me, baby. You want me?"

I nod.

"I want to hear you fucking say it."

"Okay, *Hellcat*, where did this devilish side of you come from?" I tease, trying to get out of my head.

He smirks ignoring my question. "Hmm. I like that."

Then he gives his best impression of a needy girl panting for dick, "I need you to fuck me, Hellcat."

He looks back at me, biting his bottom lip with a panty-dropping smile. Well, it would be if I was wearing any. I give him a challenging look, and he leans over me, pushing two fingers inside me, rubbing my G-spot with quick, forceful motions, and I cry out.

"Say it," he orders, watching my face, pushing into me harder, causing me to hold my breath and my eyes roll back in my head. Then he jerks them out, leaving me empty.

"Okay, okay," I pant. "I need you to fuck me, Hellcat! Please!" It sounds ridiculous coming out of my mouth.

"That's my good girl."

Sparks go off in my head and my stomach flutters.

Holy fuck. Totally worth it!

My mind goes feral, wanting more. I reach for him, dragging my nails across his skin. Satisfied, he removes his fingers, lifts my legs to my chest, and holds them there as he lines himself up.

Fuck!

Hurriedly, I place both hands on his chest, "Wait! What about-"

He cuts me off with a low growl, "Don't fucking care." He pushes inside of me with a loud groan.

"Fuuuck." My head smacks the ground, all rationality leaving, replaced with pure bliss as he reaches the deepest parts of me.

He starts slow, coating his whole length in my wetness, then picks up his pace, using the ground and my thighs as leverage to get a better angle. He fucks me hard and fast, his dick rubbing inside me perfectly, and his eyes squeezed shut.

I look down to where we meet, and my stomach drops with embarrassment. His eyes attempt to follow mine, but I grab his face, forcing his eyes up.

No. No. No.

Are you fucking kidding me?

He slows down, and his brows pinch together.

"What's wrong?"

"I uh- I got a birth control IUD implanted today, and I wasn't supposed to have sex yet. It can cause some... bleeding," My heart is racing. How much more embarrassing could today get? "I promise it's not period blood." I try to reassure him, worried he is going to freak out.

He looks down to see the blood. I go to move from under him, but he stops me, pushing on my stomach and holding me into place.

"You think a little blood scares me?" He looks at me with an unreadable expression. "As long as you're not in pain, I'm not stopping until you cum all over my dick."

"No, I'm not hurting, and I've been taking my pills this past week, but they said-"

Grabbing my jaw tightly, he shuts me up with a forceful kiss. "Then I don't give a fuck. Hang on tight, beautiful." Before his sentence can fully register, he pushes my legs back up and slams back into me.

He grabs my hand gripping his thigh, and brings it to my clit, instructing me to help the process along. I do as he says, rubbing myself as he fucks me perfectly, the smell of copper and sex in the air. I revel in the bliss, letting reality slip away.

No grief or pain anywhere to be seen.

I just can't get enough of how he feels inside me and how different he is from anything I have ever known. It feels immense, earth-shakingly amazing.

"Fuuuuuck!" I rub my clit furiously, needing the friction more than I have ever needed it in my life. I look down, mid-orgasm, seeing why it feels so explosive.

I squirted. Everywhere.

Finn's eyes widen, and he looks up at me and I freeze.

"Damn, that's so fucking sexy," he growls before standing and stroking himself, wanting to come on me.

Once I catch my breath, I crawl to his feet, looking up at him as I take his crimson-coated cock in my hand, giving it a few strokes before opening my mouth and gliding him along my warm tongue. He gives me another look of surprise, before his head falls back.

One of his hands rests on his lower back, and the other on my head, not pushing, just following my motions. Letting me show what I can do on my own. What I want to do for him.

Within seconds he's stiffening, cursing as he grips my shoulders. His warm, salty cum shoots down my throat, mixing with the coppery tinge. His body shaking in my grasp.

I gather it all, pull away from him, and stick out my tongue to show his cum mixed with the blood that coated his dick and now my face, no doubt. I can smell the copper stronger than before, so it must be on my nose too.

He steadies himself and rakes a hand through his hair as I swallow us down.

"Christ. You are either going to make or break us," he mumbles.

Us? Me and him?

I push that loaded question back for another day as he helps me to my feet, and we get dressed. He shakes off the towel, and we return the way we came, soaking in the comfortable silence.

Stopping by the tree I was originally sitting under, he picks up my lighter and blunt, pocketing them.

"Hey!"

"What, my dick didn't get you high enough?"

I pause. My head is clear for the time being.

Touche, Hellcat.

Readjusting our clothes, we realize we are covered in blood. So Finn takes my hand, pulling me towards the community lake showers. They are disgusting, crawling with bugs, mold growing everywhere, but it will have to do.

It's better than staying in our current appearance.

Ignoring the decrepit environment, we step inside the shower and let the lukewarm water cascade over us. I untie my bikini, letting it fall to the ground. Finn's eyes travel over my breasts and down the rest of my body as my shorts fall next.

"God, you are fucking breathtaking," he murmurs, and I fail to hide my smile.

We take a few minutes to wash the crimson off our skin, and I don't miss his eyes constantly roaming my body. The weight of his stare makes me wish he would take me again, right here, but he doesn't. He leaves the small room, and I check to ensure I'm not bleeding. Stepping out of the shower after, I put on my washed suit, and walk out to meet him.

He's smoking a cigarette, his back to me. Leaning against the building, with wet black hair falling in his eyes, he looks like a walking billboard ad for a sex shop. The tips of withered feathers on the back of his lower neck poke out of the collar of his shirt.

Interesting. I guess I haven't ever seen his backside in the light, now that I think about it. Curiosity bubbles in my chest as I think about any other small details I may have missed and what the rest of that tattoo looks like.

He turns around to see me undressing him with my eyes.

"Like what you see, kitty cat?" he teases.

The nicknames are never ending with this one.

"Kitty cat?" I raise a brow, not liking how small the name makes me feel.

"Well, if I'm your Hellcat, you can be my kitty cat," he teases, and I almost cringe at how he says it.

"I am not a *kitty cat*." I protest, letting him hear the disgust in my tone. That nickname makes me sound so defenseless.

"Hmm," he hums, holding the silence for a long moment. Then crosses his arms, and I catch myself staring intently at the muscles rippling in his arms. "How about Angel?"

I shoot him a look of annoyance.

"The angel that will set the world on fire."

I pause and stare at him with a new blank expression. My mind wanders, trying to place where I have heard that phrase before.

"It's funny... because of your fascination with-"

"Yeah, I got it, asshole," I snip at him, realizing the joke as soon as he said it.

He steps closer and trails a finger down my left arm, tracing my cut. I hide my wince and look at his face. His brows bunch together before he looks into my eyes. "Wanna tell me the story here?"

I push him back a step, dropping my arms. "I already told you. It's a long story."

He pulls me closer and grips my chin. "We have time, Angel. Spill it. Or I'll use my dick to get you to say what I want again."

I rub my thighs together, trying to soothe the ache he just caused by one sentence.

He raises an eyebrow at me, and I sigh.

"Had to go see my mom. Didn't go well," I say, chewing my lip. He doesn't say anything, so I continue. "She's on her normal summer bender. She didn't want to see me... or hear from me. She pushed me against a mirror, and it shattered."

His jaw tightens, and his fingers tilt my chin up, brushing against the faint shadow Lance left weeks ago with his fingertips.

"And here?"

I drop my head, hating that he is bringing all of this up.

"That one was from Lance. I told you that."

His features turn ice cold as he steps away and paces like I have personally offended him. "Right."

"I'm fine."

"Amelia, I will be damned if I let anyone lay a hand on you and get away with it. You may not be mine yet, but I will protect you like you are. Do you understand me?"

Yet?

"I have to go. I'll see you around, Angel."

And just like that, he leaves.

Eventually I head down to the beach to find him, but he's gone. Changing route, I grab my phone and search for JJ, finding her getting her tan on a little further away from everyone. I shake my towel out and plop down beside her, sighing.

"Hey, sister. Are you good now? You were gone for a hot minute."

"Yeah, I do feel better," I half-lie.

I lay down on my stomach and untie my top to avoid tan lines. I don't tell her about what just happened or the storm in my mind trying to convince me that I did something wrong for Finn to act like that.

I'm almost asleep, lulled by the distant chatter and music mixing in the breeze, when I suddenly feel eyes on me. I pick my head up, looking around but not seeing anyone.

For a moment, my heart leaps and hopes that with the shore nearly empty, I would be able to see *him* watching me. But find no one noticeably looking my way. With an internal sigh, I lay my head back down.

"Amelia?"

A girl with short curly hair and tan skin walks towards us in a neon pink bikini. "It is you! We met at Finn's party.

"I'm-"

"Emma," I say with a forced smile.

We met while me and JJ were dancing. She accidentally bumped into me, sloshing her drink all over the floor, barely missing everyone's clothes. She's a perky little thing that I seem only able to handle in small doses.

"Yeah!" she squeals, and JJ cringes, letting out a laugh to cover it up.

"What's up, girly?" I say in my best *OMG girl* voice to match hers.

"Well, I was hanging out with the guys over there, and I heard them mention an after-party tonight and just wanted to extend the invite! It will be at Ian Davis's house. He's a friend of Finn's!"

Before I can accept or deny, she blows us a kiss and sashays away.

JJ and I look at each other for a minute and simultaneously snort a laugh, spitting a little. That girl is a lot.

I text Finn to ensure it's cool if we come. And by the time he answers, we are wrapping up our tanning session, heading to put our stuff back under the tent and cool off in the water. I get that weird feeling that someone is watching me, but a crowd of people makes it impossible to find the source. I keep looking until the alert on my phone calls my attention.

Finn:

Hey cutie.. sorry to leave in a hurry earlier and yes we just planned it as I was leaving. You BETTER be there 10 sharp baby

Finn:

I can swing by to pick you up if you want to come but Tyler is taking JJ on a date tonight

Although I'm slightly annoyed that he left without so much of a decent explanation, I smile that he offered to come get me. I turn to JJ with a pout.

"Finn says you're going on a date with Tyler, so you won't be going to the party?"

"God, they gossip like girls. He literally just asked me, and I haven't even answered yet."

"You should go. You haven't been on a real date in a long time, and Finn said he would pick me up, so I'll be fine."

"You sure? What if Lance is there?"

It's a valid question, but since Finn knows my story and the party's at his friend's house, I'm sure he could make Lance leave if I pointed him out.

"I think Finn could take care of the situation better than you or I could," I laugh.

"Good point."

I send Finn a text letting him know to pick me up at 10 then put my phone under my towel to protect it from the heat. We spend the next hour or so cooling off in the water before heading home, utterly exhausted and desperate for a nap.

Amelia

My alarm goes off at eight, giving me two hours to get ready. My social battery is nearly empty, but I can't bail. I take a proper shower, blow dry my hair, and style it in loose waves that fall down my back. I do my makeup, going easy on the eyes but popping a matte red lipstick. Then I search my closet for a good outfit to complement it. I decided on a pair of fishnet leggings under high-waisted black shorts, a red bralette-style top, and my black combat boots.

When I look down at my phone, I see I have five minutes until Finn gets here to pick me up. I shove my pipe and lighter into my pocket, hoping I can buy some off someone tonight, as usual. While I'm at it, I pop another Xanax too. I'm having some unexpected anxiety about not having JJ beside me.

My phone rings, and I answer to a delicious voice purring on the other end. "I'm here, baby."

"Coming!" I sing-song, absolutely adoring when he calls me that.

JJ gone, I grab my phone and lock the door behind me.

Finn is holding the passenger door of a beautiful deep purple, sixties Mustang. His fitted black shirt, ripped jeans, and backward ball cap makes him look edible. I'm practically salivating at the mouth just looking at him, like we didn't just fuck in the woods hours ago. I take in the whole picture, and let out a whistle as I climb in.

He rounds the car and gets in, looking at me like he will pounce on me at any second.

"You like her?" he asks, running his tongue over his bottom lip.

"Very sexy," I say, playing along with his tease.

He leans over the console and kisses me hard and fast. "So are you." He runs his hands over the dash. "Just got her out of the shop I work at. I built her from the ground up. Well, with help."

I give him a look of impressiveness as I take in the worried smile on his face. Maybe he thinks I don't trust his skills.

Oh, but I do. I trust all of this man's skills. Sexual pun absolutely intended.

One hand on the wheel, the other on my thigh, and we are off. Finn blares classic rock from the 90s with the windows down for the short drive to Ian's house. I let the music vibrate through me, and the wind pulls my thoughts away on a whim.

When I finally open my eyes, I see Finn taking quick glances to look at me with a wide smile. I smile back and turn my head to look at the familiar house as we pull through the gates. It's the same house the party was at.

We park, hop out, and Finn pulls me inside the house like he owns the place. He doesn't bother to introduce me to anyone, knowing that I'm not one who enjoys much of that. Instead, he leads me to a couch closest to the beer pong table, kisses the top of my head.

"I need my good luck charm close," he whispers. He casts me a wink as he pulls away and walks towards the table where his blonde partner from last time is waiting for him, seemingly impatiently.

I watch him play, laugh, and enjoy himself for so long that I forget everything around me. Seeing him so carefree makes me so envious that I can't do it as easily. Those moments are rare for me, and I often have to be coerced into action before the joy becomes known and takes over.

This party is more relaxed than the last but just as crowded so I haven't moved. I know I needed to get out, but the thrill just isn't there tonight. Deciding that trying to force it is useless, I glance around for something to occupy myself with other than ogling Finn.

Spotting a plastic baggy next to Finn's keys on an end table, I scoot closer. Smiling as I see my name scribbled on the front of it, I take it and empty a small amount of the contents into my palm, rolling the bud over in my hand. Taking my time to enjoy the process, I pick pieces off and discard the small stems onto the bag next to me. Fingers working from memory as I listen to the conversations around me. My eyes stay focused on the task at hand. I hate that I enjoy the act so much when someone I now beg myself to hate taught me.

Retrieving my miniature pipe and lighter from my pocket, I fill the small hole and heat the bud. I take a long drag, attempting to ease the small part of my mind that refused to let go in the car ride over here. Only hitting it twice, I lean back in my seat and blow the smoke into the air above me, watching as it swirls and twists, then disappears into nothing. I envy it, tired of waiting for the moment my heart can no longer withstand the contortion it's constantly under and just... gives.

I let myself ride the buzz, eyes closing and skin tingling. My thoughts fade into incoherent sounds. Suddenly, the air shifts. My face warms familiarly, and my eyes fly back open as my heart picks up pace.

For the past few years, my anxiety sometimes makes my highs tilt more to the paranoid side, and with my recent circumstances, I am a little on edge. I can't help but think my intuition was trying to warn me that the person I held close was nothing I thought he was. I dart my gaze around, searching. My vision blurs, my brain trying to catch up with what my eyes see around me.

I still, letting my eyes focus on Emma walking in my direction with that cheesy ass smile she always wears plastered to her overly plump lips.

I am really not in the mood to talk.

She holds out her hand, offering me a new drink, and I accept it with a smile. She may be unreasonably chipper, but overall, she's a nice girl, so I can't be rude solely because she slightly annoys me.

"Wanna go outside? I think I saw a tree-house, and you look bored," she asks, tilting her head to the side, making her dirty blonde hair trickle over her cheek. Her straightened curls, making her hair longer and her overall appearance seemingly a tad more preppy. Her pink lipstick is smudged, and her cheeks are flushed. Obviously she had no problem finding something to occupy her time tonight.

I chuckle and give her a nod, nervously flicking my favorite lighter in my hand. I might as well indulge her, right? I haven't been in a tree-house since I was fourteen when JJ and I snuck out to lose our virginity. So I can't lie and say I don't have a small thrill from the idea.

We go out the backdoor, and as the cool night air hits my skin, a shiver rakes through me. I spot the tree-house sitting in a huge oak tree in the back corner of the yard, and it looks like it's been here for a good twenty years.

Emma's arm tucks me under her shoulder with a gentle squeeze. "What's wrong, girl? You look like you would rather shove forks in your eyes than be here."

I force a smile, trying to prove us both wrong. "No, it's not that. I'm just..." I pause, searching for the right words as my brain seriously lags. "Stressed."

On top of Finn's odd behavior before he left the lake, I still haven't gone to the pharmacy to pick up my prescription to get rid of Lance's parting gift.

She hums a sound of understanding. The chatter from the house grows faint the further we walk, and the silence is both unsettling and calming.

"I'm sure you are," she says in a strange tone, but I disregard it.

Coming up under the big oak tree, I look up, taking in the carvings on the stairs. I toss the rest of my drink back, throw my cup behind me, and climb up the ladder with a smile from ear to ear, testing the strength of the steps as I ascend them.

"It's expected when the man you are so in love with is keeping secrets," Emma says from below and I falter on the last step.

Secrets?

My stomach sinks as I make it just high enough to see inside the tree-house and my eyes lock on Lance.

Before I can retreat, I'm being hauled up to the floor by my arm with the gash in it. I cringe at the small amount of pain and look down at Emma, about to beg her for help.

"Have fun, bitch."

Before I can process what the fuck is happening, Lance is squeezing my cheeks with enough force to bruise, redirecting my head towards him.

"Told you I'd be seeing you again."

"So you had to hide in here like some fucking creep?" I nearly yell, still trying to make sense of what the fuck just happened.

"Lower your fucking voice!" he snaps, looking nine shades of pissed and anxious. "I have a surprise for you." The side of his lips curl and my gut churns. "A private one."

"I don't want anything from you," I choke out, reaching behind, feeling for the exit. He grabs my wrist with a punishing grip before I can make contact.

"Oh, but I want something from you."

I try to break his grip, but he only pulls me closer.

"I hear you've been fucking someone else," he says, inches from my ear and sounding like the most vile human on the face of the earth. "Such a little hypocrite."

"That's none of your goddamn business. We aren't together," I grind out.

"You can't fuck me away, drug me away, or burn me away." He licks my earlobe.

He did notice; he just didn't care.

My heart aches in desperation, and I swear I feel my soul crack in two.

I part my lips to speak or scream, but no sound comes, and my head gets heavy.

No. No. No. God, please, no.

My eyes go wide as my vision gets fuzzy, and he chuckles.

God, please, no.

"Desperate times call for desperate measures, sweetie," he says, patting my cheek. "You won't go to sleep just yet, but you will be immobile for a good while. Since you wanted to make things difficult, I had to be sure you cooperated and listened. You won't fuck this up for me."

Bile rises in my throat; I want to fucking die.

He pulls me into the corner, away from the door, and lowers his voice to ensure no one can hear him. "I'll be keeping a close eye on you, but I no longer want to pretend I want you. It's more, what I can get from you."

Fear spikes through me as he gives my legs a forceful tug, and I fall flat on my back, my head banging against the floor.

Taking his time, he shuts the hatch before turning back to me. He yanks my shorts to my ankles and rips my fishnets.

Tucking his fingers in my panties, he watches my face like he enjoys the fear. Eyes dark and glassy, full of hate, bearing no resemblance to the man I love.

Loved.

I squeeze my eyes shut, imprisoned in my own body, completely at his mercy. Willing myself to go anywhere but here, as I have so many times before. Dissociation can be a gift. I guess I never really realized it for what it was... until now.

I let my head fall to the side, focusing on the carvings on the walls, similar to those on the ladder. Initials and shapes. I try to make out the images, using them as a distraction. A bird, multiple stick figures, and initials I don't recognize. I sift through my brain, trying to make connections. Then I spot *Jones,* and what little progress I was making comes crashing down.

Finn.

I want to cry out for him. I want him to come for me, but if I have learned anything in this life so far, it's that you cannot rely on someone to save you. You have to protect and avenge yourself.

I refuse to look at Lance, and a single tear rolls down my cheek as I give one last effort, urging my body to do something, anything.

Then, I accept defeat.

Lance grunts, yanking my top down so hard the strap breaks. He frees his dick as he stares at my chest, stroking himself.

Spitting on his length, he spreads it around, and pushes my legs open with force so hard my hip might just break. Lining himself at my entrance, his head touches my most intimate part, making me crawl inside myself, hiding in shame and embarrassment.

He slams to the hilt in one punishing thrust. And pain racks through my body at the unwanted intrusion and his too hard grip on my thighs.

He picks up his pace, coming down to force a kiss, smearing my lipstick.

I close my eyes tight, hot tears streaming freely down my cheeks. Painfully aware the boy I once loved is raping me.

"Open your eyes and look at me," he demands and I hate that I obey. "I know you're not as miserable as you're pretending to be. I know you love it, Mel." He smirks. "I always get you in the mood once you give in."

I don't listen. Letting the voice in my head and my heartbeat drown the sounds of his thrusts.

You deserve this. This is your punishment.

"Fucking hell, Amelia," he says, annoyed like I am ruining this for him. Pulling out of me, he flips me over, my cheek slamming into the hard wood, scraping the skin. I can hear him work himself with grunts before I feel him slam back into me.

My body rocks back and forth, against the hard floor until he finally pulls out rapidly, his hot cum landing on my back.

A flash of light fills the room, followed by the sound of a camera click and the *swoop* of a message being sent.

Crawling to my side, he puts himself back in his jeans before leaning to my ear. "I'll be seeing you."

He opens the hatch and descends with a chuckle, leaving me drugged with my pants down, his cum on my back, and bile threatening to spill out.

Just as Lance comes into my line of sight through the tree-house entrance, someone tackle's him and starts pounding the shit out of his face.

A sick grin I can't muster ghosts my lips.

Die, motherfucker.

The loud party fills with cries and gasps at the commotion below me.

"*If you ever touch her again-*" a voice growls, his raven-black hair shinning in the moonlight.

My heart beats harder in my chest. *Finn.*

Leave him. Please, come get me.

Please.

Darkness pulls me into the abyss, and I finally leave reality behind.

Amelia

When I wake up in a tandom bed, panic surges through me once more. My arms twitch searching my surroundings with tired muscles.

I find Finn sitting next to me in a chair, his head down, thumb gently rolling over my hand. Feeling me move, he looks at me and then jerks to his feet, helping me sit up.

"How are you feeling?" his voice cracks painfully like he knows there is no positive answer I can give.

I stare at him, unsure of how to answer.

Do I lie and tell him I'm fine? Or do I tell him that right now, I feel like I want to claw my own skin off and end my life? Surely that's not the answer he wants.

"Can you get to the shower?" he asks me in a low voice, sounding unsure.

I hesitate but then nod. I want to scrub this feeling away.

With his help, I make my way to the bathroom. He stands outside the shower and helps me wash, gently scrubbing my skin. I push his hand firmer into my skin, instructing him to scrub harder. My skin aches, but I ignore it, wanting to feel Finn's pressure on me instead of the ghost of Lance still lingering in the emptiness.

He pauses at my pubic bone, and I guide his hand lower. I don't look at the red and purple skin I know is down there. There is nothing sexual about the contact. I make him scrub with enough force to make my eyes spill tears. I assume he understands what I am doing, but the looks of pity he gives me just pisses me off.

I cut my eyes at him, still not wanting to talk. I need him to wash Lance's touches from my skin. He has to be the one to do it because I cannot allow myself to become fearful of his contact.

I spread my legs further, and the warm soapy water burns the tear I just realized was down there.

"Motherfucker," Finn mumbles, and I look up to the ceiling, the feeling in my chest indescribable as I stand there naked and broken, bleeding between my legs.

He rinses me off and helps me step out of the shower. As he squats down to dry my legs, I notice his hands trembling.

I don't want to be treated like I'm going to break, but that's precisely how he looks at me as he takes in the already-forming bruises on my thighs and hips.

"I'm okay, Finn," I say in a whisper, my throat scratchy and sore.

"I... words will never be enough to tell you how sorry I am for not getting to you before he-."

He looks up at me, and even though his anger is clear, a single tear slips from his eye.

Grabbing his face, I brush it off his cheek with my thumb, and he leans into my touch. I close my eyes and he lifts me up, laying me down on pillows that smell like him. He runs his hands down every inch of my skin, pressing firmly.

"*I* am here. You are *mine*."

His voice settles me, contrasting to the fear as his hands linger on the bruises. My wrists, my thighs, my cheek. My pubic area.

"*My* touch replaces his. He is not here. Never again."

"I am yours," I say softly, placing my hand on his, feeling every vein and texture that makes it him.

"Yes, baby," he mumbles, brushing my swollen cheek with his fingers, his lips attempting to curl into a half-hearted smile.

"He is not here," I repeat, keeping my eyes locked on Finn's, watching as they soften, the stress leaving his body as I relax into him.

Sitting me up, he dresses me in some of his oversized clothes and climbs on the bed, curling around me and holding my face tightly to his chest. The pressure grounds me as his smell surrounds me.

***

We lay there for what felt like an hour focusing on the sound of his breathing, matching my own, keeping me from spiraling. My head on his stomach, hair sprawled out over his chest.

He combs through my wet hair soothingly. Long enough for my breathing to resume a normal pattern.

My eyes are heavy when he sits up, the air chilling the place warmed by his body touching mine. "I'm going to run to the store and get you some Pedialyte and Ibuprofen.

The party's over, so don't worry about anyone coming in. It's just my boys here now." He touches my face, forcing my eyes to his. "You are safe here."

I want to beg him to stay, but I don't. As much as I appreciate his comfort, I have to learn to be on my own. Now, more than ever.

He walks out, and the second the door closes, the voice comes back, whispering everything Lance said. I shove the pillow over my head, trying to block it out.

I have a surprise for you.

I'll be seeing you.

I know you love it.

His cruel eyes invade my thoughts, and I lurch over the side of the bed, vomiting into the small trash can next to it.

I wipe my mouth, gasping for air, and sob.

Taking a few breaths, I steady myself, sit up, and search for my phone. I look over the room and come up short. JJ's probably blowing up my phone.

I sit there for a few minutes, telling myself I need to go back to sleep, but the room's emptiness becomes too much.

Taking the bag from the trash can, I head down the stairs, steadying myself with the handrail as I shakily place one foot in front of the other ignoring the ache that is everywhere. Finally making it to the bottom floor, I stumble towards the living area, tossing the trash bag into the garbage as I pass through the kitchen.

I find my phone where I left it on the couch and see it's about three A.M.

Three hours.

I don't see any missed calls or texts.

Okay, that's not usual.

Flipping to JJ's chat, I see about ten messages from her and a reply from "me."

Me:
Hey, it's Finn. She passed
out for the night and is
crashing here. She's okay.

JJ:

I scoff at Finn's message. He was just trying to minimize my stress right now, but the idea that I am okay is laughable. I'm in the calm before the storm, knowing it's only a matter of time before I break.

But the thought of calling her right now and explaining makes me want to throw up again, but I miss her and need the comfort of my own bed. I need to process and reach the next step on my own.

I startle as the front door opens, jerking around to find Finn.

My eyes trail over his body, soaking in how good he looks in black T-shirts that fit just a little too tight, and I am instantly disgusted with myself.

How the fuck could I be thinking things like that right now?

"Hey...Uh..," I start, fumbling on my words, "Can you just take me home?"

"No. You're not leaving." he says flatly, stopping in front of me.

"Why? I.. I need to go. And I... I can't stay here," I stammer out, my head pounding.

"You need someone to keep that prick away from you, to take care of you, and it isn't going to be your mom.. or yourself."

"So it's supposed to be you, then?" I say with an attitude, hurt that he just used the ammo about my mom and mental health that I gave him weeks ago. "Fuck off."

"Yes. Among others."

Others?

I don't need a whole fucking crew of babysitters. It's not that I don't want to be looked after; I don't want to be seen when I finally lose my shit. A person can only take so much, and this...this is my breaking point. I'm only waiting for it to register fully.

Minutes pass as I hold his piercing stare, challenging those dark green eyes. Earlier, I could have sworn they were hazel, but there is no hint of brown within them. Had I imagined the dark caramel color before?

He turns around to pace the floor, rubbing his head, and I see the tip of the tattooed wing poking out of his shirt. He sighs and scrubs his hands over his face.

"Can I at least get the Ibuprofen you bought then, asshole?" I gripe, begging for the opportunity to leave. I'll walk out of here and call JJ on the way.

He scoffs, "Yeah, let me get that from the car. Don't fucking go anywhere, Angel."

He walks outside, slamming the sliding door, making me jump again.

Yeah right. Talk about a fucking mood swing with that one.

Maybe it's another sign, one, I might listen to before shit goes sideways.

You will never find someone to truly love you.

You are a magnet for failure.

My heart starts racing, and I know I'm about to have a panic attack.

Unable to remember if I brought my purse, I walk to the bathroom and fumble through the medicine cabinet, praying I find something to take the edge off before I leave.

Fuck Finn's permission.

I finally find a bottle of Benzos and let out a sigh of relief. I crush two on the counter using the pill bottle and quickly snort them so they enter my bloodstream faster.

Willing the mental and physical pain to subside, I sink down to my knees. Sparing a few minutes to cry, thinking about where the fuck my life is headed and what the hell I did to deserve any of this.

Not wanting to get caught, I slug out of the bathroom, holding onto the walls as I return to my phone. Just as I enter the kitchen, Finn comes in the front door holding the shopping bag.

He cocks his head at me sideways, looking at me curiously.

"Amelia...what's wrong?" His eyes flick around the house then back to me as if searching for an intruder.

He turns to the side, locking the door, and my eyes land on his neck.

Where's his tattoo?

I stare for a minute, silently scanning his body, and my brain feels like an old staticky T.V.

He walks up to me, cups my face, tilts my head slightly, and kisses my cheek softly. "Come on, baby. Let's go lay down. You shouldn't be up right now."

I stare into his eyes.

His very deep-brown eyes.

A tear slips free and trails down my cheek. The voice in my head chants once more and confusion ripples through me. My mind goes straight to my mother. Maybe, like her, I am finally losing my shit.

"Crazy" the voice whispers.

I hear the back opening, but I don't move, still trying to process what my head is doing to me.

Finn's eyes widen as they fall back down to mine. He closes them tightly and sighs like he realizes something I don't.

"You were supposed to wait," he says, looking over my shoulder.

I turn around to face the same direction, and my heart sinks.

Finn?

"Wha..." I try to speak, but I'm getting progressively dizzier, and the only thing that makes sense is that I don't want to be here. Thinking is too much. Breathing is too much.

Everything is too much.

I stumble, and Finn catches me against his chest, tilting my chin to look at him. Worry etched across his face, but all I can think about is how I want to dive into his eyes and never leave. They hold so much love, like I can see the entirety of who he is just by the way he is looking at me right now, all the anger from moments ago gone.

Why can't I ever stick to my guns when someone shows me a reason to leave just because they showed me a reason to stay?

"Did you take something, baby?"

"Yeah. Probably shouldn't have since I was drugged earlier, but I couldn't stand to hear his voice." I get progressively dizzier, and my vision gets spotty, causing my stomach to whirl.

"I- I'm not feeling so hot, though. You might be right about me not being able to take care of m- me." I laugh, my voice slurring, suddenly realizing just how far I have tumbled down the rabbit hole recently.

I am just like her.

"I never said..." Finn starts to protest but stops and shoots a sharp glare at impostor Finn across the room.

Can he see him too?

I turn my head to look at said impostor, who shrugs.

"Oops," he smirks at Finn. "Now might be a good time to explain to her that you have a twin, *brother*."

His eyes land on me, and I scan his body.

Almost everything about him is identical to Finn, except for his eyes and tattoo. There is also the slight muscle difference and facial structure, but you would never know unless they were standing in the same room or you knew them well enough.

"I'm Carlisle," he says in a low sultry voice with a wink and no shame. Then it registers somewhere in my mind as I think back to the behavior at the lake.

It was him?

The harder I try to think, the more my head throbs. The room spins and I feel like I am going to hurl.

Carlisle's stare instantly changes from purposely sexual to fierce and angry. He walks over and pulls my right eye open wide with two fingers, and I feel my eyes rolling in the back of my head.

"Angel, how much did you-"

Blackness creeps in as my body goes limp, fully collapsing in Finn's arms. Just as everything goes black, I hear two deep voices collaboratively sigh, "Fuck."

Carlisle

Earlier the same day at the lake...

I storm out of the woods, seeing red, as I make it back to my car. I yank my phone out of my front seat and call my brother.

"Hello?" he asks, calm as day.

I hear chatter around him and know that he's still down by the water I didn't make it to. My knuckles grip my phone so hard I'm surprised it doesn't crack.

"Get your fucking ass up here now. I'm parked on the left."

That's all I give him before ending the call. I close my eyes and try to calm my breathing. Minutes later, Finn is opening the passenger side door of my baby-blue 1969 Chevrolet Chevelle.

"What's got your panties in a twist, dude?" he asks with a pissed tone. "I want you to come down there and meet Mel officially."

"Already did," I say, keeping my eyes on the water in front of me, thinking about the way her perfect lips looked wrapped around my cock.

She had me wrapped around her finger the minute she looked at me with those big green eyes and sucked me in deeper into her world as she begged me to thoroughly fuck her.

"I was walking down there when I saw her walking into the woods with a blunt and a fucking depressing look on her face," I blurt out, turning my head to him, letting my anger shine bright.

I knew Amelia Mason's face. I recognized it instantly when Finn showed me a picture of them.

"You wanna tell me why the fuck you let her go off to smoke by herself, knowing that she self-harms? And from the looks of the gash on her arm, has had a really shitty day?"

His face contorts with pain. "I didn't know that's what she was going to do, but I'm not gonna force her to be anyone she isn't, Lyle. I watch her to make sure she isn't in such a dark place that she would take it too far, but we all have our vices." He gives me a pointed look. "If I tried to stop her, control her, she would push me away."

I scoot further away from him, leaning my back on the car door so I can face him fully. "Interesting theory considering she didn't push me away when I slapped the lighter out of her cute little hands mid-burn. Then fucked her so hard she forgot what had her so wound up."

He goes still, the air between us thickening, and I can feel the rage rolling off him in waves as what I have done registers. "You did what?!"

I shrug casually, barely giving a fuck that I screwed his girl. No girl ever stays around long enough for it to matter. Bros over hoes, and all that.

"She thought I was you, and I kept her from hurting herself. I fail to see the issue here."

"The issue is that she had sex with you, thinking it was me." He run's his hands through his damp hair before slamming them into the steering wheel. "I care about her! How much do you think she will trust either of us when she finds out?"

He says she's been controlled her whole life. If not by her mother or the fucker that had her heart for years, then by her thoughts and emotions. I can see she is strong willed, but her soul is fractured. A hit too hard, and it just might shatter. But I'm still struggling to feel remorseful.

"It would have taken two fucking seconds, Carlisle. We have to explain before she figures it out herself and shit blows up. Call Ian and tell him to get the word out that we are throwing a party at the house tonight," he says, already working this out in his head.

"If it would have taken two fucking seconds why haven't you planned to tell her before now?"

He holds my stare, not backing down. "It was best for everyone that she didn't know about you until I thought she could stay. Until I thought you might be ready for her to stay."

My jaw tightens. "Don't act like she is staying," I say defensively.

I know how this plays out. Though, I can't lie and say I don't see his reasons.

I'm already obsessed with her.

Finn

Now...

After making sure Amelia was still breathing and wasn't going to overdose, I tucked her in my bed upstairs and head back down to kill my brother.

"Do you realize how much you just fucked with her head?!" I yell at Lyle, not fearing prying ears. "I told you to leave until she was ready!"

"Oh, give it a rest. Big fucking whoop, she didn't know you had a twin. She has bigger shit to deal with right now!" He fires back, apparently as worked up as I am, "And as much as you want to hate me for shaking the foundation of whatever y'all have together, she's not staying."

"She could."

The room falls silent for a moment. "Besides," Lyle continues, "she could tell something seemed different with *'you'* when it was *me*. She can decipher who was who now that she knows."

"You willing to test that theory?" I ask, smelling a challenge and still pissed enough that I don't have to hide the desire for him to be wrong. The rules are, you lose, you get your shit rocked.

"Absolutely!" he quips back, moving closer into my space, now nose to nose with me.

Although it will kill me if she enjoyed being with my brother, part of me hopes she knows me and what I would and wouldn't say or do to her.

Lyle can be a complete dick sometimes. That seems to be her type, though.

So where does that leave me?

Regardless of the outcome, win or lose, Lyle is going to get his shit rocked.

"Can you two put your dicks away? There is a much bigger issue that needs to be handled," Ian groans, toying with his lip ring nervously.

He's never been very good at hiding his inner thoughts or ambitions.

"What are we going to do with Lance?" I ask the group, agreeing that we need to focus on the bigger problem at hand.

Blank stares and empty silence fill the room as we explore the options and our internal battles.

Ian tracked them on surveillance to the local hospital, Trinity General, using his tech skills. He was basically crawling through the front doors. Just in case the fear of God we put into him wasn't enough, Ian made sure to make the call.

One we make frequently to the hospital coordinators to ensure they know to keep their fat lips shut unless they want a lawsuit. One threatening to air that the hospital has multiple employees guilty of negligence and malpractice.

What Lance has done, in our home no less, means we have a choice to make. Leave it where it stands, or right it our way. There's usually no question about handling such disrespect, but for some reason I am putting Amelia's feelings above our vow.

I try to convince myself that it has to be done, and if she can't stomach it, it won't matter. But my heart screams otherwise.

Relaxing into the couch, I let out a long breath as I fight my internal battle. I am pissed the fuck off, but thoughts of her seem to calm the raging waves.

My body twitches with the need to rush up those stairs and hold her. To run my fingers through her hair and stare at the perfect features of her face, squished by the palm of her. I want to be there when she wakes up. I never want to let another day pass where she wakes up alone or scared again.

Fuck. What has she done to me?

I am breaking the one rule I swore myself to keep.

Don't care enough for it to hurt when she's gone.

But it already hurts.

I need her to stay.

I have to convince them to do this.

I lift my gaze, finding Lyle's smug expression gone, taken over by a look of pure anger. I wonder what he read on my face.

You would think after studying human behavior, I would be better at manipulating my own. But truth is, I've always been a very transparent person.

I scrub over my face before looking at Silas, pacing around the room.

"We need to eat something and sober up before we make any decisions, or we might do something we regret," Ian states.

"I wouldn't regret a damn thing." Silas mumbles, barely loud enough for us to hear.

He never does.

Ian gets up to throw a frozen pizza in the oven, and we all look at each other.

There's no way in hell any of us are getting any sleep right now. Which also means there is no chance of me sneaking back into my room to lie next to her. They would see it for what it is.

I'm attached to her.

Silas leaves the room once Ian comes back, returning to his cave, our in-home gym. The dude would marry his punching bag if it had a vagina. Come to think of it, that might be his only option with how much he enjoys getting overly physical in the bedroom. Maybe we should give the heavy bitch a name.

The rest of us avoid eye contact, but the room's energy reads clear. We're all thinking the same thing.

What the fuck happens now?

Amelia

I wake up to complete silence, in someone else's t-shirt. Again, having no idea where I am. Panic overrides my body for a minute before it all comes rushing back. The fear. The pain.

The embarrassment.

I look around the room and take in the vaguely familiar dark walls and navy blue comforter. I'm still at Finn's friend's house. Ian, I think.

I smooth my hand over the soft fabric on the bed to avoid touching my skin. My feet tingle with the need to rush downstairs to find Finn. That would be clingy, wouldn't it?

Picking at the lint balls on the bed, I contemplate how to handle this.

I could casually walk down the stairs and out the front door, never discussing this again. I could find Finn and cry a river into his arms. I could compartmentalize and pretend that what has happened doesn't bother me in the least. Yeah, that sounds good.

When in doubt, stick to what you know.

Isn't that a thing people say?

I swing my feet over the side of the bed and place them firmly on the floor. One foot in front of the other. I slowly turn the knob as stealthily as possible. I step into the hallway, and it feels as if the temperature drops five degrees. It's silent too, like I'm the only one here.

Doors line the hall, and a memory flies to the front of my mind.

Finn has a twin.

Curiosity takes over, and I walk downstairs faster than I was previously moving.

The sun is going down, the low orange light filling the house.

I slept all day?

That must be why, other than the dull aching pain of bruises, I feel better. Clearheaded. I haven't been able to sleep that well in years, not that I am thankful for last night's events.

I round the bottom of the stairs and see Finn passed out on a familiar couch that has been moved back to its seemingly rightful place in a smaller area. At least, I think it's Finn, though I'm not sure now, and I can't decide if I hate that.

I find the blonde-haired guy that's always with Finn lying on the other end of the couch. His mouth wide open, shaggy hair splayed messily every which way. I inch closer, rounding the end to get a better view of the second couch that dons another onyx-haired man lying face down, feet hanging off the end. I walk closer, carefully stepping lightly to get a better look.

Tattoo.

This is the brother.

Carlisle?

I give a fake cough.

Carlisle stirs then hurriedly sits up once he sees me. He reaches over and slaps Finn on the head, startling him awake. Finn then slaps the blonde beside him. And I try to fight back a smile at the domino effect, but fail and end up beaming with enjoyment at the sight before me.

"Well, she's smiling, so that must be a good sign, right?" Ian says, casting a wink at Finn.

"Ian, Jesus." Finn says back with his brows scrunched.

"So this is your house?" I ask Ian, looking around at the beautiful place he calls home.

"My house officially, but a home to all of us." He smiles brightly, and I realize it's my first time seeing it. It's contagious. One of those smiles that are so big that it makes the room seem to brighten every time you see it.

"Us?" I ask nervously. How many freaking guys live here.

"Me, Finn, Carlisle, and Silas." Ian says, leaning back on the couch, stretching his arms out along the back before rocking his head side to side to crack it. It instantly makes me want to do the same.

"Silas?" I ask.

"Present," a heavy voice says, coming into the living room, shirtless and covered in sweat. Silas is a few inches taller than the other boys, tattooed from head to toe, and absolutely ripped. I bet I could use his abs as a washboard... or a cheese grater.

I stare as we walk into the room, but he doesn't make eye contact. Just plops in a chair and props his head in his hand, giving a little dismissive wave. I see his face head-on, and realize I have seen him before.

He's the guy that roid-raged the night I met Finn.

Finn's soft voice pulls me back in, and the tone underlining his words has my stomach clenching. "Mel...we need to talk about yesterday."

I cross my arms. I'm not sure why this requires a whole ass family meeting, but there was no way I was going to be able to convince them to leave it alone. In any other situation, I may have tossed up both middle fingers and unkindly left the building. But right now, I feel something I can't explain. Something safe; familiar. Not in the sense that I have felt it before, but perhaps in another life.

"Okay," I agree.

Seeing Finn in the same room with his brother has my head swimming. His eyes watch mine flick back and forth between them.

"Well, for starters, I want to apologize for how you met Carlisle. Officially and unofficially," he says, as I pick at my fingers.

I only nod in acceptance. I'm not entirely sure how to feel or what to say about anything that happened yesterday.

Carlisle shifts in his seat and motions to his brother. "I told you it wasn't a big deal. She's stronger than you give her credit for." His eyes darken as they move to me, and the weight now has me shifting uncomfortably at the feeling it gives me, one that comes all too soon. My guard slips.

"Excuse me?" I throw my words angrily at Carlisle. "You having sex with me under false pretenses was pretty fucked."

There is so much emotion inside of me that wants to spill out in anger, but there's nothing else that he's done to earn it. Honestly, I'm not even sure I am mad at Carlisle. Maybe irritated, like how you feel towards a child who misbehaves.

I stay unmoving, despite his unrelenting stare that seems to undress me. He doesn't even flinch at my words.

"You got a point," he says, fighting a smile that proves he is not entirely remorseful, if at all. "That was out of character for me if it makes a difference, so I hope you do forgive me." He tilts his head, and I don't miss his tongue's subtle dip over his bottom lip.

Whatever confidence juice this man mixes in his protein shakes, I need some.

The pieces of memories fall into place, and I now feel like I have the upper hand.

"I was having a pretty off day too. I hope you do forgive me." I mimic his head tilt and move my hand between my legs to fake an itch. I had tried to warn him about my infection, but he cut me off without any idea of what I was going to say.

Carlisle looks at me curiously, and Finn chokes on a laugh as I finish my next sentence. "Maybe you'll learn not to stick things where they don't belong."

Carlisle looks between us both, a little salty that he is not on the inside of this joke.

Deciding I am going to let him stew on that for a minute or two, I plop down on the coffee table in front of them and cross my legs. I lean back on my hands, trying to act like the reason for doing so is not from the pain between my legs.

"Well, she obviously put two and two together and knew when it was me, so pay up," Carlisle says smugly, trying to hide the bother he still feels.

I guess that one time was the only time. I was kind of hoping that there was another.

Both twins stand and close the gap between their bodies. Finn's right fist connects with Carlisle's jaw just as he is getting his guard up and I slap my hand to my mouth in shock.

Finn growls over the sounds of his brother's groans. "That was for the both of us. The rules are that she would have to point it out directly. Sit the fuck down."

Carlisle squares his shoulders and wipes his split lip. "Okay, that was fair."

Seeing my opening, I take it, no longer caring about the other ears in the room. "Yes, and it's also fair that you need to get tested for Chlamydia, courtesy of Lance. Which you could have prevented if you would have let me talk before you fucked me."

All eyes turn to me, and it takes everything in me not to throw up at the words that just came out of my mouth.

Carlisle's mouth goes slack momentarily. Then busts out laughing.

Is he actually laughing? Who laughs at that?

I look at Finn, the words written all over my face, and he shakes his head.

"Oh, Angel. There might be hope for you yet," Carlisle says on an exhale through his dying laughter.

My stomach warms at the use of his nickname for me, and the memories of him panting it whisper in the back of my mind. That sex was hot, and honestly, it may be a little fucked, but I'm not *that* mad about it. Though, that doesn't mean I am entirely okay with it. Finn looks at me curiously, and my eyes drop to the floor, instantly feeling guilty for enjoying my time with Carlisle.

"Don't go back on all those filthy words now," Carlisle teases, enjoying the discomfort he is inflicting. He looks at his brother. "There is a difference in the way we choose to protect her and fuck her. I wonder which she prefers."

I take Finn's hand in mine, moving to his side. "If you were educated in female anatomy as much as you are in arrogance, you would know that my interest in Finn was the reason for my enjoyment with you. I don't want or need anything from you."

Liar.

Finn's fingers tighten around my own as he flips his brother the bird with his other hand.

"Keep telling yourself that," Carlisle grins.

"So, you both screwed her? That's fucking awesome," Silas finally speaks, his voice sounding murderous.

I look at him with a glare. "Slut shaming, are we?"

"Not exactly, love." He gives a sarcastic smile. "Can we move on, please?"

Another dick with a pretty face. Great.

"So, why didn't you just tell me you were Finn's twin?" I ask Carlisle, truly interested in why he didn't if it was supposedly out of character for him.

"Well, once I saw you hurting, I acted on impulse, which is normal for me. And honestly, after you called me Finn, I wanted to see how you would react to figuring it out. Call it sibling rivalry." His eyes ignite with that same challenging darkness as if he is testing me.

"So, you like to play with people, huh?" I ask him with a glare.

"No, babe. I like to see someone's potential. Their mind's strength," he replies, leaning forward with a devilish grin.

His lips touch my ear as he whispers low so no one else can hear, but my eyes meet Silas's. "I know I showed you new parts of yourself in those woods. I could see the awe all over your face, just as you could see it on mine."

"Enough!" Silas's fist slams into the wooden table, causing it to shake beneath me. My body jumps, and I gasp before I can hide the fear.

The room falls silent, and all eyes are on me.

My body flashes with a wave of heat, and I clear my throat. "Okay, next topic, please."

"You are handling last night surprisingly well, considering what it entailed." Ian interjects, pushing his shaggy blonde hair back just before Finn slaps him upside the head.

"Well," I explain, "It's not exactly the first time Lance has forced me to have sex or rough-handled me. Just the first time I realized what all the times before really were." Dropping my head, I look at my hands, picking at my nails nervously. "Though it's the first time he has intentionally drugged me, and...the first time I tried to fight him off."

I'm not ashamed of the actions of another person. You can't control what someone else does or says, only how you react. That's what I'm ashamed of. I never fought back or left.

"Coward." The voice whispers in my head, and I swallow, trying to force it back down.

I finally lift my head to see the boys staring at me, frozen and pained.

"The night I broke things off, he started by trying to get me to stay, but his words changed when I didn't back down. He got angry and violent." I rub the back of my neck, playing with a piece of hair while I try to recall exactly what he had said. "Last night, he said he wanted something from me and sent someone a picture of me... after."

They sit there silent for a minute, and my chest constricts at all the things they could be thinking about me.

Silas stands up abruptly. "I've got better places to be. Fill me in on the important shit later."

"Oh, I'm sorry. Is me being drugged and assaulted boring you?" I crow at him, hurt that my vulnerability is once again pushed aside.

"No, the fact that you have no spine does."

I stare at his back as he walks away, heading deeper into the house.

Tears sting my eyes as his words ring true. I hate that I eye fucked him for even a second.

"Don't mind him. He's a dick," Finn says, leaning forward to wipe a tear rolling down my cheek.

"So, how did he get you out there? I would think you have a bit more sense than to let him take you up there after his initial threats and abuse," Ian asks, crossing one ankle over the other leg and leaning forward in curiosity.

"This girl I met the same night I met Finn at the party. She gave me a drink, and I guess she slipped something in it. It was her idea to go out there." I look up at Finn. "She found me after I smoked the weed you left for me."

Finn's brows furrow. "Baby, I didn't leave you anything."

I laugh painfully, shaking my head at the floor, "God, I am so fucking stupid."

Finn's fingers find my knee, caressing softly as everyone realizes what happened.

"What is her name?" Ian's soft voice asks.

"Emma."

Ian's brow furrows. "Emma Anthony?" He looks over to Finn with an expression I can't read.

"Yeah.. why?"

Finn rubs a hand over his face and Carlisle's eyes go wide.

"Son. Of. A. Bitch," Carlisle says in a flat tone.

"She fucking walked right out the door. Right under our noses," Ian says defeatedly.

"I'm going to kill that bitch," Carlisle says.

"Chill the fuck out, Lyle. We will handle her, but right now, we need to figure out what the hell Lance wants from her and why Emma even helped him."

Lyle? Cute nickname, Hellcat.

"Why? I don't have much to offer, so what could he possibly take that would be worth anything?" They just stare at me. "And can't we just write Emma off as a shady cunt and move past all of this," I plead.

"Angel, I know you don't know us too well yet, but when people fuck with the ones we care about, they are dealt with," Carlisle says, moving a piece of hair behind my ear and kissing my cheek before walking away.

I hold my breath, not moving a muscle. He's right. I don't know them. Not really. I know the bare minimum about Finn but not nearly as much as they all now know about me.

Wait.

"People you care about?"

He winks at me and walks away without clarifying or retracting. If the feeling he sends to my stomach is any indication, I'm in deep shit with these two.

Carlisle

A gross joy takes over as I walk away from Amelia, thinking of the last time we had to plan an epic revenge plot to bury someone's sorry ass. I've been itching to get into some trouble again and beating the fuck out of Lance last night didn't even begin to scratch the itch.

I meet Silas in the gym, ready to blow off some pent-up frustration, partially because I want to beat Lance into the damn ground and partly because the whole time Amelia was battling me, I couldn't help but memorize the exact color of her eyes.

I don't know what it is that I feel for Amelia; I just know that when I see her scared, crying, or hating herself, I want to do whatever I can to help her evade it. I have seen her around over the years, yet never once noticed the fire inside of her.

According to Finn, she has spent her whole life trying to be what other people want her to be, never showing that fire. If there will ever be a time in her life when that changes, it's now. She doesn't realize she has so much potential to bring anyone to their knees at her mercy. She certainly did with Finn.

She tried so hard to convince us she didn't feel something different when she was with me. We both know it's not true, but I'll play along.

I open the gym doors, grab my gloves, and meet Silas at his punching bag. I go around the opposite side and stop the bag with my hands, peering around the side.

His skin is flushed red and dripping sweat. He avoids me, grabs his water bottle, and begins pacing.

"What's got you so worked up, Si?"

It's always been clear when something bothers him, he disappears into this gym for hours. I step in front of him, blocking the path he is pacing with a knowing look.

"Nothing," he snips at me finally, sitting in one of the chairs against the wall.

"Come on, man, we've known each other for over ten years. I know when something has got your panties in a twist." He avoids looking at me, his eyes cold and distant. "You almost had a stroke when you heard me and Finn banged Amelia."

Wait.

"Is that what's bothering you? You like her?"

He stands abruptly, moving towards me, swinging and landing a right hook on the bag hanging from the ceiling.

"I don't give a shit who either of you is banging, and what she does is between her, God, and her gyno." He swings a series of punches, grunts coming out in short breaths.

I scoff at him. "Okay, dick. Then what's your fucking problem?"

He stops the bag and throws off his gloves. "The problem is that you two are getting in too deep with her. You know she can't stay."

"She's different."

He tosses me an amused look, "No, she's not. She's a lost puppy."

Amelia is broken, sad, and scared, but she is also so much more. So much is under that surface, just waiting to be tapped into. I know it.

The four of us were once that lost puppy.

"Did you forget what you once looked like, Si? What makes her any different?"

Finn

"Where is she, anyway?" Lyle asks, looking around the house after he and Silas walk into the middle of my conversation with Ian.

"I sent her back home to spend some time with JJ," I answer without looking at him.

He rushes a few steps toward me as he growls. "Ex-fucking-scuse me? What if Lance is stalking her fine ass? Or worse, wants to get his hands on her again?"

I know I'm not anything more than sex to her, but she apparently has both of us by the nuts. It seems that we can't help but want to do everything we can to keep her near.

Ian seems not to care either way, and Silas looks like he's going to crawl out of his skin every time she's mentioned. I figured giving her some time to herself would do us all some good to sort out how we feel about her hanging around.

"Calm down, *Hellcat*. I put my number in her speed dial if she needed anything, and after being...assaulted." I can't even say the word. "I don't think what she needs is multiple penises in the same room with her."

"Give me her number. I don't give a fuck what you think she needs," Carlisle says, pulling out his phone. "Obviously, you aren't a great judge in that matter."

"Why would you need it?" I cock an eyebrow, choosing to ignore his comment.

"Maybe she likes my dick more than whatever it is you bring to the table," he says dismissively waving to me. "She might wanna booty call me. Considering I didn't even give her everything I got, maybe I'll really show her what I can do to that tight little body, and she will lose your number altogether, hmm?"

He stands and mimes, bending her over, licking his hand, swiping over her pussy, then throws his head back, moaning while he thrusts into the air.

"Caveman," I state blandly, but fear turns in my belly as I think about the possibility of Amelia choosing my brother and pushing me away.

She has told me her life story. She trusts me. Does that mean she likes me as a person? *I care about her.*

I was teasing when I told her I would give her whatever it was that she wanted from me, but what if I want to give her more? Could I be selfish? Assertive?

Would she run from me, fearful of being controlled?

No. I couldn't do that to her. This has to be her choice, or it won't work. They won't allow it to work unless it is. I will let her decide what she wants in her own time, and make myself okay with it, even if it's less than what I want.

What do I want?

Fuck. Get a grip, Finn. You've known her a couple of weeks, and you are acting like a love-sick puppy.

Lyle just looks at me, waiting for my phone with an outstretched hand.

"Whatever, but don't whine to me when she turns you down again," I say, handing my phone to him. "Maybe she can read you and knows you are going to come running to her for more, and she can't wait to laugh in your face."

He takes her number, then smiles at me. "Oh, I won't have to ask her for anything. She will be begging for another ride."

I roll my eyes. He's always been a cocky shit. Ironic since we have the same face. He may be a little more muscular than me from boxing regularly, but we are physically equal in every other aspect.

"She's not a chew toy. Show some respect," Ian chimes in, looking up from his phone. "Backtracking to what we were talking about. I can't find anything in the public database that gives any insight into what Lance wants from her."

"She's not safe until we know what his motives are, and apparently he's smarter enough to not run around flaunting them," Lyle agrees as he types on his phone.

"I can start by scanning the house for bugs and watching our security cameras. Not saying he made it in the house, but Emma could have placed something," Ian says.

We all nod, but Silas looks like he's barely listening.

You spend so long with someone, and you begin to see the signs.

His absence has been increasingly frequent, and lately, he seems to barely tolerate being around anyone. Whatever or whoever has got him so wound up better be ready for the explosion that is bound to come soon.

Amelia

JJ had a million questions, and I answered them to the best of my ability. She was plagued with the same feelings I had preceded by guilt. So, most of the past few days have been spent with her cuddling me in a tiny bed.

I made time and treated my tear and STI. I tried to convince myself that it was just another day of picking up the pieces that someone left behind. And I was successful until the second night when I woke up in a cold sweat. My legs were clenched, my muscles ached, and tears ran down my face. My first nightmare.

Five days of doing nothing and five days of wishing I was with Finn but not being able to pick up the phone other than replying to a text to let him know that I was still okay.

But am I really?

Being trapped in your head but unable to do anything about your situation is the stuff of nightmares. I don't know what awaits after death, but I know what I felt in those moments was hell.

My bruises are still visible, and my body still aches.

I want to be near Finn, but the idea of his comforting touches turning into something more makes me want to crawl out of my skin. This body is tainted, no longer feeling like my own.

Will he see me that way too...

The way he looked at me after the shower, like I was a broken toy...

An aggressive knock startles me, bringing me out of my rabbit hole of thoughts. JJ's parents are on a summer trip, and we weren't expecting visitors.

I walk warily to the door, peering through the peephole finding no one there. Unlocking the door, I pull it open just a crack.

A small box with a red bow tied neatly around it sits at my feet. A small tag hangs off the side, addressing it to me.

I freeze unsure if I should pick it up or leave it be. But curiosity gets the better of me.

Looking left and right for any sign of the person who may have left it I bend down and pick it. Up. Then quickly lock the door behind me.

I set the box on the couch between me and JJ and lift the lid. My stomach turning sour at the sight.

A picture of me the day we moved out of the dorm stares up at me with *'Can't hide'* written across it.

Signed... Lance.

"What the actual fuck is wrong with him?" JJ asks, her face turned up in disgust.

Another knock sounds at the door and I jump. JJ sits up straight, swinging her legs off, sending me a panicked look.

Sweat beads on my forehead, and I sit there, unmoving.

Another three knocks have me jumping to my feet.

I walk to the door and pause with my hand on the knob. In a moment of clarity, I rush to the kitchen, grab a knife, and return to the door. In a ready position, I slowly turn the knob and quickly yank it open, ready to pounce.

Quickly deflating as a familiar, smirking, raven-haired man leans up against the frame. His head falls to the knife, eyes guarded by sunglasses, and my shoulders drop, a sigh leaving my mouth in relief.

"Jesus Christ, you almost got stabbed."

He chuckles and moves inside the apartment, taking a look around.

I turn to JJ, and she smashes the box and picture between the cushions.

"Why didn't you?" he asks as he wanders around, inspecting pictures on display.

"Stab you? Because I know you?"

He spins to face me, raising a single brow. "You sure?"

"Wait," I say, holding up my empty hand and stepping back. "Which twin are you?"

He inches closer, making my heart thunder in my chest. "Why? You think one of us would hurt you?" His tone is both curious and accusing.

He's wearing a hoodie, so trying to search the back of his neck wouldn't do me any good.

His tone sounds like Finn asking if Carlisle has given me a reason to think he would hurt me, but his body language and the way he's teasing me sounds like Carlisle.

Finn wouldn't play games with me - I don't think. But I don't think Carlisle knows where JJ lives.

I shake my head nervously, and he inches closer.

I can feel JJ's stare, watching the interesting interaction.

He's so close now that my chest brushes his as it rises and falls, getting faster by the second.

"Wanna kiss me and see if you can figure it out?" He's inches from my lips.

"Yes!" JJ giggles, trying to answer for me.

I turn and give her a look, and the twin chuckles low, thoroughly enjoying this.

Before I can deny, his hand snakes around my waist, pulling me flush against him, crashing his lips against mine. My stomach sinks, but I don't pull away, even as every nerve in my body screams. His other hand cups my jaw and slides down my neck firmly as his kiss deepens.

His tongue explores every inch of my mouth. Elegant but demanding motions immediately telling me who this is. My whole body gets hot, and my heart feels like it's going to give out. He traps my bottom lip between his teeth, and I swear I see a grin.

He releases my lip, and my fingers brush the tender skin. He smiles freely and wickedly. "What's the verdict?"

I drop my hand, nervously picking at the bottom of my shorts, "Hellcat."

He turns his back and walks to the couch.

Did I guess wrong? *Shit*. I just screwed up.

"I left an impression, did I?"

He plops down, making himself at home, laying his head on the pillow I was just using. I let out a sigh of relief. He tilts his head and inhales. "Mmm... smells like you. Can I have this?"

Creep.

I roll my eyes then remember JJ is still here. I turn to face her, and she's smiling like an idiot.

"Damn. That was hot. Like *Wattpad* hot. I want my own sexy twins to play with." She giggles, with a pout.

I freeze, thinking about the fact that I just kissed Carlisle. Part of me knew it wasn't Finn, and that same part of me currently hates myself. I should have made him leave the second I knew.

"Relax, Angel. Just a little fun and Finn knows I am here. I rock-paper-scissored him for it, and I'm sure he's not a complete idiot." He smirks. "And can see that you might be a little into me too."

I walk over next to him, arms crossed and annoyed. "You rock-paper-scissored to see who got to come over?" I ask, biting back a laugh at the childish games. That familiar excitement sends tingles throughout my body.

"Absolutely, and I didn't hear you object to my statement," he points out, pulling me towards him.

I push off him, smoothing my shirt back down, "Consider this me objecting. How's that infection?"

JJ clears her throat. "I'm going to make myself scarce." Pointing a thumb to the door, she heads out, giving me a blushing smile, fisting the box and picture in her hand.

"Thanks, JJ. And remember, whatever you're hiding, secrets don't make friends," Carlisle sing-songs like he has known her his whole life, and she laughs nervously, widening her eyes at me. "Uh, just nudes for Tyler."

Door closed, he looks up at me with hooded eyes. "Treated. If you don't want me here, I'll leave." He waits for a moment before speaking again. "But I want you to know the day at the lake, I didn't find you intentionally. I didn't plan to sink myself into that tight pussy, but I won't say I'm sorry."

I don't move and don't speak.

"So," he continues, "Will you let me keep you company, or are you going to keep wallowing in self-pity like a child?"

Sighing, I sit next to him. "Fine. You're a dick." The side of his mouth tips up, and I quickly glare a look that could kill. "If you make a penis joke, I will castrate you."

Laughing, he holds his palms up in surrender.

"You're not getting laid, so why are you here?"

He tilts his head. "Do you really think I'm that shallow?"

He doesn't want me to answer that.

"I am not here to convince you to have sex with me." He grabs my hand, his thumb rubbing over the back of it. "I was thinking about watching a movie, eating some pizza, and taking a nap."

A genuine smile curls on my face, and the strangeness of the feeling causes it to disappear just as quickly. I agree, letting him choose the action-packed movie as I order delivery.

An hour later, we are lying in my bed. I am stuffed full of supreme pizza and dozing off from the feeling of normalcy when a hand lands across my stomach and pulls me closer into the curve of a large, warm body. Carlisle's steady breath warms my hair, and I stop breathing. I wait a long minute to make sure he isn't going to turn this into something more, and then I give in.

Sleeping peacefully for the first time in nearly a week.

***

I wake to my hair being brushed from my face, the strands tickling my nose as they pass.

"You know you drool when you sleep?" Carlisle whispers, his embarrassing claim not matching his tone's adoration.

I wipe my chin, finding evidence and scrunching my nose. "I blame it on finally sleeping well."

He props his head up, looking at me with a sense of achievement that is credited. Being alone has not been serving me as well as I thought, and as much as I hate to admit it, Carlisle is undoubtedly the reason for my drool. Feeling the emotion crawling up my throat, I tilt my head further down.

"You don't have to hide from me, Amelia." His soft voice brings comfort. The kind that calms your heart and tears open the wounds you so desperately tried to hold together. He pulls me closer, the pressure of his hug releasing everything I hadn't let free.

It's too much.

Tears stain my cheeks and his maroon hoodie.

He says nothing, letting me cry until I am good and embarrassed, though feeling better.

His fingers brush mine. "I want to really hold you."

A statement with a hidden question. *Is it okay?*

"Is Finn okay with this?"

This. Me laying next to his brother, my heart beating faster every time he touches me. My heart screaming for both of them. Was Finn okay with that?

"Yes. He wouldn't have let me come if he wasn't."

I check my phone to see if Finn has replied to my earlier message. It's warranted for me not to trust Carlisle, so I asked if his story was true. It is.

My mind swirls, trying to determine what I feel after confirming. We only agreed to friends with benefits. That's all we are.

I swallow. My body feels like a bag of bricks as I scoot closer, resting my head on his chest.

He grabs one of my legs and swings it over his waist. His chest hardens, and I can't tell if he flexed or tensed. He places his hand on my thigh, then immediately moves to my lower back and then up a little more.

"I'm not going to lose my shit from human contact, Carlisle."

He chuckles, always enjoying my snarky retorts. "I just don't want to... trigger anything."

I tilt my head up, our lips only a few inches apart. "I don't know what those boundaries are... or if I even have them."

I have gotten sick at the idea of having sex, but it's because, in my head, Lance is always there. But having Carlisle's hands touching me, I think the only nerves I have are about making a stupid mistake.

My eyes drift down to his perfectly pink lips. Then, ever so softly, I press my lips to his, gently deepening it as his lips part, allowing me in.

Stop! My head shouts, and I nearly leap off of him.

"I- I am sorry." I sit up, pulling myself from his body, the heat overwhelming.

"You have nothing to apologize for." His brows furrow then raise, realization dawning, "I won't bite unless you want me to."

My eyes narrow, and I wipe my remaining tears.

"Look, I won't lie and say that I don't feel something for you, but I am not that kind of man. If you want to be just friends, I can do that. And if you want more, I can do that too." He leans, pressing his lips to my temple.

I sit still, contemplating making him leave before something happens that I'll regret.

He's right. Finn and I aren't exclusive, but I can't lie and say I wish we were. I also can't deny the way Carlisle makes me feel.

His intense eyes draw me in, sinking me deep into something so wild and alluring. I swallow hard, trying to ignore my need for his hands to slide over another inch and touch my waist.

"Can I ask you a question?" he whispers. Sweat forms on my neck as I silently nod. "Do you enjoy comfort or challenges?"

I chew my lip, contemplating his question. "Comfort."

"You're lying."

"Excuse me?"

"You find peace in comfort because you are scared of challenges. Scared of failing."

My lips gap in defense. "I am not scared. I just..."

"You have never dared to do something for yourself that scared you. Prove me wrong."

I grind my teeth, annoyed and angry at his truth.

Truth coming from a man who knows nothing about me. Not really.

"I see how bad you want to, but you refuse to let yourself have it." His hand lifts from the bed, hovering as it slowly moves closer to my hip. He makes contact and I stop breathing.

"Do you trust me?"

"No," I answer truthfully, earning a low chuckle.

"Will you try if I promise it will not ruin things between you and my brother?"

I nod, barely noticeable.

What the hell am I doing?

His hand inches slowly up the curve of my side and under my baggy t-shirt.

I close my eyes, reaching for his hand to stop him.

"Eyes on me."

I open them, trying to determine what part of this is freaking me out. He pulls me over on top of him, my legs straddling his waist, his hard erection pressing into me firmly.

"Carlisle," I beg, fear shaking in my hands and legs.

"You have no idea how bad I've been waiting for you to say my name like that. I can't wait to hear you moan it."

Oh, sweet baby Jesus and all that is holy.

"I don't know if I can do this."

"I was joking. Halfway. Try for me, baby, and we can stop whenever you need to. This is for you."

I nod, both nervous and anxious, fully riding the high he is giving me, and not believing for a second that this is *only* for me. His hands grasp my hips firmly, moving my hips slowly against him.

I ignore the dull ache and warning telling me to stop before I cause irreparable mental damage, determined to see where it is he wants to take me. The friction feels all too good.

I start moving my hips on my own accord, humming quietly, my eyes remaining locked on his.

His grip on me tightens, and he stills my body. Moving one hand to grab my ass while the other grabs the back of my neck to pull me down lower to him. Eyes darting back and forth between mine.

"Why do you do that?"

"Do what?" he whispers, the warm air of his breath brushing my lips, causing a tingle between my legs.

"You look into my eyes like you are searching for something."

"Because I am," he says, pushing my chest back with a solid hand until I am the one laying on my back then he crawls on top of me, slowly, allowing me enough time to adjust to the newly feared position.

"And what exactly are you looking for?"

His tone is low and sexy, dripping with desire. "Your fire, my Angel."

My fire?

His Angel?

This feels wrong. Wrong, but so so good.

He tilts his head to the side, leaving soft kisses down my neck, pulling my shirt over my head. I suck in a breath between my teeth, and he lifts back up to look at me.

"Is this okay?"

Confirming, I encourage his hands to keep moving. Surprisingly, as long as I can see him, I am okay.

Am I strong or fucked-up?

"There you go, baby. I want to see the fire that you hide inside. Demand what you want and take nothing less. To be who you are and own your shit."

His words grip my heart and twist. That's why he stopped me from burning myself. He doesn't want me to let my demons win or even co-exist. He wants to see my fire.

My fight.

Me taking control, demanding what I want instead of letting the hurt rule me. I have never fought back because of the fear of being alone when my demands were heard. He wants that to change.

He continues his journey across my skin. Running the tips of his fingers down my arms, across my stomach, down my thighs, and back up again.

"So soft," he murmurs, kissing my skin everywhere but where I want him to.

The heat of his words and soft touches has made my thighs slick. I pinch my eyes closed, and he grabs my chin.

"I want you to look at me. Watch me worship this beautiful body like a temple. I want you to see how fucking much I am obsessed with you."

His demands aren't controlling; they are encouraging. Meant to build me up, not lock me in. Without the fear of thinking he might want me to be perfectly put-together, I'm left with only the burning ache of desire.

I give him a nod, letting him know I am okay, as I watch him slide back down the length of the bed, taking my shorts and panties with him in one swift motion.

He grabs the underneath of my knees and pushes my legs up to my stomach, giving him a clear view of my dripping wet pussy. He lets out a pained growl and looks directly at me as he swipes a finger through my lips.

"Are you this fucking wet all the time?"

I lick my dry lips before shaking my head.

"Hm, so right now, this is all for me, then?"

I nod, slightly fearing his next moves but trusting him to do this right.

"Use your words," he demands, drawing me out of my shell, sending chills through my body.

"Y-yes. I am wet for you."

He kisses me softly as he slowly separates my legs. I don't stop him. Not yet.

Right here, right now, I am wearing my discolored skin like a giant *fuck you* to the universe.

His fingers brush my heat then travel back to my thighs, allowing me to adjust. The need grows stronger as he teases me over and over again with the same motions. I arch my hips, signaling to him that I want more. That I need more.

He grins as he slips two fingers inside of me ever so slowly. My head goes back and a foreign sound comes from my mouth at the intrusion. I tense, throwing my lids back open.

"I'm right here."

He pleasures me, curling his fingers, moving them in and out carefully but demandingly. My breathing becomes labored, his matching, as I feel my orgasm quickly build.

"Fuck," I say on exhale.

"Tell me how good it feels," he instructs.

"So fucking good," I say, letting the words flow out of me in abandon.

"When you come, I want my name being screamed from those beautiful lips."

"Wait," I choke out, and he stills, fingers still inside me.

"If you want it, baby. Take it."

My God, this man and his filthy words.

He must be able to read my decision all over my face because he leans down to my neck, sucking and biting the sensitive skin, giving me one last chance to decide if I want to finish.

I moan and then he is moving his fingers in and out, his palm rubbing my clit as I start to ride his hand. I fall head first into my orgasm, and scream so loud my voice cracks.

"Fuck, Carlisle!"

"Good girl," he praises, pulling his fingers out of me and then licking them clean. "Goddamn, I don't think I'll ever get tired of feeling your pussy tighten or my name on your lips."

I sit up and my head drops, eyes fearfully meeting the bulge in his jeans. He lifts my chin back up.

"No, Angel. This time was all about showing you the strength you have, a man could never take away." He grabs me around the waist with one arm and falls back with me in his arms. "Challenge conquered."

"Thank you," I say in a low voice, not sure of the correct response to an act like that.

"Amelia, I just want you to see what I see. You are not weak. You will set fire to the world," he says, repeating his joke from the first time we met, but this time, there is no humor to be found in his voice. "And I'll be the hellcat kneeling at your feet if that's where you want me." He turns my head to his. "It's where I want to be."

Amelia

I wake up to a quiet humming noise and the sun's fading glow coming through the curtains. We had fallen asleep again.

Realizing the humming noise is coming from JJ's bed, I look over and see her curled up facing the wall with her earbuds in. I can't help the smile that comes at noticing her attempt to give us privacy in her own bedroom.

Turning, I look to my left, a set of eyes already on me.

"You are such a creep," I say, shoving Carlisle's face away. He lets it fall against the pillow but bounces and brings himself right back to me.

"I can see why my brother might want to keep you all to himself."

"Do you usually go after the girls he sleeps with?" I tease, rubbing my fingertips over his five o'clock stubble.

"Do you usually fall for twin brothers?"

"I haven't fallen, and stop deflecting."

He looks at me with a determined glint in his eye, "No, because we don't tend to keep them around long enough."

Oh.

"However, it seems we have changed our rules. You are staying with us. Permanently." He hovers over my body, then slides lower between my legs and parts them. His eyes fill with lust, his rough hands running up my thighs. His index finger brushes the scars partially hidden by new marks that will eventually fade to nothing and I suck in a breath.

"I told you, even though you're not ready to be mine, I would protect you like you already are. I meant that." My heart lurches and he grips my thighs firmly, a fierce darkness taking over his expression. "I won't control you in the aspect of determining who you are, but nothing will hurt you. Foreign or domestic."

I look down and swallow the lump in my throat as his words dawn on me and his promise takes root.

"I- I like the pain because I can control it," I say honestly, trying to defend myself. "Pain inflicted by me to take back the control others had over me."

Then it registers.

Even though my body is still echoing with pain, I was in control of the discomfort when Carlisle touched me. I allowed it. I made it happen - pushed for it. I wanted it to hurt again, but by my own wishes.

He lets out a sigh and lays his head on my thighs, fingers still brushing my mutilated skin.

"Angel, pain is a part of life. It shapes us just as much as love and laughter. You don't have to forget, but you have too much fight to think that you have to resort to this to move on. You control how you respond to what happens to you, and that is where your power lies." He kisses my thighs with the tenderest pecks.

"Our scars make us who we are. They are a reminder of where we have been. Let these remind you of what you have overcome, not what has overcome you."

My breathing gets shallow, a lump forming in my throat. My eyes burn as the first tear falls.

Sitting up, he pulls me into his lap.

"God, baby. No. Please don't cry. You are killing me." Pressing his forehead to mine, he whispers, "Please don't hurt yourself anymore. I don't think I can take it."

I sink into his embrace and inhale a deep breath before speaking. "I barely know you, and I've had a lifetime of pain. I would want to make an effort to keep that promise for my sake just as much as to please you, but that's easier said than done."

"I will be able to help." He kisses the top of my head. "You'll be living with me after all."

I pull back and pinch my brows in confusion. But he just grins a smile that could bring any girl to her knees.

"I told you. You are staying with us. Quite literally."

I laugh, half thinking he's joking, but he doesn't even crack a smile.

"I can't leave JJ to live with the four of you," I say flatly.

He's lost his mind.

"I wasn't asking," he says sternly, grabbing my full attention. "Finn may allow you to do whatever you want without regard to the cost, but I will not."

My jaw falls slack at his bluntness and sudden change in tone.

"It's the smartest choice all the way around. Safe. We protect what is ours."

There it is again.

Claim.

"I am not yours or anyone else's."

Maybe Finn's, but as he pointed out, we haven't declared anything officially.

"You keep telling yourself that, darlin."

Yeah, I'm trying.

"Two weeks," I say, considering the mini vacation.

"If claiming that makes you feel better, sure. Two weeks." He smiles, flashing those perfect white teeth at me.

"What if I refuse?" I ask, curiosity getting the better of me.

He leans in and gently kisses my neck, making me shiver.

"You can either walk to my car, or I can carry your ass out."

Despite what might be my better judgment, I agree and begin packing. Silent expressions pass between Carlisle and I as I throw clothes into my bag. He watches me contently and shows his appreciation for certain items of clothing. I scoff a little louder than intended when he lets out an exaggerated breath of air at my handful of panties.

JJ stirs awake, rubbing her eyes, letting out a groan with her stretch. She spots my bag and looks up at me confused. "Where are you going?"

Carlisle answers before I can, and I use the freedom from his gaze to slide the bottle of pills into my bag.

"She's gonna come to stay with us for a little while. You and Tyler are welcome to come over whenever you'd like. Just give one of us a heads up."

She looks between us and gives a filthy smile. "Riiight. Wouldn't want to walk in on any unholy fornication going on between you, Finn, and my best friend."

My cheeks burn, and Carlisle's chest shakes with laughter. "Intriguing thought, JJ, but I don't think sweet Finn would be willing to share Mel's sexy ass once she's in his bed, and Miss Thing has made it clear that *she's not interested in my dick anymore.*"

"But would you be willing?" It slips from my mouth before I can stop it.

His eyes darken with intrigue. "I'm down for all kinds of filthy things, baby."

My head gets dizzy, and my mouth goes dry as I take a minute to fantasize.

JJ laughs, filling the silence as I try to catch my breath and bring myself back down to earth. "Well, I might have to stop by now. Text me and have fun. I'm sure I'll see you soon."

I give her a smile and a nod before wrapping her in a tight hug. I kiss her on the cheek, then I'm out the door with Carlisle on my heels. I get in his car, throwing my bags in the backseat. It smells like men's cologne and weed.

"You smoke in here?" I ask as he slides into the driver's seat.

"Who do you think gave Finn that good-ass bud for you?" Well, in hindsight, that makes sense. "He said you liked to smoke to help with stress, so I gave him the good stuff as a gift for you. I was supposed to officially meet you that day since y'all are becoming more than a fling."

It clicks into place as he explains the timeline, and I push aside the mention of Finn already telling him he wants more with me.

I cross my arms defensively. "You gifted that to me and then took it back before you left."

"Yeah, that was shitty, huh? Misplaced anger."

I place my hand on top of his where it lies on the gear shift, trying to return the comfort. *What really bothered him that day?*

I make a mental note to figure that out another time.

Back at Ian's house, Carlisle shows me upstairs to an empty guest room.

"We all have our own room here, so I'll have to show you around, so you don't accidentally walk into the lion's den."

Lion's den?

"This one is yours to do whatever you want with, and we have another one for JJ if she wants to come to crash sometimes if you start drowning in testosterone."

Finn walks in, and a smile brighter than the sun shines at me. "Hey, baby! I missed you."

He hugs me tight and kisses me three times on my cheek.

My stomach sinks. *I have to tell him.*

"I see he convinced you to come stay awhile?" he asks, looking over his shoulder at Carlisle propped against the wall by the door.

"Oh, I can be *very* persuasive."

Finn doesn't miss his innuendo, and I start sweating. He looks back at me, and his face falls.

Fuck me.

"Are you... mad at me?" I ask nervously, fearing this trip has ended before it's even begun.

He trails a finger down my cheek and smiles lightly.

"Never. Whatever you need right now is solely your decision."

Finn looks at me with all the adoration in the world, leaving my head swarming with a million questions.

"If you care about me enough to have me here, why don't you care that your brother touched me?"

His jaw twitches, and he takes a step away from me. "I didn't say that I don't care. The thought of his hands on what is mine makes me slightly murderous, but I am willing to share if that's what you want.

"Share?"

They both look at me, but it's Finn who says, "If you want more than benefits from one of us, you get the four of us completely."

Amelia

Fresh out of the shower, I throw on a baggy shirt and panties, getting ready to climb into the queen bed I have all to myself now that the guys are occupied.

Fuck it's been a long day.

I spend some time unwinding and organizing my things. Finishing up, I throw a few things into the closet, I hear a thundering voice from downstairs causes me to jump a little.

"Amelia Mason! Get your fucking ass down here, now!"

Excuse me?

Rage burns through me as I walk out of my room and look over the railing. Silas is standing on the bottom floor, looking up at me. His expression turns sour.

"Are you deaf?"

"Are you a dick to compensate for the inches you lack?" I retort, making my way down the stairs to get in his face.

"What is your fucking problem with me?"

"My problem is that I called a meeting, and you took your sweet ass time." He glares.

"You said *family* meeting, didn't think that included me."

"When you are actively fucking your way through the family, shit involves you." The look of disgust is evident on his face as he looks down at my bare legs.

Embarrassment for my lack of pants creeps up until I look past his arm to see Carlisle looking at me with a pointed look.

Own your shit.

"Jealous?" I quip, looking back to Silas, and square my shoulders, causing my shirt to ride up slightly.

"Hardly." He looks down at my thighs again and then back to my eyes. "I don't make it a habit to put my dick in the same used-up hole that theirs have been in," he says before turning away and sitting in the same chair as last time.

I hold back a reaction to his insult and head to the couch, to an open spot between the twins.

Finn pulls me into his lap like it is my rightful place. He says nothing, but his embrace calms me.

"We need to catch Amelia up on my dad," Silas tells the guys while successfully talking around me like a child.

"Why?" Ian asks, almost afraid.

"His release date is years away," Finn adds from behind me.

I scrunch my brows in confusion.

"Something tells me he has other plans." Silas says, pulling a piece of paper from his back pocket and laying it down on the table. A sketch of an hourglass with the bottom half nearly full shows. Inside a man is drowning in sand reaching up for help.

All it's telling me is his father is a creepy ass lunatic that needs to spend more time in art class.

But the guys seem to read it differently. Each of them shares looks of fret and despair, adjusting in their seats and scrubbing some part of their body stressfully.

Something tells me if any of them have a hair trigger, this is it. No one says anything, and I don't ask, choosing not to gamble.

I stare at the image for a long time, artistically critiquing the lines and shading while simultaneously reading the message it depicts. Someone is running out of time in a very lethal way.

Eventually, I look up at Silas. He's already looking at me. The whole time I was reading the image, deep inside my thoughts, he was watching me.

"My father is a dangerous man who went to prison for abuse while drunk off his ass. It was not his first offense, just the first that we got him behind bars for. I'm not sure when, but he is planning on busting out. We will be his first targets."

"Okay?" But I don't understand how that pertains to me. I am not part of their group. What would his father want with me?

"Like I said, with you actively dropping your panties for my boys and them having no desire of you going anywhere, you might be on his radar as a way to fuck with them. It wouldn't be the first time."

Panic set's in, but my heart stings.

I'm not the first.

They've done this before, and it didn't end well.

Taking a deep breath I wrangle my emotions.

"Okay, so is this you all asking me to stay or leave?" I ask timidly, knowing the latter would make more sense logically, but my heart screams for them to want me to stay.

"You have to decide for yourself. Are you scared?" Ian asks me, and the look of curiosity is new for him. For the first time, he appears to be interested in more than logistics.

"No. I want to stay," I say looking around. "But do you all want me here?"

"What does that matter if you know what you want and the door has been opened?" Ian speaks again.

"Because I want to know which men in this room have a personal interest in me staying here and which ones would be less burdened by my absence."

Finn kisses my shoulder, confirming what I already knew. I look at Ian with a pointed stare, and despite the discomfort on his face, he smiles sweetly.

"I don't mind. You are welcome here. Plus, you aren't as hard on the eyes as these three."

Carlisle winks at Ian. "Don't pretend you haven't stared at our dicks just as much as the pussy they were going into."

My jealous bone tingles as I listen to their banter over their sexual history.

I turn to Silas for his answer, but he looks at his friends. "This isn't going to work."

"You haven't even tried giving it a chance. Ian is, so why won't you?" Finn asks, his voice both irritated and sorrowful.

Silas squares his shoulders then glares at me. They're cold, despite the warm color of them.

"I'm not going to stroke your ego. I have seen my dad hurt enough people in my lifetime, and I don't care to add another. It has nothing to do with your pussy and the poor places you decide to put it. You will stay until he is no longer a threat. Not a minute longer or shorter." Without another word, he walks out into the backyard.

Ian coughs, breaking the silence hanging in the large room. "Alrighty then, I guess the meeting is adjourned."

"God, he's a prick. How do you three put up with that?"

"Well, he's never commented on my pussy, so that makes it easier," Carlisle snorts.

I jerk my leg out in an attempt to kick him, but he catches my ankle and presses his lips to it, staring at my pink lace panties now showing. "Hot damn."

"I'll say," Finn says. "You know how hard I was fighting an erection, seeing her go nose to nose with Silas with her ass cheeks hanging out?"

Ian's face turns a shade of pink.

I realize now that from where I was standing earlier, Ian had a perfect few of everything on display during my brief argument with Silas.

My cheeks heat, and I tug my shirt down, wiggling back and forth to get it under me. Finn stills my hips, his dick now filling the gap between my thighs.

"I didn't mind the challenge. You're not the only one with kinks that developed from parental trauma," Ian chimes in, and I feel the color drain from my face.

Standing abruptly, I turn around, fisting my shirt by my sides. "What the hell, Finn. Did you tell everyone in this house that I fucked you then spilled all my issues? Did you tell them how I cling to you so much? That I must get off on you wanting to take care of me because mommy and boyfriend didn't?"

My eyes fill with tears, but I keep them open, willing the tears not to fall. I spin to Carlisle, and his face is scrunched slightly.

"And what the fuck did *you* say? That I loved you taking control of my pain? That I liked being dirty because mommy forced me always to be perfect?"

"It wasn't like that," Finn defends, "I didn't say anything about you to Ian and Silas until after the party when I had to explain who you were to me and what the hell happened. Lyle explained how he got mixed into it too. It was all factual to cover all the bases after some shit happened, not gossip."

"It wasn't yours to share." Anger and betrayal stoke my fire, burning my heart. "Y'all could have summarized vaguely or even waited for me to explain." My head spins, as my heartbeats loudly in my ears.

Ease the pain. Burn.

"I want to go to Barnes & Noble tomorrow." I change the subject refusing to look at the twins and just stare down at my nails picking them, a nervous tick. "So, one of you needs to get my car so I can drive myself."

"I'll get it tonight, but you need one of us with you when you leave here," Finn says quietly.

"I-"

"I don't want *anything* from you!" I say making a point to hold up a finger in Carlisle's face.

"I have to go to my dad's office tomorrow. If you want to tag along, we can stop by the store on the way home." Ian avoids my eyes as if he is just as flustered as I am.

"Fine. As long as you leave me the fuck alone once we are there."

Fuck. So far, this sucks.

Did I really just offer to bring her to the bookstore?

I pay close attention to her body language and the words that fall out of her mouth, still trying to determine what it is about her that intrigues me.

I pissed her off with my comment, but it wasn't intentional - just a sensitive subject, I guess.

She didn't seem like the kind of person to be private, but clearly, I made a bad judgment call with this one.

"You got it, sweet cheeks," I purr at her as her hips sway with every step she takes up the stairs.

She keeps walking but turns her head to see me propping my head up on my hands, making eyes at her ass. She rolls her eyes and pulls her shirt back down.

I know I'll hate myself for that later, but damn, she looks good walking away.

Christ.

"So, why are you going to see your dad after two years of no communication?" Finn asks once Amelia is out of earshot.

"Caught that, did you?" I run my hands through my hair and down my face, distorting the skin on my cheeks.

My dad hates that I didn't want to be a lawyer and follow in his footsteps. Never missing a chance to tell me all the ways I'm a failure and disgrace to the Davis name. But my mom refused to let him cut me off, so we compromised. At eighteen, I would move into one of our houses and only speak to my father if it was an absolute necessity.

I held my ground and chased my dreams; parents be damned.

"I checked the cameras after last weekend, and I saw Emma go upstairs. So, I went to check for bugs, but my damn RF detector finally shit out on me. So I have to go ask him where he put all my stuff when I left. Bastard won't answer my calls."

Not that I actually want to speak to the asshole or give him any preconceived idea that I give a shit about him. Really, I'm just going to make a scene.

"You need backup?" Lyle asks.

"Nah, I'll have the firecracker upstairs with me."

"Hell hath no fury," he mumbles.

Yeah, we could be in for more than we can handle with this one.

"Do you really think this time will be different if it gets that far?" I ask in a low voice.

"She's different." Lyle's answer is short and to the point.

She is.

Even I can see that truth no matter how much I try to deny it. There is something about her. Something that beckons you closer, promising all that you have ever dreamed of, if only you took the time to deserve it.

Are anyone's hands ever clean enough to deserve such a thing?

Amelia

I Immediately head upstairs to my room and shut the door. I turn a playlist to shuffle and put in my earbuds and climb underneath the covers, ready for this day to be over. I can't forgive myself for being so fragmented.

Moments come where I don't even feel like I am in the room. Like I'm a ghost floating through a fake world, unable to figure out where I am meant to be or why I feel the way I do. Why was I destined to live this life when clearly I was not built to withstand it?

One of my favorite letters comes to mind, and I begin sobbing softly.

"She's the girl whose smile isn't always real. She's the girl that cares a little too much what you say. She's the girl that will love you with every inch of herself. She's the girl that will watch the stars with you at night. She's the girl that will give you her entire heart.. and someday she will find someone to handle her with care."

A summary from Julie Martinez to describe the girl that will forever bring me to my knees.

Please, for me, never give up on someday, Mel.

- Not Him

I held that letter so close to my chest the night I found it, wishing I could engrave the words on my heart—another letter left without so much as a clue as to who left it. But I didn't care because I had someone out there that saw everything about me as enough.

I thought that I would find *him* eventually.

Finn and Carlisle are great, but I don't think anyone could ever measure up to *him*. How could they?

I have had years to perfect him in my head. Maybe he should stay that way. Forever something good and unchanging.

Finn left to get Amelia's car, and Ian returned to his cave, the muffled sounds of his guitar blasting. I am so glad he got that room soundproofed. I have never been able to sleep much at night but when he couldn't sleep either, he would wake up everyone in the damn house. We left it alone for a long time because it brought him peace, and well, it is his house, but eventually, we caved and made him do something about it if he demanded that we all see it as *our* house.

Heading back into the main living area, I decide I need a drink to process all the ways my world is crumbling around me yet again after so much effort to keep it whole.

It was foolish to think the darkness wouldn't follow me.

Maybe something in my past lives has damned me to live this life, never able to outrun the anguish that hunts me and those I love. I wish I could say seeing my father was the only source of my affliction, but I would be lying. I love my friends as my brothers. In my eyes, they *are* my brothers. I trust them with my life.

But we don't always tell each other everything, and this one thing would stay mine - at least for now.

I saunter up the stairs, careful to remain quiet as I head to my room. Soft cries leaking from her room stop me.

I must be a masochist.

Pressing my ear to the door, I strain to listen.

After moments of silence, I turn the doorknob as slowly as possible, hoping to go unnoticed.

She's facing the wall, and her body shakes softly. The familiar soft hum of music, and I know she is shutting the world out, as she has so many times before. I stay unmoving, listening to the pain being expelled from this girl who does not deserve anything she has been dealt.

I stay for longer than I care to admit, torturing myself as I watch such a familiar act.

My feet inch closer, despite my head screaming not to. Her petite frame stills as if she feels my nearing presence. Letting my rationality take over, I quickly slip from her room and back into my own.

I sit on my largely empty bed, fisting the half-empty bottle of whiskey, for only a moment before deciding I need to leave. I can't spend another minute of this night in the same house as her. Feeling her so close and knowing she has never been further away.

I slip my keys in my pocket, grab my bottle, and head for the door.

My spine tingles, knowing someone is watching me and quickly roll over to face the door as I suck in a breath. I don't want anyone to hear or see me like this.

Yes, you do. You want someone to come sweep you out of here and make everything okay. The voice in the back of my head lingers.

The reality is I don't need that. I'll cry out everything I've been pushing down, and once I'm done, I'll pick myself up and move on like I always do.

I wipe the remaining wetness from my cheeks and swing my legs over the side of the bed. Opening the door, I look to the side and find the hall empty, all doors closed. I only make it a few steps before my body slams to a halt.

Clutching my chest, I look up to see Silas's brown eyes piercing my own. My hand brushes the top of his abs with each hard exhale. His breathing stays perfectly even as I attempt to catch my own.

"Were–were you in my room?" I ask, doing my best to hide my erratic nerves.

His eyes slowly travel down the length of my body, stopping at my bare thighs once more. Though this time, there is something different.

When he looks back up, his brows are scrunched, causing wrinkles in the skin. I notice a glossy tint in his eyes and slightly pink whites.

"Why did it have to be you?" His voice is stern, and my heart aches at the familiar resentment in his tone, whiskey on his breath.

He's drunk.

"Am I really that bad?" I ask softly.

The state he's in isn't one I want to fight with and tonight, I don't think I have any left in me. I want to know what he really thinks of me.

He grabs a piece of my hair and trails down to the ends. "If I said yes, would it make you leave?" His eyes follow the water drops that fall and trail down my skin. My chest heaves under his heavy stare. "If so," his eyes lock on mine, "then, yes."

He snaps out of the trance he seemed to be in moments ago and walks past me, bumping my shoulder leaving me dumbfounded.

I tell myself I don't care what Silas thinks of me. I'm not seeking his approval.

But it's the feeling that his question leaves - A question I have asked myself.

Why me?

She's the girl whose smile isn't always real. She's the girl that cares a little too much what you say. She's the girl that will love you with every inch of herself. She's the girl that will watch the stars with you at night. She's the girl that will give you her entire heart.. and someday she will find someone to handle her with care."

A summary from Julie Martinez to describe the girl that will forever bring me to my knees.

Please, for me, never give up on someday, Mel.

-Not Him

Ian

I stayed up late playing. Music is how I express myself. It can make you feel every emotion. Can carry you back in time or hold your dreams. It can take you away on a high or help keep you grounded when you feel yourself drifting away. It can hide your secrets or confess what you want to say.

Last night, it was undecided what kept my fingers strumming over my guitar strings until I was cross-eyed and sweating. Thank God for soundproof padded walls, or I might have given the idea I was in need of an exorcism. I'm not thrilled about seeing my dad or hearing his usual bullshit, but I'm intrigued to spend the day with Amelia. The thought of her and the place she may have here plagued my mind all hours of the night.

At first, I couldn't see her appeal, but now I'm thinking there may be something worth my attention. But she isn't the helpless, naïve, attention-seeker I thought. Then her demeanor changed, as if Lyle reminded her of her true self. It wasn't forced, only hidden.

If Silas hurt her feelings, she didn't show it. And she didn't cower or pout when he didn't want her, even as she stood in front of him, half-naked. She wasn't even half-naked to get our attention; she was wearing what she wanted because she fucking wanted to.

It stirred feelings that haven't been around for a while, and I'm not entirely sure I'm ready for it.

Shaking my head, I try to focus on the morning ahead, but my mind falls back to her. Here.

I can see why someone would hurt another out of selflessness now.

Finn brought her staying with us up wisely and with great caution. But really it devolved into a lot of screaming and gloved fists flying.

Carlisle, though the most conflicted, was the first on board. I think he sees her as an experiment.

Curiosity had me agreeing next. Something new and surprising told me I needed to see this out.

Requiring a unanimous vote, we waited for Silas to come around. After last night it's clear his decision ultimately rested on the fact that he couldn't risk another life at his father's hands, despite his weariness of history repeating itself.

Given the chance, I think Si will put his father, ten feet under, dump four feet of dirt in, then plant a fake coffin before filling up the rest and marking it with a blank headstone. Nickolas underestimated us once. He would be a fool to do it again.

But now she had made it clear she wanted to be here, it was final.

We were doing this.

Even if we lose a part of ourselves.

Again.

Closing my eyes I take a deep breath, steadying myself.

The smell of bacon lures me out of bed and into the kitchen, where I find Lyle in his usual place cooking breakfast. Si looks like he's nursing a hangover, sitting at the island bar with his head flat against the cold surface.

Guess I wasn't the only one fighting internal battles last night.

I walk by Silas and squeeze his shoulder. "You alright, man?"

He grumbles, and I chuckle.

I don't necessarily enjoy his pain, but I am enjoying that Amelia clearly gets under his skin.

The death stare she continues to give the back of his head as she spills into the room says they didn't rectify that wrong foot they got off on.

She and Finn plop down on a stool next to me, the latter looking more miserable than she did last night. And I can't help but wonder if she slept any better. And if she didn't, which parts of her new life kept her awake.

It's clear the slightest sign of rejection can upset her, but I'm not entirely sure if it's approval she seeks or just acceptance.

Her face brightens slightly at the sight of our usual morning routine, and I struggle to look away. A small slightly crooked smile that slides into place like a missing puzzle piece.

"Carlisle. I didn't know you could cook," she says, grinning wide.

I guess her mood from last night has dissipated.

"Someone has to feed four growing men," he tosses over his shoulder.

"Oh, please, mister culinary master," I snort, "Don't act like cooking is some great burden you carry."

Amelia gasps in disbelief. Honestly, looking at him, you would think he could burn water, so her reaction has merit.

Lyle turns around and pops his hip out, mimicking a sassy stance that she would hold if she were standing.

"What makes you think I can't be as good in the kitchen as I am between your legs?"

Halfway to the fridge, she grabs and throws a kitchen towel at him. Catching it, he rolls it up and pops her thigh.

"We all have our passions, love. We all put in work at the shop, but that, too, is primarily mine. Outside of that, I like mastering food, Finn is into psychology, Ian's into music, and Silas - boxing."

She looks around at us like a museum of art. Her green eyes float around before they focus on me as if deciding I was the most interesting reveal.

I feel naked like she stripped me bare and is poking me with a stick. I don't look away, letting those green eyes lull me into their open field and imagine a cool breeze whipping around us as I lean in to kiss her...

"Music, huh?" she asks, looking at me like she's genuinely surprised. "Maybe you can show me sometime."

"I don't share my music." I give her a flat stare, her words sparking a memory I guard, and her posture hardens.

"Okay, you don't have to be a douche about it." She says it guardedly, trying to hide her embarrassment of overstepping.

With how much she enjoys learning about us, she'll find our triggers soon. I wonder if she will push the buttons she finds or if she will be wise and avoid them.

"It was just a fact. Why would I share something personal with someone I don't know?"

Silas laughs, the sound muffled from below his crossed arms, where his head rests.

She does her best to shrug it off and not look at Finn to rescue her.

She might last longer here than I projected.

She walks behind Lyle at the stove and snatches a piece of bacon from the skillet.

"Careful, it's hot," he warns her urgently and reaches for her hand. The hot grease pops, but it must miss her wrist. Shoving the hot bacon into her mouth, she chews it openly.

"I know."

Lyle gives her an alluring look, different from the one last night.

I wonder what this one says.

"Give it a rest," she groans, turning her back to him, but before she can round the island, Silas speaks up.

"Get me the Ibuprofen from the cabinet to your left."

"Oh, sure." She smiles at him as if she has wholeheartedly forgiven or forgotten the way he spoke to her last night. Once again, my question of acceptance or approval crosses my mind. Grabbing the bottle out of the cabinet, she throws it at him with full force, hitting him right in the middle of his forehead with a *thud*. The pills rattle as the small bottle falls to the floor.

"Do you have a fucking problem?" he bellows, arms bulging as he grips the countertop.

"If I said yes, would it make you leave? If so, then yes," she beams back with a big smile.

I almost snort coffee out of my nose. That was not what I was expecting from her. I like it.

No one has fucked with Silas like that, except for us, and been inclined to tell the story. They often end up with a broken jaw or teeth knocked out. A year ago, he broke both of someone's hands. Regardless of the punishment for disrespecting Silas, it's clear that if you refuse to keep your mouth shut about it, we all come back for more.

Yet here she is royally pissed, standing toe to toe with him, and I am thoroughly enticed to see more of it. Maybe, like me, she chooses to hold that side of herself close, only using it when necessary.

His stare goes cold, steam almost coming from his ears as he grinds his teeth, leaning down to pick up the pills. He takes them with a swig of orange juice and leaves towards the gym, stalking like a child that isn't getting their way.

"On that note," I laugh. "It's time to go. Go get dressed and meet me at the car in ten."

"Joy," she tosses over her shoulder sarcastically as she leaves.

I smile to myself. This could make for a fun day of pissing off my dad.

***

Amelia takes twenty minutes, and during that time, I decide she does like pushing boundaries. She climbs into the car wearing tight jeans and a crop top paired with neon slip-on vans. I catch myself staring at every detail of her body wondering what conclusion Finn has come up with about who she is.

Slinging the seat belt over her, she slumps in the seat. It's clear she has no desire for small talk making herself busy with her phone instead. Her petite fingers quickly brush over the screen as she types, and the simple task holds my attention.

She doesn't notice my lingering gaze that rests on her face, and for the first time, I wish she would. I want to tell her how beautiful she is, but I say nothing and return my focus to our goals for today.

The entire drive to Davis Due Process is silent except for the punk rock playing at a low volume and the loud thoughts in my head that keep pushing me closer to the edge of saying something. Anything.

Then her phone rings with a Facetime call from JJ. I don't hide the smirk curling on the side of my mouth at her choice of ringtone. The chorus of *I Will Not Bow by Breaking Benjamin.*

She narrows her eyes at me. It seems I need to make up for the first impression she has concluded of me. I need her to want to be around me, and right now, she seems almost as irritated with my presence as she is by Silas's. I contemplate my next moves as her sweet voice answers the call.

"Hey girl, what's up?" Her voice shows no tone of the attitude half an hour ago. She picks at her jeans and listens to her best friend's response.

Which one of us is making her nervous?

"Hey, Mel. Uh- Ian's family business is the Davis law firm, right?"

She looks at me and answers hesitantly after I nod.

"Yeah, why?"

"Because I just saw Emma walking out of there."

We exchange *what the fuck* looks.

"Maybe she's scared about that shit with Lance and is lawyering up in case you reported it?" JJ offers.

"Yeah, maybe... Okay, thanks, girl. I'll let the boys know."

There it is. She's been thinking about it. All of us.

She is feeling us all out before making a decision, and so far, I am not convincing her to stay. Despite everything my head is telling me about how this could end, I need her to stay.

She ends the call, rambling about how she always trusts the wrong people. I want to tell her, even though it sucks, it only means you see the world through rose-colored glasses and that it's something worth cherishing.

The reality is that you will often be wrong and accept snakes into your garden, but holding on to that purity in your heart is nothing to criticize. For most people, once you have been burned enough times, your heart hardens, and you trust no one.

I watch her curl into her shell and blame herself for being so naïve in a way that seems to be a pattern for her, and decide not to tell her any of that. Letting rationality win this round, I convince myself that I need to hold back and let this run its course without being talked down.

"Don't worry, we will look into Emma. You can help too."

"How? I don't know anything about the shady bitch."

"Emma Anthony is known for doing whatever she wants, just because she can. Be that starting gossip, backstabbing a friend for her gain, or even breaking up relationships by sleeping with a taken man," I tell her the details most people know.

A few minutes later we walk into the twenty-story building, and my breathing gets shallow as the elevator takes us to the top floor.

I attempt to regain control over my breathing, not wanting my father to see how much he still affects me. I say he doesn't, but the words that spill into my music beg to differ.

Amelia frowns when she notices. Despite my reluctance, I allow her to see a part of me.

"I just, uh, haven't seen him in a couple of years. He hates my guts because he was prepared to pass his empire down to a level-headed, self-preserving businessman. Instead, he got one that thinks our justice system is wack, suits are itchy, and hates publicity." I force a fake laugh, and she smiles, but it doesn't meet her eyes. "Oh, and I want to be a musician, which means I will amount to nothing if I can't stand being in front of crowds, ultimately proving him right."

"Fuck parents and their expectations." She straightens her shoulders and walks out as the doors open, but I'm held in place for a moment as I watch her.

We were raised by people who had a preconceived idea of who we should be so they could be proud of us.

She's resentful.

I step out after her, the too-quiet, too-clean office bringing a sense of unease. Our shoes softly squeak against the freshly waxed floor as we make our way to the front desk, where a bright-eyed blonde sits.

"Mr. Davis," the receptionist squeaks with a tight smile. She clears her throat and picks up the phone. "Mr. Davis, your son is here to see you." She waits a minute, and then her face turns a shade of pink. "Uh, Ian. Ian Davis is here to see you, Sir."

That's grand.

Jameson Davis does not claim an unworthy son. But that doesn't change that I still carry the family name, as well as all the ties that come with it.

"He'll see you now," she says with a tinge of sadness.

I flash a menacing grin, and we travel down the long hall to his glass cubicle at the end. I don't bother to knock, pushing the heavy door open for Amelia and closing it behind myself.

"To what do I owe this embarrassing and unwanted encounter?" My father leans against the front of his desk crossing his arms. He has no need to pretend when no other eyes are on him, and no ears can hear through the soundproof walls. His eyes drift to Amelia, and I see his lip twitch slightly. "And why, pray tell, is *she* here?"

"Amelia. We met years ago. Damian's daughter. He used to work for you," she reintroduces, reaching for his hand, but he declines, leaving her hand awkwardly extended for a few moments before she drops it, and her face falls.

I place my hand on her back, and she straightens, reading the room, and I swear I can feel the change in her attitude.

"She's with me, but you shouldn't worry about things that no longer concern you. I came for the rest of my stuff. Where did you put it?."

I never had anything to do with this part of my family name. Years ago, I left with as much as the four of us could haul in one load and nothing more. No direct contact since that day, and I'm reminded why by his *High Lord* attitude.

"It concerns me when my son comes into my business with trash on his arm. Bad for business."

Amelia laughs sharply, and his eyes round as they dart to her.

"So, now he's your son? Funny. You don't give a shit about him unless you deem his actions so bad that they might affect your image. I thought it was that very reason that you disowned him. See, now I'm confused." She finishes her verbal lashing with a mocking pout, and he looks back at me with utter disbelief.

"You think I'm going to defend you?" I ask. "She makes an excellent point. Tell me where my shit is, and we will be on our way. I don't want to be here any more than you want me here."

He swallows hard before speaking. "The basement. Get it and get out. Don't come back here. Ever."

He could deny me access to the building, but he never has, and I don't think he ever really would. How stupid of him.

She flips him the bird, and I am following right on her heels, a genuine smile glued where a flat line usually sits.

Maybe Finn is right.

I watch as her hips sway with every step she takes to our destination, and I have to readjust my dick as I think about all the trouble we could get into with her.

I could love this woman so hard.

***

She was perfectly focused searching for an unknown item, and I couldn't help but stare at her, as I got what I needed, along with what fit in the trunk of Finn's car.

"That was hilarious," I comment with a laugh as we slide back into the car, "The middle finger, Mel? How very trashy of you."

She slaps me on the arm. "What do you mean? I'm currently intertwined with brothers and rooming with four men. That's very classy."

Intertwined. Wishful thinking seeps deeper and deeper into my mind as I watch her out of the corner of my eye, as she, no doubt, rolls that information over in her head. She chews on her lip nervously as she gently nods her head to the low music playing through the speakers.

"What do you think of me?" she finally works up the nerve to ask.

"What makes my opinion different from your mother's or a complete stranger's?"

She pauses. "Nothing, but it doesn't make me want to know the answer any less."

Acceptance. She wants to know if we welcome who she is, not if we approve of her. If we didn't welcome her, would she leave?

"I am still trying to figure that out. You intrigue me, and that's saying something."

She nods thoughtfully then begins to watch the passing buildings out of the passenger window. "Do you think I am stupid for wanting to stay at the house when I think that I have feelings for both of them?"

My heart beats faster.

"Personally, no, but only you can decide if it is. You need to figure out what kind of future you see for yourself and if the four of us could play a part in that."

My heart is in my throat. I want her to hear everything I didn't say. I want us to be in her future, but at the same time, I'm terrified for her to want to be.

I keep my eyes on the road, but I can feel her looking me over.

"Can I ask you something now?"

Her eyes are still on me as she nods.

"Are you trying to imagine what your life could look like with the four of us loving you?"

I turn into the bookstore's parking lot and shift into park before turning in my seat to face her fully.

She chews on the inside of her cheek but doesn't look away. The struggle she is fighting to turn away from me written all over her face. She inhales deeply, and my eyes fall to her chest. The air around us thickens, and she slowly nods. I move only a few inches closer to her, and she stops breathing.

"To give you a better picture, you should know we all fuck very differently." My eyes fall to her lips, and she softly rolls them into her mouth. "And when we love someone, we love so hard that we will die for them. We would worship our girl in every sense of the word. Is that something you would like?"

Please say yes.

I want to hear her soft, nervous voice whisper that she wants everything we have to offer.

She says nothing, taking that with her to chew on as she claws out of the car and races into the store like she couldn't escape from me fast enough.

I follow her in but head to the music section to flip through old vinyl, trying to give her space while still tracking what genre she chooses to explore. I watch her turn into an aisle marked young adult fiction as I flick through the classics. I wait for her to reappear at the end but she darts into the erotica section across the walkway. Thoroughly intrigued, I slowly stalk towards her, trying to seem still occupied with my own interests.

When I finally reach her, she's curled in a chair in the back with her nose in a book. I take the long way around and sneak up behind her. Peeking over her shoulder seeing words like "moan" and "trembling" send blood rushing to my dick.

Finn's nickname for her comes to mind. *Dirty girl, indeed.*

"Whatcha reading?" I whisper in her ear.

She nearly jumps out of her skin and scrambles to her feet, spinning around to face me.

"Fuck, Ian. I thought our deal was you leave me alone?"

That was until our recent discussion and her choice in reading material. Now my deal has changed. I walk around the chair to her and peer down at the book's title, trying to read it through her fingers. Something about *Multiples*.

"Why are you embarrassed about your choice of material?" I lean down to her ear again and hear her breathing catch. "Doing some research before you decide?"

She shoves me back, "Fuck off."

"It's just a question," I shrug.

She turns her back and walks to put the book back, but I follow and stop her hand.

"Tell me about your book?" I whisper, my dick now pulsing with need.

"No."

"Are you always this mean, or is something else bothering you? Perhaps sexual frustration?"

"Is that what's bothering *you*?" She looks down pointedly.

Busted.

"Caught me," I whisper, leaning in against her neck, hear breath catching again.

"Ian."

"If I slipped my hand inside your jeans, would you be innocent?" I grip her hip, barely restraining the horrible urge to press myself into her.

"I.. we can't.."

Her voice trembles, and a cold wash flows over me as I take in her body. I'm scaring her.

"I'm sorry. You're right."

God damn myself.

I move my hand from the shelf, and she rushes away from me and probably straight out of the store. I collapse into the chair she was previously sitting in, cursing myself for letting my strength slip and being so fucking stupid.

Those horrible memories come flooding back, and I begin to doubt everything today has made me believe. I'm not sure I could let her in completely, no matter how much I believe she could be perfect for what we need. It seems I need to take my own advice and decide what my future looks like.

I want the small talk with her. I want to know what makes her smile and what she does when she's happy. I want to find out just how similar or different we are and explore all the terrifying possibilities that truth holds. I want to tell her that I like she is staying with us. That I want her to stay longer.

That I can picture a future with her.

But would I ever allow it?

I buy the book she was reading and find her waiting for me in the car. Honestly, I'm surprised she didn't try walking home to avoid being back in a confined space with me.

I place the book in her lap as an apology gift. She remains impassive.

"Words are not enough to tell you how sorry I am. I wasn't thinking."

She finally turns to look at me. The gloss coating her eyes and black streaks under them makes me want to rip my heart out. I stare out the windshield and grip the wheel tightly,

"Can we start over?"

She nervously picks at her fingers, having nothing left to say. A silent tear rolls down her cheek and her hands tremble in her lap.

I drop my hand to the shifter, ready to take us back to the house when her hand falls on top of mine. She doesn't look at me, but I feel peace wash over me that I have only ever felt when I play music.

Amelia

It's almost dinner time when we get home. Everyone is on the back patio, drinking, the music just loud enough that you can have regular conversations.

Finn comes over to hug me from behind while Carlisle chooses a new playlist. "Did you have fun?"

I nod and accept the kiss he plants on the side of my face, but this time it feels different. It feels loaded and temporary. He looks over my shoulder to Ian and scrunches his brows at whatever facial response he gets.

"JJ called earlier. Said she saw Emma leaving DDP," Ian explains.

The boys suddenly look interested and fully invested in whatever is about to come out of his mouth next.

"I'm going to hack his security footage and see if I can figure out why she was there. It may be nothing."

"None of you have slept with that bitch, right?" I scrunch up my face.

"Would you be jealous?" Finn asks.

"Protective?" Carlisle follows, biting his lower lip like that would be the hottest thing ever.

"No. Just would make me not want to be near any of you ever again." I wink in Finn's direction, completely ignoring Carlisle.

"Okay, okay. No, none of us have slept with her. She's way too fucking perky. Even for me." I can't hold back the chuckle as Finn says exactly what JJ and I have already joked about.

"I would have loved to see you knock that bitch out," Carlisle pouts.

Silas leans back in his chair and nods at me. "That one, fighting? I've seen puppy dogs with more fight instinct than her."

Finn holds up his hand at Silas. "She's been through shit, Si. She can learn. You had to start somewhere too, so don't go there." His eyes soften as he glances at me before looking back to Silas. "Once she knows how to swing, we can watch her give Emma what she fucking deserves. Give her a chance."

Unspoken words pass between them.

"I like the fucking sound of that." Carlisle smiles. "I volunteer to train you. Silas would probably just fuck with you the whole time. You need to learn how to fight, not how to be a dick."

"Yeah, and you would just try to fuck me."

Carlisle shrugs, but when I'm the only one looking at him, he cuts his eyes at me, reminding me of the help he promised with no strings attached. As much as I want to keep distance between us, I know I have to be reasonable.

"Fine. When do we start?"

"Not tonight," Finn says. "Tonight we drink our worries away, eat some damn good food, and I'm going to dance with my girl."

He turns up the music and pulls me to his chest. Spinning and dipping, he guides me as we dance around the back patio. After about the third song, I need a break to catch my breath.

Ian takes my place with Finn, and everyone laughs as their bromance is showcased.

I had to get another drink, willing my buzz to thrive, when Carlisle gives me a proposition. "Shots, and then we shake our asses?"

"Wait! I have a question!" I shout a little louder than intended, and they all pause, waiting for me to continue. "Can someone please elaborate on the fact that Finn told me if I want to really be with one of you, I have to accept all four of you assholes?"

I can't even say the word *relationship* because the thought of it nearly makes me dry heave.

Carlisle grins, but it's Finn who speaks. "Exactly that. Once Nickolas is no longer a threat, and you want to stay for more than an occasional fuck, you have to be willing to be in a relationship with all of us."

Yeah, that's what I thought he meant.

What the actual fuck?

"I don't want any fucking right now and damn sure don't want any relationships. I guess I'll be gone once I am released from protection services." I try to leave it alone as I dig through the cooler mindlessly, but I can't. I stand back up. "You always share the girls you date?"

"If everyone agrees, yes," Ian says, shoving his hands in his pockets.

"And how many times have you done this?" I ask, looking at them all like they are entirely insane.

"The offer has only been used once, for a short time." Ian says, his eyes flicking to Carlisle for a split second.

I roll the idea over in my head, trying to imagine all of them working together to love the same woman. The image is both hard to picture and intriguing enough that it has curiosity and anxiety swirling through every inch of my body.

"And everyone has agreed to try it again?" I ask, looking around at them while trying to maintain a calm composure.

No one denies my question.

"Wanna give it a shot tonight?" Ian asks, a glint of hope in his eyes.

Deciding I'm not nearly drunk enough for this, I take the shot out of Carlisle's hand and throw it back. I give an awkward thumbs up, agreeing and motioning for the party to commence.

We throw back a few more shots, and things start to seem less intense. I loosen up and ride the high of not being in my own head. The playlist shifts, and the four of us bounce around, sweating, and yelling the lyrics with our hearts, leaving only Silas sitting by himself.

I glance over to see Ian with his eyes closed and his head bouncing with sentiment as if *Sucker for Pain* speaks to his soul. He looks so caught up in the song's emotion, like he feels every note in his soul, and I watch in awe.

Finn is pretending he's performing in a packed arena and I nudge Lyle to get his attention. We join in on the concert, singing to the empty backyard illuminated by twinkling lights strung above.

The song transitions to *Neighbors Know My Name*.

"I love this song!" I slur, heading to Carlisle in what I hope is a sexy walk, doing my best to get into the character of a woman that is with more than one man.

He raises a brow at me, questioning what I am doing and I fist the collar of his shirt trailing a finger down the center of his chest.

"I won't bite unless you want me to."

Hiccup.

I sway my hips and run my hands up and down his chest. His eyes are glued to mine and flare with mischief. Turning around, Finn is staring at me with a daring look. I spread my legs slightly and bend to grab my knees, placing my ass directly to Carlisle's crotch. This is the second hard dick I have felt today, and zero is the number of dicks I wanted to feel today.

Though right now, I'm not hating it.

I slowly grind in circles on him as he grabs my hips firmly and guides the motions. I stay focused on Finn's face that looks torn between ripping his brother off me and pulling his dick out to stroke it as he watches.

I hear a deep but quiet moan come from behind me. "Fuck".

"Keep your dick under control," Finn groans out painfully but with order, and my stomach swirls with the demand.

"For now," Carlisle responds, making his hopes clear. Or maybe he's stating a fact.

I smile and pick up my head to see Silas still sitting in his chair where he has been all night, tossing back drinks. I keep dancing as his eyes roam my body seeming to strip me bare. I know every red flag I've found should be telling me to run, but all I can hear is my heartbeat in my ears and my gut screaming to take a chance on something new.

When he finally meets my eyes, he looks at me like he doesn't know if he wants to come closer or throw up.

I want to know what having all four of them would feel like. Call this a trial run. In my head, I know with Silas in the equation, there is no chance this could possibly get far. He has made no effort to even be my friend, much less anything more. I'm sure he only agreed to appease the rest of them, seeing me like damage that taints his home, or him. I'm nothing more than an inconvenience. Here for protection and nothing more.

But I take my chances and let my drunken state throw out all rationalization. At the end of the day, I will know that I took action for the first time in my damn life.

I curl my finger at him in a motion to summon him. He doesn't move, and I fight the embarrassment that threatens my cheeks.

He finally tilts his head to the side, looks me up and down again slowly, then mimics the motion I had just given him as he slumps down further in his chair. His shirt rides up, showing off the tan, tattooed skin of his lower stomach and the half-exposed v-line that is all too enticing.

My feet swing into motion, and as soon as I am close enough for him to reach me, he spins me around and pulls me into his lap. The other boys cast me a quick glance like they are just as surprised as I am. Then they look away, resuming their own goofy dancing to the next song as if this is something meant to be only between Silas and me.

"You shouldn't be doing this so soon," Silas says in a low, slurred voice.

Body heavy, I lean back, resting my head on his large shoulder. "Just a little fun. Carlisle showed me I'm fine if I'm making my own choices."

His chest rumbles against my back, and for a second, I think he is going to throw me off him, but he only relaxes further into the chair. I don't pay attention to the lyrics, just the beat, as I lazily grind my ass on Silas's lap, my anxiety waiting for him to dump me onto my face or try to take control. He doesn't strike me as the kind of person that likes to just sit there.

He lets out a few quiet grunts under his breath, and I feel a bulge grow underneath me. Three dicks now.

I swallow hard as he runs his hands down my arms, where they are braced on each side of the chair.

"You can touch me," I whisper. My words are thick and don't sound like my own.

Slowly, he moves his hands up the sides of my stomach.

My skin chills everywhere he touches, the liquid courage warming me back up. I move to stand so I can turn around and straddle him, but he stops me with a firm grasp and pulls me back down.

"You don't get to leave my lap until I say so."

I let out a small chuckle that I got him hard, despite how much he apparently despises me.

"I was just going to turn around to face you to get a better position."

I feel his breath on my neck as he sits up and his lips brushing the sensitive skin below my ear. "I can't be staring at your perfect face while you dry fuck my dick."

Oh, shit.

I restart my hips, trying to grasp that he complimented me. He gathers my long hair off my back, tosses it over my left shoulder, then rubs a flat hand down my bare back. His calloused fingers clash with my soft skin perfectly, like they were always meant to complement each other. I'm still wearing my crop top from earlier but opted to change into loose shorts before we came out. His hands reach around to my stomach, lightly dragging his fingers across the warm skin, down to my leg.

I am trying like hell to keep my composure, but I can already feel my panties sliding back and forth with my arousal, and my center aches with the need for contact. I hate the feeling just as much as I love it.

As if hearing my thoughts, he runs his fingers up the inside of my thigh, and my motions falter, as does my heart. He grips my thigh hard enough that I yelp and freeze, but none of the other guys notice. They are horse-playing, making dares and challenges regarding dance moves.

"You made this choice. Keep fucking moving," Silas orders in a low growl that does filthy things to my mind and I obey.

The hand that was resting on the arm of the chair comes down to mirror his other on my thigh. I watch as he spreads his fingers wide so his thumb snakes under my shorts, resting on the edge of my panties.

My heart pounds and my clit is pulsing with the need for friction.

I look up again to see if any of the guys are looking my way. Maybe one might come steal me away to play their game and save me from whatever the fuck I am getting myself into, but no. They are completely lost in the fun they are having. I see Carlisle attempt to do a move and fall flat on his ass, and the other two look like they are going to piss themselves from laughing.

"Don't look at them. Focus., Silas says and gives my inner thighs a tight squeeze.

His thumb is so close to my pussy that I can't help the frustrated moan from the pressure an inch away from where I need it. I do as he says and, once again, working my ass around and around against his strained jeans. It feels so good that I do it harder, using his legs to press him right where I need it. My head goes back, and Silas mumbles in approval, "Holy fuck."

Warmth blooms in my belly, my head pops back up, and nervousness sets in as I realize what is about to happen. I continue to move lifting myself a little higher so the friction isn't so perfect.

But Silas grabs my hips and pulls me down hard, not having it one bit.

"I.."

"I can feel your body begging for it. Come for me." His voice is shaking with restraint, and I can almost feel his dick throbbing.

My head reels with his words, but my orgasm is building so fast I don't think I could stop it if I tried.

Silas rubs his thumbs right outside my lips, and I grind my core on the hard length of his bulge.

Within seconds, I come, squeezing his thighs and shutting my mouth so muffled whimpers are all you can hear. He pulls his hands off my thighs, picks me up by the waist, and stands me on my feet, spinning me so that I am facing him.

He tilts my chin up with two fingers and strokes my jaw.

"Good girl," is all he says before he leaves me alone with a fresh orgasm still gently pulsing through me.

When Carlisle called me a good girl, I couldn't get him in me deep enough, wanting to devour everything he had to offer and beg for more. This time, I feel equally as dirty. That felt so good. Too good to leave me feeling used and embarrassed, but here I am.

"I'm going to bed, guys," Silas tells the rest of them before entering the house.

After he is gone, I rejoin the group, and we carry on like nothing happened, thankful none of them address what just happened. As far as I'm concerned, I don't want it to happen again.

We follow inside a little later, stumbling in and laughing as we bump into things left and right. We help each other up the stairs, cracking up as we all almost fall backward. We fumble into our rooms, and I manage to take a shower before falling into bed. I can't say the same for them. I'm not sure Ian even made it to the bed at all.

I sat down at my window and tortured myself some more, watching her laugh and dance with each of the boys, as if what I gave her didn't phase her. Her hands wrapped around their necks, and their hands wandered her perfect body as she moved in hypnotic motions, including Ian.

I watched as they talked off to the side, smiling and laughing, seeming to cross a new marker. His gaze lingered. I saw the conflict as his head turned over what his heart was no doubt feeling.

And here I was, wishing to be any of them.

I sat here for a little longer after they all came stumbling back inside continuing to stare at the backyard, at the tree-house.

That fucking tree-house.

I hate myself for being too concerned with getting her out of my head that night. If I hadn't caved and kept my eyes on her, I could have ended that shit before it began.

I have kept enough distance in the past that I can still see her, but when she looks around, she won't suspect it's me. Though now I'm forced in closer proximity, and I'm reveling in the pain. I know the shit she has endured more clearly than *anyone* in this house, so I will let her take what she wants from me, but she can never have me.

I might kill myself in the process, but I will make sure of it.

I have to.

Once the house is silent, I walk down the hall to the fifth door and press my ear against the wood. I hear her even breathing and slight snoring. I open the door excruciatingly slow, closing it behind me, and inch towards her bed.

She is passed out on top of the covers, still wrapped in her towel. I shake my head and get a T-shirt out of her closet. I'm not sure how she would react if she woke up right now.

Still, I gently unwrap her towel and pull it out from under her. She barely budges. I slip the baggy shirt over her head and pull her arms through. Then gently pull the comforter from under her and slip her legs under it.

I look at her resting face, and my heart feels heavy with regret. I climb up behind her and pull her into me.

"I am so fucking sorry, Mel," I whisper into the dark.

She turns over to face me and mumbles, "Finn?" as she nuzzles her face into my chest.

I don't answer.

That hurt.

Instead, I lean down and kiss her head and close my eyes, wishing for my reality to be anything more than what it is.

Just a few minutes.

Fingers brush the bare skin of my stomach and nudge me back into consciousness. I nuzzle closer, wiggling my butt back into the warm frame behind me.

"Stop moving your fucking ass, Amelia," a voice that does not belong to Finn grumbles into my hair.

I still, then slowly look down at the arm splayed across my stomach and see a collage of tattoos.

Silas.

Sitting up quickly, I yank the covers off him, thankfully revealing his fully clothed body.

"Relax, Mel. We didn't do anything. Other than you getting off on my lap outside." He props his hands behind his head and he looks at me smugly.

Everything about this situation is irritating. His expression. His comment. His use of my nickname. I stare at him blankly, still trying to figure out why the hell he was cuddling me.

"Why the fuck are you in my bed? And while we're on that topic, what was that about last night?" I demand, hoping he can't read how I truly feel about that time with him.

He slides off the bed casually and turns to look at me with a smirk. "Someone had to keep you from choking on your own vomit." He stands silent for a moment, and I clench my jaw.

I wait for him to answer the second part of my question, my temper growing hotter by the second. I am not a morning person; it is too early for his shit.

Enjoying my frustration, he grins wider. "As for last night, I saw how hard you were trying to let them convince you that this *thing* could work and wanted to see how fast you would jump on my dick if given the chance. Even when you know damn well that, despite my efforts to make them happy, I have no interest in you staying here."

I know he is purposely trying to hurt me. He wants to get under my skin, and it is working. I don't know what it is about his claim that bothers me so much. Maybe it's the truth behind it.

Part of me wants my place here to work. Who wouldn't want to be loved like that? However, it's becoming abundantly clear that if it has to be all or nothing, I will not find my future here. Silas seems incapable of love and full of blinding and unwarranted hatred. Continuing to show me that I am not welcomed here by him.

"Fuck you." I spit at his back as he leaves.

Last night, I was more *me* than I have been in a week, and it felt good. Now, that feeling is tainted by Silas's words re-branding the memory as one of weakness and stupidity.

Why didn't I laugh in his face like he is always doing to me when he called me to him? A seriously missed opportunity, now looking back.

I take a shower, feeling the need to wash myself after knowing Silas was in my bed all night. I don't think about how well I slept, dreaming about my MIA secret admirer. I don't think about what I may have said to Silas in my drunken haze or how, for a moment, I was happy with the thought that he was going to apologize and turn over a new leaf.

Except I do.

I think about all of that on replay the entire thirty minutes it takes me to shower. I spend most of the time scrubbing between my legs like I have once again been taken advantage of, that no amount of cleaning will make me feel clean.

Reluctantly, I force myself out of the shower and back into my room. I brush out my wet hair, throw on some spandex shorts and a shirt, brush my teeth, and head downstairs.

Waiting for the rest of the boys to spill out of their rooms, I walk to the front porch for some sun to call JJ.

I close the front door behind me and stop, frozen in fear as I stare at a little box, tied with a red bow, at my feet.

Coming to my senses, I scoop it up, peering inside the windows to be sure no one is watching before I take the lid off.

I immediately gag at the sight. A note sits atop a used condom.

WHILE UR KEEPING THEIR DICK WARM, RUBIE IS DOIN THE SAME TO MINE. DONT WORRY, I USED A CONDOM THIS TIME, BABY.

-LANCE

Disgust floods my body And I quickly close the box, tossing it in the trash, rushing back inside.

I dial JJ and she answers the video chat on the second ring, takes one look at my face, and dramatically questions me.

"Biiitch. What happened?"

I comb my fingers through my hair with a snort, trying to clear my head. Not ready to tell her I got another box.

"Oh, you know, just the aftermath of being a whore."

She scrunches her brows in confusion at my snarky response and I let some tension leave on my next exhale.

"Sorry, just in my head about an... opportunity that was thrown in my lap last night."

I do my best to focus on last night and not what I just saw.

"An opportunity to be a whore?" She lifts her brow.

"Oh, my God! You're fucking both twins!" she shouts loud enough for the entire neighborhood to hear her.

I give her a half-smirk, and she reads between the lines.

"You're fucking all of them?!"

"JJ," I scold her in a hushed tone. "No. I'm not fucking anyone right now."

This time she's quieter but still louder than I'd like.

"But you *want* to fuck all of them? And they gave you the opportunity?"

I roll my eyes dramatically and hear Silas grunt across the open room in the kitchen.

He doesn't look up from stirring his coffee as he mumbles, "She's quick, isn't she?"

I groan frustratedly. She is supposed to be helping, and right now, she is most definitely not. So, I half-lie.

"No, I don't want to screw all of them. It was just brought up in discussion last night."

I choose to leave out the finality of the discussion.

She fantasizes for me, trying to lighten the mood in her own way about how creative I could get with temporarily living with four men that are sexually charged. I let her go wild deciding not to ruin it for her by explaining that I would rather stab my eyes out with a serrated knife than sleep with Silas.

She turns the conversation to her and tells me that although she misses me, she has had so much fun with Tyler in the two days since I left. Hearing that eases my guilt, but it doesn't ease the dull ache in my chest.

I miss her. We have lived together for years and are basically glued at the hip. I am happy for her, though. We both needed a little more independence to find ourselves.

I end the call, tossing my phone on the couch with a groan.

Silas takes a slow sip and follows it with the sound of him sucking his teeth then sighing. He sets his cup down on the table and braces his arms on either side of it. Giving me a look that says exactly what my head is already telling me.

Liar, liar.

I quickly find something else in the room to look at before I actually do stab him. Something pulls my eyes back to him. He winks, and I rip my eyes away again. The asshole is toying with me.

"You're looking better this morning," Ian says walking in then winks at me. "We were a little sloshy last night."

"But so fucking fun." Finn says, coming in next.

I grumble as I stand from the couch and move to Finn for a hug. He holds me tight, squeezing my thighs and making me cry out in pain. "Sore?"

"Yeah, asshole. It must have been all the dancing." I laugh.

We danced for hours, and I enjoyed every minute of it. I have always loved any kind of dancing. Doing it, watching it, learning it, teaching it. Everything about dancing makes me feel a type of freedom I don't find in anything else.

"You think it could have been all that grinding you did on Silas?" Finn pulls me in tighter, and I love that he knew I was about to shove him.

I decide to take a different route, knowing Silas is standing close by.

"You know, he supposedly despises me but so desperately wanted my ass rubbing on his cock. Last night and again this morning. I think I even heard him jacking off to me when we came in last night."

Finn chuckles and releases me before he heads for the kitchen. He moves past Silas, who is now glaring at me.

I look through his large frame and watch as Finn takes out materials to cook pancakes.

"Hey, money maker," Ian says, drawing my attention away from the mess Finn is making, "I'm going to do some hacking today. You wanna come hang out? Silas and the boys are gonna be at the shop all day, so I just figured I'd offer something you might enjoy more."

"Are you referring to me as a hooker, Ian Davis?" I cross my arms defensively, and his face pales. He has a certain adorable factor when he squirms.

"No, uh, just joking about how comfortable you were with your... dancing skills last night."

Finn smiles over his shoulder. "A talent we all enjoyed witnessing."

Oh, dear God. Please tell me I didn't.

"I didn't, uh-"

"Clothes stayed on for the most part, but you did put on quite the show. You can blame Carlisle for the money comment." Finn grins, nodding towards the stairs.

"What did Carlisle do?" Carlisle asks, wearing nothing but a pair of underwear as he prances into the living room.

"Threw money at Mel," Finn repeats.

"And she loved every minute of it." Carlisle confirms casually, moving to the coffee machine.

I move next to Ian and he slings his arm over my shoulder. "Well, as flattering as the nickname is, let's not make that one stick, and I'll agree to hang with you today." I give a big smile, and his shoulders release the tension they had been holding.

Aside from the fact that I would enjoy a day to read, I am not sure being surrounded by grease and machinery is my idea of a fun way to nurse a hangover.

After stuffing my face with food and fucking with Finn about not cooking as well as Carlisle, I return to my room and find my book. Stepping back into the hall, I hear a muffled groan coming from the bathroom.

I quickly peer down over the railing to see if any of the others had heard. They all remain too occupied with their conversations. I turn back towards the door and momentarily stand still, wondering if that sound is what I think it is.

No, he wouldn't be doing that so loud, with nothing but a door separating him from the rest of us. I inch closer, clenching my book harder with every step, and lean into the door. The sound of running water is all I hear for a long moment before it comes again, but this time, a name follows.

"Meda," he groans, barely audible, long and drawn out, like... he finished.

Oh my God. Oh my God.

I swallow hard and rush back down the stairs as fast as I can without drawing too much attention. I shouldn't have stopped. Just as I throw myself into a bar stool, nearly knocking over into Ian, the shower shuts off, and Silas emerges. Conversations continue, merely background noise as I watch Silas walk to his room through my lashes.

Who the hell is Meda?

And why is that the one fact that bothers me the most?

I vaguely hear Ian explain his plan to hack into the law firm's security system. I get lost, a dark cloud casting over me, causing me to check out mentally. A sick feeling builds in my stomach; nothing feels right or good now.

I know this feeling all too well—the downward spiral after a manic episode.

The highs of finally feeling happy are almost worth the epically shitty lows. They come quick and unannounced, and all I want to do is crawl out of my skin. I overthink every choice I have recently made and try to determine if it is right or wrong. I let the fear make me sick, physically making me unable to enjoy anything until the next high comes or something distracts me enough for a short while.

"Mel?" Finn's brown eyes are looking at me curiously.

Seeing that I wasn't listening, he repeats himself.

"The shop. Would you want to come to see it later? Let us share something that we love with you?"

Warmness tries to nudge out the cold, gloomy feeling that consumes me but fails. Still I force a smile. I really would love that and don't want him to think otherwise.

"We work on our own time. We restore and sell the cars we don't want to keep," Carlisle adds. "I just started a new project. Maybe you can swing by one day and give your opinion on the paint and interior."

Seeing how his face lights up, how could I say no?

WHILE UR KEEPING THEIR DICK WARM, RUBIE
IS DOIN THE SAME TO MINE. DONT WORRY,
I USED A CONDOM THIS TIME, BABY.
-LANCE

Amelia

I plop down on Ian's bed, book in hand, and take a look around. His room mirrors mine a lot. He has notes and music sheets pinned all around the walls in chaos like as soon as it hits him, he has to write and find a place it fits well with. I'm sure he has some kind of system to determine where he puts things, but I don't ask. His desk with multiple monitors on it has some sort of music app pulled up. Another is flashing random green codes, which he probably uses for his super-spy stuff. The middle is blank like it should have a screensaver, but he has nothing to put there.

"What do you think?"

"I like it. I wasn't sure what to expect, but this fits you." I lean back on his pillows, and he sits in his desk chair but keeps it turned towards me. "A bedroom tells you a lot about the person."

"Well, I hope it tells you good things." He sounds a little nervous but continues, "You're the first person I have ever let come in here."

I sit up a little and look at him curiously. "Why me?"

He runs his hand through his hair. "Well, I guess I want you to see who I am. To learn who I am on the inside. You might have gotten the wrong idea about me from our encounter at the store."

I laugh nervously, matching his energy. I feel like I'm in high school again, my palms are sweating, and I feel awkward.

"Is that right? Well, what do you think I assumed about you?"

"That I'm a pompous dick just looking for a quick fuck."

He's not entirely off the mark. "Explain why that's wrong."

He moves to the bed and sits in front of me. Then takes a deep breath and lays back on the bed, staring at the ceiling.

"For starters, I haven't had sex in over four months. I don't want power and popularity. I want love and genuineness. I was never attracted to the kind of girls that would fall all over me, making it obvious they just wanted to fuck. I want a girl that cares about the bigger things in life. Someone that fights for her dream, her respect, her strength. I wanted someone I could relate to and share myself with. I'm a private person, but I want to find someone to share my little world with." He turns to look at me, and I am in awe of the glimpse of this secret person no one gets to see.

"I am honored to be the first person you wanted up here, but I don't see why I would be someone you chose to share that with. I jumped into bed with Finn the first night you met me."

I pick at my skin nervously. For some reason, I want so badly to be the person Ian chooses to open up to, but I don't want to be the one to let him down.

"I thought the same thing at first, honestly, but then I realized you didn't come in that night looking for sex. You came in there with the sole intention of having fun with JJ. Days passed, and I started to see everything about you that I didn't see before. Then, you shut me down, standing up for what you needed when I was too stupid to remember it."

He turns to face me a little more. "You have pain, some of which I can relate to, and you showed me that with my dad. You stood up to him in a way I did years ago, and seeing the satisfaction on your face made me so fucking proud to know you and have the chance to be more. I was overwhelmed. Feeling things I haven't felt in a long time."

My heart warms at his words. Hearing him talk about me as a person and tip-toeing around me is a breath of fresh air.

"I will forever hate how I acted towards you, but I hope that we can put that past us. That you let me show you who I am. I know I am dying to know who you are." His soft smile tells me everything I need to know.

"I would like that."

I lay back on his pillows again and wince as my body aches. He takes my left leg in his hands and squeezes softly. I wince at the pain that feels all too good.

"You know, I can give you a rub if you want."

I quirk my brow, and he laughs. "Not in a sexual way. Massages are always kind of sexual, but I promise that's not my goal."

"Pinky promise?" I ask, and he looks amused. "Well, since we are getting to know each other, to me, a pinky promise seals a promise, and breaking it is the worst thing you could do."

He sits upright and holds out his pinky, "I love that. Okay. Pinky promise."

We interlock little fingers like little kids, and nostalgia rocks the smile that was on my face.

"Damian and I used to make pinky promises, so it means a lot to me. Childish, I know." I shrug.

"Having something that grounds you to the innocence of your childhood is not silly. It's beautiful."

"It's not the childhood I miss... just him. Damian is half of the reason I knew there had to be something better out there for me. He was always there for me, showing me that unconditional love existed."

Ian smiles softly and leaves to grab lotion, and I take my shirt off, lying face down on his bed in my sports bra and spandex. I inhale deeply and appreciate the scent that is Ian.

He comes back into the room and freezes.

Crap, was that weird?

Did he see me sniffing his bed?

"What?"

He scrubs his hand over his face and chews on his bottom lip. "Uh, nothing. Half-naked woman in my bed for the first time, and I'm about to rub lotion all over her without making it sexual. Easy day."

"I can put my shirt back on if it makes it less weird. I'm sorry, I-"

"You will do no such thing. New, but not weird. We will just have to ignore the raging hard-on I have right now."

He climbs onto the bed and situates behind me to where he has leverage over my body. He warms up some lotion with the friction of his hands and begins to rub my thighs and calves.

He was absolutely right. Feeling his hands glide over my skin is inherently sexual. I *cannot* read my book right now.

"Can I hear about your music? I know you said you don't share it, but maybe you can tell me about it?"

He pauses for a long moment, and I begin to wonder if that is a button I need to stop pushing. Then he speaks.

"Uh, well, I started playing in high school. Self-taught with YouTube. I loved being able to put different cords together in my own way, creating something of my own. Eventually, I started writing songs and using it as an outlet to express the things I couldn't say. The anger and sadness from my dad, the joy of following my dreams, the loneliness of the world..." He trails off, as he continues to rub my legs.

"I think I might share my music someday, but some songs will forever stay private. Some parts of your soul have to stay protected from the evil in the world."

"That makes sense. I think I have pushed the fight down inside me for so long because I was scared that my anger would push people away from me and tarnish that last part of my soul that still has love to give. Setting yourself free isn't easy for someone who has been taught their whole life to please someone else."

I close my eyes, enjoying his soft hands rubbing my tight muscles.

"Can I talk to you about something? If it's too personal, you can decline to answer."

I nod silently, and anxiety fills my stomach.

"You eat Xanax like candy, and I see how hard you try to drown out your pain. That can be a very slippery slope. I'm sure Lyle could make you some edibles as substitutions."

I roll over on my back so he can rub the front of my legs, and I can look at him while we talk.

"And whose idea was this?"

"Just mine. I'm sorry if I upset you. I just..."

I give him a soft smile of reassurance. Truthfully, knowing he noticed and cared enough to say something would entirely outweigh him overstepping a boundary.

"You didn't. I know the pills aren't good to rely on like I do, but it's the only way I've managed to keep my word with Carlisle. I told him I would do my best to stop... burning myself."

I have been trying hard to keep that promise to him, but it has resulted in me taking my pills at double the pace I was previously.

He looks down at my thighs and rubs his hands over my scars, and it takes everything in me not to pull away. His face scrunches.

"Ah, I see. I'm glad Lyle stepped in on that, but would you be willing to try to make a deal with me too?"

I let out a long sigh. "I don't see why not."

I close my eyes as he continues to rub deep on my upper thighs, feeling more at ease with my answer. My gut churns at the thought of giving up my defenses that I have grown so comfortable with, but I know he's right.

I think about my mom's mental state and substance dependency, and I know that's where I could end up soon if I don't get some kind of help to deal with my demons - the self-loathing, the guilt, the broken heart.

Ian rubs his hands to the top of my thighs and around to the back of them, cupping my ass with his index finger and thumb. My thoughts disappear as I focus solely on his hands gliding and groping all over my skin. He moves up to my stomach, squirting some lotion directly onto my skin, and I jump at the abrupt cold.

"Sorry," he chuckles,

He smooths the lotion all over my belly, then brings his hands down to the top of my shorts. Laying his hands firmly on my sides and pushing up, He digs his thumb into my stomach just right. As he nears my chest, he slides his hands outwards, gliding over my sides and to my back. He pulls up, lifting my back a few inches off the bed. Then shifts his weight to drag his hands down the length of my back while digging his fingertips into my skin again.

It feels so good that I groan arching my back to compliment his fingers as he starts the motion over at my stomach.

"Baby, you're gonna have to stop making those sounds," he almost begs with a certain gentleness that makes me wonder how he possibly fits in with the other three men that live here.

Half of my groans are because of the relief the other half is because his hands roaming every inch of me except for my lady bits has got me aching to be touched.

For a split second, I think about their offer once more.

He grabs my hands and pulls me to sit up, then wraps his arm around my hips and pulls me into his lap in one quick motion. His thighs put me a little taller than him, so my chin is level with the top of his head. He runs his hands up the back of my neck and into my hair with a slight tug, and my head falls back. His hands glide firmly back down to my hips and squeeze.

My body arches, making my covered breasts an inch from his face, and I moan again, gripping his shoulders.

Fuck, his hands feel so good in every way. All I can think about is how good they would feel between my legs and tightly squeezing my breasts.

"I'm trying real hard to keep my promise, but you are turning me the fuck on right now. So responsive to my touches." He breathes into my shoulder heavily, and I am overly aware of his dick hardening under me.

His hands stop, and his breathing is unsteady like he is trying to regain his composure with great effort.

My chest rises and falls a little faster than normal, and I feel the wetness hidden behind fabric.

He looks up at me, and we sit there, chests heaving, hormones raging. The room is silent, our lips are inches apart. My eyes fall to his lip ring, and my lips part slightly, inviting him in.

"Okay, massage session is over," he says before grabbing my neck and forcing me closer with a tight squeeze. A whimper falls from my lips as I fall into the depths of his blue eyes.

They are the deepest parts of the ocean and the highest reaches of the sky. They are like the bluest beaches, soothing and terrifying. Inviting and captivating. He watches me back for a moment, and then his lips crash into mine.

I part my lips even more, allowing his kiss to deepen. His tongue slips in and I slide my hips forward. He takes control, pushing me back and forth. The delicious friction I had been aching for moments ago delivered being thoroughly enjoyed as I conduct my hips to follow his instructions. I moan into his mouth, and we desperately fall under a haze of frantic movements and pants.

Ian pulls back abruptly.

"I want to make it clear that it is extremely hard for me to stop this right now, but we need to." I lean forward and lick up the side of his neck. "Amelia," he growls. "I want to fuck you so bad it hurts, but this is not the right time."

I put my forehead to his and exhale with a smile, and it falls, emotions tipping from one extreme to another.

"What is wrong with me?"

"What?" he asks, shocked by my question.

"It's only been a week."

He tilts my chin, forcing me to look at him. "Not a damn thing is wrong with you. There is no rule book on coping, and whatever, whenever you are ready, is entirely up to you."

He wraps me tighter in his arms, and I sink into him, trying to force his words to ring true. He brushes my hair behind my ear. "Let's go do some illegal shit."

Dragging me to the edge of the bed by my leg, he hauls me into his lap at his desk. He starts typing in codes that make no sense, but I let him do his thing. It takes a few minutes of rapid keystrokes before he gets to what he is searching for, but with his arms on either side of me and his chin resting on my shoulder, I don't mind one bit.

"There we are," he says, scooting me to one of his legs so he can lean in closer.

He does some clicking and a few more codes to pull up yesterday's footage. It's rewinding at a high speed, but when he spots Emma's blond ponytail walking into the lobby, he stops it. He presses play and clicks through the different cameras, following her as she walks.

She gets into the elevator and goes straight to his dad's office. They talk for a bit, but there is no audio.

Ian almost looks defeated when he realizes he isn't going to be able to try to read her lips because her back is to the camera, and his dad is sitting silently. Just when Ian leans back in the chair, Emma gets up and rounds the glass desk. Ian springs back to an upright position, and we lean in a little closer, anxious to see what will happen next.

"What is she-?"

Emma strips her clothes off in a hurry, and Jameson proceeds to place her on the desk. He begins to take his pants off, and Ian clicks the screen off, knowing where that was going.

"What the fuck?"

Ian's eyes come to mine, "What the fuck is right. My dad is having an affair."

Amelia

Heading to the shop, my head falls back against the seat, and I close my eyes, listening to the old rock pouring out of the speakers. My mind begins to wander, and before I can stop it, whispers of doubt telling me I'll never be enough betray the foundation Ian just laid. The downward spiral continues.

I shove my demons back in their box and plaster a smile on my face like armor once again as we pull up to a little red metal building with front glass windows. Carlisle is working under a car while the other two pass a joint back and forth. When we push through the door, Silas and Finn turn to us.

Finn rushes to me and spins me around in a hug like he always does.

"What are y'all doing here?" he asks, looking over my shoulder. I try not to let it irritate me that when it comes down to the nitty gritty, they talk around me.

"Emma is screwing my dad, which is not a likely coincidence." Ian says passively, though his fists ball at his side.

It falls silent, the only sound coming from the creeper Carlisle is laid on, scraping across the floor as he rolls out from under the car.

"Come again?" he asks, wiping grease off his hands before tossing the dirty rag over his shoulder. That shouldn't be as sexy as it just was.

"Maybe she has been trying to whore herself into protection in case Mel presses charges like JJ suggested," Finn says.

Carlisle rubs his hand through his hair, the grease making it stand up. "But why would she even play a part in Lance's shit so openly if she knew it would be possible? She would have had to have known she couldn't be touched. Both of them, actually."

"Not that anyone asked me, but Jameson was very uncomfortable with me being at the law firm yesterday." I speak up demanding they acknowledge that I'm here.

Silas grins. "I can't say that I disagree with his judgment."

I smile back sweetly. "Your opinion will be relevant if I ever give a single fuck." I dig in my invisible pockets and show him my hands come up empty. I fake a pout and turn my flat palm into a fist, then flip him the bird with a wink. "Eat shit."

"If I wanted to eat your pussy, I would."

"And the day I want to be underwhelmed while you motorboat my labia, I know where to find you. Shut the fuck up so the grown-ups can talk."

He says nothing, and Carlisle chokes on his laughter before Ian continues with a shit-eating grin. "Well, I scanned the house before we came here, and it didn't pick up anything, so we still don't know what Lance is trying to get if not intel,"

I cross my arms and tilt my chin. "Well, I say it's time for that fighting rash course. That way, the next time I see her, the bitch will eat my fist."

"Oh, fuck yeah," Carlisle cheers.

***

"So, where is the beauty you wanted me to look at?" I ask, looking around.

Carlisle scrubs the back of his neck. "Well, not so much of a beauty just yet." He takes my hand and brings me through the shop, the other guys following close behind. Down the hall and around the corner into another open room with tarps lining the walls. Awestruck, I stare at the paint room walls, taking in all the different colors of over-spray that overlap.

"Uh, the car is over there, babe." Finn jokes.

I spin around to the hunk of metal in the middle of the room. The build looks familiar, and I can appreciate its beauty, but my knowledge is limited. "Do you plan on selling this one," I ask, dragging my hand down the old worn paint and circling the back.

"No. I was thinking it could be yours."

I stop, my feet frozen in place. There is something so beautiful about his offer and yet just as terrifying. This is personal for him.

"I know you don't like to drive, but I saw how much you liked mine, and well... your Chevy Cruze is just embarrassing."

Now, I can see the Chevelle hiding under the rusted and falling-off pieces. I cross my arms, "What's wrong with my car? Silas doesn't drive a classic either."

"Silas also isn't sucking Lyle's dick," Silas mumbles, and I jerk my head so fast the room spins.

"Wanna say that again?" I ask, stepping closer, my rage just about boiling over. "I have had just about enough of the stick that seems super glued up your ass."

His nostrils flare and his shoulders square. "If you're feeling froggy, *leap.*"

I lunge and Ian catches me mid-air as my fist swings, missing my target's cheek by half an inch. My vision blurs, blood booming in my ears. A deathly rageful voice muttering encouraging obscurities.

"Stop, stop, stop," Ian chants, setting me back on the ground and walking me backward. He spins around, tucking me behind him, glaring at Silas.

Finn steps between them and shoves Silas towards the exit. "You need to get a fucking grip."

Silas stands unmoving as he looks at each of his friends, skipping over me. There is something in his expression that seems pleading. It's not anger towards me that fills the room; it's something louder and more agonizing. Unspoken words and nameless looks are passed around in a silent language I don't speak. I can spot the ache in Finn's casted glance towards the exit.

Silas spins on his heel, taking that feeling with him on his exit. The second Silas is gone, the room feels lighter. Not entirely in the sense of being easier to manage, more that something is missing.

Silas never seemed the kind of man to take an order from anyone, but without another word of protest, he did. Coming from anyone else, his response would have been completely different. Their dynamic is more than friends or even *family*. It is something entirely different.

Loyalty without exceptions and respect beyond measure.

I keep my eyes low, a cold feeling of embarrassment washing over me. I have never lashed out like that. Never been the one to fight in a situation where flight was an option. There is just something about Silas that provokes me.

His problem with me has become personal, and I will not let him ruin a chance at being happy, whatever that may look like.

He has made it my mission to make him see me as an equal human being. I have a heart and a story. And he will listen and see me for who I am.

"I'm glad to see you are finding your fire," Carlisle chuckles, lifting a weight from my shoulders.

The pride in his eyes nearly brings me to my knees. For the first time, I acted and demanded more.

I regain my composure and slide into Ian's lap in the car's front seat. Or at least what's left of a seat.

"Black interior. Green exterior." I run my hand along the steering wheel, envisioning the car being my own and what I would want it to look like.

Damian would have loved those choices too.

"Green?" Carlisle asks. Surprise underlines his tone like he was expecting something different. "What shade of green?"

I motion for him to come over, and he leans in, resting his arm on the frame. I take out my phone and snap a picture of him. I zoom in and flip it around to show him. "This color."

He smiles, looking at the blown-up picture of his own eye. "You are a real sap, you know that?" Kissing me on the cheek, he takes my phone and moves to the corner of the room to take a color swatch.

A vibrant earthy green. Like leaves that cast a sound so soothing as the wind rushes through them. A sound that could quiet the mind if you only let it. Green, like Carlisle's eyes.

A phone rings from the main room, and Finn grumbles something about an old man being persistent on a project. He kisses me so hard that I press back into Ian's body, before he leaves.

My mind absorbs the feeling and conjures up intriguing scenarios after his lips leave mine. I have to readjust in Ian's lap and catch the breath stolen from my lungs. If Ian noticed or felt anything similar to what I did, he didn't give a sign. His fingers just rest on my thighs and tap every now and again.

Carlisle calls me over to check the paint color.

"It's perfect." I can already imagine it on the car when it is fully restored. I'm not sure how long it takes them to complete a project like this, but I hope I am more confident in driving by the time it's ready. It would be a shame for such hard work on a classic to sit idly in a driveway.

I drift around the room and finish inspecting the paint-dusted tarps hanging on each of the walls. Trying to find shapes and letters within them.

"So you like art?" Ian asks, looking at me through the empty frame of the windshield. I climb onto the roof of the car and continue looking around.

"I do. One of the few things I genuinely enjoy. Painting, reading, music." All things I found a little slice of heaven in while being forced to try to become more than I was.

It was never enough to just be a child. I needed a list of talents and hobbies. Things my mother could brag about to bring more attention to how much of a wonderful mother she was. They were never my own, not really.

Nothing in my life is.

Ian hums, seeming to get lost in his thoughts just as much.

"You show me yours, and I'll show you mine?" I ask, trying to encourage him to talk more about his music. I want to know everything about the process. The type of music he likes playing the most. Why he is scared to perform. What he feels when he plays or writes.

"Mel," he whispers, and I take the hint that I am being shut down again.

I'm not bothered he doesn't like sharing his music. I have a few things I would like to keep to myself too. But now that I know I was the first woman to be in his room, I want to be the first he shares his music with too.

Lyle hands me my phone and unbuckles his pants.

I slap his hands before he gets the zipper down.

"Not that, you perv." A sound of whining and laughter pours out of me.

"Come on. If Ian doesn't want to play, I do!" He rushes for my leg, and I slide further onto the hood and off the side. I back up, laughing, trying not to trip over empty cans of paint and beer bottles as he stalks toward me.

"Care for another challenge, love?"

"No! I don't want your dick!" I turn, taking off running, still laughing so hard my sides burn.

There is a truth to what I tell him.

They have been guiding me back into being okay with certain types of contact, but I don't think I am actually ready to have sex. I worry that once I am in the act or once I have finished, that dark and dirty feeling will come rolling in. Dragging me back down the few pegs I have climbed. I don't want to lose that progress. I can't lose it.

Hands loop around me, pulling me back, and we crash onto the car's hood.

"You know that's a damn lie," Carlisle growls, kissing where my shirt has ridden up. It feels good, and he's right, but I still deny it. He peers up at Ian in question, and I follow his eyes over my shoulder.

Ian shrugs, leaning back smugly. "You heard her. She wanted to see mine, not yours."

I narrow my eyes, and he flashes a shit-eating grin that tells me I'm in trouble.

"Tell him what you told me, baby. Tell him how you were grinding on me earlier. How bad you want to feel it for real." Ian subtly rubs his hand across his dick, "That it's not his dick you want right now."

Oh, this bitch is playing dirty.

I look back at Lyle, and his eyes darken as he looks at me through his lashes. "You tell me that shit, and I will make you beg."

My stomach sinks and flutters. The warmness between us dips lower, making my clit tingle, and I clench my thighs as subtly as possible.

"It's true. I want to feel Ian's dick inside me right now just as much as I did earlier."

Half true.

The thought did cross my mind, but only for a moment. Maybe two.

Carlisle growls, pulling me off the hood, bending me over, pressing my chest to the dirty metal. The fingers of his right hand loop into my shorts, pausing with great effort. "Last chance to tell the truth, Angel."

Fingers brush my left thigh, rubbing soft circles in place, reminding me who it is behind me. Reminding me this is my chance to tell him no. But this isn't abrupt or unwarranted. I want this just as badly as he does. I'm practically shaking with anticipation.

Exhaling, I ready myself to leap. Reaching down, I place my palm on top of his.

Needing no further permission or explanation, he pulls my shorts down and yanks my panties to the side. Burying his face between my legs, tasting everything I have waiting for him.

I gasp, and Ian's eyes sparkle with delight. Two fingers press inside me, gliding easily from my arousal.

Carlisle leans back kissing my thigh. "Seems you two may have had a little fun earlier, no?"

I breathe out, sounding more like a moan than an answer.

"Did Ian not want to play with my poor girl?" He teases like he already knows Ian would have stopped it before things went too far.

Ian's eyes become more challenging, daring me to play along or maybe to choose my answer carefully.

"He told me not yet," I rasp as Carlisle's skilled fingers work me over. I can feel myself dripping down my thighs now, and I want so badly to rub them together to give my clit the friction it's begging for.

"How very sad. You want to come so bad." He uses his other hand to press two fingers to my clit, and all of my tension peaks. "I can only imagine how bad you wanted it earlier."

"I do." I pant harder and harder, balling my fists on the hood, keeping my eyes on Ian. Just as I am about to come, Carlisle rips his finger away.

"Lyle!" I protest turning to look at him.

He stands, leaning over my shoulder to look at Ian.

"Tell me again. Ian wasn't nice enough to make you come, but you still want him right now?"

I try to figure out the rules of this game. "Y-yes." I say, trying to figure out the rules of this game.

He starts moving his fingers inside me again, this time pressing his thumb into my ass. I look back at Ian, seeing him rub his dick through his shorts.

Lyle builds my orgasm up again, sweat beading on my temple and lower back. It's hot, and everything is too much.

The way I can feel Carlisle's breaths on my damp skin. The way the hard metal is rubbing against me. Ian's eyes locked on mine, filled with so many emotions. The sounds of my pants and pleas as I beg for release in the middle of the open shop.

"What do you want him to do right now?" Carlisle asks against my cheek.

"I don't know." I mutter, unable to think properly, losing sight of the game.

He yanks his fingers out again just as I tighten around him.

"Lyle!" I yell, beyond frustrated now.

He rubs my lower lips with flat fingers for a few moments, allowing the buzz to whither before he pushes into me again, moving his fingers fast and with a purpose.

"Try again."

"I want him to touch me," I pant, and he yanks my hair, forcing my head back at a painful angle.

"If you want him so bad, beg for it."

"Please, Ian. I want you to touch me," I beg, watching Ian to see what he does with the request.

To my surprise, he slides out of the car and between it and my body. Leaning back on the car, he lifts me up to straddle his lap, my clit pressed perfectly to his clothed shaft. Lyle pushes his finger back into me, his other hand moving around to the front of my neck.

"Ride him," he rumbles, the sound making my pussy throb.

Ian grabs my hips, and I lock eyes with him, moving my hips along his swollen length, and holy shit, he feels huge. The twins are by no means small, but I can't even find the head of Ian's dick as I grind on him.

Lyle pulls me back against his chest, kissing me hard as his fingers work overtime, while Ian's hands roam to my breasts. I tilt my head back down, all of us watching as his shorts darken underneath me.

I ride Carlisle's fingers and dry fuck Ian's lap, imagining again what it would feel like to have two of them at once. My orgasm builds easily, having been denied multiple times, and I fall apart in their arms. My eyes meeting Ian's warm stare as he watches every micro-expression I make. I pulse around Carlisle's fingers and dig mine into Ian's shoulders. His mouth falls open, and he looks almost pained as his eyes fall to my mouth, watching the little whimpers leave it.

Carlisle pulls his fingers out of me, pulling my head back and wiping them across my lips. "The next time that you want a dick in you, it will be mine."

I swallow hard.

He bites the small of my neck hard enough to make me whimper, then cold air rushes my skin at his absence.

Ian stares at me for a long minute before giving me a soft smile that speaks a thousand words and nothing at all at the same time. There is so much just below the surface that he keeps on lockdown. I don't like it. They know everything about me, and I am still learning the basics about them.

He cups my chin with his thumb and index finger, parting my lips. I lick the tip of his thumb, inviting him in but not forcing it. He leans in, running his tongue over my wet lips, tasting me on them. Then, dipping his tongue into my mouth, our lips mold like puzzle pieces, and every inch of my skin tingles.

He has just become my second mission.

Amelia

I have never been presented with the opportunity to fight anyone. I was never in situations that would ever lead to it. Except when I got detention in high school for slamming a girl's head into a brick wall after learning she was spreading rumors about me. That was the first time I felt the rush of letting my anger take control.

I shove that part of me down deep, but you can only escape a drug for so long when it lives inside you. And here I am about to dig that part of myself back up and fully explore it.

The nervousness and fear I expected are drowned out with anticipation.

The guys want to see this part of me.

I feel like they need to see it. They need to see that I am more than my past and the scared little bitch I have molded into. I am fully embracing this change and want to prove to them that I am worth it.

I change into clean shorts and a sports bra after a much-needed cold shower and head down to the gym. Pushing through the door, I find the boys in gym shorts and shirtless.

"Now, this is a sight I could get used to."

Carlisle walks over. "Easy killer, we are here to teach you how to punch properly so you don't hurt yourself."

His fingers tease the mark he left on my neck as I pull my hair into a ponytail. I want more of them. I want them everywhere.

Seeing a mark left by them is a constant reminder that they want me here. Marks of possession, I'm theirs now.

Not officially, but I want to be. If it doesn't work out, I will cut my losses and move on, but I feel like I am learning something about myself here and owe it to myself to see it through.

Carlisle grabs some kind of padding that straps onto his hands. He moves in front of me, and the other guys give us some space. "Have you ever fought anyone before?"

I scratch at my scalp with a half-laugh. "Uh, only if you consider slamming some bitch's head into a brick wall in the ninth-grade fighting."

Lyle snorts, and his entire chest shakes with laughter.

"Damn, you crazy... but no."

Silas moves, and all the anger he was radiating earlier seems to be gone. He is covered in sweat and water. Most likely coming here to blow off whatever was bothering him. He steps in front of me. "Now, you are going to want to mimic my stance."

I take in the positioning of his feet and shoulders, then mirror him, trying to avoid saying the snarky retort that came to mind. If he is trying to play nice, I guess I can too.

"Always keep your guard up like this." He pulls his fists up in front of his face, and I nod, following his instructions. "Okay, good. After every punch, your arms need to come back to this position so your face is protected if they swing back and you can't dodge it." I nod and he continues. "Now, watch how I throw my punch."

He slowly extends his fist, rotating at the hips. My eyes seem to focus on his lower half longer than they should. I take in the deep cuts of his body and the line of hair trailing into his shorts.

He shows me a few times slowly then puts it all together. "Your turn. Remember you want to punch through your target, not into it."

I practice a few times slowly and look for his approval. He may be a dick, but he knows how to fight, and it seems in here, he is all business. His awards plastering the walls echo my conclusion.

Silas nods, confirming my motions are correct. I feel the pride and confidence wash over me as I approach Carlisle.

He holds the targets out for me and smiles. "Go for it."

I get my footing right, pull my guard up, and take a deep breath to calm myself. I am shaking with nervousness, but I know none of the boys would laugh at me if I mess up.

Well, maybe Silas.

I have a hard time reading him and guessing what he would and would not do. And he is constantly surprising me.

I take a swing, picturing Lance's face, then resume my guard position for feedback.

"Good." Silas nods. "Now put more force behind it. Use your body's momentum to help hit harder. It's all in the hips."

I nod and try again, this time using his tip.

"Perfect. Again."

We do this for hours. They critique me on little flaws here and there, but overall, they seem satisfied.

That feeling of pride takes over again as each of them commends me, and my heart thunders in my chest.

The guys take turns doing drills with each other while I practice with Carlisle, and I watch them on my breaks taking mental notes to better myself on the next round. It would take me years to be able to fight like them, but Carlisle's right. Right now, all I need to know is how to throw a punch.

Silas was right too, I can't hesitate - a moment of hesitation would cost me everything in a serious situation. Though it's something I will need to practice to conquer.

I watch Ian and Carlisle spar with laughter and playful banter, their eyes occasionally flicking to me, each time lingering longer than before.

Even though I am enjoying the rush, my body starts shaking with exhaustion, and my moves get sloppy. There was no more progress that I could make for today. I opt to take another shower and leave them to finish on their own. They allow me to leave with a smile at that.

They really are proud of me.

***

Just as I step under the hot water, the bathroom door opens, and Finn steps inside.

"Can I help you?" I tease.

"I figured I would join you, saving water and all that. I could use some help reaching those hard-to-reach places."

I hum a sarcastic sound but open the shower door wider for him to step in. He stands behind me reaching for the soap in front of me. His naked body presses to mine, and for the first time, his touch causes me to stall. I spin, needing to see him, and he turns me back around.

"You don't need to see me. Feel my presence."

I swallow. Focusing on the smell of his sweat and body wash and the sound of the water, I set my foundation. I wiggle my toes in the water, forcing myself to feel where I am.

Finn softly places his hand on my hip, covering a bruise, and I focus on his hand. *Darker. Veinier. Finn's.*

His lips find my shoulder, his hair visible from the corner of my eye.

Longer. Softer.

He runs a soapy rag down my back. Taking his time, he washes every inch of my backside, paying special attention to my ass. My center begins to throb with every touch, and my chest grows heavy with desire. I turn to face him, offering him my front side. His eyes trail up and down my bare body before he resumes washing me.

"You are so fucking perfect, Amelia."

I meet his eyes as he sinks into a crouching position below me.

He takes my leg and props it up on his knee. "You know. The night I met you, I would have never thought you would become so special to me."

A smile spreads across my face. "We have only known each other a few weeks, Finn. I can't possibly be that special to you in such a short time."

He looks up at me, his brown eyes as golden as the brightest autumn leaves, and begins washing my calf.

"Time is everything and nothing at the same time. You can know someone for years and never love them, and you can meet someone new and fall within weeks. Time is something we can never get enough of, but time does not determine when you can do or feel something."

"Finn Jones, are you telling me you are falling for me?" I tease.

He rubs the soapy cloth up my thigh and grins. "Was it not clear? I hate when I am not around you. I crave your smile, your laugh, your kiss. Your touch. Weeks ago, I wasn't looking for anything but a good time, and now, I can't imagine ever being happy without you."

He washes my other leg and stands up. "You have my heart. Promise you won't break it?"

My heart pounds, and I feel a lump form in my throat.

Am I ready for this?

Weeks ago, I was in a relationship that broke me down to nothing. Now I have this man that is everything Lance isn't, offering to give me his heart?

They say the right timing never comes. You just have to take the leap and hope to God they catch you when you fall.

I'm leaping.

"Pinky promise that I'll try my best," I answer him truthfully.

Finn smiles at me, wrapping his pinky around mine.

"I have a lot of baggage." I look down, but he tilts my chin to look at him. "I am a broken human, but as long as you are patient with me, I am not going anywhere. I want to do this."

He swiftly changes places with me, pinning me against the shower wall. His hands travel down my body, and he squeezes my ass firmly. He hoists me up, and I wrap my legs around him without so much as a second thought.

"That's cute. You do understand that even flat-out telling us to leave you alone would not easily result in any of us actually doing that, right?" He presses his hot body against mine, holding me to the wall, and I exhale a needy breath. He spends long minutes nipping and sucking at my skin, before I'm being hauled out of the shower.

***

I curl in closer to Finn on his bed staring at the ceiling. He's been passed out for a little while, but thoughts of all the wonderfully horribly ways I'm going to fuck up my current situation flood my mind. Not only the possibility of getting them hurt from whatever they are getting into with my issue with Lance and Emma. But also my traitorous and dishonest heart still thinking about *Him* and why he stopped caring about me.

I inhale deeply, hoping Finn's smell will soothe me. I focus on my breathing and the sound of the fan whirring, trying to ground myself. Though it doesn't seem to be working.

Frustrated, I slip on some shorts and head down the stairs, looking to keep myself busy with something. My heart races as I try to rationalize with myself, but the fear takes over, and my head becomes overwhelmed. I slowly walk over to my purse, second-guessing myself the whole way. I made a deal.

I hesitate, only for a moment, then cave. I reach in, find my bottle, and pop the cap off. Dumping it over, finding it empty.

Ian.

I pace back and forth, trying to clear my head. I fumble through my purse again and pull out the lighter, desperate for something to channel this feeling into. My hand freezes mid-air, hearing something outside.

I inch towards the glass of the back door and peer through the dark. The boys turned off the fairy lights, so nothing but my reflection stares back at me.

Against all rational thinking, I slowly slide the door open and inch outside. As I step over the threshold, I grow hyperaware that I'm completely unarmed and am shaking too much to put up any kind of fight with the training I received today.

I'm royally fucked if someone is out here.

I turn around to retreat, maybe grab a knife from the kitchen, or maybe just because I am a coward that can't even prove a point to herself. I stop, feeling a presence behind me. My body goes cold despite the warmness radiating into my back, and fear tears through me.

Before I can yank the door open, a hand wraps around my mouth, and I'm being hauled back into the yard.

No. No. No. Not the tree-house...

Tears stream down my face, and a voice growls in my ear. "When will you stop running?"

Silas.

He throws me to the ground, and I land face first, barely catching myself, preventing my face from meeting the dirt. I flip over and crawl backward, desperate to put distance between him and me as my fear grows with every step he takes towards me, a dead look in his eyes.

"Do you realize how pathetic and meek you look?" Silas asks, a look of disgust smeared on his face.

"What the fuck is wrong with you?!" I shout back, letting him see my terror and anger. I scramble to my feet, and with every step he takes toward me, I step back.

"Are you scared of me?" he asks, tilting his head to the side.

With only the moon lighting up certain areas of his face and highlighting the whites of his eyes, he embodies evil well. I don't answer his question.

He moves towards me in a quick motion, raising a hand. I flinch hard, turning my head, bracing myself for the impact.

"Amelia." he says flatly, his tone now softer than before but still firm.

I open my eyes to see his hand still held in the air.

"Do you really think I would hit you?"

Just like that, I was back to my old self. No progress made.

"After everything you learned today, your first instinct was to run, and the second was to cower and accept the blow."

I brace myself and take in his face once again, finding disappointment. His eyes relaxed - softened. I don't speak. What could I possibly say to explain that one day of learning how to defend myself is not going to override years of abuse.

He sighs heavily. "Hit me."

My face twists into confusion.

"You heard me. No gloves. Hit me." He pats his stomach, and I roll my eyes.

I spin on my heel to walk away from more of his stupid mind games, but he grabs my wrist, spinning me back again, and I slam into his chest. My heart races, and I find my eyes locked on my hand lying on his chest. Heat radiates off him.

"I'm not fucking around, Amelia!" His voice thunders in my face, and tears start streaming down it. "Good. I need you to hate me. Fucking hit me like you do."

Anger rushes through me.

What is his fucking problem?

I can't handle people yelling at me. Lance used to scream at me every time I tried to stand up for myself. My mother used to scream at me when I made a mistake, and this, this feels exactly like that.

Before I can think about what I'm doing, I take a step back, pull my arm back slightly, and throw everything I have into my punch. I connect with skin right and his head jerks to the side.

I pull my fist to my chest in shock at what I just did. Shaking my hand out, I try to soothe the burning fire in my knuckles.

Fuck, that hurts, but felt so damn good.

He looks down at me with wide eyes, and for a minute, I am worried he is about to go off on me. But a toothy smile takes over, and he laughs deep in his belly. I look at him like he's insane, but his laugh only continues. I must have lost my mind, bursting into laughter as well.

"I knew she was in there somewhere. You just have to stop pushing her down when you are scared." He plops down on the grass and lays back without a care in the world.

I hesitate before walking next to him and doing the same.

The dewy grass dampens my clothes as I lay flush with the ground.

"You are fucking crazy," I say, dropping my shoulders and the weight that was on them.

"Tell me something I haven't heard before." He chuckles. "For what it's worth, it wasn't a bad hit."

"Why did you scare me like that?"

He shrugs. "Spur of the moment. I was out here lying in the grass when I heard you in the kitchen. I wanted to see if you would fight if you thought it was someone who was going to hurt you."

"I mean, I see the logic in that, but you have to see how fucked-up that is too?"

He chuckles. "Yeah, but I knew you could handle it. Despite what you might think, I wouldn't intentionally hurt you."

Sitting up, I hug my knees. "Right. Because you are backing their choice to want me here."

I don't ask because I know that has to be why. He doesn't care about me personally. He's just tolerating me because the other boys care about me.

"Partially, yes."

I look down at him in confusion once again. Does he ever just say what he's thinking?

"And the other part?" I ask, almost annoyed that I have to dig for such basic answers.

I turn away when it's clear that he isn't going to answer.

After a long silence, he speaks, his raspy voice quiet in the night air. "Do you think monsters are born or made?"

"Are you drunk again?"

He doesn't answer, waiting for me instead.

"I think they are made. Monsters are created based on the circumstances forced on them. No one is hard-wired to be an evil person." I don't look at him, but I can feel his stare on me. "Can I ask you something now?"

"Sure."

"How did y'all meet? What made y'all so close?" I expect another shallow answer, but I hope for more.

"I met the twins in seventh grade. Some asshole had them cornered in the bathroom. I still had fresh cuts hidden under a hoodie from the night before, but I beat the breaks off that guy. I don't like bullies."

I glance over my shoulder, seeing him staring up at the night sky.

"I started boxing at a young age and learned to defend myself as best as I could against a grown man. I taught the twins, and they took me in when I could get away from Nickolas." A smile ghosts on his lips and my stomach flips at the sight.

"Their uncle didn't mind. He didn't have any blood kids, but he loved us all like we were his own."

Silas sits up, mirroring my position but keeps his eyes on the stars. "We met Ian not long after. I caught him hacking into the school files, downloading everything for his own personal enjoyment. He likes to know everything about everyone, and me being the shit starter I am, thought having him around could be fun." He laughs lightly at the memory.

"We pulled some epic pranks with the school's social media and bypassed a lot of the work we had to do to graduate. Ian was outcast by his family. The rest was history. We became brothers. And nothing matters more than the family we made."

I smile at that. "I'm glad y'all found each other. Some people spend their whole life waiting for a love like that."

A shooting star passes overhead and I watch as Silas closes his eyes. Silence fills the space between us, comfortable and full of hope.

"So, why were you out here so late anyway?"

"I have trouble sleeping. I like to come out here and look at the stars." He pauses, seeming to get lost in thought. "The silence of the night is peaceful."

I snap my head to look at him, surprised at the similarity.

"I'm human, Mel. Maybe not a very good one due to the circumstances forced on me, but I do bleed red."

"You are not a monster, Silas. Yes, an asshole, but you don't hurt people without good reason." My words were meant to comfort him from the demons I see behind his tired eyes, but it seemed to do the opposite.

"Does selfishness fall in the good reasons category?" he asks, getting to his feet.

I do the same. "I think it would depend on the reward."

He solemnly nods. "What were you so flustered about?"

"I feel... lost... on how I am supposed to adjust. When I know I am ready and what I want."

For a moment, the world feels lighter as he takes my hand.

"No choice you make could be wrong. The next time you are at that crossroads, don't talk yourself down. See where it takes you. One way or another, you will find your way out of the woods," he pulls his hand away, "and if you have decided you want to stay... you chose wrong. You can't be happy here."

Carlisle

It's Saturday night, and we decided to go dancing, per Amelia's request. She wanted to go out with JJ, and we decided she wasn't going without us.

We all dressed in jeans, combat boots, and a nice shirt, and sat on the couch waiting for Mel to finish getting ready.

"So are we going to be the overprotective boyfriends that guard her all night, or are we going to let her have some fun without us up her ass?" Finn asks the group.

"Up her ass? Now there's a thought." I quip, and Ian almost spits his drink all over Silas.

"I say, let her have fun, and we watch from the sidelines until she needs us," Ian says, wiping his face and the dribbles on the table.

Of course, the little perv wants to *watch*.

Silas nods in agreement, he seems to have an issue being in forced proximity to her. Though I can't see why when all I want to do is see her naked in my bed.

She has been bouncing between mine and Finn's bed.

Claiming it's only because she sleeps better than she does alone. Sweet girl still seems to struggle with speaking up and being honest about what she wants. Of course, given the chance, I would keep her all to myself, but denying her happiness with my brothers is not something I could ever do to her or them.

I dream of the days to come when she rules over each of our hearts.

We are making great progress though. Each night, she grows a little more comfortable with our touches. Every night she climbs into my bed wearing only her T-shirt and panties, my dick instantly hardens. I should be commended for the restraint I have shown. No other woman has gotten that from me.

Fuck I'm pussy-whipped.

Seeing her in a tight little dress tonight is going to have me aching to be between her legs, eating her sweet cunt before I bury myself inside of her.

Finally she comes down the stairs wearing a short-fitted red dress, her long black hair gently curled in waves, with black heels wrapping around her ankles. Her dress dips low in the front, showing off just enough cleavage to draw the attention of every man in the room, but not quite enough to make me want to cut the eyes out of every man who looks. Maybe just assault with a deadly weapon.

As soon as she hits the bottom step, I motion my finger for her to spin around, my knees already growing weak from the sight of her. She twirls in a quick circle, and her scent wafts my face, wrapping around my body, seeping into my soul. I inhale deeply, wanting to absorb every drop of the coconut, almond butter, and rose that surrounds her.

When her backside becomes visible, I see the back of her dress is open, covering just her ass, and I nearly fall at her feet.

"Fuck me." I exhale, unable to hold in my appreciation of the woman standing before me.

"You be a good boy, and I just might," she says with a cheeky smile, and my stomach sinks like the fucking Titanic.

She better not be fucking with me.

I growl low, giving her ass a smack as she walks past me to the middle of the circle we have formed.

"Y'all like it?" Her voice is so soft and sweet, completely contrasting the vibes she is giving off. We all take her in, silent for a long moment as she shifts on her feet, waiting for our approval. The focused and pained looks on their faces say we all are having the same thoughts.

"Changing plans," Silas says, surprising all of us, and the way Amelia's lip pouts when she is not getting the whole picture is so fucking adorable.

"I don't want to change plans or clothes."

"Oh, no. That's not happening. You can wear whatever you want. We can fight," I say, and I see the excitement in her eyes. She may seem timid at times, but she is as bloodthirsty as we are under that exterior.

"We just decided that you are not going to be left alone at all tonight," Finn says, pulling her into his side. "No fucking way. One of us will be right next to you at all times."

He might as well piss on her.

"Someone might snatch you up. I know I want to." I say, chomping my teeth at her.

She rolls her eyes but doesn't try to fight us on the decision and I understand her a little deeper. It's not control that she fears. It's the diminishment of who she is. She enjoys belonging to someone entirely - having someone love who she is so much that they wouldn't dare risk letting her slip through the cracks.

"If I didn't want all of you right next to me all night, I wouldn't have let you come at all. Now, quit being cavemen, and let's go."

All of us.

She doesn't wait for us to answer as she heads for the door. I throw a sarcastic face at Silas, and he returns it.

Like she had a choice.

Maybe she loves that little fact.

***

As soon as we open the door to the bar, rap music and loud commotion fill the air. You can barely hear yourself think. The floor is scattered with moving disco lights, and the entire building is dimly lit, setting the vibe for everyone that came here to get drunk, laid, or both. The smell of weed passes in the air around us, and my lips curl into a smile when I see Mel's nose wiggle, trying to sniff it out.

Our IDs are checked and a neon orange band is wrapped around our wrists, stating that we are over the age of twenty-one. Except for Amelia, who gets a black X on the back of each hand, identifying her as underage. She doesn't mind, though. Her choice of poison isn't found in a liquor bottle. Though, if she wanted to drink, it would take one word to make it happen.

We pick a table in the corner where we can see the dance floor and bar. She will have eyes on her all night, including ones that don't belong to the men she lives with.

JJ and Tyler find us the second we sit down.

"Girl, you really have a whole reverse harem thing going on here. I'm kind of jealous." She looks at Tyler and wags her brows.

"Um, no. I don't think so," he laughs.

"Hey, it's not for everyone," I shrug. What we decide to do is not anyone's business but our own, but when my Angel decides she wants to belong to us, the whole world will fucking know it.

Tyler claps his hand on Finn's shoulder and shakes it slightly. "Props to you, dude. I don't share."

It annoys me that he spoke that part only to Finn, like just because he fucked her first, he was the one that decided it.

We get some drinks in us, making small talk while the girls have their own separate conversations about makeup or sex or whatever it is girls talk about.

Eventually, JJ stands to drag Mel to the dance floor. She hesitates and looks over to me for acknowledgment.

My heart leaps right out of my goddamn chest and into her hands. I give her a nod, and she moves to the edge of the dance floor, staying as close as she can to us.

Good girl.

Our eyes follow them as she grinds on her best friend, her dress stopping at the curve of her perfectly round ass. I'm pretty sure we all have to readjust ourselves. Realizing Tyler is watching, too, Finn playfully punches his arm.

"Your eyes better be on your own girl."

"Or I'll cut them out of your head," Silas chimes in.

Tyler laughs, "Fuck, y'all really are all in love with that girl, huh?"

Love or obsession, I'm not sure, but she's definitely got my balls in her grip.

I have done this once before, but the level of possessiveness taken with Amelia is entirely new. We have never cared if someone screwed a girl that one of us had been with, but the thought of someone even getting close to Mel makes me see red. And it wouldn't change even if things go south, or she chooses to leave.

What I feel for Amelia is so deep, on a molecular level, that it hurts to think about a day when she wouldn't be near. I have always been told that you will know love when you feel it because it walks a thin line next to pain.

"Hey, cuties, what are you doing here?" a woman purrs.

I look over to see Emma fucking Anthony sit on Ian's lap and lean forward to tug on Silas's shirt, rubbing her ass on Ian in the process. Ian has never been harsh about his rejections. So, I am surprised when he yanks her head back, a red ribbon falling out of her hair.

"Get the fuck off of me, bitch." He shoves her off of his lap and into Silas's hard frame, who just shoves her again, this time, to the side, landing straight into a Amelia's fist.

Her punch was perfect, knocking Emma straight to her ass. The utter pride that floods me has got to be a sign that I more than just *like* Amelia, and a smile beams on my face at that realization alone.

JJ steps back as Amelia stands over Emma throwing punch after punch, firm as a brick wall. Not a single shake in her movements. No hesitation or fear.

Emma's eyes close, and her body goes limp, blood smeared across her face and skimpy clothes.

Silas pulls Amelia off, looping his arms around her firmly, and Ian steps in front of her, grabbing her face.

"You got her, babe. Breathe."

Her eyes are unfocused, and her breathing is uneven.

It takes a minute, but her breathing slows, and she steps out of Silas's loosened hold. Finn yanks Emma to her feet and throws her in a chair. A bouncer walks over, only to receive a wave of Ian's hand in dismissal.

This place is run by a man who deals on the side, so the Davis family is not exactly who they want to fuck with. And everyone knows that Ian can pull strings to get what he wants.

Emma regains consciousness and wipes her bloody mouth onto the back of her hand. Mel fucked her up good. Her face is already swelling, and the cuts on her nose and cheekbones steadily seep small amounts of blood.

"What's the prob?" Emma coos, holding her bravado. "You haven't fucked these two yet, so I figured they were fair game."

She barely got that last word out before Amelia slaps her across the face, probably making her head spin.

"They all belong to me." She steps closer, leaning down and getting in Emma's face. "How about we take this somewhere a little more private? I actually have a few things to ask you since you were kind enough to stop by."

She looks at Ian, and he flags the owner over. "We are going to need to use your supply closet for a little bit. We won't say anything about what we find down there if you don't." He gives the man a wink, and he nods back nervously before scurrying away.

The 'supply closet' is a decent-sized room with huge stacks of cocaine in the back corner. The entire area smells like piss. There is no telling what kind of shit goes on down here, but we are about to add on to that list. We get Emma tied to a chair and back away from Amelia to lean against the wall.

"We are here if you need us, baby, but this is all you," Silas says, and Mel freezes.

Dammit, Silas. You choose now to let your feelings slip?

She needs her mind right.

"Take what she owes you and *own* that shit." Amelia meets my eyes and smiles, releasing a steady breath.

There she is.

She straightens her back and saunters to Emma, not a crack in her armor to be seen.

"This is how this is going to go. You can answer, or I can beat the fuck out of you."

Emma spits blood at her, and Amelia slaps her across the face again, the sound echoing through the small room.

"Fuck!" Emma gasps, fighting her restraints, likely wanting to rub the sting.

"Now," Amelia exhales. "First, why assume that I haven't had sex with two of the guys? That hurt my feelings." She tilts her head to the side, looking amusingly vile.

"I'm not explaining shit to you, slut!" Emma yells, and Amelia jabs her right in the nose this time, blood spurting out, staining both of their skin.

Emma's eyes water, and she sobs, breaking the wall she was holding up.

"Try again."

"Fine." She breathes out, trying to stifle her cries before continuing. "Lance said he knew you were only banging the twins and wanted me to try to fuck the other two."

What the fuck?

"How and why?" I can see the tension in her shoulders. Even now, Lance refuses to let her have a moment of peace. My eyes fall to her hands, seeing them still steady. She's not scared.

She's pissed.

Emma shakes her head, receiving a growl of frustration from Mel.

"What is his fucking end game?" She's practically yelling now as she grabs Emma's face with one hand, squeezing so hard her fingertips turn white.

"I don't know!" Emma yells between gritted teeth.

Wham! Amelia lands a solid punch to the face.

Emma starts violently crying, sucking in breaths between words. "I don't fucking know! I don't know. I don't know"

"How about an easier one? Why are you screwing Jameson Davis?"

Emma's eyes bug out of her head then go to Ian.

He gives a wicked smile in return. Sweet Ian doesn't like to get his hands dirty but don't mistake him for gentle or domesticated. He knows how to play dirty when it counts.

Emma's eyes dart back to the one in charge. "I swear it has nothing to do with Lance's shit. I met Jameson when I became his intern, and we started sleeping together a few months ago. He told me I had to help Lance keep an eye on you, but that was it! I don't know how Lance gets information or why! It was Lance's idea to drug you. I tried to say no, but he told me he would out me and Jameson if I didn't play the part. Please, I'm sorry!"

Her word vomit is glorious, but the pure venom that takes over my girl's face is fucking sex on drugs.

"You're fucking *sorry*?! Do you know what he did to me that night?!"

Emma doesn't answer. Her head falls, and her cries come freely.

Amelia turns to us, her chest heaving with each breath, accenting the sweat and blood dripping between her breasts. "I can't stand to look at her anymore."

We untie Emma but leave her in the basement and head back up. She begs and pleads for forgiveness, but it falls on deaf ears.

JJ looks like she just saw a ghost as she takes in Amelia, and the blood splatter along her hands, arms, chest, and neck.

"I'm okay," she confirms with heaving breaths.

JJ stands frozen for a moment. "What have you gotten yourself into? Did they make you do this?"

I see it the second the words meet her ears. She hardens, and you can almost see a heart-string connecting her to her best friend snap in half.

JJ looks around at us warily, but as her eyes land on Silas, she reaches for Mel's hand. She tries to pull her away, if only a few steps, to have a private conversation, but Mel jerks it free and steps toward Finn.

"I chose to take the initiative for once in my life. Emma helped Lance rape me. She's lucky she's not dead."

Mel doesn't watch the volume in which she speaks or the company around her. She's comfortable in knowing that she's safe with us.

JJ gives her a slow nod, but her eyes don't look any less pained at the clarification.

"We gotta go process this shit. I'll call you, I promise." Mel kisses JJ on the cheek and nods at Tyler, not waiting for a response before exiting the building, us right behind her.

Amelia

O nce I started hitting her, I couldn't stop. My demon came out to play, but this time, instead of being helpless to her terror, I welcomed her.

Hit after hit, I made Emma feel all the pain trapped inside me. I released all the hurt and torment I had endured my whole life, feeling a weight lifting as her body lay helpless underneath mine.

Not a smither of regret plagues me.

I finally allowed every part of myself to show, no longer hiding my rage in fear of someone else's feelings or the outcome.

Rage boiled over until Ian's eyes pierced my soul. His gentle voice and praise-filled words soothing my rage back into submission.

I enjoyed wreaking havoc far more than I think I should have.

Back home, I lay on the bigger couch, trying to calm my racing mind. Ian comes to sit at the end, lifting my legs and placing them on his lap. He rubs his hands along one of my calves, and the touch instantly stills my thoughts, bringing all of my attention to how his skin feels on mine.

"That was insane," Carlisle says, sitting on the smaller couch, reaching for my bruised knuckles.

"Which part?" I ask, turning my head towards him, a headache forming.

"Partially watching you beat the brakes off of her." Carlisle smirks. "It happened so fast, and it was so fucking sexy. I have a boner again just thinking about it."

I laugh and sit up, making room for Finn.

He grabs my shoulder and lays me back down, gently stroking my hair.

Silas sits in his usual spot in the big chair, his forehead creased with tension. "The other part being that Jameson told her to help Lance. The fuck is that about?"

"I don't know." Ian rubs his jaw in frustration. "But we can find out. Now that we have proof of his affair, we can use that to get some answers."

I pinch my eyebrows together. "You are going to blackmail your own dad?"

He looks at me with a wary, forced smile, "What has he done for me to think twice?"

Right. We share the same burden of parents forcing their idea of perfection onto us. I wonder if I would do the same to my mother if it became necessary.

"So, how do we want to do this?" Finn asks, sounding as exhausted as I feel.

"I say we make a scene," Silas says, crossing his arms with a mischievous grin. "Embarrass the fuck out of him in front of all his rich ass friends. His embarrassment of a son and all his no-good friends is enough to taint his million-dollar reputation."

"Of course you would," Ian laughs before he continues, "He has the annual black-and-white gala next week. We can make an appearance and drop our bomb. Tell him he has to meet us the following day in private. He will be more likely to comply if he doesn't have to be seen with me."

The idea of pissing Jameson off thrills me, but I have never been to a formal event, much less have anything remotely acceptable to wear to a black-and-white gala.

"Hold on. We just found out that whatever Lance wants from Mel, your dad is tied into it somehow, and you want to wait an entire week to figure out why?" Finn asks. "What if that's too long, and whatever Lance wants from her is happening soon?"

Good point. That lingering question keeps me up at night.

"That's a reasonable question," Silas says, "but with all of us here and someone with Amelia at all times, Lance wouldn't get very far."

"That is, if what he wants has to do with her physically," Finn says, making an excellent point. "Emma said Lance needed to keep an eye on her. That doesn't necessarily mean he needs to touch her physically again." He looks at Ian. "It would be nice if we could hack Lance's phone."

"I'll see what I can do." Ian looks at me. "So, do you want to do this sooner? It's up to you."

I take a minute to think. I can't for the life of me think what Lance could want from me if it isn't physical. Maybe money, but all of Damian's funds were wired to my mom's account. I know Damian would have meant for some of his money to go to me. After all, he was sending me money weekly to help while I was in school. I guess he never thought my mother would go off the rails and keep every penny for herself.

But if Lance wanted money, using me to get to her wouldn't be the way to do it, and he knows that. I am at a loss, and quite frankly, I am tired of dwelling on it.

"You know what," I finally say, "I say screw it. I'm tired of giving the bastard any of my energy. There is nothing readily available for him to take or use me for, so I say we wait until next weekend, and in the meantime, we go do something fun."

Ian smiles at me, and Carlisle looks at me like the sun is shining out of my ass.

"Atta girl." he says.

"How about we go to the lake house at Gypsie's for the week?" Ian looks around at each of us in question.

"Hell, yes!" Carlisle praises.

He claimed a lake house too? "Seeing this one in a bikini? Yes, sir," Finn jokes, trailing a hand down the center of my chest to my stomach. I tilt my head back to look at him and wink. He leans down, his lips inches from mine, and whispers, "Stop trying to get me hard."

I part my lips, and his meet mine, his tongue slipping between them. He kisses me hard, cupping the underside of my chin with his hand. I let out a quiet moan as our kiss turns sloppy.

"Come on, man. I know we are all picturing her half-naked on the sand. Don't make it weird by giving us all a hard-on." Carlisle whines, and I smile against Finn's lips.

He pulls away with a laugh. "Okay, it's a plan."

Thunder cracks outside, and I race to the back door. I stand there, watching the rain fall softly. I'm so consumed by the peace it brings that it takes me a moment to realize Carlisle is standing next to me. Watching me. The wind picks up, and the trees start to dance in a rhythmic motion.

"You like the rain?" he asks as if he has found a common interest between us.

I nod and crack the door so I can hear the sound of it falling a little better. Leaning my cheek against the glass, I close my eyes.

My mother always said rain was the tears of angels because someone somewhere had just died. I never believed her. How could something so comforting to me be something devastating on a much larger scale?

I choose to think of rain as a whisper. A reminder that good can still come, even when the drought seems endless.

Carlisle's hands snake around my ankles, and then he is taking my shoes off. His discarded nearby, along with his socks. He takes my hand with the biggest smile on his face and pulls me out of the house and into the middle of the yard.

Stretching my arms out to the sides, I tilt my head back, letting the water drench me and the dress I'm wearing.

The rain falls harder and faster. I spin and twirl like a little kid, laughing carelessly as wet grass and mud coat my feet.

Carlisle pulls me into him, and together, we fall flat on our backs. As I wipe the dripping water from my eyes to look at him, lightning flashes across the sky lighting his features. His hair is matted to his forehead, and his chest is heaving with deep breaths.

"Shh," he says with a finger pressed to his lips.

I listen for the part I love the most.

Pow!

Thunder cracks again, and I jump. It always scares me in an exhilarating way. I know it's coming, and the sooner it does, the closer the danger. I wonder what it is about the thunder that causes the same smile on Lyle's face.

He rolls on top of me, the water from his hair dripping onto my forehead. His wet lips crash into mine frantically, and I drink him in. Our heads bob and turn as he kisses me as deeply as he can. I frame his face with my hands and give back as much as he gives me.

Lightning flashes again, and I smile against his mouth as I silently count the seconds.

Pow!

He times it just right and whispers the sound against my mouth. I tilt my head farther up to feel the rain on my face again, and laughter consumes me as Carlisle sticks his tongue out to taste the rain. I laugh hard, and I know this moment is one I will never forget.

For the first time in a long time, I am laughing purely from enjoying something so childlike - so pure.

It's the first time I've seen Carlisle in his own light. He is not just the twin that likes to play games and push boundaries. He is a man that thrives in chaos and enjoys playing in the rain. And he's sharing that with me.

Finn, Silas, and Ian watch us when we sit up to face the back door. I don't try to read their expressions because, right now, nothing else matters. My hope has come, and I intend to stay out here until the dark skies have nothing left to offer.

Then, when the rain stops, I might write a letter.

***

I stare at the pen and paper and debate on writing something to *him*. My damp hair drips onto the paper, blue lines smearing like they do with tears. I can't leave a note and tell him where we are going. The wrong person could find it. If *he* is still watching, he will find me. He followed me to the dorms, to JJ's house in the summer, and he left me letters a few times when I was out in public. So he will find me again.

I tap my pen on the hard top of my new dresser. It's been a little over two weeks since I have heard from *him*. And so much has changed. Despite *him* not answering my last letter, I want to write another and tell him everything about the new life I'm forming here.

I know he would be happy for me, but I still hope he would be jealous of the guys. I conjure the idea of *him* reading my letter and rushing to me, finally whisking me away like I have wished he would for years. Only now, I'm not entirely sure I would want *him* to.

I drop the pen onto the paper and walk away from it. Tossing a week's worth of clothes into my bag, I zip it and race back down the stairs, not nearly moving fast enough to match my elation. Maybe this will actually feel like a summer vacation now.

"Let's go!" I sing-song to the boys.

They flow down the stairs one after the other, shaking their heads at me or laughing.

"You would think we locked her inside the house for a week, and this is her first outing," Silas says sarcastically. I give him a shove as he passes me, and he looks at me like I'm an alien.

I heard him call me baby last night, but when I looked at him, he didn't seem the smallest bit apologetic. Though maybe I misread the progress I thought I was seeing between us. After all, he did tell me to do better at hating him when I thought we might become friends. Sure, he annoys the ever-loving fuck out of me sometimes, but *hate* is a strong word.

"Relax, Alpha, it was playful. Not a challenge for dominance." I hold my hands up in surrender, and he grabs them, pulling them above my head, pushing me back against the wall.

My head hits the wall with a thud, and he lowers his head to be eye-to-eye with me. I swear I hear him inhale through his nose like he's smelling me.

"What a shame," he says in a slow husky tone.

He releases me and walks away, leaving me frozen with my chest heaving. The other guys chuckle, but no one says anything. I smooth the dry clothes while clearing my throat.

"What car are we taking?" I ask.

"Well, we can be crammed in one car, or we can split up, and half of us ride in the truck," Finn answers.

"Truck?" I had only seen two of the boys' cars and thought maybe the other two were at their shop.

"Yeah, we keep it in the garage," Ian says. And now I feel stupid for not obviously suspecting that.

"It's awesome. It has the best sound system," Ian continues, tilting his head back with his mouth open. I laugh at his music-gasm induced purely by the thought of it.

"I'm down," I say, walking towards him. I wrap my arms around him and look up half expecting him to tense or be awkward about it. But he pulls me closer and kisses me on the forehead.

We grab our bags and lock the house up. Ian walks to the truck and opens the passenger door for me. The dark blue frame sits on huge tires that require me to use the step to get in. I get situated and toss my bag in the back seat. The back door opens, and Ian climbs in, shutting it behind him.

"What are you doing?"

"Oh, it isn't my truck," he says, looking amused.

Before he can elaborate further, the driver's side door opens, and Silas slides in.

Ian leans up and props his chin on the back of my seat. "It's Si's."

I lean towards Ian, getting an inch from his face, and glare at him. "You tricked me."

He closes the space between us, presses his lips to mine, and nips my bottom one with his teeth. "Don't worry, love. He won't bite unless you ask him to... usually. But we are gonna have some fun."

I look over to Silas and raise a brow. "Does this one even know how to have true fun?"

Silas starts the truck with a loud rumble and returns my expression.

"If you want fun, I'll show you how big boys have fun, but don't complain when you don't like what you get." I cross my arms, and he laughs. "Don't say I didn't warn you."

Carlisle and Finn open the door and hop on the step in sync. "Gotta get a kiss before the drive. Can we get you halfway?" Finn asks, leaning in close.

"Maybe," I say before I give him the kiss he was asking for.

"Hey Lyle, wanna hit Dead Man's Curve? Mel wants to have some *fun*," Silas asks with that evil smile he wears all too well.

Carlisle freezes for just a moment. He looks from Silas to his brother and then to Ian. Finally, he turns to me with a challenging expression. His ebony hair falls into his eyes as he holds onto the truck's roof. He looks like a wet dream, and I clench my thighs as he leans inside the cabin.

"Better buckle up, Angel, and show me what you're made of."

Fuck.

He pulls my seat belt down and over my chest, his body brushing mine, his smell invading my nose. God, he smells so fucking good. Like coconut, coffee, and leather with a hint of weed. He runs his hand up my thigh and squeezes as he kisses me, then retreats from the truck.

Both boys flash me a wink at the same time before shutting the door. If that won't make your pussy throb, I don't know what will.

We pull out of the driveway, and Ian instantly leans forward to connect his Bluetooth.

"What makes this fun for you, but a test for me?" I ask in the silence, liking nothing about the sound of Dead Man's Curve.

"Some things you will know when you see them, others are kept hidden until they are yanked to light." Silas replies without looking at me.

I groan, "Fuck, why are you always so cryptic."

"Why do you reveal your pain only once you are in a secluded place?"

Instead of getting embarrassed, I keep my tone level.

"Because I like that only I know it's happening."

He nods like he has made a point. "Some things are kept hidden because there is more beauty when someone discovers the truth on their own."

I take a minute to think on his words while Ian picks a song. Silas is an ass most of the time, but he chooses moments to show me parts of him. The stuff with his dad had him building a wall around himself to keep anything from hurting him again. Though, now it seems he is waiting for someone to figure him out. To break it down.

The speakers in the truck begin to rattle as "*Take What You Want*" by Post Malone and Ozzy Osbourne pours into the truck, filling the silence of past pain and unanswered prayers.

Fitting.

I let the music flow through me as I dance along with the beat. Pretending to give a full-blown concert to the windshield in front of me, pouring my entire heart into the lyrics.

Silas looks over at me, and fuck me; he actually *smiles*.

Hands grab my shoulders from behind and yank me back against the seat. A hot breath travels up my neck to my ear.

"Do you know how fucking hot it is watching you doing that?" Ian asks.

I turn my head to the side. "If you keep getting that close to my neck, we are going to have another issue with our promise."

He nips my earlobe and leans back in his seat as the next song comes on.

His playlist is all over the place, switching from old and new rock, 90s R&B, rap from every decade, love songs, and even some pop. We sing and dance for the next hour and a half, thoroughly enjoying ourselves.

The truck begins to slow down, and Silas nods his head toward my door. Just as I turn my head, my window is rolled down, and the truck is moving left into the other lane. The twins pull up next to us in Carlisle's car, blaring *"Crazy Bitch"* by Buckcherry.

Ian laughs as the boys sing it to me, and Finn turns around in his seat to hump the back.

"You ready, baby?" Ian asks as the boys gas it.

My head slams against the seat, and my heart drops out of my ass. Ian reaches around the seat and wraps his arms around me. I claw the shit out of his arm as we do a hundred and ten down the straightaway, side by side.

I am freaking out from the speed and that we are in the lane for oncoming traffic. I stare forward into the trail of our headlights and I can't see the road anymore. A caution sign for a curve and a cliff flies by.

I look at Silas who only laughs maniacally.

"Silas?" I question nervously in a loud cry. We don't slow down And I am about to throw up.

"Silas! Slow down!"

The curve is coming up fast, and on the right side is a steep drop to death.

When we are close enough, Silas and Carlisle yank the emergency break and drift around the steep turn side by side.

The boys yell excitedly, but my own scream is louder than them all. My body slams against the door, and I smell rubber burning. I lock my eyes shut, and every muscle in my body stiffens as another sound of pure terror rips through my throat. All of my worst fears flash before my eyes, and I picture this ending in a blood-stained road.

My body jerks back and forth as we straighten back out. Both vehicles slow down and pull to the side of the road, and they are all laughing. I look around like I have no idea what the hell just happened, my chest heaving with every breath I force myself to take.

"What? Not the kind of fun you wanted?" Silas taunts me.

I stare at him for a few seconds before bursting into hysterical laughter. I look down to see blood on my fingers from my nails digging into Ian's arms. I release him and hold my hands in front of my face, laughing even harder.

"Great man. You broke her." Ian groans exasperatedly.

I laugh even harder at that. My fear of car wrecks fully lashing out, and I am shaking violently. My brain feels like mush, and there's sweat dripping down my back.

They stare at me silently, and the longer I look around at them, the harder I laugh.

It takes me a good three minutes to regain composure. I inhale all the air my lungs will allow.

"No. That was fucking terrifying, and you all are horrible for that, but I think I... loved it."

I have been so fucking scared to be the cause of an accident in a car, my mother's hatred only solidifying the reasoning, but now it doesn't feel as impossible to escape.

Shit happens, but that doesn't mean you should let it stop you from living. Fear is a liar, and destiny is a conceited bitch.

Carlisle smiles at me, every white tooth visible in the dim lighting.

"That's my fucking girl!" He hops out of his car and yanks my door open. "I am so fucking obsessed with you, Amelia!" he practically yells at me. Then he grabs my face and kisses me long and hard. He pulls away, and I am left panting harder than before.

"You do something to me, girl. I just... God, you set me on fire, and I cannot get enough."

A feeling of comfort warms me, and I kiss him again, showing him my response. No second-guessing.

It's funny how something so small can mean so much to someone. I look past Carlisle and into his car.

Finn is smiling huge, giving me a little nod. I bask in the adrenaline that is still swimming through my veins, now mixed with adoration for the Jones brothers.

Amelia

We get back on the road, and Ian leans forward to turn the music back up. "You wanna come back here with me?"

I unbuckle my seat belt and climb over the console into the back seat.

"Hey, handsome." I smile flirtatiously, and Silas scoffs, watching me through the rearview mirror.

"Grow up and fuck off, Silas." I retort.

Ian chuckles, "Yeah, what she said."

I see Silas cast him a glare through the mirror, and I stick my tongue out at him.

"You're a child," he says, sounding annoyed.

"Well, I guess that makes you a pedophile with how much you want to fuck me," I tease.

"Keep dreaming, sweetheart."

"That you are a pedophile? *Wow*, you are sick." I lean closer to Ian, his chest shaking with silent laughter.

Silas's shoulders rise and fall faster, a clear sign I'm getting under his skin.

Ian strokes my cheek. "You look tired. Wanna take a nap? We have about an hour left."

I agree graciously as I stretch out and lay my head in his lap, utterly exhausted. He runs his fingers through my hair lazily with one hand and types on his phone with the other. My eyelids suddenly feel heavy, and sleep begs me to come, but as Ian holds his phone screen in front of my face, I keep my eyes open for a few more moments to read the message.

I'm proud of you. I wanted to stop them at first but we all needed to see how you would react. You handled that shit like a champ babe. I'm not even mad about you cutting my arm. Kinda a turn-on.

I turn my head to look up at him, and he is smiling shyly. I pull his phone out of his hand, flipping it over to use the light, inspecting the crescent-shaped marks on his skin before gently kissing them. Placing his phone on the seat, I roll back over, tucking his hand to my chest. His body stills for a moment, but finally relaxes, continuing his gentle strokes through my hair, massaging my scalp. I let my eyes finally fall shut, dragged into a peaceful sleep within seconds. No demons to be heard.

***

Ian gently rubs my shoulder, and I groan. "We are here, but I can carry you in if you want to sleep."

I nod and lift my head for him to slide out of the truck. I sit up fully and lean out, reaching for him. He pulls me into his arms, and I wrap my legs around him, laying my head in the crook of his neck. His arms cross under my butt, and he grips my thighs.

"Pinky promise," he whispers into my ear.

I relax into him and inhale his scent deeply. His smell is subtle and almost earthy, with hints of bergamot.

He carries me into the lake house laying me gently on a bed after pulling back the cover.

"They are bringing in the bags if you want to change." He says, running a hand through his shaggy blonde hair.

"Yeah, I can't sleep in pants and have to take a shower, or I feel gross."

"So, I carried you in for nothing then." He laughs and shakes his head as he walks out. "I'll start the shower."

I follow him out of the room and around the corner into the bathroom.

"I wouldn't say for nothing." I definitely didn't hate the feeling of him holding me like that.

"You are something else. Towels are in the cabinet, and soaps are in there. Nothing girly, so I hope you don't mind smelling like a guy."

The rest of the boys pass by the open door with bags over their shoulders. I reach to grab my bag from Finn, but he pulls away. "I'll pick something out for you. Go ahead and get in."

They continue walking, heading for their rooms. I grab the hem of my shirt, and Ian's eyes freeze at the small of my stomach showing.

"Staying for the show?"

His eyes reach mine, and he exhales loudly. "Oh, how bad I want to say yes, but I'm already in trouble knowing you don't sleep with pants on."

My brows pinch in question.

"There are only three rooms here, meaning you have to room with one of us. We like you, but none of us are sleeping on the floor or couch, love."

"That's alright. But who said I had to sleep in your room?"

"Well, I was thinking that you and I could spend some time together. You don't have to sleep with me, though." He taps his fingers against his thigh nervously.

"I don't mind." I lean in and kiss him on the cheek, understanding he wants me in there with him but still needs to take things slow.

"Well, I'll leave you to it." I don't miss the pink color of his cheeks before he leaves, shutting the door behind him.

I make quick use of the shower, washing with one of the gel body washes. I step out as a knock hits the door.

"I got your clothes, Mel," Finn says through the door. I reach for a towel and wrap it around my body.

"You can come in."

The door swings open, steam rolling out of the room. He extends his arm, handing me the tee and panties. "You smell like Lyle."

Guess that bottle was his.

"Thank you." I say as I reach for the clothes, letting my towel fall to the floor. Finn releases my clothes into my grip, his stare is frozen on my bare skin.

"Oh, sweet baby Jesus," he says, breathless.

Footsteps fall quickly down the hall. "I wanna see!" a voice yells, and Carlisle slides past in his socks, gripping the door frame to pull himself back to center.

"Ah, shit," he says in the same tone, matching Finn's gaze.

"Can I help you, boys?" I prop a hand on my hip as water drops trail down my skin onto the floor.

"Absolutely, you can," they answer harmoniously.

"I can think of at least three things that could help me right now," Carlisle adds.

I bend down and pick up my towel.

"Yeah?" I ask, slowly walking towards them, placing a hand on each of their chests.

"How will I ever choose who to sleep with tonight?"

I lean in and flick my tongue against Finn's lips, and he groans. I move to Carlisle and trail my tongue up his neck, and he does the same.

"Hm, now that I think of it, I'll take Ian up on his offer to stay in his room this week."

"All week?!" Carlisle asks. "Yep. Call this punishment for the way I met you. Now get out."

With my hand still on their chests, I shove them backward at the same time and shut the door, turning the lock, a laugh tickling my throat.

"That wasn't my fault!" Finn bellows.

"Tough shit. Should have told me sooner."

"This is not fair!" He yells back, laughing.

I slip on my clothes and open the door to see them both standing with their arms crossed, exasperated looks on their faces. I give a wink and walk towards Ian's room.

They follow behind me and stop at the door like I am going to tell them I was just kidding.

"Shoo. I'm tired. Make me breakfast in bed and then take me swimming, and I'll think about changing the terms." I give them both a kiss and shut the door.

"This is your fault, dumbass!" Finn snarks from behind the closed door.

A thud comes from the other side of the door and Carlisle groans, laughing through the pain of the hit.

"This woman," Carlisle says exhaustively, and I can picture him running his hand through his hair.

I smile in success, then turn to see Ian laying in bed one hand propping up his head. "I am scared for the days I might be on the receiving end of your attitude. You are a sassy little shit."

"So you plan on keeping me around then?" I crawl into bed and mirror his body, propping my head to level our eyes.

"I just might have to. Those two are like toddlers fighting over their favorite toy." He pulls me in close wrapping his arms around me.

"I know you now have plans to go swimming tomorrow, but I plan on getting some one-on-one time with you while we are here. Maybe sunset by the water?"

"You're sappy. You know that?"

"I have never been with anyone long enough to discover that about myself, but yes, I'm seeing the signs."

"Yes, sunset sounds lovely." I place a hand on my heart and mimic a swooned look.

Ian crawls over me and gets up to turn off the lights.

The room falls pitch black, triggering something inside of me, but I breathe through it focusing on Ian.

He fumbles back to the bed, tripping over our bags.

"Ow. Fuck," he grumbles.

Climbing back over me, he pulls the covers up and rolls me over. My back presses against his bare chest, and his legs curl under mine.

"Is this okay?"

"Stop acting like we are thirteen, and it's the first time we've touched. Cuddle me and shut up."

A low laugh rumbles against my hair, and he rests his arm on my side. "Yes, ma'am."

I feel him tilt his face down to my neck, before he inhales. "You smell like Lyle."

I smile as he pulls me closer holding me a little tighter.

I close my eyes and try to let myself drift off to sleep. I don't get very far before my thoughts start racing.

Ian's grip on me tightens, and he whispers, "Breathe, babe. Everything is fine. Stop trying to convince yourself otherwise."

I didn't realize my breathing had kept time with my pounding heart. Taking a deep breath, I place my hand on top of his.

He slides his hand under my shirt, rubbing small circles on my stomach. I focus on the touch and the smell of Ian, reminding myself that, in this moment, I am okay.

I am okay.

I tell myself over and over again until my inner monologue becomes a mumble, and I drift into sleep.

Amelia

I wake to the smell of bacon and syrup inches from my nose and open my eyes to see the twins standing before me with a tray of breakfast, and laugh. I wasn't totally convinced they would do this part of my request.

Ian stirs awake, his arm still wrapped around me.

"What time is it?" I ask.

"Almost lunch. Considering we didn't get here until almost five am, I figured we all needed more than three hours of sleep," Carlisle says with a shrug.

Good point. They do not want to see me woken up after only three hours of sleep. I am not nice to anyone if I don't get the rest I want.

"Breakfast, as ordered, and we are going swimming when we are done." My eyes shine bright with excitement, and the boys look pleased.

"You two are so whipped," Ian mumbles, still half asleep.

"Don't point fingers, pretty boy. You're well on your way." Finn says, narrowing his eyes.

Ian laughs putting a pillow over his face. "Get out. We'll meet you downstairs," he says, barely audible thanks to the fabric smashed against his mouth.

I eat what I can before giving Ian the rest to finish. I hop out of bed, comb through my tangles, and throw my hair up in a bun. Turning, I see Ian mid-bite, his eyes glued to my ass cheeks hanging out from under my t-shirt. I give him a pointed look.

"Sue me. Your ass is fucking amazing." He shrugs, continuing to shove the small piece of pancake into his mouth before readjusting his morning wood.

"You gonna come swimming with us?" I ask, half teasing a little more.

"Or what? Miss that ass in a bikini? Not a fucking chance in hell."

"So are you just gonna compliment me and stare?" I climb on the bed, moving the now empty tray out of the way and onto the bedside table.

"Is that not what a gentleman does? Is that not what you want?" he asks, sitting up and pulling me into his lap.

"The way you keep looking at me is driving me insane."

"Well then, something new and frustrating for the both of us."

The room falls silent and perfectly still, other than his fingers tapping rhythmically on my thighs. He watches his own fingers as they dance further up, closer to the lace of my panties.

It takes every ounce of strength I have to push off of him.

"Okay, let's get dressed. I'm ready to go swimming!" I chirp, slapping him on the leg and ripping the blankets back.

"Fuck, it's cold!" he protests, reaching around me to smack my ass. I yelp and jump off the bed.

"Let's go! Let's go! Let's go!" I chant, doing a little hopping dance to my bag to grab my red bikini, T-shirt, and toothbrush. I continue out of the room all the way to the bathroom as Ian groans and shuffles out of bed.

It would have been easy to let that go further, but the last thing I want to do is have my impulsiveness ruin this if he was to regret it being too soon.

I change my clothes and quickly brush my teeth, then skip to the kitchen where the rest of the boys are.

"God, she's chipper," Silas mumbles, sipping coffee, "Who fucked her?"

"Mr. Grinch," I snarl.

Ian comes down the hall holding a stack of towels and a small bag.

"If we don't go now, she's likely to go without us," he says with humor in his tone.

The twins stand up from their stools.

Matching swimming trunks.

The day I met Carlisle, they were wearing the same ones and, spotting the difference between them was impossible. But now I could easily point out many things that are not like the others.

"What's so funny?" Finn scowls at me.

"The fact that you two still coordinate clothes like your mommy is dressing you for first grade."

"Easy!" Carlisle protests.

"Come on, you are in your mid-twenties and still wear matching swim trunks?"

"Our uncle has a sense of humor," Finn says, "He always buys us matching clothes as a joke, and it just kind of carried into our adult lives. He still sends us packages, and we play into it, sending him a picture of us holding hands."

I nod, still amused and unable to hide the humor or sarcasm in my tone. "Adorable."

"Alright, judgey, let's go get some sun." Finn steps forward, poking me in the stomach playfully.

Ian squeezes my shoulder, and I look at Silas. "Are you coming, grumpy? Or are you gonna stay here and find something to punch for fun?"

He smiles wickedly, "Oh, I think I can find *something* fun to do out there. There is a cliff that I just might push you off of."

"Ha, you're hilarious."

The sun greets me, as I walk out the back door, warming my skin, the fresh air blowing across my face. I inhale, and a sense of excitement thrills me. There are miles between me and the place of so much pain, and I have a week to soak it up. Looking around, I take in the beautiful houses lined next to ours. There are docks leading to the water in front of each. Further down, in the water, to the right, a large cliff sits in the distance.

I take off my T-shirt and sprint down the dock. Reaching the end, I jump high and front flip into the water. The coldness surrounds me as I go under, feeling utterly amazing. As I surface, I wipe the water from my face and tread water, looking at the guys. All four are standing side by side, staring at me.

"We are in so much shit," Carlisle laughs, and Finn nods with a slightly slack jaw. Ian runs his hand through his hair with a baffled grin, and Silas has his usual unreadable flat expression.

Finn grunts and runs my way, jumping into the water, nearly landing on top of me.

As he breaks the surface, he wraps his arms around me and kisses me deeply. We sink just below the surface, but he doesn't break our kiss until I shove him away to come up for air. I suck in the needed breath he stole from my lungs and clear the water from my eyes with a laugh.

Finn shakes his hair, slinging water in my eyes. I wipe my face, only to be met with another wave of water as soon as my eyes reopen. I cast him a stare that asks where he found the audacity to be a child, but laughter consumes me as I return the motion, drowning his face with the dirty lake water. He pushes above the surface, gaining a few inches above me before he dips in for another kiss. My heart soars at the playfulness.

I look up to see the other guys standing at the end of the dock, and my cheeks flush under the weight of their stares. There is something new and heavy about this moment. For them, though, this is somewhat familiar. I know nothing about her, but the thought of this being déjà vu for them has my stomach in knots.

Ian reaches for my hand and pulls me out of the water up onto the dock.

"Stay present, baby," he whispers into my ear before we stand up.

I smile, and my eyes drift over his shoulder to Silas. His eyebrows are slightly scrunched, looking almost pained.

Carlisle's voice hums behind me, "Are you into trying another adrenaline high?" He nods his head to the side, and I turn to see him referencing the cliff.

Intrigue fills me. The drive around Dead Man's Curve filled me with something I had never had before, and I didn't hate it. Maybe this would be like that. The difference is that this time, it's a fear of hurting myself, not others.

"I don't know," I answer nervously.

"It's terrifying in the best ways." Carlisle reassures.

I look between the boys and back to the cliff.

"Told you she would have to be pushed," Silas points out.

My blood turns hot, and for some reason, I feel like I have something to prove. It's not abnormal for me to want to please everyone, but when it comes to Silas, I just want to prove him wrong. I want to prove to him that I am not the scared little girl who won't do anything she's not sure of, just as a *fuck you*.

I stand my ground, and I cast a challenging glare his way. "Let's do it."

Carlisle takes off for the cliff, Silas following behind him.

Ian grabs my hand and spins me to face him once more, "You have nothing to prove to him or anyone else."

"I do," I say, "I have something to prove to myself, and if it shuts him the hell up, it's a win-win."

He gives me a smile, and together we walk down the shoreline with Finn. I look over at him, and he grins.

"You know, the fact that he even bothers to fuck with you means that he has an interest in you." I audibly laugh at that. "I'm serious. I'm not saying I know how he's feeling, but I've never seen him so hell-bent on pissing a woman off."

I have had my fill of men that seemingly get off on my pain. I don't need someone like that in my life so he can shove his "interest" right up his ass. Though without him, I may lose them all.

"Silas has been through a lot, Mel." Finn shrugs. "I'm not saying his actions are always right or excusable, but keep that in mind before deciding he is beyond all hope."

I don't say anything, and we walk in silence for the remaining few minutes. There is nothing awkward about it. It's a peaceful silence - a rarity for me.

Climbing up the cliff, I hear a scream, and my heart leaps out of my chest. My head jerks towards the water to see Carlisle in mid-air, arms flailing. He takes a solid four seconds to hit the water.

My gut churns and my eyes stay fixated on the disturbed water, waiting for him to surface again.

"Breathe, Mel. It's scary the first time, but each jump after gets easier," Finn reassures me.

"Just make sure you bend your knees so you don't hurt yourself," Ian says as he continues climbing next to me.

"Not helping."

The closer we get to the top, the more I feel like I am going to throw up. I search for my backbone and silently talk myself up.

Silas goes next just as we reach the top. He takes a running start, and as he jumps off, he does a backflip. He comes up from the water howling with laughter. I can see the smile on his face all the way up here.

And I want to see it again and again.

"Do you want me to jump with you for the first time?" Finn asks, taking me in his arms.

Silas is not around to poke fun at me, so I accept. I told them I had something to prove to myself, not Silas - completely contradicting what I had told myself moments before. It's both, but I won't admit that to anyone else.

I nod, and without hesitation, he reaches lower on my thighs and hauls my body onto his. On instinct, I wrap my legs and arms around him. He inches to the edge with my back facing the water and pauses.

"Take a deep breath but keep your eyes open. The next one is all you."

I nod and squeeze my body flush with his. He counts down, and I take a deep breath.

He pushes off with both feet, and we begin free-falling through the air. My stomach flips, and I squeeze even tighter, trying my best not to choke him. He yells excitedly, but I stay silent, holding my breath all the way down. We crash into the water, shooting down deeper below the surface than I have ever been.

The water muffles all sounds around me, and I look up to the water glistening from the sun above us. We both swim towards the glimmering surface, coming up for air. I push my wet hair back, and smile ridiculously.

Finn shakes his wet hair and runs a hand through it. "Did you like that?"

"I did," I beam.

"Good. Now you go solo." I hear his words, but my eyes drift to his shoulder, where the water drips down his tan skin, and butterflies flutter in my belly. "Stop eye fucking me, Mel, or I am going to have to rip that bikini off of you, let it sink to the bottom of this lake, and make you walk out of this water butt-ass-naked."

I swim towards him and run my hands down his chest and along his trunks. "Is that a challenge?"

He chuckles, "As much as I would enjoy the sight, I think Silas might keel over."

"Hm, I see that as a pro, not a con." Not that I see why he has such an issue with my lack of clothes.

"Are you two going to move?" Ian yells down at us. We look up at him and laugh, ending our moment and swimming to shore. We begin our climb up the cliff and take it slow as the guys jump off one after another, yelling with joy, free-falling into the water below.

"I like seeing you smile this much," Finn says, grabbing my attention. "The night I met you, you were so determined to have a good time, and now it seems to come easy."

"Well, I think that has a lot to do with the company I've been keeping."

He stops walking and leans against a large rock. "I'm glad you enjoy staying with us. We enjoy having you around. You can stay longer than required for your safety."

"Yeah, we do!" Ian yells, running up from behind us, scaling the rocks faster than what would be considered safe.

"I could look at that ass every day and never get tired of it!" Carlisle follows with an exaggerated growling noise.

I narrow my eyes at them as they come up, smacking my ass simultaneously.

"Pervs," I grind out, resuming my climb.

"Oh, don't act like you don't eat that shit up. There's no shame in wanting to be owned." Carlisle winks at me and I gulp.

Owned?

I think about that word and that I enjoy how much they constantly touch and show possession over me. Every time I move, there they are. Feeling wanted is new to me and I may be addicted to it. I'm itching to see how far they would take *owning* me if I gave in.

Leap.

"How long are we talking?" I ask Finn.

"Indefinitely, or as long as you want."

Those are the same thing. I no longer feel like a booty call overstaying her welcome.

Here, with them, I feel... at home.

We reach the top where Silas was waiting and they all step back. I guess it's my turn. Ian gives me two thumbs up in the nerdiest way. I step towards the edge and calm my breathing.

Slow. In and out.

"We are going to be here forever," Silas groans. "Someone just push her."

I turn around and glare at him, "You are such a fucking dick. Didn't your parents ever teach you any manners?" As soon as the words leave my lips, I realize what I said.

"No, my mother abandoned me for drugs and my father beat the shit out of me every day for over ten years. Sorry to disappoint, little monster." His eyes darken and he challenges my stare right back.

He only ever tries to cut me down, so I'm not sure why I feel so bad about my comment. He shows no sign that I hurt him, but I wonder silently if under the surface, that cut him deep. Maybe I wish it would, if only to have someone relate to my own pain.

"Hm, shame." I simply say, turning back around. "Just shut the fuck up and give me a damn minute, Mr. Perfect."

He doesn't say anything more, but I hear commotion as the boys likely joke behind me.

I look out over the water, focusing on the stillness and the calmness of the scarce clouds passing overhead. Taking a deep breath, I push off with one foot.

My stomach flips again. I pull my knees up, and this time, I close my eyes. Wanting to enjoy the rush of falling - the moments where nothing is touching my body but air. My heart feels wide open, my soul free.

I crash into the water and am welcomed back up by the sounds of cheering coming from my guys.

All of them.

Amelia radiates with happiness, floating on her back, soaking in her victory. The guys are whistling and clapping for her, and I find myself smiling, unyieldingly. I turn finding Ian grinning slightly, though he looks away fast and I steel my face.

"Do y'all think she could be a good fit?" I ask, letting my mask slip just a little.

They turn to me with blank faces.

"I mean, once she really knows us, she could do worse than run." I shrug, leaning against the large rock behind me. "Were risking a lot more than heartbreak here."

"I have no doubt she could be the perfect fit," Finn says.

Neither do I.

"If she's given the chance to rise to the occasion," Ian says, scooping a pebble off the ground and tossing it out into the water, away from Amelia.

I wait for the ripples, using the time to fill the silence. My throat tightens at the reality that my best friends are already falling for her.

"I'm gonna sit on the bank, guys!" Amelia yells from below. I move to peer over the edge, watching as she gets comfortable in the sand.

"Why are you so hard on her, Si?" Lyle asks, taking my spot against the rock.

"You of all people feel the need to ask that? How are you so quick to fall in love again when it ended so bad last time?"

He shrugs, smiling at the ground like a love-sick idiot. "Amelia feels like home, peace. And even if we blow this to shit, she'll never not feel like home. Nothing could keep me from her now."

I chew my lip and nod slowly, trying to find the right words as his truth sinks in. "It's like looking in a mirror... seeing my past. It's haunting."

"You have to let her show you who she can be," Finn says. "Let her in deep enough to love those guarded parts of yourself."

He firmly grips my shoulder, locking his eyes with mine. "We're all broken, brother. But she's not fragile."

Carlisle

I set all the necessary baking materials for brownies on the counter while waiting for Mel to finish her shower. I set the THC oil next to everything and hop onto the counter as Ian walks in, a towel slung low on his hips.

"You taking my advice?" he asks, nodding towards the supplies.

I quirk a brow. "Getting her high to see if she'll let me put it in her ass again?"

He scoffs a laugh, opening the fridge and retrieving a beer. "Yeah, that's what I suggested she needed. Your dick in her ass."

I shrug and accept the beer he passes to me, popping the top and flicking the lid somewhere onto the floor. "I think anyone would enjoy my dick in their ass." I swig a drink with a grin.

Ian's motions falter and he doesn't look at me again, taking his beer with him on his way to his room. "Don't fuck this up. She doesn't need to be dependent on pills."

Ian has always been the most level-headed of us. He never talks about it, especially with me, but falling for Mel was hard for him. Loving someone new almost overshadowed by fear of losing another person we care about, so of course he won't let her continue her pill problem.

Mel comes in wearing a tank top with no bra and pajama pants. Her wet hair is in a bun, and her face shines subtly. She watches the ground, positioning herself between my legs, and the smell of her skincare products wafts under my nose. Resting her forehead on my stomach, she wraps her hands around my waist.

I massage her arms and kiss the top of her head. "You ready to make some brownies so good they will make you question the best sex you've ever had?"

She gives me a nod and spins, walking to the mirroring counter where everything is placed without so much as looking at me.

I narrow my eyes at the back of her head. *Something is off.* I slide off the counter and pull the brownie box from her hand as soon as she picks it up. She continues to keep her eyes low and passes me the measuring cup.

Knowing what I'll find, I tilt her chin up, revealing the red puffiness of her eyes. I clench my jaw, and something pangs in my chest.

"Why?"

Her voice is shallow and quiet. "It's nothing, I promise."

"That's not what I asked. Why are you crying? I thought we were having a good time?" I pull her closer and force her to wrap her arms around me. I do the same, putting pressure on her back, pressing her chest firmly to my stomach.

Her shoulders droop. "We are." She thinks for a moment, and I give her the time she needs to find her words. "I didn't want you to see because I don't even know why I was crying. Sometimes it just comes, like my body is exhausted from holding everything in."

I bend and scoop my hands under her ass, picking her up. Her legs instinctively wrap around me and I set her on the countertop and frame her face with my hands. "So why cry in the shower when you could have come to one of us?"

"Cries are distorted by the sound of the water, and tears are washed away as fast as they fall. It's like you aren't really crying if there is no proof." She shrugs.

"Is that like if a tree falls and no one is around, does it still make a sound?" My lips begin to curl in a smirk, but falls as her features turn scorned.

"Don't trivialize my pain. I was being transparent with you, and you made it a joke." She shoves my chest and attempts to slide from the counter.

God, I am fucking this up.

I let her see the remorse on my face. "You've had enough change in the last few weeks to give any sane person whiplash. But you're fully capable of handling it better than most. There is no room for tears when there are people that need to bleed. Feel your emotions when it's done."

She rubs her pink eyes and nods again. "Like I said, I'm fine. I just needed a release for my frustrations."

There you go, Angel.

"Okay then. Let's make a mess and have some fun."

She smiles, and it seems genuine. I pull my phone from my pocket and turn my playlist on shuffle to help with the good vibes. She stays sitting on the counter, measuring out the milk, oil, and eggs. While I pour the brownie powder into a large mixing bowl, and she hands me what I need one by one. As the minutes pass, I can feel her mood shifting into a better place. She preheats the oven while I mix the THC into the batter and then pour it into the pan.

I swipe my finger along the edge of the bowl and wipe a smudge of chocolate on her nose. She darts her tongue out, trying to lick it off. The tip of her tongue making contact with the tip of her nose.

"No wonder you suck dick so good. You have a long ass tongue."

She wipes the rest off with her finger and swipes it down my nose. "Let me see you do it."

"You want to see me suck dick?" I smirk.

She curls her lip. "Are you capable of not being a perv for any amount of time?"

"Nope, sorry." I pull her to the edge of the counter, and I love the laugh it brings out of her. "But do you?"

"Want to see you suck dick? Are you serious?" She laughs harder, but I detect a hint of nervousness within the humor.

The oven beeps, and I quickly slide the pan in, set the timer, and retake my place between her thighs.

I bend at the waist and prop my head in my hands between her legs, looking up at her emerald-green eyes. "If you asked, I might do it."

Curiosity shines in her eyes.

Filthy, filthy girl.

"If you still want to see my tongue, I'd be happy to remind you what it feels like too."

She lifts her thighs hooking her legs over my shoulders. Leaning back on her hands, she readjusts her thighs on each side of my head.

"You know what I've been thinking about since I found out it was you in the woods?"

I begin to get lost in the haze that her lustful voice lures me into. I hum a curious sound. Her ankles cross slowly, then, in a swift motion, she grips my head with both hands and clenches her thighs around my skull.

"If I could kill you by crushing you between my thighs." She grunts, expelling every amount of force she has.

I let her think she's winning for a minute, tugging on her thighs like I'm trying to escape but can't. Then, I reach between her upper thighs and dig my fingers in to tickle her. Her grip lessens as she bursts into laughter, and I slip my head out of her hold.

I grip her around her back, my other hand wrapping around her throat. Lifting her from the counter, I usher her body to the floor, protecting her from the impact. Straddling her, I lower my face to hers.

"If you really want to kill me, you'll have to try harder than that. Might think about hitting the gym, but we both know you enjoy fucking me way too much to get rid of me."

I squeeze my grip tighter around her throat and crash my lips to hers for a bruising kiss. She welcomes me, giving back as much as I give.

I come in the front door after running some errands and immediately freeze at the sight in front of me.

An empty pan of brownies on the floor and Mel and Lyle nearly naked, sprawled on the couch with blankets laughing their asses off. They fall silent when they hear the door shut behind me. Their heads jerk in my direction, and the room fills with momentary silence.

"Uh, what's going on in *here*?" I say with a laugh. It only makes them burst into laughter again.

"Mel is experiencing pot brownies for the first time. Be glad you didn't come in here about ten minutes ago."

Ah, they're stoned.

She giggles and pulls the blanket up higher on her bare chest. "Ian wants me to use edibles instead of antipsychotics. What do you think, Dr. Jones?"

Moving to her, I lean down and kiss her cheek, neck, and chest. "I can agree. Though, if you get naked every time, we may end up with an unusually high body count."

She scrunches her brows. "What's the normal count?"

I give her a wink in response. Then I kick off my shoes and slide behind her on the couch. She settles into me and her eyes flutter closed.

"I'm gonna take a nap. Stay with me?"

Resting my head above hers, I the smell of my shampoo in her hair. "Always, baby."

Silas

My gaze falls back to Amelia and the thin scraps of material she calls a bikini. She insists on suntanning on the deck, and we join her outside because there is no way in fuck we are leaving her alone. Next to her Lyle leans up, stripping his shirt off to tan with her, causing her to adjust her straps.

My eyes trail down her body, and the beast inside me growls. The damn thing should be a crime. It hugs her subtle curves in all the right places, covering her small breasts nicely. Bottoms lightly cutting into her toned but not flat stomach, accenting the transition to her thick hips and ass, falling more between her cheeks than on top of them.

The snake tattoo slithers down the length of her spine nearly meeting the tail of the dragon hugging her side. Wings outstretched, about to take flight.

Burn marks peek out from the inside of her thighs as she lays face down on the long chair. She isn't trying to hide them anymore; not from any of us, at least. Despite the way I have treated her, she still feels comfortable enough around me to let me see who she really is.

Though, I know her more than anyone.

I watched her make a lot of them.

Pain inside my chest forces me to look away and busy myself with finding a chair. Sitting, I lean back in a still upright chair and close my eyes, as the pain takes me back all those years ago.

Sneaking out of Ian's house, I begin the forbidden walk to the other side of town. My truck is loud, and I don't want to alert anyone of my absence... or presence. Praying the three hours it takes will give me time to rationalize with the parts of myself that enjoy this torture.

Feeling pain isn't enough, I have to make myself see things that dig the knife in a little deeper, scaring my heart as a constant reminder of the monster my father made me.

No matter how many times he beat me for showing human emotions, I could never keep him out completely. I could only build my walls so high. Shove my emotions down so far. I boxed and fucked them away, but it could only ever do so much.

The human and monster inside me fight for dominance, leading me to her house to the pain of a girl who deserved none.

A girl who was perfect in every way, forced to her breaking point and then some. One who hid it well, just so she would be loved. But to them, she would never be enough. Always falling short in some way.

But she is my salvation and my damnation. The one I want to hold close but never can. The one I want to heal me. The one I would break.

I don't have the right.

I scale up the tree of her little light-gray brick house, climbing to the second-story window and pressing my back just to the right of it. I press my ear closer to the window she keeps cracked with the curtains pulled back. I have watched her lean up on the ledge, peering at the night sky, tears streaming down her face many times.

It's why I started lying on our lawn at night, doing the same thing, mostly thinking about her.

Her muffled cries greet me, the same as they do most nights I come over here. Though tonight they are sound different, so I turn and peer inside.

Sitting on the floor of her bedroom, she adjusts her earphones, moving the lighter to her thigh. Fresh blood dripping from a cut near the flame says this night has been particularly rough.

I watch as she finishes her ritual of pain, tossing the lighter across the floor and balling up in the fetal position. My heart aches, but my eyes refuse to move away from her shaking form. I need to watch.

I fight the urge to crawl through the window and take her into my arms. I am a stranger. A face she may have seen around, but nothing more, and that's how it needs to stay.

"Earth to Silas." Ian says, snapping his fingers in my face.

"Yeah, man?" I shake off the pain, open my eyes, and reapply my armor, similar to the woman next to me.

Ian gives me a soft smile and hands me a cold beer. He notices everything, and as much as Finn tries to decipher my behavior and Lyle tries to start conversations in boxing practice, Ian is the one who only observes. He doesn't push, just lets me know he isn't blind to the fact that I have much I don't make known.

Turning towards Amelia, he leans down, and kisses her on the cheek.

For fucks sake.

She whispers something to him, and he almost stumbles over his own feet.

"Dammit, Mel. You make me nervous like a fifteen-year-old boy with his first crush."

I was thinking the exact same fucking thing. He went from being annoyed with basically all women, to making googly eyes every time she breathes.

She giggles, and it takes everything inside me not to react when she sucks her bottom lip between her teeth and looks up at Ian in the most submissive way.

He exhales slowly and reaches to unclip her top. "Damn, where the fuck is my game?" he mumbles.

Finn and Carlisle laugh.

"Use it or lose it. Watch and learn, brother." Carlisle stands up, steps inside the house for a moment, then returns with his grinder and blunt wraps. He straddles Amelia's chair and lifts her legs over his.

My throat tightens as I watch his hands glide up her thighs and grip her hips, lifting them and sliding himself forward so her ass is right in his lap.

He rubs his hands over her ass and up her bare back, causing a little sigh to escape her lips. "It seems I'm in need of a table to roll on. Mind if I use your ass?"

"It'd be my pleasure, as long as you share when you're done." She wiggles her ass, and a low groan rumbles in my throat.

"Don't worry grumpy cat, we can share. Maybe that will lighten you up a little." Mel says, jutting her bottom lip out.

"Fuck off, Mel." I retort.

God, I am losing my fucking mind. One minute I'm trying to hurt her feelings, the next, she's busting my balls and making me want to fuck her stupid.

Carlisle rolls the joint, and I pass him my lighter from my cigarette pack.

Amelia rolls to her back, holding her top to her chest motioning for the blunt once Lyle gets it lit. Her chest rises and falls as she exhales a stream of smoke. Then she passes it to me.

I take it from her, locking eyes as I hit it, and pass it to Ian. My body warms, realizing this is the first time she has really looked at me with no bullshit being said between us. My heart beats a little faster, and my fingers tingle with the need to touch her.

My lips burn to say the things I would never dare.

We make small talk as the blunt is passed around the circle again and again. Laughter fills the air as we talk about nothing of importance. It's moments like this when my guard slips and my pain fades, leaving me in peace to enjoy the company of the people I love. For a few hours, I am able to live. Able to reach the surface of the water that, in all other moments, drags me under and fills my lungs, slowly killing everything alive inside of me.

I see Amelia, carefree and smiling like she has never felt pain a day in her life, and I wonder if she, too, feels the same. Or if even now, under that shining exterior, she is still fighting the darkness.

I see how the other three look at her, and it pisses me off. I have to sit back and watch as they fawn over the girl I have longed after for years. Not that they know. It isn't fair to expect them to know something I have never voiced out loud.

I love her.

The guys knew *of* her in high school, but I knew *her*.

Being a cheerleader made her part of the crowd, but she was easily overlooked by most.

Not by me though. There was something about her that felt familiar. So, I watched her.

I found her school schedule and walked the same halls she did. Watching her go through the motions of an average high school girl for weeks. She was a ray of sunshine. But there was something I was missing. I couldn't help but wonder who she was when no one was looking.

My answer came one day after school. I stayed late to avoid going home, sitting in my car, the tint so dark she couldn't have seen me.

She climbed into her car, sank in the seat, and cried her heart out. A bone-shaking, heart-wrenching meltdown. The kind that only comes to those who have felt true pain in one way or another. It was the first time I saw her pull out the lighter. This girl who seemed to have the perfect life was so broken at fifteen, and I had to know why.

Watching her with Lance led me to understand part of it. She had given her heart of gold to the wrong man. He didn't care about her. Doing the bare minimum just to keep her around.

Her light dulled over time, and I wanted so badly to help her. The unknown stopping me every time. Would I would snuff her light out completely or would she burn brighter with the challenge of loving someone just as broken?

I still wonder.

I lingered after graduation, my interest in her growing to something more. She became all I could think about. Any time we had parties, I searched for her. Hoping she would show up so I could get my high. And if she wasn't there, I would find a girl that resembled her and fuck her like she was.

But the anger and frustration became too much. I become so angry with my life that I enjoyed seeing her at my mercy. I needed to be on the other side, watching someone else resemble what I looked like all those years. But it always had to be her, always pretending she was the one to take it. The one to understand who I am.

Other times, she showed. She smoked, drank, and told herself everything was okay. Sometimes Lance came with her, but even then, she was often alone. On the nights she came alone, she would get so fucked-up I would have to make sure she was taken care of and made it home safely.

I nearly killed the few guys that made any kind of comment about her being an easy lay, pointing out that she was barely cognitive. Less abrasive comments were rewarded with a busted-up face. Always picked a fight to mask my true reasons.

She began to grow into herself. She got her braces off and her curves filled out. No longer having a problem being noticed, but she didn't take care of herself. Lyle was right about that. She was hurting and seemingly had no care for what happened to her. But I did.

Then Damian died, and I had failed her. I knew that any hope of one day having a place in her life was over. I would hurt her more than help her, so I could never be more than what I was now. I heard her heart shattering from outside that window each time I climbed that tree. And I ached with the need to fix it.

I dreamed of the day she would notice how much I cared - hear the echo of my soul begging to be near to hers. I dreamed of the day she would smile when she saw me and of the moments she would let me hold her close. I wasn't stupid enough to think that dream could ever come true. I had to be the villain in her story.

Now, her happiness is here.

She may fall for one of them, maybe all of them, and despite what we've told her, I would let her be happy with only them. If they made her happy, I would let her take them from me. Maybe then I could be content with leaving her be, knowing they will love her as fiercely as I would.

Lost in laughter, her top slips a bit, and she gasps, pulling her knees to her chest. With a nice buzz blurring the lines, I walk behind her, and she gives me a nervous smile as I pass her side.

Kneeling down I grab the dangling straps. My fingers brushing her bare skin as I re-clip the back of her top. She stiffens and I trail my fingers down her spine. My heart racing as my rough fingers contrast the soft skin I have longed to touch. I hear her suck in a small gasp, and I smile to myself.

She is affected by me just as much as I am by her. I wonder if she hates herself for that.

Her phone chimes, and I grab it from the ground next to her. I type in her code, and she looks at me like I have three heads. But I've watched her enough to figure it out. She never changes it.

She craves controlled consistency in any form she can get. Finn taught me that little sign pointing out the same thing about me and my obsessive routines. It brings a sense of tranquility, controlling something in your life when you have experienced trauma.

I look at the message.

Lance:
I alwys luvd u in red, baby

What the actual fuck?

I look at Amelia, my anger must be all over my face. Her face falls, and she places her head on her knees in defeat. Looking back to the phone, I scroll up, seeing many messages she hasn't replied to.

Lance:
Emma always did have a big mouth ;p

Lance:
I know u think abt me while ur in his bed

Youll never forget me baby

Lance:
Left standin alone after he made u cum.

Ouch. Bet that hurts :(

Lance:

U honestly think staying
with them is goin to solve
anything??

Lance:

Scaredy cat scaredy cat

I see u.

I casually lower the phone trying to hold on to my composure. "Dinner time," I order, motioning for everyone to follow me inside.

I get a few curious glances, but no one protests, reading the room and understanding the cues.

"What the fuck is this?" I demand, locking the door behind us.

She exhales and runs her hands through her hair.

"Nothing. He is just fucking with me."

The guys look confused, so I pass the phone around.

"When we have thought he was nowhere to be found, you have fucking proof of him stalking you since before you moved in." I glare at her.

She groans. "It's not that big of a deal."

"It is!" I counter. "Is this the only form of contact?"

Her eyes fall to the floor, giving her answer.

"Amelia..." Finn trails off.

She sighs. "He sent me a few creepy boxes with red ribbons, at JJ's and the house."

My head nearly explodes.

"But he hasn't touched me so it's not an issue!" Amelia says, trying to calm me.

"That's what JJ was hiding when I came to get you? That was months ago," Lyle says, his irritation growing. "And the red ribbon Emma was wearing. It was right in front of my fucking face."

"How could you not tell us?" Finn asks.

"It's nothing. No big deal–"

Ian holds a hand up. "The issue is that we don't know *why* he's watching you," he says. "And most importantly, he's fucking with what's ours now."

"He was at our fucking house and you said nothing." I struggle to keep my composure, fists balled at my side.

She doesn't say anything, but her eyes say it all. She is used to him tormenting her, and she is tired of fighting.

Lyle must see it too. "Baby, we don't let that shit slide. You should have told us he has been close by so we could beat his fucking ass. Stop cowering to him. You're giving him the power he wants."

He walks over to her and takes her face in his hands. "Dig deep and stand the fuck up for yourself."

She flinches slightly but doesn't get defensive. Just sits up a little straighter, and Lyle gives her a nod.

"Let's give the little leech an invite." Finn beams with a wicked grin. "Party here tomorrow night. Everyone's invited. We know he's watching. Let's make sure he hears."

Silas

I find Mel in the backyard a few hours later, going to fucking town on a pillow she duct taped to a tree. The bun on top of her head bobs with the angry motions of each strike. Her form is good, and my heart swells with pride, but the asshole in me wants to correct the few mistakes she's making.

Her bikini strings sway with her movements, brushing the tops of the shorts she put on over her bottoms.

Shame. I would have loved to watch her bottoms ride up and her ass shake as she worked out.

She has her earbuds in, so it takes nearly no effort at all to make her jump when I come up from behind and wrap my hand around her wrist. Spinning her, I pin her against the tree. The surprise in her eyes quickly washes away, replaced with irritation.

I take out one of her earbuds. "You're pulling your punches. You're not going to hurt anyone training like that."

She snarls at me attempting to push out of my hold.

"What's got your panties in a twist anyway?"

My eyes fall on her breasts, trickled with sweat, moving with her rapid breaths.

"Right now, you," she says not a hint of playfulness in her tone.

I raise my palms in defense. Then pin her again when she tries to move away. This time, I move in closer, pinning her with my body.

"Are you telling me that I have an effect on your panties, little monster?"

"God, you are insufferable. Go away." She holds my stare, not backing down. "I'm sure there are tons of poor desperate freshmen crawling around, begging for some asshole to rock their world for a solid two minutes."

I snort a laugh. "Lighten up. Look." This time I allow her to turn and resume her stance. I stand behind her wrapping one hand around her wrist, the other on her hip. I guide her motions, forcing her hips to turn as her arm glides through the air.

"Punch through, not at, and don't hold anything back. If you're hitting, it's with the purpose of breaking a bone."

We rock back and forth together, going through the motions over and over again until she gets the feel of it. Her eyes fall to my hand laying on her hip, and I dig my fingers in a little firmer. The sound of my heartbeat grows louder in my ear, and my dick swells in my shorts. I don't back up or try to hide it. I want her to see what she does to me, despite everything I have told her.

The scent of her sweat greets me as I press my cheek to the side of her head, whispering just above her ear. "All your power is in your hips."

She turns slowly towards me and peers up through her thick lashes. "I think I need a human target. Trees don't exactly give like human flesh does."

I smile wide, accepting her invite. Moving a few steps back, I take my stance and hold my palms up as targets. She gets into place, and I don't miss the small flutter of her eyes that brush over my slight bulge. Her eyes meet mine, and I give her a nod, letting her know I'm ready.

She swings straight for my jaw and I swiftly lean to the side and block her fist with my forearm.

I give her a stern look. "Play nice, Amelia."

She returns with a wicked grin, followed by another jab straight for my gut. She lands it, and I grunt at the impact, the pride on her face clear as day. And I'm beginning to enjoy this a little too much. I'm rock solid and raging with the need for this to escalate.

I square my shoulder and throw her an easy punch. She dodges it and comes up for an uppercut. I block it and give her another that grazes her arm.

"Come on, baby. I know you can do better than that."

She turns backward, stepping and spinning back in my direction on one foot, kicking the other through the air. I catch her ankle under my arm and *tsk* her like a child. "That's not playing by the rules."

She uses my hold on her leg to jump up and grab onto my shoulders, slamming her other knee up into my chin, knocking my balance off. I see stars and release her, only to be met with her firm hand sweeping my legs out from under me.

My head slams against the ground with a thud.

What the fuck just happened?

She steps over me, trying to catch her breath. "Since when do we play by the rules around here?" She smiles, genuinely enjoying this.

"Where the fuck did you learn to do that?"

She shrugs and begins her walk back to the house. "Summer camp. Thanks for the tips, though. I feel much better."

Those were the few months out of the year I wasn't always available to keep tabs on her. I made trips when I could but staying was nearly impossible without drawing attention to myself.

What the fuck else did she learn at summer camps?

***

After we shower, Lyle starts dinner, as the rest of us pile onto the couch.

"So, were you bullshitting when you needed us to teach you to throw a punch?" I ask.

"No. I really did need that. I only knew how to do that move outside from watching some guy fuck around one year. I wasn't even sure I could do it."

I narrow my eyes, not entirely sure she's telling the truth.

"What other useful skills did you learn?" I want to know, but my mind instantly wonders if she had been fucking guys all summer long, learning *useful skills* my dick is aching to feel.

"I don't know." She picks at her fingers nervously. "Some archery, forging, target practice with paintball guns. Things like that."

I nod, but barely hear her. Still thinking about the fact that I may have missed some serious opportunities to be with her before any real shit in our lives happened and that someone else filled that spot. I'm tumbling down that rabbit hole when Finn pulls her into his lap.

I watch the way she responds to his hands on her. She's only wearing an oversized t-shirt and panties now, giving me a full view when he separates her legs and runs his hands down her thighs. My eyes are glued to the blue lace between her legs, and I feel my dick swell in my shorts. She blushes and tries to pull her legs back together, but he stops her.

"Don't worry, babe. He likes to watch," Finn whispers in her ear, and her eyes pierce mine.

Fuck.

I have watched her masturbate through her window and even have boring-ass sex with Lance. But right now, I am barely able to hold my composure. The way she looks me in the eye with a challenge and my best friend's hand pleasing her, might be what finally pushes me over the edge.

I can't let them see my weakness for her, so I can't say no. She might get hurt by the rejection, but they would see it for what it was. It never mattered who it was when I watched because, in my head, she was always Mel, and he was always me.

I lean back into the couch and uncross my legs, letting her see my bulge. Her throat bobs when she swallows, then her body relaxes into Finns. Her eyes flicker back and forth between Ian and me.

Her wet hair clings to her neck as she tilts her head back. Little whimpers escape as one of Finn's hands moves up rubbing her through her panties.

"Guys, come on! That's not fair!" Lyle yells from the kitchen.

She grips the sides of the chair grinding her hips softly, begging for more.

"You like that, baby?" Finn groans.

"Uh-huh," she answers breathlessly.

His fingers slip inside her panties, and I silently curse him for not pulling them to the side so I can see her bare. He rubs her from top to bottom, likely spreading her arousal. His wrist curves down as he pushes his fingers inside her, and she moans more intensely. She wiggles and writhes in his hand as he works her at a steady speed. I glance to my left at Ian as he readjusts himself, watching her intently with a grin.

"More," she breathes out in a plea.

Dammit, she's trying to kill me.

I have to fight the urge to pull my dick out of my shorts and stroke myself as I picture her riding me, but my face might give away my inner thoughts, and I just can't risk that.

I have to keep the wall between us standing.

I have to.

She's a wet mess with Finn's fingers deep inside her as Lyle walks in. "Dinner's rea- oh, fuck."

Finn pulls his hand away, and she yanks her head to the side and whines at him.

"We can finish this later." He winks at her, and together, they stand up.

"Well, I hope you fuckers enjoy the food," Lyle says, butt hurt.

Ian runs his fingers through his hair and looks at me with an eyebrow raised.

"What?" I growl, but he just tosses me a look like he is tired of my shit.

"Fuck off."

He laughs but leaves it alone, following everyone to the kitchen.

I don't know what he thinks he knows, but he better sure as shit keep his theories to himself.

We head into the kitchen and I fix a plate of loaded nachos, but the only thing I can think of is how hard I'm going to beat my dick tonight.

***

Mel opens the back door and steps outside, us all following behind her. A box with a red ribbon sits at her feet and she makes an effort not to show it affects her. She pics it up and tosses it over her shoulder to me.

"He doesn't know when to give up, does he?" she says, hoping to bait Lance from wherever he's hiding.

I open the lid and grin at his efforts. A syringe and vile sit on a note.

I SAVED SOME FOR U. UR ALWAYS MORE FUN WHEN UR FUCKED UP. TELL YOUR LIL BOYFRIENDS THANK YOU FOR BEATING THE SHIT OUT OF EMMA SO I DIDNT HAVE TO.

-LANCE

I toss it in the trash. "Cute. You're next, bitch!" I yell.

Ian pulls Mel into him, and she giggles dramatically as he kisses down her neck. She pulls out her phone and dials JJ.

"Hey, babes. I tried to call earlier, but I'm at their lake house. We're gonna have a party tomorrow night. Wanna come?" She pauses for a moment then continues, "Yeah, girl. It's fucking awesome up here. Invite whoever. The guys said they are gonna call the usual crew."

About two hundred people were going to be here. We just had to make sure Lance would too.

Amelia turns around and hangs all over Ian. Her free hand wraps around the back of his neck playing with his hair as she listens to JJ talk. She hums an approving half-focused answer to whatever is said while molding her body flush with Ian's. Her hips grind against his leg subtly, and I don't miss how Ian's eyes roll in his head as she tugs on his hair.

"Yeah, it's going good. I am really happy with them. We get into all kinds of binds together." Finn snorts at her double meaning but continues to undress her with his eyes as she dry-fucks Ian for God and everyone to see.

I miss the last few things said, too enticed by how her hand drifts between their bodies, stroking Ian through his shorts. She ends the call with a kiss on Ian's cheek and leads him back inside, seemingly fully intent on finishing what she's started.

We follow behind them and she tries to walk away from Ian, but he holds her in place. "You know, you could have picked one of the twins. Why did you choose me to rub all over?"

"Well, I figured if Lance thought I was having sex with three of you, he might get his panties in a bunch. He may not have cared about me, but he was always a controlling dick." She rubs a hand down his chest. "Or maybe, I just wanted it to be you."

His eyes flash with delight, then he spins her towards me and holds her in place. "What? Silas isn't even a contender?" He asks, fucking with the both of us while passing his hands over the inside of her thighs.

She steps away from Ian and towards me. "No."

I fake a sad puppy-dog expression and twist it into a grin. "Awe, now you hurt my feelings." She looks annoyed, so I continue, "It would have been more believable. Desperate and slutty is my type." I drag my eyes down her body while turning my nose up in disgust. "Usually."

Smack.

My cheek stings, and it takes me a minute to register that she just bitch slapped me. That comment was out of line, and it physically hurt to get out, but I needed to amp up her distaste for me. She doesn't say anything else, just turns on her heel and goes straight to Finn's bedroom.

"Why the fuck would you say that?" Ian rages.

"Seriously, Si. That was fucked, even for you." Finn lashes.

I place my cold exterior on. "Oh, for fucks sake, it was a joke. She'll get over it. Props to you for teaching her to react, Lyle."

I walk out and to my bedroom. Before I shut the door, Finn yells after me, "You are such a prick!"

Yeah, I know.

My heart aches with the sting of my words. Years of watching words tear her down - chip away at her soul - and here I am, contributing to her pain. But what choice do I have? I either to make her hate me now, hurt her little by little, or let myself get close to her and watch it burn to the fucking ground all at once.

I am too fucking sober to think about this. Retrieving my pre-rolled blunt from my pocket, I open my window and stare into the starry black sky, just as Amelia did when her strength was shaken and her mind a mess. I blow my smoke out the window and listen to the wind blowing against the water. I inhale, letting it fog my mind and remove everything that hurts.

Before I met the twins, I spent so long begging for the pain to stop. Begging for someone to be there. I had someone that loved me, but I lost her too. Day in and day out, my father beat me for any reason he could think of. If I cried or couldn't complete manual labor, I needed a lesson in toughening up. If I was late getting home or left dishes in the sink, I needed a lesson in responsibility. If he couldn't think of a reason, it was because I was a *disrespectful little shit.*

The boys would rescue me whenever they could get me out without getting caught. They lived with their uncle, and he wasn't fond of me sneaking over there and him risking the charge of kidnapping or harboring a runaway - whatever the fuck they would label it as. The nights they couldn't get away with it, I had to go back home, and the beatings were worse. The reasoning - I couldn't man up and was running like a little bitch.

The wise words of Nickolas Steele.

I spend about two hours steadily smoking, getting a good enough buzz that all my cares disappear into the night. I stop thinking about all the damage my father has done to me, about all the pain Amelia has endured, about Lance and whatever the fuck his issue is, and about the choice I have to make.

Then, I make a call.

***

I wait until the house is silent, before heading to the kitchen. I eat a whole box of brownies and start on the chips. Footsteps near and I pause. I look up to see Amelia walking in, her puffy eyes dazed and pointed at the floor. The chip bag rustles, and she startles. Her red eyes meet mine, and her face twists in pain. My eyes fall to the table, my high fading slightly.

I look back up to see her reaching in the open snack cabinet, stretching on her tip-py-toes. Her shirt rises, and my gaze slips to the blue panties peeking out. Her firm ass cheeks tease me, jiggling slightly as she bounces, trying to reach the cookies on the top shelf but falling short. I move quickly, coming up behind her. My body presses to hers as I reach above her head, retrieving her target.

She stiffens, and I can feel the tension between us. I place the cookies on the counter and let my hands fall to my sides. Fighting my own movement, my fingertips brush her hips, and she quivers in response. My breaths get heavier as I drag the tips of my fingers up higher, pulling her shirt up with them. She doesn't move an inch. Leaning in close, I let my warm breath hit her neck.

"Why the fuck are you wearing shit like this."

"I didn't know you were down here," she says breathlessly, and I can't help but imagine her sounding like that under me, naked and begging for more.

"Yet, you didn't turn around once you did," I growl in a low tone. "You are so fucking-"

I stop myself, not letting the words fall from my mouth, letting my throat burn with everything I wish I could say.

She turns slowly and peers up at me. Her beautiful emerald eyes so close to mine. My heart grows heavy as I take in the puffiness around them.

"-attention seeking."

I force my features passive, and quickly grab her hips, picking her up and tossing her on the counter. I spread her knees and swipe my hand along her center, pleased to find them wet.

"You are fucking soaked," I growl, purposefully tinting my tone with disgust. I take my wet fingers and bring them to my mouth, sucking them clean. Her mouth falls open slightly as she watches the motion intently. "So, did one of them get you like this, or are you still turned on by someone who doesn't want you?"

Her chest rises and falls, short breaths of anger expelling onto my skin. I keep going, needing the burn.

"Is that why you stayed with Lance for so long? You loved boring-ass missionary sex with someone who only stayed with you because you were something wet and tight to slip his cock in? Did you enjoy being embarrassed? Did it turn you on to see the annoyance on his face whenever you simply spoke to him?"

Tears pool in her eyes, and I can see her willing them not to fall. They will - they always did. I glide my hands under her shirt, slowly rubbing up her sides, savoring every moment.

A single tear slides down her cheek, and I scoff to hide the hurt of seeing her cry because of me. She wipes it away in a swift motion as if it's acid. I dig my nails into her sides and drag them down, scraping her and making her whimper in pain.

"You are a used-up piece of ass with mommy issues. I don't want you, so get that through your thick, fucked-up head."

I lean in, inches from her lips, and can smell the men's body wash she used. I want to kiss her so much it hurts. Her eyes are wide, tears now slipping from them in quick repetition. Her chest rises and falls faster than mine now that I am in my element.

"Go fuck one of your boyfriends and stay the fuck away from me." Pushing off the counter, I leave for my room.

A moment later, she calls after me, "You know you may say that, but the hard cock in your jeans says something different. Either you are lying to me, to yourself, or you like inflicting pain on a deeper level than most. You are as fucked-up in the head as I am."

I turn back towards her slowly. "Maybe there's more to the darkness than the fearful ebony surface."

I wish you could see there is more to me than the abrasive person I make you see. That your happiness can be found in many unexpected shapes, deep within the darkness that threatens you.

She looks at me for a moment, her features soft before they turn scorned.

"Fuck you and your riddles, Silas."

I SAVED SOME FOR U. UR ALWAYS MORE
FUN WHEN UR FUCKED UP. TELL YOUR LIL
BOYFRIENDS THANK YOU FOR BEATING THE
SHIT OUT OF EMMA SO I DIDNT HAVE TO.
-LANCE

Amelia

I shut the door behind me and press my back against it trying to catch my breath. I could smell the weed like a cloud around him, and hoped I would walk away unscathed. My panties were still damp from Finn's little show earlier, but I can't deny that the rest was all for him.

Silas Fucking Steele, the asshole that has made me cry more than once now, had gotten me wet.

He had me aching for it.

What's wrong with me?

Do I truly enjoy hurting myself so much that I would walk into that trap? I feel him stare at me and I see him tense when I brush by. Then he speaks to me like I am the lowest trash on the planet. I rub my hands under my shirt, feeling the torn skin and liking the burn.

I wait until I think he has gone back to his room and has had enough time to go to sleep before I open the door once more. Sliding back into the hallway, I tiptoe down to his door and press my ear softly to the crack.

I don't know why, but I need to know if he is just as shaken up by our encounter as I am. He's hiding something from me, and I am determined to figure out what it is.

Hearing a grunt, I turn the knob slowly, and it glides open an inch without a sound. I swallow hard as I see him on top of a girl I don't recognize. She's naked and on her stomach, bound at her hands and feet. His hand is wrapped around her mouth, pulling her head back at what appears to be a painful angle as he thrusts into her.

I stand there, frozen, as I watch him roughly fuck her. He uses his other hand to grip her shoulder, using it as leverage to go deeper. She whimpers and groans. Each sound she makes fuels him to go harder. My eyes fall to where they meet, and I see color coating her thigh.

Red.

Blood.

My heart beats as hard and painful as his thrusts, and then it nearly stops completely.

"Amelia." The name leaves his lips so sensually. My name. I want to close the door, but I want to stay even more. I want to witness him fucking her, pretending it's me.

"I know you're watching."

I pull the door shut as fast as lightning and sprint back to Ian's room.

Oh, God. Oh, God.

I shut the door behind me and immediately climb back into bed with Ian. He wraps one arm around me and pulls me closer, tucking the other between my thighs.

"You are freezing," he whines against my hair with a raspy voice.

"Sorry, I went to the kitchen."

I'm still trying to catch my breath. Hoping he can't feel my heart racing.

"Run into Silas?" My muscles stiffen.

"I can smell him on you."

If he heard us talking or knows what just happened, he's not commenting on it.

"Noth- Nothing happened. Not really." I stammer.

He chuckles softly and tightens his hold on me. "Chill, babe, just an observation."

"Oh."

"I think you could be good for him." Finn's voice is deep and raspy, and I silently wish he would keep talking.

"Why do you say that?" I turn to face him, but he doesn't open his eyes.

"Just an observation." He smirks, and I groan.

I roll back to my side and nuzzle into my pillow that smells like Ian. Calmness surrounds me, and I am wrapped in comfort, but blissful sleep evades me.

***

The sunlight wakes me, pouring low through the windows, and I groan. I am not an early riser, nor will I ever be.

"Rise and shine, Sleeping Beauty," Ian sing-songs, pushing my hair away from my face. "Come on, babe, we got a party to plan and an asshole to beat the shit out of."

The last part of his sentence makes me smile internally, but the sun has just come up, which means it's the ass crack of dawn, so I am *not* getting out of this bed yet.

He tries to pull the blanket back, but I snatch it out of his hands in a swift motion and yank it back up around my face. "Ian, you are cute, but I will fucking kill you if you don't leave me alone for another hour. Maybe two just because you're being annoying."

He mumbles something under his breath, but I can't make it out. Slipping out of the room, he leaves me alone to drift back asleep. But now that I'm awake, my mind sparks to life, and my thoughts drifts back six years ago as I think about Lance being here tonight.

I walk into the high school early in the morning, tears streaming down my face. I push through the girl's locker room door and find my usual spot in the furthest bathroom stall. I sit on the toilet and slip in my earbuds to drown out the world around me for the next half-hour.

Eventually students will start pouring in soon so I reach into my bag, searching for makeup to conceal the truth. Putting my feet down with a long exhale, I wipe my eyes, take my earbuds out, and begin fixing myself.

As I'm finger-combing my hair out, a piece of paper slides under the door, and I freeze. A golf ball forms in my throat, and I hold my breath like it will make me invisible. I wait for the steps of my deliverer to fade and the heavy door to bang shut before grabbing the note from the floor. I flip it open.

AMELIA,
YOU ARE WORTHY. YOU ARE ENOUGH. YOU ARE PERFECT.
- NOT HIM.

What the hell?

I pause for a minute, then cram everything back into my bag before dashing out of the stall. Just as I reach the locker room door and yank it open, the first bell rings and the halls flood with bodies. I scan the halls, searching for suspects, but it's useless.

He's already lost in the crowd.

My heart warms at the memory of that first note.

I hear the guys downstairs, and I can't hide my smile. I may not ever find *him*, but I might have found something better. Someone once told me in order to form the perfect man, you would need three. Combine three men's pros, and you would have enough good to overlook the bad. I have my three, maybe four. If you consider sexual tension with a caveman a possible fourth.

Prancing into the living room I find Finn and wrap my arms around him from behind while looking for any evidence that Silas's visitor is still here.

"Well, hello, grumpy. I heard you were very mean to our sweet Ian this morning." Finn laughs.

I grumble giving him a tighter squeeze, finding myself glad the mystery woman is gone and no longer invading my territory.

"I seriously doubt any feelings were hurt by little ole me." I don't look at Silas, but the words were meant for him too.

Ian gently shakes with laughter. "Well, the next time you need to be woken up in the morning, I call nose-goes." He puts his finger to his nose, and I scrunch my own.

"You must not have woken her upright," Finn says, and I don't have to see his face to know he is doing some kind of douchey eyebrow wag.

My phone chimes, and I pull it out from my shorts. Lance's name flashes across the screen, and my heart sinks.

Lance:

> See u tonight baby! Wear somethin sexy and I might just go back on my word abt the last time bein the last ;)

Bile rises to my throat, and my heartbeat pounds in my ears. My vision gets spotty, and my knees grow weak.

"Mel, don't let him do that. Not anymore," Carlisle says, taking the phone from my hand and guiding me to lean against the couch.

His features turn fierce as he reads the text.

"I'm going to fucking kill him." He turns to the nearest wall and pushes a hole into the sheetrock.

I flinch at the sound, and he runs his hands through his hair before dropping them to his side, his face white as a ghost.

He takes my face in his hands. "God, I'm sorry. I wasn't thinking. I'm sorry."

I force a smile letting him know I'm okay. This was the plan. Lance is baiting me. We all know that, and we expected him to try to rattle me. The guys wear looks of concern and anger and I take a moment to breathe.

"Okay then, we have a party set up for," Ian says.

I set out, opening all the doors and windows, letting the cool breeze blow through the house. I walk through the back doors to take a smoke break before I truly begin, snagging one of the boy's packs on the way out.

Suddenly, I am being yanked to the side and thrown against the wall. Silas bends down, inches from my face.

"What did I tell you about wearing shit like this?" he growls irritatedly.

"You're not my daddy," I retort pushing against his hold, but he doesn't budge.

He leans closer and nips my jaw, and I fight to silence the whimper that wants to leave my body.

"Oh, but I could be. I hear that I make a great one where it counts."

I scoff, trying to keep that idea out of my head. I attempt to push him away again, but he doesn't budge.

Moments pass as we stare at each other, and I wonder if his mind is in the same place mine is. His eyes dark gray eyes swim with lowlights of blue and black.

"On another note, believe me when I say, I will kill Lance if he even attempts to touch you like that again. Lyle might just hurt him, but I am not him."

I pause, only for a moment, at his choice of words.

He pulls his hand up and holds a blunt in front of my face.

"And this will be more effective for what you are looking for." He tucks it in the top of my tank top and leaves without any mention of last night.

I slide down the wall as Ian walks outside and crouches down next to me, and my mind begins picking apart how Silas's actions correlate so nastily to Lance's.

"What's going on in that head of yours?"

I flick the lighter on and watch the flames for a long moment before finally lighting the blunt. The urge to burn is there, but I push it down. I take a long drag and let my head fall back as I think of how to answer that question.

"All the time or just in this particular moment of fuckery?"

My head is usually a constant flow of chatter. Worries and questions take root, and no matter how much I tell myself I'm being irrational and stressing about things I can't change, it doesn't end. Maybe I'll just go mad one day and become friends with the chaos.

"You know," Ian says after a long silence, "I've been writing a new song."

Not so subtle redirection, but I appreciate what he is trying to do, so I indulge.

"Yeah? You gonna tell me what it's about?"

His eyes shine excitedly. "I was thinking I'll just let you hear it one day."

I give him a look of shock and pure adoration.

"What's the catch?"

"The catch is that you have to help me write the lyrics."

Write the lyrics of a song? He has got to be joking.

"That's my condition. If you want to see inside me, I get to see inside you."

I can't say it's the worst idea. Romantic and bonding, if nothing else.

"Well, I won't turn down that offer or a challenge."

He stands up in front of me and pulls me to my feet.

"There's our girl."

Heat spreads throughout my body.

Our girl. He's claimed me too.

The pride I feel when they say that makes me want to step out of my comfort zone every chance I get. I put the blunt out and leave it on the table when we walk back in.

"I'm gonna set up in my room. Create a flyer, hack the University's contact list, and post everywhere." He gives me a kiss on the head and goes back to our room, leaving the door open.

While we wait for Lyle and Silas to return with party supplies, Finn turns on his Bluetooth speaker and starts playing some 1990s and 2000s country music. I sway over to where Finn leans against the kitchen counter and wrap my arms around his body, bringing my hands down to his firm ass.

"You know what we need tonight? A karaoke stage."

He chuckles, "Oh yeah? Are you wanting to give or receive a performance, dirty girl?"

"Get me drunk enough, and I might give all kinds of things."

Brining my hands to the front of his body I trail them down his chest, stopping at his pants tucking my fingers inside the waistband. He tilts his head back slightly, and his eyes fall closed with a groan.

"God, you make me want to do filthy things to you."

I unbutton his jeans without breaking eye contact and sink to my knees. He looks over his shoulder towards Ian's open door and back down to me with lust. He doesn't say anything, so I tug his pants down his legs, and his dick springs free. Nothing but arousal fills me at the sight.

I lick up the underside of his length then suck the tip into my mouth. He groans in pleasure, and his hands tangle through my hair. I suck him up and down a few times to get him thoroughly lubed, then sink down as far as I can, opening my throat to let him in.

"Fuck," he growls in a hushed tone.

Using his words as encouragement, I work him over, flicking and swirling my tongue on his head. Twisting my right hand on his shaft. His breathing turns shallow, and his hand tightens in my hair.

"Yes, just like that."

I moan, his cock in my mouth, spit pooling and dripping from where we connect.

"You like being praised?" he asks, pulling my head back roughly, forcing me to look at him. I nod the best I can, and a wicked grin pulls at his lips.

"Of fucking course you do. You want to be a good girl? You want me to tell you how good it feels inside that pretty little mouth?"

I work him faster, giving him my answer. He pulls away, my lips smacking as he leaves them. Spinning us sideways, he pulls my panties down my legs with no hesitation. He pulls my right leg out of the puddle of clothes at my feet and hikes it up on the counter. I gasp as his open mouth presses against my center, licking me intensely from opening to clit. The air thickens with low grunts and groans, but the music plays loud enough to cover them up.

He pushes two fingers inside me and fucks me with

them, rubbing just the right spot. The delicious pressure builds in my lower stomach, making me feel like I am going to pee. Finn licks my clit faster, and my legs shake.

"Wait, I'm gonna come." I whimper as I struggle to breathe. I don't squirt every time, and I haven't with Finn yet, but I can feel it building.

"Wait, wait, wait," I chant, but he doesn't stop; not even as Ian walks out and the front door opens behind me.

I hear Carlisle chuckle behind me, and I jerk.

"Oh no, don't stop at the best part. Yank your fingers out of her just as she comes."

Finn does as instructed, fucking me fast and hard with his fingers. I stop holding it back and encourage it to come, the sensation too much to bear. My legs shake as I grip his hair, my orgasm coming just as he yanks his fingers out of me, brushing the topside on his exit. I shake, scream, and grip the counter and Finn's head as liquid streams down my leg. Placing my flat fingertips on myself, I rub vigorously to soothe the sensation, as he sits there watching in awe.

My heart races as they watch me pull my panties back up. I look over at Ian, and he is sucking on his lips to hide his grin. Finn pulls his own pants back up but pulls his shirt off and wipes his face off with it. I snatch it out of his hands, and he snatches it back.

"Hell no, this is my first squirt shirt. I'm keeping this bitch forever."

I roll my eyes and cross my arms, turning to face the other two.

"You just had to comment?"

Carlisle walks over to me, swipes a hand up my still wet thigh, and licks his fingers.

"You decide to give a show; spectators are allowed to cheer you on. That shit is hot. Nothing to hide, Angel."

"How did you know to do that?" Finn asks him.

"Well, after the first time she did it, I watched some porn on it and paid more attention to how they got her there."

I mean, props to him for doing research on my account, but don't men know that a lot of that shit is fake?

The guys laugh, and he shrugs. "Hey, laugh all you want, assholes, it worked, didn't it? I wanted to know how to make her do that every time."

Silas drops the shopping bags on the couch, grabs himself a beer, and raises it. "You all are fucking idiots, but cheers to getting her to spread her legs so easily again."

He walks outside to sit in the patio chairs, and I follow him, shutting the doors behind us, giving us a small sense of privacy.

"You want me to stay away from you, but you seem to keep putting yourself in my way. You stand around long enough to get an eyeful every time I have my pants down and then make some shitty comment about how nasty I am. What the fuck do you want from me? No bullshit."

Silas crosses his legs lazily and closes his eyes, and I spot a fresh cut along the inside of his left palm. The blood I saw on the girl last night was his.

He hurt himself.

"If you want some of us, you get all of us. Be thankful that spank bank material is all I want from you." He takes a long swig from his bottle. "Now, go the fuck away before I decide I don't want you here at all. Just one sentence, and you're gone. That's all it'll take." He says it without a hint that he's bluffing.

I scoff exasperatedly and leave him outside. I slam the door behind me and lock it.

I hope he gets sun poisoning.

Amelia,
you are worthy. you are
enough. you are perfect.

—Not Him

Amelia

Ian shows us the flyer he posted everywhere possible. It's simple and to the point. Address and the guy's names, surrounded by little cartoon images of bongs, beer, dicks, and asses. Classy. We all have a good laugh at it, finishing up the last touches with the sound system and microphones that Ian orchestrated.

"What do you think he will do tonight?" I ask looking at the ground, afraid the guys will see how shaken I am.

I am not scared of Lance, but I can't lie and say that I'm not scared of what he would do to me if he were able to get me alone. He isn't stupid enough to hurt me in the middle of a crowd or with any of the guys around.

Then again, I guess I never really knew him. My mind tangles in all the scenarios that could happen tonight.

"There is no telling, but we won't let him hurt you. That's for damn sure," Finn says.

"If he wants to watch you, we can give him a damn good show," Carlisle says, grinding on the back of the couch.

"Who says he even cares in that way?" I laugh out, trying to cover the hurt that swells in my throat.

"He may be the lowest fucking scum on the planet, but he spent three years with you. I promise it will bother him to see you happy with us," Carlisle says.

Part of me hopes he's right. I want to be able to rub it in his fucking face that I am just fine without him.

***

Hours pass, and people will start showing up any minute..

A soft voice comes from behind where I stand alone on the back porch, looking over the water.

"Let's make tonight's main goal about having some much-needed fun. Let loose and enjoy yourself, and if fuck face decides to get stupid, we will handle it." I turn to see Ian holding out his hand. "I'm not usually the violent type, but for you, I'll make an exception. But stay by one of us all night, just in case."

I relax my fists, and shake out my nerves. "I wouldn't leave y'all's side even if he wasn't showing up."

Ian takes my hand and leads me back inside. He hooks his phone up to the Bluetooth speaker, and classic rock pours from the speakers, rattling the house, tickling my bare feet.

My bikini peaks out under ripped blue jean shorts and loose crop top. Silas had built a bonfire out back after he disappeared earlier, so we decided to add night swimming to the list of festivities. The porch light doesn't reach all the way to the water, and although you don't have to have light to swim, it makes it a lot less creepy in a lake.

I fix myself a drink and sit between Ian and Finn on the couch, as Carlisle opens the front door to welcome the first wave of party-goers. Just having them near helps calm my erratic heartbeat and still my nerves, a hand on each of their legs like a throne.

Everything is going to be fine.

Lance was just being a dick. He didn't have the balls to do anything but lie and manipulate. He has nothing to hold over me anymore, but I still have this pit in the bottom of my stomach that says something is going to go wrong tonight.

Within the hour, the house and yard are flooded with over a hundred people. JJ showed up with Tyler, and are now in the back, making out by fire. We talked briefly when she arrived, catching up on the past week, and she scolded me for not telling her that I was leaving town to come up here.

Finn looks over his shoulder through the open back door where she and Tyler are in perfect view. Their form is mostly shadows, but the fire illuminates enough to see her dry-humping him.

"I'll have what he's having, please."

I scrunch my nose at him and slap his leg. "You gotta beat me at flip cup first."

Ian laughs from my other side. "Now this, I have to see. Rematch to see if she really is better than you."

Finn cuts his eyes at Ian. "Who is to say I didn't just let her win, like the gentleman I am."

"I call bullshit," Ian says pulling me into him. "So how about let's play teams so there is no chivalry on the table. I call Amelia."

Finn raises a brow. "Oh, it's gonna be like that, is it?"

Ian hauls me into his lap and runs his hands down my thighs, heat pricking the area as they glide across my freshly shaved skin.

"Pick your teammate Finnegan Jones, and pick wisely because we are about to bend you over like our bitch. And when we do, you owe us a punishment of our choosing."

"Finnegan?" I almost spit my drink, trying not to laugh.

"Fuck off." Finn charges, clearly not appreciating Ian's use of his full name. "I'll be back. This is war," he grumbles as he walks away.

I turn in Ian's lap and straddle him with bent knees.

"That was cruel," I say, laughter tingeing my tone.

He smirks and leans in, his lips an inch from mine and his warm breath teasing the skin. "Is that why you are laughing? You enjoy cruelty? Pain?"

My nose brushes his, and I look down to break our eye contact. "One of my favorite authors once said pain is pretty to the people who have too much of it."

He tilts my chin up with his index finger. "Cry Havoc and let slip the dogs of war."

My eyes go wide. "You read-"

"Porn? Written by women? You bet your fine ass I do. They know what they are talking about."

And he gave me so much shit at Barnes and Noble.

My body shakes with laughter. "I was going to say dark romance, but yeah, porn is fitting, too, I guess."

He shrugs, "I like it. It may not always be a completely realistic plot, but it is comforting to be taken out of this world and dragged into another where there is an explanation for the pain, and in the end, love prevails. Plus, it's a hell of a lot better than watching it."

I listen to him talk about all the reasons he likes to read romances and who his favorite authors are. We talk about books we have both read and which are our favorites. We are deep into giving each other recommendations when I hear someone clear their throat behind me. I slide off of Ian's lap and face the two men standing in front of me.

Finn and Silas.

Great.

Ian scoffs, "You're kidding. He looks so hammered already that he might just fall over if a stiff breeze blows through."

"Get the fuck up, and let's do this." Silas's eyes are bloodshot, and he is slightly swaying from side to side. "I heard there were punishments involved."

"Oh, I see," Ian muses, "You chose him because he is such a dick that with the motivation of humiliating someone, he might just play a good game?"

I stand up and brush past Silas roughly. "There is no question who that person is." I round behind Finn and stand on my toes to hook my chin over his shoulder.

"You want to play dirty, I can do that."

I stop Silas on the way to the table where Amelia is setting up for the game. I speak low so that bystanders are less likely to hear, "What the hell did you do to piss her off so much?"

He narrows his eyes and gives me a dismissive tone, "Who said I did anything. We don't like each other, end of story."

Oh, for fucks sake.

"Give me a fucking break Si, I don't ask questions, but I'm not as fucking blind as the other two dipshits. If they paid any amount of attention to you two, they would clearly see what I see. You don't have to tell me anything you don't want to, but you are killing yourself. Get your shit together before you do something you'll regret."

Anyone with a pair of eyes can see his emotional state is declining rapidly, and it doesn't take a rocket scientist to line up the facts. He needs to either voice what the issue is or grow the fuck up. Him being a dick or spiraling is not going to do anything but hurt all of us. What does he expect to happen if she chooses to stay around?

He scrubs his face with both hands and mumbles as he continues walking, "That's what I'm trying to do."

I shake my head and follow suit.

"Alrighty, boys, let's do this," Mel says confidently.

I take my position next to Amelia, and the other two mirror us, Finn standing in front of Amelia. Tyler and JJ are now standing at the end of the table. "Wanna ref again, Tyler? This one is going to be a bit more intense than the last."

He agrees and takes his position, checking to make sure everyone is ready before giving the word. Finn and Amelia fly down the table, neck and neck.

"At least Amelia decided to make someone work to get laid this time instead of handing it out for free," Silas snarks, slurring his words.

Irritation makes me clench my teeth, and I see Amelia falter.

She is on her second to last cup, and she yells at me, "Hey Ian, how good are you under pressure?"

I raise a brow but don't waste a second to think, "Uh, pretty good. Raised by a businessman and all that."

She lands her cup and moves to her last one, throwing the liquid back just as Finn moves to his last cup and picks it up.

"Good, we are about to play dirty."

I take my starting position and watch her intensely, waiting for that cup to land on its head. The second it does I rip my cup from the table, and the race is on.

"Go, go, go!" Amelia chants, her smile wider than ever.

I fumble with my cup, unable to land it, and now on try number four. I grumble under my voice, and a gentler one whispers near me, "Stay focused."

Amelia looks down at her wet shirt and loudly groans, "Gosh, my shirt is soaked now."

I don't dare look over at her, knowing exactly where her devilish mind is headed. I glance up at Silas, seeing his eyes on her while he drinks his next cup. He looks back down at the table and starts flipping. I look slightly to the left and see Finn raising an amused brow at her.

"Oh god!" Amelia gasps, "My top!"

I laugh under my breath.

Evil little thing.

Finn rushes around the table, "Fucking hell!"

Silas stiffens, and his motions pause as he falls into her trap, allowing me to land my last cup.

I shout in excitement and turn to see exactly what she was doing. Her shirt dangles in one hand, and her other is clasped around her chest, bikini strings dangling by her side. Her arm barely holding the fabric covering her nipples in place.

Finn makes it to her a split second later, spinning her to face him so that no one gets a show.

She grins maniacally. "Sorry, I must not have tightened it enough and snagged it when I took my shirt off."

Finn smiles and shakes his head at her. "You are in so much trouble for that one, dirty girl."

I laugh to myself. A typical move for a girl, and usually, it wouldn't phase any of us, but this girl, she's a different story.

Even for Silas, clearly.

He never spares women a second glance unless he is spiraling and needs a quick fuck. Sometimes it's random, and sometimes he seeks out girls with dark hair and a petite frame...

I swear the other two are fucking idiots if they don't see it. I thought it was just a coincidence Amelia had a lot of the same features as the girls Silas clung to, but then I paid just a little more attention, and the pieces started to fall into place. She means something to him that he isn't sharing and apparently isn't coping well with.

We all follow her and JJ back into the house as they laugh and giggle to each other. They plop down on the couch and intertwine their legs, hands resting on each other.

"So, what kind of reward do we want?" I ask her.

"No, no." Finn wags his finger. "You cheated. Null and void."

Amelia opens her mouth to protest, but I beat her to it. "Nah, you heard her. It was an accident. You, on the other hand, picked Silas just to try to throw her off her game because we can all see how much he pisses her off. We won. Pay up."

Amelia tosses me a smirk and looks back to the men in question, crossing her arms.

Finn rolls his eyes playfully, and Silas starts to walk off.

"Where do you think you're going?" she orders him.

"I know you are going to make him do some shit like bend you over the hood of his car or eat your little cunt until you can't walk, and I have no desire to participate in anything of that nature."

Finn wags his eyebrows, "Not much of a punishment if you ask me. Maybe she wants a reward rather than giving a punishment. She's all about rewards." He says the last part a little lower, and JJ laughs under her breath, looking away like it will make her not present for this conversation.

"Oh, no. I definitely want to punish, and it is not going to be sex-related, so why don't you hang back for a bit, Si," Amelia says.

Oh, this is going to be good.

She looks around the room, taking a minute to think of the perfect plan, then summons me closer with a finger. I lean in close, and she whispers in my ear the best she can. With the music still loud and her quickly getting drunk, it's not as quiet as she had hoped, but I don't think anyone other than JJ can hear her.

I stand back up straight and chuckle. "Ah yes, I think that will do nicely."

She instructs them to stay put while I head to Silas's room. I know that kinky fuck will have exactly what I'm looking for. I rummage around in his drawers, finally finding his small stash he keeps here for parties, likely not even a quarter of what he keeps back home. I stroll back in, finding Amelia and JJ's faces inches from each others, their lips brushing slightly as they drag it out, teasing. Lyle has joined the other guys, and they are all watching the girls.

"What is happening here?" I ask. Curiosity nips at my mind.

Is Amelia bisexual?

Tyler speaks up, "Silas told Amelia he wasn't going to play along in his own dicky way, something about her being boring and predictable."

So, this is her proving him wrong? I can't say I hate it.

Their lips part simultaneously, and then they collide, slowly moving like they are savoring every second of it. Amelia and JJ separate and look around at us.

"How's that for boring and predictable?"

Silas scoffs, "Being promiscuous does not prove me wrong; it actually supports my earlier statement as well as the fact that you have broken a rule."

The rule that nothing intimate happens with anyone other than the five of us.

Her face falls, and she looks between the twins, then over at me. We exchange looks, reading each other, and then Lyle shrugs. "This is a one-time exception. She gave us time to stop it if any of us were uncomfortable with it."

Her lips turn up slightly, and then her eyes flash with delight as she sees the blindfolds and edible body paint in my hands.

Silas sees the same thing a second later. "What the fuck are you doing with my shit?"

"This is for your punishments. Unless you are too boring and predictable and refuse."

Amelia stands up, takes the black blindfolds from my hands, and walks behind Finn. She drapes it across his eyes and ties it firmly behind his head. Silas watches her fingers as they glide down Finn's sides to the bottom of his shirt, then pull it up over his head.

Tyler whistles, and Finn bites his lip playfully, giving a little dance. "You like what you see, big boy?"

Amelia leans in close to his ear and gives it a little tug with her teeth. "Sorry, Tyler, I don't share my men."

"But from what I hear, you like that they share you," Tyler chuckles.

Lyle grabs the front of his shirt, "We like you, Tyler, but don't get it twisted. I will still knock the fuck out of you if you say some shit like that again."

Tyler's face goes taut, "Sorry man, it was a joke."

Lyle stares at him for another moment, then releases him with a pat on the chest.

Amelia still stands behind Finn, who is still blind to everything around him. None of us had to even question that Lyle could handle that comment. Silas didn't move a step, but all his muscles are tight, his shoulders nearly up to his ears.

Amelia steps behind him and brings the blindfold around his face, just as she had done to Finn.

Her next words come out choppy. "Uh, you're too tall for me to reach, so you'll... have to do it yourself or bend down."

He pulls his shirt over his head, and tons of girls' eyes shift his way, drooling over the body of a very fit boxer, adorned in tattoos and scars, just like they always do. No matter how much of an ass he is, they still look at him like they would strip down naked if given half a chance.

My mind shifts to Amelia, and my heart beats a little faster as I find her eyes not on the two shirtless men next to her, but on me, holding out her hand for the remaining supplies. Thrill courses through her and manifests in little childlike bounces.

I pass her the paint, and she hands one to JJ, nodding toward Silas. JJ looks at Tyler and motions for her to draw a giant penis.

Well, I guess he has no qualms with her painting another man's chest.

"Ready, boys?" JJ asks.

"This might be cold," the girls say together.

Silas puts his hand out, grabbing JJ's wrist with perfect aim.

"Relax. I don't particularly want to touch you with a ten-foot pole, but I think I can enjoy the sight of something even if I don't particularly like it for what it is."

Amelia bites back a laugh and gives a wink, then opens the pink jar of paint. JJ opens the green, and they get to work, dipping the brushes and creating their designs on each man. They swap colors a few times to add details that stand out a bit more than their primary color.

Lyle and I take turns whispering ideas into their ears and chuckling as the masterpieces come to completion. The girls take a few steps back, dramatically wiping their brows, panting, and nodding in approval.

Finn has dual-colored spirals around each nipple and a stem going down, resembling a lollipop. In the center of his chest, it reads, 'I know you wanna take a lick' in 3D bubble letters.

Silas has a veiny, hairy dick from his chest to his belly button, filled with pink jizz. He has the words 'I'm a dick, but I still want you to suck mine' written half on one side, half on the other. At the bottom, right in the middle of his V-cut, it says, 'and say thank you.'

JJ climbs up on a chair and shouts, "Hey everyone, we have the losers of a bet taking on their punishment! Come get a good look and take lots of pictures!"

Sounds of laughter and cheers surround us. Girls crowd around and catcall the two men on display with hoots and hollers.

"Is this how it feels to be a woman? I kinda like it," Finn says, and our group laughs as he wiggles his hips a little bit.

Silas chuckles, "If this is to embarrass us, you need to up your game."

I step forward and turn, standing in line with them. I take both men's upper arms in my hands, "Oh no, dear friends. We have one more thing in store for you."

I guide them to the area we cleared for the stage and put them into place.

"Ian, for the hundredth time, I will not give you a strip tease," Silas says dramatically so everyone can hear him.

"Oh, this one isn't for me, but somehow I'll live." I clap him on the shoulder, hand them both a microphone and nod at Amelia to turn the music on. "Now, give it your all, boys, and we might throw some money if we see something we like."

The speakers vibrate as the song "*Buttons*" by *The Pussycat Dolls* pour from them.

Silas and Finn both shake their heads, nervously stepping side to side and getting into character.

Finn is a goofball through and through. This is just another day for him. For Silas, this is a rare sight. He rarely, if ever, lets himself go enough to have fun like this. It wasn't that he thought he was above such a thing. It was more of him thinking he didn't deserve to have fun like this. All the heartache and devastation he has ever felt somehow always was his fault in his own mind.

Both boys start dancing, running their hands all over their bodies, waving and writhing their hips and torsos as feminine as possible. Finn starts singing the words of the lead singer, putting on a show for a crowd that he can't see. Silas works the crowd, air thrusting, pulling his pants a touch lower and the girls go wild.

Amelia laughs and nudges JJ, both of them giggling, and I just shake my head. This girl becoming a little spitfire is going to be a wild ride, and I am fucking here for it.

Silas picks up *Snoop Dog's* part, rapping it seamlessly, and we all exchange surprised looks. They wrap up the song, panting and sweating, having given it their all. They take the blind folds off and take inventory of themselves. Silas rolls his eyes, and Finn dies of laughter, taking Amelia into his arms.

"Well, this was fun. Risking agreeing with what Silas said, it wasn't that harsh of a punishment."

She presses her lips to his, kissing him slowly and passionately.

"Oh, sweet Finnegan, for you, it was purely my reward to do this..." she trails off, bending down to lick off some of the edible paint.

"For him," she says, nodding in Silas's direction where he stands, watching them, "it was entirely different."

She pushes Finn back onto a stool, "You see; because I made him think that I was searching to embarrass him. He was so concerned with proving my choice to be inadequate that he never questioned my intentions might actually be to prove how little interest I have in wasting energy on him." She places her hands on his legs and bends down to his stomach. "How embarrassing for the man who takes delight in embarrassing others." ticking out her tongue, she glides it up the painted art again and then licks her lips clean. "Delicious."

Silas

I barely hold back my need to react, watching her all but fuck Finn right in front of me, just to spite me. I don't know if I want to pin her against the wall and scare the shit out of her or fuck her until she's begging for mercy. I told her I wasn't interested and I'm constantly a prick to her, but my little monster is persistently testing my restraint. I wonder if this is a new side to her, acting out because she is hurting and finally free to respond to the pain any way she wants, or if she can see through my lies.

I won't lie, I let myself have some fun on the stage. I'm not such a stuck up prick that I can't have genuine fun like that, but I don't do it often. The high is great, but coming down is worse than sobering up any other way. The past doesn't creep in; it busts down the fucking door and beats the shit out of me for the audacity I had.

Why should I ever be allowed to feel like that, right?

I give Amelia a smirk. "Look at you, finally developing some brains. Good girl." I step off the stage and look back at her to see her brows scrunched. "Isn't that what you like to hear for a job well done?"

She scoffs and turns her back to me. I don't wait to see what else she has in store for the boys. Grabbing the closest brunette, I pull her around the corner, into my room, and slam the door. I leave it unlocked, some dark part of me wanting Amelia to walk in and see, hating me a little more.

The girl giggles and sets her drink on the nightstand. She takes her shirt off and slides up on the bed, "I'm not gonna lie; I've been wanting this for so long."

I shove her back and yank her mini skirt down her legs.

"Shut the fuck up."

Her face pales slightly, but she does as she's told. I pull my pants down, freeing my cock, and stroke the hard-on that has been begging to be in something wet since Amelia's top came off earlier.

I flip the nameless girl over and slap her little ass. She gasps loudly, and I groan, closing my eyes picturing *her* lying under me instead. I lift her hips, giving me a clear view of her. I reach up, wrapping one hand around the girl's neck and squeezing tightly, letting my frustration seep out. She whimpers something, choking on the air and ending my daydream that has barely started.

"What the fuck is your problem?" I bark, letting go of my grip.

"Y- you are squeezing a little too hard."

I have zero fucking patience right now. "This isn't going to be a soft fuck. If you aren't okay with that, get the hell out, and I'll find someone that is." I would never force a woman into my bed. She always has the power to say stop, and I would. Maybe not with ease, but I would.

"N- no. Keep going," she squeaks out.

Pathetic, just like the rest of them.

I resume my hold on her just as it was before and use my other hand to stick two fingers in her mouth, getting them wet. I pull them out, yank her panties to the side, and wipe the saliva up and down her bare pussy. The mix of her own lube and spit get her ready, and without warning, I shove my fingers inside her, twisting then moving them rapidly. She grunts and pants in pleasure. I picture *her* again, *her* whispering my name, begging for me to be inside her. My cock throbs, and my balls ache.

Once the girl's pussy is dripping, I remove my fingers and dig in my nightstand for a condom. I tear it open, roll it on, and in one thrust, fill her with my cock. I am not small by any means, and I don't take it easy most of the time. I almost take joy in hoping it hurts just a little, but this girl doesn't cry out; she only moans.

"Oh, God. Yes, Silas." Her whiny voice causes my haze to falter.

"Shut. The. Fuck. Up," I say again after each thrust. I yank her head back then slap her across the cheek; this time, she yelps in pain. A feral growl rumbles in my throat as my desire spikes. "I hope that hurt. Maybe you'll learn to do as you're told."

My father's voice thunders in my head, only encouraging me to cause more damage. I grab the pillow from beside me, turn her head to lay flat and place the pillow on top, cutting off her air the way my dad had done to me time and time again.

I picture Amelia again, telling me how much she loves being the only one for me. How she loves to take away my pain. That she will take whatever I give her. I speed up, chasing my orgasm. I throw the pillow off, gather the girl's hair into my fist, and slam into her as hard as I can, again and again. She sucks in gulps of air but doesn't protest.

I keep my eyes shut, picturing my little monster. Sucking me. Riding me. Crying out for me. My orgasm tears through me, and as soon as it fades, I pull out, throw the condom in the trash and pull my jeans back on.

The girl rolls over and gives me a confused look. "I- I didn't come yet," she says shyly.

I don't spare her a glance while I fasten my button.

"Did I ask?"

She scoffs, pulls her clothes back on, and yanks the door open. "You are fucking unbelievable."

The door slams, and I sink onto the bed, exhausted with myself. My head falls into my hands, and my thoughts turn dark. Sometimes I love that I don't allow people to really see me, but other times my heart aches with a hollowness, and I wonder what it would feel like to fill it. The room grows quiet, the muffled chatter and music coming from behind the door. I focus my ears and listen for any signs of Amelia, hoping proof of her presence will soothe me.

A crash sounds from outside, and I hear Lyle yelling a stream of cuss words. I stand from my bed and straighten myself up, taking my time to put my no-give-a-fuck look in place. Lyle probably knocked some overly drunk bastard out for acting a fool.

He's a very skilled fighter and can handle his own. He's leaner, and that makes him quick. He moves so fast, that when he lands a hit, it rocks their shit. I usually only step in to throw the sorry fuckers around and out once they are good and bloody, just for good measure.

He can take care of himself, but those are my boys, and I would protect them with my life. If anyone fucks with them, they will damn well understand they messed with me too.

I casually stroll back into the living area as Ian runs towards the back door. He stops abruptly, spotting me. "He's here, and he's not alone! Let's fucking go!"

He?

Fuck me.

Lance.

We jog through the house and out the back door.

"No one saw them come in, but he waited until there was enough room between her and Lyle to grab her," Ian says.

As soon as we walk through the open back doors, I see them. Lance holds a hand full of Amelia's hair with one hand and another around her arms, pinning them down to her chest. I can see the fear in her eyes as he drags her down the wooden pier. The light from the fire casts a dim light halfway down it, but the end is almost pitch black.

I take a single second to assess the situation, looking further right and seeing Lyle fighting to get to her but being slowed down by one of Lance's guys. Closer to the water, Finn is on top of another man, knocking his head to the side over and over again. Fists fly and blood sprays. The crowd gasps and huddles just close enough to watch. Everyone knows not to intervene in our business, and I don't have time to clear them out like I usually do.

I step to run towards Amelia, but Ian stops me, grabbing my arm. I look at him with fury, surely blazing in my eyes.

"I need his phone," he says sharply.

I give him a nod and run faster than I ever have in my entire life. I choke down the fear and guilt that threatens to spill out of my mouth. Lance's face disappears into the dark as he backs further down the wooden area.

"Lance, I will fucking kill you!" I yell after him.

"Oh, come on, we're just having some fun," he laughs back.

I slow into a walk, entering the dark, not knowing where the edges are. The clouds shift, allowing the moon to cast just enough light for me to see their bodies.

"Can't you take a hint? She doesn't want you anymore." I say, trying to engage in conversation to slow his unknown plans but treading carefully so I don't push him to act faster.

He leans in closer to her face, and I can see her flinch from the six feet away that now separates us.

"Seems she doesn't want you either. I think I might have ruined her taste for assholes. Sorry about that." He gives her a soft kiss on her cheek, and my fists tighten.

"I don't expect you to know the meaning of family, but I stand by my boys and what they care about."

He laughs like I said something amusing. "You do know how closely I've had my eye on her, don't you? I needed all the juicy details, so you can only imagine the pieces I've put together. Have they?" He nods in my direction, motioning at the boys behind me, but I don't dare take my eyes off him to look.

"And why was it that you needed all that again? Must have slipped my mind," I ask.

"*Tsk. Tsk.* Can't be revealing secrets now. Don't worry. You all will know soon enough."

I hesitate to think of my next move. She can swim, but if they both go in, he might try to drown her. Without moving my head, I look lower at the ground. Beer bottles lay scattered next to a few pieces of discarded clothes.

I give him a nod and a sigh before allowing a dark smile to crawl across my lips.

"You know, my boys seem occupied, and my lay tonight didn't really cut it for me. So, how about we shine some light on the situation so I can see these games you are wanting to play."

A mischievous grin crosses his face. "Amelia, baby, would you be a dear and grab my phone from my front right pocket?"

She does as he says, shaking as he tilts her body in his grasp and digs her hand into the pocket, retrieving it. She slides up, turning the light on. He squats with her, allowing her to set it down.

The light shines up on her face and I can see wet streaks staining her cheeks, her eyes now pinched shut.

"I was thinking about a little truth or dare. Amelia always loved that game, didn't you, baby?" Fresh tears spill from her closed eyes and he yanks her hair harder, and she whimpers, nodding.

My nails dig into my palms, damn near breaking the skin.

"Alrighty then, questions about my plans are off-limits. Silas, truth or dare. Now remember, if you don't complete your turn, there is a consequence."

I force another grin. "Dare."

He hums as if he needs to think about what he would want. "Take her shorts off."

I slowly walk towards her, her eyes still closed and my head screaming. I take a knee in front of her and tuck my fingers into the front of her blue jean shorts. She sucks in a breath, and my heart sinks. I don't look at her as I unbutton them and slide them down, leaving her in black cotton panties. No swimsuit bottoms, she obviously had no intention of taking her shorts off in front of everyone here. I stand and let my right hand rub up her leg on the way up, putting on a show in the worst way.

"My turn. Amelia, truth or dare," I say darkly.

She opens her eyes and looks directly at me with a hollow stare. "Truth," she chokes out.

I cock my head to the side. "Do I make you wet?"

She searches my eyes, but I hide my emotion carefully. I hold her stare and step closer.

"Don't lie," I whisper, "or do. The consequence might be more fun."

Her throat bobs as she swallows. "Sometimes," she whispers quietly.

Lance chuckles. "All that hell she gave me about fucking other people, and now here she is wanting to fuck four men at the same time. Fucking slut."

Her hands shake a little harder than before, and I know she won't be able to take this much longer.

"Your turn" I cross my arms and wait for her to speak.

"Silas, truth or dare."

"You already know. Give me the best dare you got, little monster." I dig my eyes into hers, praying she sees my hidden words.

"Let me think for a minute," she whimpers.

I take my eyes off her and look around as if annoyed. I land my gaze on a bottle and hold it there for a minute then bring them back to her sharply. She looks down to where I was, and her eyes widen.

There you go, baby.

"I want you to fuck me on the dock while Lance watches."

I look at Lance with a shit-eating grin, but my stomach flips as her words take root in my head.

"See my point," he scoffs.

"It's just amusing at this point." I confirm.

"Let's give the bitch what she wants." He leans into her. "Answer this first. Why do you want this?"

She turns her head to look at him. "Because I've wanted to fuck him for weeks, and I want to see how you will react."

He hums. "I think you want to fuck him because you want to feel the way I did, fucking whoever I wanted, still having another person wrapped around your finger. Is that right?" She gives a little nod, and he smiles in victory. "I will not be moving very far away, so don't think you are going to run."

My phone rings in my pocket, and I pull it out, holding out a finger. "Hold on, gotta take this." I put it on speakerphone for full effect, trying to convince him that I am completely on board. "Hey Finn, what's up?"

"We beat the fuck out of these two and through them in the ditch out front. Where is Amelia?"

"Don't worry, I got this handled. We just need a minute to breathe. Go ahead and send everyone home, and we will meet y'all inside in a bit to watch *Algol* like planned."

"Got it," he replies without hesitation and ends the call.

I step into them and gently grab her arm.

"Trust me, I'm not letting her go anywhere. I know she wants this." I cringe at the words I know he has said to her in other forms, knowing that it cut her deep for another person to say them.

Lance loosens his grip on her, and I pull her into me. I turn us so I am facing the house. I push my body into her with all of my weight and place one of my feet behind her, tripping her and swiftly moving her to the ground. I slip my hand behind her head at the last second, protecting it from slamming against the ground.

Lance squats down to the right of us and holds his light up. His flat expression shines like a thing of nightmares, his eyes void of any emotion for what I might do to her.

Her eyes drift from his face to mine, seeing the same cold features. I try to soften my eyes, but it's a gesture that's unfamiliar to me. I'm not sure I'm even capable of it. I guide my hands up and down her legs, and my heart races.

"Take her top off. She has great nipples," Lance's voice rumbles low. He stays perched only a few feet away as I move my hands up her body to the sides of her stomach, feeling the plush of it.

My dick grows harder, my fantasies invading my mind. My adrenaline spikes making me want to tear her clothes off and fuck her so hard she wakes up all the neighboring houses. I shove it down. This is not how it would happen.

I take her face in my hand gently and then force my grip harder, jerking her head towards me.

"Truth. Do you want this?" I spread her legs wider and settle between them, then lean in so close to her face that her soft lips brush mine.

I wonder how they would feel wrapped around my cock or sucking on my neck. How her perfect teeth would feel sinking into my skin as hard as she could. Maybe she would make me bleed. My cock strains against my clothes, and I groan when she rubs her hands up my arms and settles them on my shoulders.

"I do."

Her eyes shine with something I can't quite place. It's almost a feeling of déjà vu. Like we have known each other our whole lives. I see touches of lust and fear mixing with a lingering sense of trust. For a moment, it's just us out here. Nowhere to go. Nothing to do but be with each other. The way I have always wanted it.

Lance shifts beside us and the moment ends in a flash, forced back into reality. Her hands tighten on me, and she lowers her chin, taking in my body hovering above hers. Our hips are the only other thing touching. Just a few layers of fabric separating us. I grind into her roughly, and her head lifts back up, a quiet moan slipping from her. Seeing her respond to me makes it nearly impossible to stay focused on the task at hand.

"I want to fuck you until you can't walk, and I want proof of how much you want me on my body. I want the guys to know without asking. Let me see that anger that I love so much." I move my hands to her top and pull it up over her breasts, exposing them to the warm air.

She looks at Lance nervously.

"Don't look at him. I'm the one about to bury my dick in you. He doesn't want you. He wants to see you like this for his own sick games."

She looks back at me and watches my hands as they knead her tits. She groans and wiggles under me slightly. I lower my head and lick a trail from the center of her stomach up to her chest. She moans louder, and I groan, barely hanging on.

"Keep moaning like that. Show him how much I turn you on." I take the phone and shine it on her center to find a wet spot on her panties, glistening skin next to them. "Oh yeah, you want this bad, don't you, little monster?"

I place the light back on the ground above her head and out of the way. I rub my hands on the inside of her thighs, careful to not touch the spot begging for it. She winces as my palms glide over her scars.

"P-please. Touch me," she begs, breathing heavily and writhing. I love the way it sounds, but there is too much tainting the pain in her voice for me to enjoy it.

"I will do what I want when I want. And right now, I want you to flip over." I move to the side of her body and grab her sides, flipping her to the left. I unzip my pants and lean into her, grinding again. Lance sits flat, getting comfortable.

I lean on top of her, getting in her ear blocking Lance's view of the other side of us. I quietly move a nearby beer bottle to her hands, making it appear that I'm just feeling her up. "Swing hard and don't miss."

Leaning back, I grab her hips and pull them up. She sits back, grabs the bottle, and swings over her chest to the right, connecting with Lance's head. The bottle breaks and Lance falls to the side.

"Go!" I yell, pushing her to her feet and towards the house, tossing her shorts after her.

"You stupid bitch! Fuck the plan. I will beat the shit out of you," Lance grumbles as he's getting to his feet.

Amelia struggles to get her clothes back on, not wanting anyone still here to see her in her current state and I step in front of Lance, blocking his way.

"You won't do shit if I break every bone in your body."

He gets to his feet and stumbles towards me. Blood drips down his face from a gash that must be in his hair. He pulls a knife from his back pocket and lunges for me. He slashes across my face in quick motions, barely missing my eye, with one hand and throws a hook with the other.

I stumble back, giving him an open path. Amelia had started running but not soon or fast enough. He is feet from her as I throw a bottle at his head, making him stumble. He lurches forward on his downfall, grabbing Amelia by the ankle, pulling her down with him.

Her face slams into the ground hitting the broken glass scattered all around. I grab the phone lying on the ground and sprint, closing the space between them and me. He flips her over, climbs on top of her, and holds the knife under her chin.

"Stop! If you come any closer, I might just do something hasty."

I freeze.

"Get the fuck off of me, you fucking creep!" Amelia yells in his face.

He moves the blade to her face, cutting a shallow slice down her cheek like mine. "Oh baby, that hurt. I just want to have some fun. You never were any fun." He frowns and then smiles, licking the blood from her skin.

She gags, crying, "God, you are disgusting!"

I step closer, and he points the tip of the knife in the center of her chest. "Test me, Silas. I dare you"

Now that we are further down the dock, I can see more of his face. His pupils are blown, and his face is sunken in.

He's high and strung out.

"You know, no one would miss a druggy going nowhere in life if you mysteriously went missing," I say.

He laughs, dragging the blade down Amelia's stomach, and she cries out in agony and my heart cracks.

"Oh, I am going places," he says.

I step closer while he's focused on the blood covering Amelia's chest, tears spilling from her eyes.

"She is my ticket out of this shithole town," he mumbles, barely audible.

"So you can't kill her. How is she supposed to help you?" I step closer, and he slashes her arm, "I said stay the fuck back, bitch!"

Amelia wails, screaming louder than before.

"Shut the fuck up!" He slashes across her chest, and she screams louder and louder. Blood seeps out, and her eyes flutter shut from shock.

Fuck.

"Stop, Lance! You're going too far!"

He looks down at her, taking in the trickling blood coming from the wounds he created.

"You're right. He said I gotta keep her alive to get my big break." Lance sits back, seeming to dissociate.

I lunge at him, shoving him away from Amelia and pinning him down.

Punch after punch, I rock his head sideways. Splitting skin, blood spraying, bone cracking. The guys come rushing out of the trees, the yard now void of other people.

I dig Lance's cell phone out of my back pocket and toss it at Ian, "Make it quick."

Lance lays unconscious, face swelling and almost unrecognizable.

Finn and Carlisle squat down next to Amelia, and I stand. "No. I got her."

A lump forms in my throat as I take in all the cuts and already-forming bruises overlapping the ones that were almost gone.

"I got you, baby." I scoop her into my arms and look at the boys. "He mentioned someone giving him orders. Don't throw him out just yet. I'm not done with him."

I take Amelia inside and into the bathroom, her limp body curled into mine, her chest rising and falling softly. Struggling to balance her in my arms, I reach into the cabinet and grab a washcloth. I wet it and sit us on the cold floor with her between my legs and head leaned back onto my chest. I press the rag to her face gently, wiping off the blood in slow strokes, then move to her chest, doing the same. Her eyes flutter open, and she winces. I pull back and wait for her next movements. I don't want my touches to cause her any more stress. She looks around, down at her body, and then up at me.

"I- uh, we need to get you cleaned up. Can I help you?"

She gives me a little nod and starts to lean up. I help her, putting her arm over my shoulder and getting her to her feet. Bringing her to the side of the tub, I set her down.

"Soaking won't be sanitary, so you need to take a shower. I'll lower the pressure, but it is still going to sting."

She gives me a small smile and raises a brow.

Right.

Pain junky.

I walk back to her and pull her up from under the arms. She wobbles a little, then finds her footing. I squat down in front of her.

"Do you want to do this yourself? I don't want you to..." I trail off, unable to find the right words.

She looks down at me, and her eyes pool. She doesn't protest, just looks back up and stands up straighter.

I help her out of her clothes, doing my best to keep them from rubbing against her raw skin. Once she is fully bare, I take my time assessing her skin. Noting every cut and scrape, picking little shards of glass stuck in her skin. She doesn't flinch or move. Just stands there, her eyes hollow, her body as still as death. I stand once I am finished and reach for her hand.

"Amelia," I say in a low tone, my voice shaking and

nervous.

She turns away from me and steps into the shower. "I know you don't *really* care. Just leave."

Oh, how wrong you are, baby.

I sigh and shut the glass door behind her, leaving her be. I stop at the bathroom door, and my spine stiffens.

No.

I have stood by long enough. I have watched her have to pick herself up off the floor time and time again.

No more.

I walk back to the shower and pull the door open. She looks at me, shocked, as I step into the water, fully clothed.

"What are you doing?!"

I pull her naked body into mine and hold her tight.

"You can act tough all you want, but we both know you need this."

She tries to push away from me, but I only hold her tighter. She grumbles and curses me, telling me to get out, but I don't move. Her body finally gives out, and her head falls into my chest. Soft sobs fill the small room, and her body gently shakes with sorrow.

"Shh," I soothe her, stroking her wet hair, "I'm here. Always."

She falls harder into me, and we slide slowly onto the shower floor. I hold her in my arms as she cries, curled up in a ball. The water mists onto us, turning pink as our blood washes down the drain.

After long minutes, her cries stop, and her body stills.

"I just want you to know I didn't want to do that. It damn near killed me."

She looks up at me and squints her eyes.

"All of it?"

"No. Not all of it."

Although my mind goes straight to those moments of her under me, the moment doesn't turn sexual. She's hurt as a result of mine and another man's actions.

She turns, places her back against my chest, and pulls her knees to her chest.

"Can I ask you a question?" she says quietly.

I rest my hands on the floor, giving her some space.

"Sure. But don't ask questions you don't want the answer to."

She is quiet for so long, I think she changed her mind, but then she speaks.

"Why do you act like I am such an inconvenience to your life if you are doing this right now?"

My head rests against the wall, and I watch the steam roll through the air as I think about what she's asking and how I want to answer.

"You are not an inconvenience, Amelia. I am just very broken." I move my hands around her legs, "You don't need my approval of who you are and how you love."

We sit in the warm silence for a while, but I don't mind it. I'll give her all the time she needs.

I help her out of the shower once she's ready, and my wet clothes soak the floor.

"I'll get us fresh clothes and the first-aid kit."

I wrap her in a towel and leave her sitting on the toilet. On my way back, I find the boys sitting on the couch with a bound Lance on a wooden chair, barely conscious. I give the boys a nod and open the bathroom door.

Amelia stands there in front of the full-length mirror, naked. I swallow hard and force my feet to move. I place her clothes on the sink and watch her as she drags her fingers across every mark on her skin.

"Do you think they will scar?" she asks, tilting her head to the side.

I move to her and begin applying ointment and bandages.

"I don't think any of them need stitches, so they should fade over time."

She hums and turns, giving me a better angle at the deeper ones on her arms and chest.

A single tear drops from her eye, and she inhales shakily. "I wouldn't mind if they did. Scars are a reminder of what we have been through." She looks at me, but her eyes are unfocused and dazed.

"Yes, they are proof that we made it through." I finish up and stand to my feet.

She turns back to the mirror and rubs the inside of her thigh, feeling the rough skin there.

"Or proof of what killed us when we don't."

I want so badly to wrap her in my arms and scream at her for even thinking that. She will always make it through. I will always be right behind her to make sure of it.

"You will."

She scoffs and begins pulling on her clothes. "I'm not like you, Silas. I don't have a bottomless pit where I can shove all my emotions to become a heartless monster whenever I please."

Pain flashes over my face, and within a second, it's gone. I force myself back into my shell, preparing myself for the next words that leave my mouth. "Maybe you should. We won't coddle you forever. Grow a fucking spine and do something about your own problems, then you can cry in the dark when it's over."

She slices me with her eyes, "Guess good ole asshole Silas is back."

I step closer and run a finger down her spine, "Oh babe, he never left."

She pulls away and slips her shirt over her bare chest, then wraps her arms around herself.

"Oh, don't play modest now when you were begging for me an hour ago and laying on me naked minutes ago."

Her jaw clenches. "You know that was just for show, for both of us. You only enjoyed my pain of enduring it."

I graze my bottom lip with my teeth. "Oh? And what about the shower?"

She was vulnerable and needed me, and I'm using it against her.

"Get out." She points to the closed door behind me, and I grin.

"Didn't you say monsters were made? Stay here long enough and you might just become one."

"Get. Out," she growls shoving me back.

I let her, taking steps back, then she slams the door in my face. I linger outside the door, listening to her movements. Cabinets slam, and sniffles become more prevalent as she lets her emotions loose. I hear the sound of the sink being turned on before the porcelain toilet lid slams against the tank. I fist my hands against my eyes and rest my forehead on the wall as I listen to her throw up every bit of the contents in her stomach.

My face isn't the one she will want to see when she cleans herself up and finally faces what is waiting for her in our living room, but I wait for her anyway. Silent in the shadows, always making sure that if she falls, she has someone to catch her.

And when she is ready, I will stand behind her, ready to rain Hell down on any sorry motherfucker in her way.

Amelia

Humming buzzes in my ears and drowns out the commotion. Dissociating, I float, not completely gone but not entirely here.

"Wake the fuck up." Carlisle's palm slaps against Lance's face, and my muscles tighten on reflex.

Lance cries out, blood spilling from his mouth. Carlisle bends at the waist, holding onto his knees, leveling himself with Lance. He tilts his head to the side, and even from the back, the act sends a chill over my skin. After spitting in his face, Carlisle moves to sit next to Finn, who's perched on the side of the couch.

Silas paces back and forth next to Lance in sweatpants with a clean white shirt, and I visualize all the blood that was on him minutes ago. His blood and my own. He cleaned up the cut on his face but didn't bother to bandage it.

My cheek burns in the many places where small cuts are scattered. I brush the bandage on my chest, the tape causing my skin to itch.

"How cognitive are you? Maybe we should let you detox for a few days for good measure," Silas grinds out, barely holding back the rage contained just below his surface.

Lance spits in his direction and is quickly rewarded with a jab to the nose, causing it to spurt fresh red blood, contrasting the dried, darker red blood that remained.

Silas stops pacing, and the atmosphere in the room quickly changes, darkness and unease casting over us.

"You mentioned someone giving you orders. Who?"

"Fuck you," Lance growls, a touch of fear in his tone.

"Finn, get my bat, would you?"

Finn does what is asked, returning with a red steel baseball bat. He stands in front of me, blocking the view of Lance. "Mel, you want to take a walk with me?"

I take my eyes off the bat, riddled with deep cuts and dried blood to look up at Finn. "No, I need this."

For a moment, it looks like he is going to argue, but then he pulls me up and sits me across his lap, his hand resting on top of mine.

"Come on, man," Lance begs, "I can't tell you who. He'll kill me."

Silas picks up the bat, swinging it over his shoulder, resting it there. "What *can* you tell me?"

His eyes bounce between all of us, and the moment they meet mine, I dig my nails into my thighs.

Finn's hands tighten around my own.

"Look, we made a deal. Fucking with her was part of it, but I can't say I wasn't enjoying it."

Carlisle stands and kicks the chair, sliding it back a few feet. "How fucked are you in the head that you can justify raping her, cutting her up, and God knows whatever else you had planned tonight?"

He plants his fist into Lance's shirt, gripping it and jerking him forward. "You better fucking say something useful to end this shit, or I swear to God, I will kill you so fucking slow that you will be begging for Hell to take you."

Silas's eyes darken, and his next words are so deadly serious that a chill crawls up my spine. "I might do it regardless."

Lance pants, looking directly at me, and the fear in his eyes reflects the way I have looked at him so many times before. If he is searching for any part of me that might beg them to stop, he will find nothing. Though watching him like this hurts, he would never get to see that fact. He deserves nothing from me but the way I sit deathly still, holding his stare like I could summon death for him myself.

Lance looks back at Carlisle. "I don't know why. I was given an opportunity for a price. I took it." He shrugs, and Carlisle seethes.

I read the look on his face, and I know it all too well. He's lying. But I say nothing. Not yet.

"You would do all this, not knowing what for, just for your own gain?" Carlisle asks.

Lance's eyes find mine once more. "I care about her, but I never felt what she did. So yeah, and I sleep just fine at night."

Silas nods, walking slowly in front of him, sucking his teeth.

My jaw clenches, and I stand. I take the bat from Silas's grip, avoiding his eyes, only watching as his large hand releases the weapon into mine. Pushing by him, I stand in front of Lance. "Let's see how well you sleep at night with a few broken bones."

I take my stance and swing hard, aiming at the side of his arm. A loud crack rips through the air followed by a deep screech of pain. I wince; the sound is blood-curdling.

Finn moves to stand behind me. He grips my thigh, reminding me of his presence, and I speak up.

"He is lying. He knows more."

Silas spins towards me and reads everything written on my face.

"You want to try that again?" he asks the bleeding shitbag in the middle of the room.

Lance begins to sob, "I can't! Please! I'll keep my distance! You can have her!"

Silas grins mischievously and steps backward, giving me full control. "Oh, I don't need your permission. I do have her, and I will continue to have her on every surface I can find. I will make her scream my name so many times she will forget you ever existed. And as far as you staying the fuck away from her, if you want to live, yeah, you will. It's not only me you need to fear."

Ian and Carlisle move closer to complete the wall behind me.

Panic floods Lance's features as I step up and raise the bat once more.

I begin to swing but halt as Lance bellows a plea.

"Wait!"

I raise my brows in question as Lance sobs frantically, trying to see through the haze of his withdrawal. Sweat and blood rolls down his agony-written face.

"He wants money and to get even. Some criminal was locked up because of Damian. I was screwing Emma, and she was helping me for a cut of the profit by trying to access the account, but that bitch's mother moved it." He nods towards me at his mention of my mother.

"Kacey. She said Amelia had it." He struggles to breathe as the words fall from his mouth. "I have his routing number and was supposed to make her life hell before getting it out of her."

Everyone goes silent, the air sucked out of it.

"My mom never gave me the money," Mel looks crestfallen.

Did her mom really set her up? Knowing what they would do to her to get the money?

My ears ring, and my throat dries. My life has been made hell because someone that my dad prosecuted did his research on where his money went after he died. If Lance had paid any attention, he would have known that I had zero access to that money.

Carlisle takes the bat from me and gently guides me backward. With one swift motion, he swings level with Lance's chest.

Crack.

Lance screams again, no doubt through broken ribs.

"How much?" Ian asks, and just as I move to speak, Lance cuts his eyes at me.

"A hundred and fifty thousand."

I can barely understand him with the blood filling his mouth.

I nearly choke as Ian speaks again. "Give me the number and consider it paid. Then, you leave her the fuck alone forever, or I swear to God your body will never be found."

No.

I couldn't let him do this. Lance can't win anything.

Ian retrieves the piece of paper from Lance's pocket, and Carlisle moves forward once again. He slips a pocket knife out of his pocket and flicks it open, moving closer and jerking Lance's head up.

"Fair is fair, *dick*." He slams the knife down into Lance's thigh and then yanks it back out. Blood spurts from the wound, and I nearly hurl as I watch him pass out.

"Get him the fuck out of here before I kill him or he bleeds out," Carlisle growls.

Finn rubs my arm and scoots me over onto the couch, but Silas interjects, "I got it. Stay here with her."

Ian tosses a phone to Silas. "Tracking and bugged. I also downloaded all the history."

Silas nods and pulls Lance up and out of the house.

Ian moves over to me and takes my limp hand in his, "Mind if I steal her for a bit?"

"Go ahead. I'll help Lyle clean up." Finn says.

I follow in hand, going out the back doors.

"Don't kill him, Si." Ian tosses over his shoulder.

"No promises," he growls, then a door slams shut, shaking the foundation of the house.

Ian walks me out the back doors and down towards the water.

No. I can't go back there.

Just as I pull back in fear, he turns slightly right, walking to the shoreline instead. I let out a breath, and he laughs lightly. "Give me some credit, Mel."

We sit at the edge of the water, about halfway between the house and the cliff and I dig my feet into the wet sand. The wind gently blows my hair, the quiet night sky whispering softly to my heart.

"I know arguing is pointless, so I'll just say thank you." I say, keeping my head straight the words coming out scratchy.

"I don't know what you are talking about. I did this for purely selfish reasons." He nudges my shoulder and scoots closer. "No, I get it. Money is not something I like to throw around, but you better believe I would do anything for you."

I place my hand on top of his in the sand as I search for my breath.

"I know you needed some air. We don't have to talk if you don't want to, but I'm not leaving you alone." He kisses the top of my head.

I sit in silence for a minute and trace designs in the sand as I attempt to sort my thoughts. "I have spent so long in silence, and I have had enough space to last a lifetime, so I think a change might be good for me."

Ian leans back on his elbows and looks at the blackness above. "Okay, how about we take turns?"

I mirror his position. "Why do you think I could be good for Silas?"

As the words fall out of my mouth, I surprise myself that he was the first thing that came to mind. He has me once again questioning everything that he has tried so hard to make me believe about him. I need to know why he seems to go back and forth, what goes on in his head, and what triggers the changes in his behavior toward me.

"Silas is a difficult person, but he's not hard to love once you get beneath his surface. He needs someone that can get under there and help him heal from the inside out. I know you see or sense it, and it's one of the things I like about you. You always try to see the good in people."

I lay back completely and rest my hands on my stomach, feeling one of the small cuts from the glass and running my nail across it. "Well, you see where that has gotten me. I don't know when to accept that an asshole is nothing more than an asshole."

Ian looks over at me and gives me a stern look. "Don't compare the two of them. They may visually have similarities, but the motive behind their actions are not even remotely related."

I focus on the north star, remembering all the nights I would wish on it with every fiber of my being. All the prayers I sent up that always went unanswered.

"Every time I think I see a glimmer of a decent person inside him, he makes it a point to prove me wrong. I have three people pushing me to fight for myself and three others who have no problem tearing down what little progress I have made. I told Silas that I'm not like him. I can't pretend I don't have feelings."

He looks at me appalled. "You told him that?" He laughs. "And you wonder why his switch flipped?"

I go over the words in my head. Yeah, they might have been a little harsh, but they were honest. You can't tell me that he doesn't know how to take someone saying something offensive.

"The two of you are more alike than you'd care to admit, and not in a bad way necessarily," Ian says. "He wants to relate to you, but he is scared. The reason, I'm not sure, but you could probably figure it out if you really wanted to. But you need to make that decision before you two kill each other."

A gust of wind blows over us, tossing sand around in its dance through the air. The smell of barbecue fills my nose, and my stomach grumbles, but the thought of eating makes me physically nauseous.

"So, why do you like looking at the night sky so much? I catch you doing it all the time," he asks.

I smile and look back up, searching the constellations for my favorite one. "It has always brought me peace. The silence contrasts the constant war inside me." My mind wanders back to high school and all the notes I used to receive. "And, as silly as it is, I used to receive anonymous letters that, some days, were the only thing that helped me make it through. One day, I received one that told me to keep wishing on my stars and one day my *Perseus* would come."

"Perseus, huh?"

I look down at my drawing in the sand, the lines mirroring the structure of the constellation. "Yeah, mythology says he saved Andromeda, the chained princess, and then killed Medusa."

His lips curl up, and his eyes shine with amusement. "Yes, I'm familiar with the story." He lays back next to me. "It is beautiful, isn't it? Such a simple thing that holds all the potential to be much more with the right beholder."

I think he is still talking about the stars, but his head is turned towards me. He pulls out a small baggie, wiggling it at me. "It will help."

Scared. Broken. Temporary. My mind whispers to me but the man sitting up right next to me keeps it at bay.

His blonde wispy hair moves slightly in the wind, and his soft pink lips touch the pipe. His long fingers flick the lighter, holding above the bowl packed with freshly ground and sorted bud. He blows the smoke up into the air, hits it again, and passes it to me.

"I'm a lightweight, so don't pick fun."

I sit up, and he lays his head in my lap, watching me inhale and exhale the sweet smoke.

"It's not about how much you smoke. It's about getting where you need to be to let go of all the shit weighing you down." I run my fingers through his soft hair and watch his hand as it moves melodically across the sand.

"You play piano?" I ask, watching his fingers tumble across the invisible keys.

"Uh, yeah," he says, realizing what he was going, "Just a tick I picked up, I guess. I hear the music in my head, and my fingers move in muscle memory. I do the same with my guitar, motioning my hand sliding over the invisible strings." I watch curiously as he shows me the motion. "It just depends on what my hands are touching and what kind of music is flowing through my mind."

I chew on the side of my lip. "What do you hear right now?"

He tilts his chin up, and his eyes shimmer in the low light of the lighter I flick on. "A soft melody. One that tells a story of pain and newfound comfort. Changes."

I flick the lighter off and on again anxiously.

"Would you hum it for me?" I lower my eyes, my chest rising in difficult breaths.

I expect him to deny my request, but he pulls my arm across his chest and splays his fingers, positioning them just on top of mine. He inhales slowly, and his fingers move, a soft hum expelling from him.

I sit there, motionless and utterly taken away by the beauty of a melody I have never heard and the delicate notes being played on my skin. I close my eyes letting it whisper its story to me.

The humming soon stops, drawing me back into myself, and I open my eyes to find him smiling up at me.

"You liked that, huh?"

"There aren't words to describe how much. I felt everything the song said and more."

He rolls onto his stomach and places his head back onto my legs. "What else did you feel?" His warm breath tickles my thighs, and the feeling travels up further, causing me to swallow forcefully.

"I, uh, I felt love, I think. I don't know if I've ever really felt it or if it's always been infatuation or co-dependence. This clung to my heart and made me feel safe, and I'd like to think that's how love feels."

His lips brush my skin as he speaks, "It is, but it can also hurt. Giving all of yourself to someone is the ultimate sacrifice." He closes his eyes tight, and I feel a wetness stream down the inside of my thigh.

"Ian?"

He sits up, wiping his cheek. "Sorry," he says with a laugh, "I uh, I just.." he trails off, and I take his hand in mine, seeing the pain hidden behind his beautiful blue eyes that appear gray in night's light.

"You can talk about her if you want."

He looks at me curiously and brushes my hair behind my ear. "You actually remind me of her. I think it's why I was so quick to grow fond of you. Isn't that sick?"

My brows pinch at the thought, "Not at all. I think it's perfectly normal to adore things that remind you of someone you love, and sometimes that thing is a person."

He nods, wiping another tear from his eyes. "I haven't let myself think about her in years. It's part of the reason I haven't wanted to be with anyone. She wasn't the type to go out looking for anything more than genuine fun. She kept to herself. Broken, but when she was happy, it was like... fireworks." A pained smile flashes and disappears as another tear falls from his eye.

"So, what happened?"

"She died years ago."

My lungs collapse, and my mouth falls slack. "Oh God, I didn't realize. I'm sor-".

He cuts me off by taking my hands and giving them a tight squeeze. "Mel, it's okay. I have had a long time to grieve, and you didn't know. But I want you to. I think it can help us all."

I try to catch my breath, "W-why?"

He pulls me into his lap carefully, and I place my knees on the ground on either side of his legs. "Because I think it's time I finally let myself move on." He tilts my chin up with his fingers. "She will always hold a place in my heart, but we were only kids at the time."

I nod my head, searching his eyes for anything that might tell me differently, but I find nothing. "Can I know who she was? She was the one you all loved?".

"No. Reina was Silas's younger sister. Car-"

"What is it with keeping siblings a secret around here?" I say, forcibly laughing. He smiles, and the weight on my chest lifts.

"She was his half-sister and had a different last name. She was a year above you."

"How did I never notice you or the twins?" They were all the same age, yet the night I met them, I couldn't place a name with any of their faces.

"Well, despite the age gap, I had a major glow-up, and the twins were home-schooled for high school so they could start working to help their uncle. Silas missed a lot of school, same as Reina."

Okay, yeah. Add on the fact that I didn't exactly pay attention to anyone outside of my circle. It makes more sense now.

I readjust in his lap, trying to take the strain off my knees. "Can I hear more about Reina? If that's okay."

He grabs my hips and stills me. "Sure. If you quit trying to make me hard."

My eyes go wide, and he chuckles at my realization and I scrunch my nose in apology.

"I only knew her for a few years, but when you live like that, every day feels like an eternity. When the twins would get Si away from his dad, we would take her too if she wasn't with her mom. I worked every day to make sure it was a good one. She liked listening to me learn how to play. She loved to dance and paint. We would have paint parties and always make a huge mess." He smiles at the memory, and I smile with him. "I tried to protect her for so long. Then one day, I was too late. After losing her, we all spiraled, but Silas never really recovered. He used to be like her. So full of life."

"How..." I try to ask him, but the words get stuck in my throat.

He taps on my legs as he had done on my arm earlier.

"Nickolas."

Oh my god.

"He was drunk and just...kept hitting her."

I sit there silent, unable to put my thoughts into words.

"Now you understand why we don't want him anywhere around you... or us, for that matter," he says solemnly, and my head drops, still gripping the reasoning behind everything that makes them the way they are.

The reason that they were all so protective when they found out about my own abuse. Why Silas is so caged off, and Ian has never sought to be close to anyone new. Why Carlisle pushes me to be stronger, and Finn observes people's behaviors. They couldn't let another loss happen.

"We all have our own reasons for being drawn to you, Mel, but don't for a second think that just because she was the initial reason that I was drawn to you, that it is the only reason that I adore you. You are you and no one else."

My heart soars, and I want so badly to kiss him.

But I hear a truck driving up, signaling that Silas is back.

Ian grabs the underside of my thighs and stands up before setting me on my feet.

I take his face in my hands and stretch on my toes to give him a kiss on the cheek. "Thank you for everything."

He smiles from ear to ear, takes my hand, and leads us back inside.

Finn

Three days later...

The early morning sun wakes me up, and the stillness of the house tells me I'm the first one awake. Needing to keep myself busy, I grab a large trash bag, tossing in the stray beer bottles lying around from the last few days. Over half are from Amelia alone.

Her wounds are looking much better, but she does her best to keep them covered, even from us. She has said very little to any of us after coming in that night.

I could visually see her mind begin to shut down as she stepped back through the threshold, her eyes glued to Lance's blood and broken glass littering the floor. A little more as we changed her bandages each night and morning. A little more as Ian worked to go through Lance's phone and deleted history. A little more once we confirmed he was still alive and was seen at the local hospital.

I don't doubt seeing more proof of him being a scumbag has made her wish he wasn't. Not to mention her own mother had set her up, knowing exactly what they would do to her when she ultimately had no money to give them.

We all tried to redirect her mind with something different. Lyle tried baking for her and tossed around the idea of a naked food fight. Ian and I offered to take her back to the cliff, trying to flood her brain with adrenaline. Even Silas offered to spar with her silently as she visualized whatever it was she needed to in order to get her head straight.

She declined each time, not giving so much as a snarky comment. A small shake or nod of her head is pretty much all we've gotten from her in response. Though, she did accept the edible candies and desserts.

She pulls away from our touches, and the look in her eyes is dark and hollow, as if she has completely checked out.

Her mind is no longer able to withstand the trauma she's endured. Everyone needs something different in times of coping, but what you say you need and what you actually need sometimes contradict themselves. We tried to give her space to help her adjust, but it isn't working for me, and from the looks of the house and her sunken eyes, it isn't working for her either. She isn't coping, she's suffocating herself intentionally.

Lyle comes crawling out of his room a while later, not looking much better than the rest of us.

I meet his eyes, hoping that maybe we've made some progress. But he shakes his head, giving me the answer I knew was coming.

It is time for a change.

She's killing herself and taking us with her in the process.

A door slams and the shower turns on. My head snaps in that direction, and Silas grumbles from the couch where he drunkenly passed out again. Ian exits his room, looking worse for wear. He has been trying harder than all of us to get her to open back up, which has resulted in him sleeping on the floor.

Ian keeps his head down, avoiding our eyes the entire twenty minutes he moves around the kitchen.

"Ian." Silas, fully awake now, growls low, challenging him to keep his mouth shut any longer.

His blue eyes lift, and his face is as pale as a sheet of paper. He looks close to vomiting right on our feet.

"She's hurting herself again."

"Excuse me?" Lyle says low and deadly.

Ian's eyes meet mine, and the pain in them is a look I never wanted to see again. He looks like he could vomit. We've seen some shit together, but things like this really fuck with him now.

"They are everywhere under her clothes, and she took a lighter in there with her."

Silas moves faster than I can blink, heading straight for the bathroom, his heavy steps quick and determined. His fist pounds on the door, no longer content with staying silent. "Open the fucking door, Amelia, or I swear to God, I will break it down."

I rush after Silas, and it takes me half a second to realize Lyle hasn't moved. He looks at me with a pained stare, and I barely hear him speak over Silas's shouted threats.

"This is all my fault," my brother croaks. "I told her to be stronger. I encouraged her to shove it down, and now she's barely holding on."

Silas's voice thunders again, "Amelia!"

She says nothing.

I hold my hand up, asking him to wait. I listen closely, needing to hear any clue as to where she's at on the other side of the door before he kicks it in. The shower water falls, nothing disturbing the pattern as it hits the floor. She's sitting still. I bend low, peering under the door, and my stomach ties itself in a knot as I see her holding the flame to her skin.

I stand, and without me stating that she is near the door, Silas kicks it in.

Lyle rushes to where she is sobbing on the floor, snatching the lighter from her hand and throwing it across the room.

"Stop, stop, stop!" he chants, pulling her into his arms, only causing more violent cries to leave her, the sound shattering my heart that beats only for her. He holds her tight, compressing her chest in an effort to soothe the panic attack. Silas takes a step forward and then stops, his brows pinched and his face turned down.

Her cries are brought to sniffles, and Ian crouches down in front of her. "This has gone too far."

Pain overrides my heart as I watch my brother's hands shake in fear.

Her reddened eyes lift to his. "I don't think I should stay here."

I see the fear form in her eyes, and now I realize what the issue is. We scared her.

I crouch next to Ian, gently wiping the tears rolling down her face. "Are you scared of us or scared by the fact that you're not?"

Her face falls, her eyes searching the floor. "I watched y'all beat him, and I said nothing because he deserved every minute. He deserved worse. Then as I watched all the videos he had, all the disgusting conversations, I realized that I wanted to be the one to do worse."

Her eyes find mine. "I wanted to kill him. I made y'all want to hurt him."

Silas's face lights up in surprise, and I don't miss the grin that teases Lyle's lips behind her. He pulls her head against his chest. "That's what makes you perfect for us."

***

She shakes her head, feeling guilty for our actions, and I look at each of my brothers as we collectively decide it's time.

We sit on the couch, huddled around her as we prepare to lay ourselves bare for her.

"We want to be completely honest with you about who we are, and once you have all the pieces, you can decide if you want to leave," I start. "You did not make us do anything. We chose this life long ago."

She looks around the room, trying to read where this is going.

"As brothers, we took two vows. The first was when we lost Reina we would never allow people like Nickolas to get away with the crimes they commit. We said we would bury whoever and whatever we needed to in order to make it right. That anything we did, we did together, always sticking by our true family. We don't play by the rules, and we always get away with it."

Her eyes watch us, reading the expressions the old memories bring forward. Each of us is haunted by different aspects. I watch for that fear to return, but I am met with only curiosity and fascination, so I continue.

"We struggled with the morality of it, wondering if we were no better than those that hurt us, but eventually, something snapped in all of us. Everywhere you look, strings are being pulled to benefit someone else, so we decided to do the same."

She sits up, nearly on the edge of her seat for the rest of our story.

Taking a deep breath I lay our lives bare.

"Ian, as Jameson's only son, owns half of his company. He has signed a temporary agreement to be a silent partner with zero interest in taking over. But we can still reap the benefits of the corrupt system his relatives have created because the last thing Jameson wants is for Ian to sell his shares to someone who believes in our justice system. Silas, in not such a legally binding way, has contacts of his own through his father's... activities. So, it goes without saying that our hands are not the cleanest, though our motives are pure."

Her throat bobs as she reads between the lines.

"We stay 'punks' to the public, and we like it to stay that way. We are not a gang, and we don't enjoy unnecessary violence, but we do deem it necessary for those that harm others in unforgivable ways, and when it comes to you, my love, everything is unforgivable."

"Which brings us to our second vow," Lyle takes over, "we took when things went really wrong with Carsyn."

"The girl you shared in a relationship before me?" she asks, her nervous ticks kicking in.

"Yes, but it is nothing like you are thinking." Lyle says. "Carsyn came into our lives when we were twenty. We were riding the high of all the fights we were getting into, all the rules we were able to bend, and she ate up all the attention she got for being the woman at our side. She wanted something official with all of us, but no amount of sex, drugs, or money was enough to cover up the truth."

Lyle shrugs. "We were playing a fucked-up version of house. I fell for her hard. Finn and Silas both wanted her for nothing but sex, and Ian was disgusted by both her presence and what we were becoming. She got angry and vindictive after the rest of us made it clear things weren't working, and Ian tried pointing out we were losing sight of what he had vowed for Reina. She started causing fights between us, pointing blame on faults and errors, trying to tear apart what she would never wholly have." Lyle drops his head, unable to stomach what came next, so I continue for him.

"Carsyn was a junky in the literal sense and for power. So, one day, after overhearing Silas was denying Nickolas's order to take over his leadership spot in a gang, she took her shot at finding that power she wanted. She found the ones in command and used her relationship with us as a bargaining chip." I glance over at Silas and he nods. "She got to join if she could draw Silas out of the shadows. She knew we wouldn't allow something to happen to her because Lyle loved her."

Right about the time Lyle looks like he's going to lose it, Amelia takes his hand, rubbing soothing strokes across the back of his hand as he has done for her many times before. Her eyes speak all the words she can't figure out how to say. She isn't jealous. She wants him to know that she is here for him, and she understands the feeling of guilt for something you had only a small control over.

I can't help the smile she brings me, as I continue.

"We showed, broken apart but ready to get her out of there and do what we needed to clear Silas of his expectancy. We fought tooth and nail to get to her, and the more we fought, the more they beat her. By the time we got to her, we were once again too late. We had lost sight of why we started doing this, and it cost us losing her and killing a dozen men to vow that the next time one of us fell in love, it was all or nothing." I look at each of my brothers. "We all would be in love with her, or on our way to it, or she couldn't stay because there is no room in what we do for blame and politics. It had to be a perfect fit. She has to love us all."

Silas' jaw twitches, his eyes not leaving Amelia's face as if she might disappear if they did.

Tears sting her eyes as she stares at the wall directly in front of her. Her fingers closing around the hand that reaches to comfort her, while her other stays with Lyle's.

In the eyes of the law, we were criminals, but in the eyes of someone who really understood, we were doing nothing more than fighting for ourselves.

She has to figure out what side of this she wants to be on.

Silas whispers in a voice softer than I have ever heard come from him before, "This is your opportunity to figure out how you truly feel. No guilt or shame."

She peers down at their intertwined hands curiously, just now realizing that it was him that had taken her hand to comfort her. "But you said that all-"

"All of us have to be in love with you or on the way to that point. Yes, and you have to feel the same," he says.

She turns to Silas. "Why admit that you have feelings for me now?"

"I was hoping I had enough time to convince you not to feel the same. I don't want this life for you."

"You have no right to try to choose for me."

He nods. "What's it going to be, little monster."

She looks at each of us and we look back at her, praying for her to say the words we want to hear. She squares her shoulders.

"I'm staying."

Finn

I open the back doors, searching for Mel, unable to find her in the house. She's sparring with the tree again. Her form is getting better, and she is learning fast. Any tips we give are immediately used over and over again until she has perfected it.

She sees me coming towards her and stops to take a water break.

"You show some real potential, you know. I don't even think Silas learned as fast as you are."

That makes her smile. "Don't tell him that. He might take it too personally," she quips.

I take in the pillow she has bound to the tree and the sweat pouring down her pinkening skin. "You do know we have a gym here, right?"

Her shoulders droop, and she props her hands on her hips. "Seriously?" she questions, still trying to slow her breathing.

I know she wouldn't enjoy the fact that I want to laugh. *Of course, Silas didn't tell her about it.*

"Where do you think Silas always disappears to?" I ask, and I see the wheels turning in her head.

"That motherfucker." She grabs her towel and water bottle, then begins quickly walking towards the house.

I follow her in, knowing I'm about to enjoy this a little too much. Once we make it through the doors, I take the lead to the back of the house. I open the gym door and hold it for her. It doesn't begin to compare to our one at home, but it has enough.

Silas is mid-workout, straddling a bench weight, pumping it up and down with sharp breaths and Amelia yells across the room at him.

"Are you fucking serious? Were you just going to keep letting me punch a goddamn tree while you used actual equipment?"

"Yep," he answers without pausing his motions.

Amelia's jaw flexes, and I swear I can see fumes rolling off her.

"You are such a prick!" she yells again, stalking toward him and kicking the bar to the floor. "Why do you have to make it so fucking hard for me to want to be around you?"

He steps over the bar and squares his shoulders in front of her.

"No bullshit. I told you I love you, but that does not mean I want you here."

"Give me one good reason?"

I can see the pain in my best friend's eyes as he speaks. I wonder if she can too. "Someone can't truly love you when they don't know the whole truth about who you are. I pray you never know."

"You need to grow up," she says angrily, tired of the push-and-pull from him.

She's staying. He's going to have to let her in eventually.

His eyes widen. "I need to grow up? That's rich coming from Ms. Titty Baby herself."

Ian and Lyle come in behind me.

"Hey, we just got back from the store. What's going on?" Ian asks.

"Smart-mouth here has her panties in a bunch," Silas answers.

Lyle shrugs and crosses his arms. "You know the rules. If there's an issue, box it out."

Amelia's head turns our way like we have lost our minds.

"We could all use the practice," I add, trying to take some of the tension out of the room.

"Get your gloves. You're so pissed at me, then you get to train with me." Silas looks to Mel, and she swallows hard.

Smart girl.

"Come at me with everything you got. Get all that anger out," he says.

Her forehead creases with worry, but she doesn't argue.

We watch her as we get into position. Amelia grunts, lunging for Silas, swinging her fist out wide. In one quick motion, he sweeps his arm over her head, grabbing the back of her neck and sweeping his leg under hers, sending her face first onto the mat.

She groans, rolling over, splaying her body on the mat.

Silas steps over her and reaches a hand out. "Try again."

She takes another approach, jabbing her arm out straight. Silas catches it, spinning her around and pinning her to his body.

"Again."

I begin sparring with Lyle, as Ian throws a few punches at the bag hanging from the ceiling. I glance over at her every few seconds, reading her body language.

She tries over and over, Silas always sending her to the floor or leveling a finger-gun to her face, and I worry I should step in, but I don't want her to think that I believe she isn't capable. She needs an escape for her anger.

She smacks the ground once more, falling straight on her back, knocking the breath out of her. Her hands swipe over her face frustratedly, as a tear falls.

I rush to her side and kneel beside her, rubbing a knuckle over her cheek to wipe her tears. "It's okay, baby. It takes time."

A firm familiar hand yanks me back.

"Tears fix nothing. Get up." Silas snarls, looking at me with disgust, then back to Amelia.

"Silas. Enough. You are being too rough with her!" I boom, standing and pushing him in the chest.

"No!" he yells, sending an echo through the room. "She needs to toughen the fuck up if she's going to be one of us. You think they are going to be gentle if they get their hands on her?" He yanks her up, her eyes red, her muscles shaking. He steps into her, "Fight me off!"

"Silas," Ian warns.

She whimpers, pushing at his chest, only for him to come right back.

"I said, fight me off!"

He mumbles hatred to her, trying to get her angry, but her half efforts show that his efforts are coming up short. His yelling is only causing her to shrink into herself.

"Enough!" Ian yells, unable to take any more.

Lyle steps up, rushing to stand between Silas and Mel's exhausted body. "You are hurting her more than helping at this point. Get a fucking grip and realize who's in front of you and who you sound like right now."

Ian is right on his heels, placing himself near Amelia for support without touching her but ready to lend his arm if she needs it.

Silas pants, his nostrils flaring, his fists balled at his sides. He knows we're right. He got carried away and lost in his head. His hands tangle in his hair, and he exhales, dropping to his knees in realization at what he was doing. Mirroring his own trauma the same way she was reacting to her own trauma.

"Mel, I'm... I'm sorry." He reaches out, brushing her leg, but she jerks away.

His head falls, and he stays kneeled before her, soaking in his guilt and frustration.

Her eyes harden, and a flame ignites within them.

Silas doesn't see her wipe the tears rolling down her pink cheeks, and he sure as hell doesn't see her foot she pulls up before smashing into his face.

He falls back onto his elbows, and she stalks towards him, pure anger on her beautiful features, and she looks like something out of my best nightmares.

"Do you know how fucking sick I am of people hurting me because of their own fucking issues and then telling me that they are *sorry*?"

His eyes nearly bug out of his head, "Mel, I-"

She draws her leg back, ready to kick him again, but he catches her heel before it can connect.

His eyes darken. "Darlin, if you kick me again, we are going to have issues."

She smiles sweetly, jerks her foot out of his hold, and lands a punch across his jaw, letting it roll off perfectly.

Lyle cheers and Silas snarls, rubbing his reddening face. "What?" Lyle shrugs. "That was a perfect and well-deserved punch."

I'd put money on the fact that Silas will get hard thinking about this later.

Deranged fucker.

"Feel better?" he grunts, standing to his feet.

Amelia flashes a huge grin and flips her tousled hair over her shoulder, smoothing it back off her sweaty face.

"I feel much better."

***

"Ian pushed back the gala we can spare another week," I tell Amelia to soothe her groaning.

She's made it clear that she still wants to go, but she isn't ready to leave the lake just yet. Anyone could understand why. Here, we can pretend all our problems are solved. The second we re-enter Acadia Creek, we are back within the borders that harbor the origin of all our pain.

"He doctored a report of a gas leak on the block and ordered an evacuation until given the all-clear, which he'll give when we were prepared to come back home."

"And his dad won't think something's up?" she asks.

"Sure there's a chance Jameson will smell a dead fish, but there's nothing he can do but wait for our game. He can pull a lot of strings, but we have better ones. Ones that are on Ian's payroll and have the same hatred for this town that we do."

"Could we live up here permanently?" Silas ogles at the water through the glass of the back door like a teenage girl fawning over Justin Bieber, and we all stare at him, shocked.

"What? I like it here."

Amelia laughs, and our gazes shift to her. She covers her mouth, and her laughter dies out, "I'm sorry. I just can't imagine you enjoying anything other than being a raging dick." She pats him on the shoulder, and he just looks at her like she has lost her fucking mind.

He grabs her hand and slams her palm down on the table, then steps into her, forcing her to look up at him. "I enjoy many other things as well. That smart mouth of yours might push me far enough that you'll experience them for yourself."

Her throat moves with her swallow, but she holds his stare, challenging him by leaning in further. "If you think you scare me, Silas Steele, think again."

Lyle moves in behind her, sweeping her long black hair over one shoulder. He pulls her head to the side and whispers into her exposed ear, his lips brushing the shell. "I don't think he was trying to scare you, love. He might be talking about pain, but it's the kind that is sweaty, erratic, and leaves you begging for more."

I can see the sweat start to glisten on her skin, and her fingers curl inward. Lyle licks up the side of her neck, and her eyes flutter closed. I tilt my head, looking under the bar, smiling at the reaction I knew she would have. She crosses her ankles and squeezes her thighs together like she does when she is too turned on to hide it.

Every girl likes a little choking and spanking, but because we have already driven down that road many times, I can only assume her mind is on something more devious.

"You wanna share those dirty thoughts, Mel?" I ask, propping my head on my hands.

Her eyes pop open, and she shoves Lyle away from where he gently bit her shoulder. "Nope. I want to go do something fun now that I can supposedly get away with anything I want."

Silas chuckles. "Almost anything, but why don't you push those boundaries and see how far you can get. I'll be sure to let you know when you find them."

She rolls her eyes, though I can see she already intends to do that.

"How about we go out for dinner and a movie?" Ian suggests, pressing a kiss to her cheek, and before she can respond, he is moving for the door.

She needs a distraction to postpone reality, so that's what we will do. Though not the way she is expecting. She is about to experience just how much we have been dying for the correct piece of our puzzle to fall into place.

***

We take our seats at a restaurant in the next city, our girl wearing a dress that is turning heads left and right, courtesy of Ian's shopping habit. He had it delivered and left it on her bed for her to find after her shower. Her thrilling remarks came bounding through the house the second she entered her room, and at that moment, none of us had ever been happier.

The material splits high on her leg, giving a great tease as she crosses her legs. The top wraps around her neck, much like I want to do with my hand, with a cut out between her breasts. She winks at me, catching me staring at the small bit of her ass showing.

"See something you want to eat?" she teases, looking back to her menu.

I pull her chair closer, the wood screeching across the marble floors, echoing through-out the expensive structure. She giggles as heads turn our way, a few of them watching in disbelief as I slip my hand through the slip of her dress to rest between her thighs. Her eyes dart around low, but she does her best to keep her composure.

"I do, indeed. Don't draw attention now, love."

I continue looking over my menu brushing the tips of my fingers along her lace panties, imagining what color she might have paired with her midnight blue dress. I feel Ian's stare as I ponder my choices.

My phone buzzes on my thigh, and I glance down to find a picture sent from Lyle into our group chat. I open it, seeing an opposite view of what I'm doing to her. I look up just as Silas nearly chokes on his water, and Lyle grins.

"Do you need help finding your meal, brother?" he asks. "Don't leave us waiting too long, or I'll handle it for you."

I push her top leg down, pull the thin material to the side, push my fingers into her, and move them in long slow strokes. Her right hand grips the tablecloth, as her left grips my wrist.

"Now, now. Play fair," Silas says, keeping his eyes down.

His phone is lying to the right of his menu, and from here, I see Lyle is now live in the group chat, Amelia's spread legs visible for each of us. I continue to play with her as I take her phone and add her to the chat. It's only fair that she gets to watch too.

I set her phone down in front of her, and my dirty girl loves the sight. Her mouth falls slack.

Using my thumb, I stroke small circles on her clit. A small moan slips just as the waitress approaches us. We all cover our phones, and she takes our orders. Each of the guys takes their time, enjoying watching Mel squirm as she desperately tries to not give anything away. The waitress looks around at us curiously as Mel cracks, slapping her hand on the table.

"Oh, God, hurry up."

Ian snorts a laugh. "Excuse her. She's just very excited to see if the reputation proceeds. Go on, baby. Tell her what you want."

Mel's eyes nearly bug out of her head, and she tightens around my fingers, begging for mercy.

"P-pasta is fine," she chokes out.

The waitress leaves with a nod, and I guarantee the poor woman is thinking she doesn't get paid enough. We uncover our phones and resume our dining entertainment. She spreads her legs further, watching her own motions on the screen.

"You know, all I can think about is you sitting on my face, drowning me in your sweet cum," Lyle says, and she whimpers.

"More," she begs in a whisper.

"You don't get to ask for shit when you thought about leaving us just yesterday. Very naughty of you," Silas says, and although her face reveals nothing, her pussy can't lie. Realizing I felt her reaction, her head slowly turns to me, as if she hasn't already admitted her feelings.

"Who do you belong to?" Ian asks, propping his

hands on the table, wanting to address that topic a little more.

She smiles wild, pure enjoyment.

"All of you."

"Good girl." Lyle praises, and she cums all over my fingers. I pull them from her and lift them above the table. She does nothing to stop me, as I bring them to my mouth, sucking the taste of her clean off. She chases her breath as she watches my fingers leave my lips.

"So fucking good."

She always tastes so sweet, and I wonder if she tastes the same to all of us or if our pallets make it unique to each of us.

We barely make it through dinner, the small talk nearly killing us after we each had stared at her dripping pussy. The innuendos and flirting never end as we talk about the movie we were going to see, how excited we would be if Amelia decided to hunt Lance down, and all the fun we are going to cause at the gala.

This time, Amelia had no shame in the way she felt. It was almost complete pleasure she took telling us she hoped Lance would show his face again. For all we know, the criminal that was making a move on the Mason name was going to go right for the Davis cooperation, attending the gala to corner Jameson when he will have his guard down, just as we had originally planned.

How perfect would it be to get to wreak havoc on them both at the same time?

As we climb back into Silas's truck, he stops her, grabbing her wrist and pinning her against the door.

"Take your panties off." His tall frame shadows her in the low light, and she looks up, tilting her head all the way back to meet his intense gaze full of lust.

She doesn't shrink or question him, just reaches her hand through the slit of her dress and begins to push the white fabric off of her hips. They stare at each other with deep focus as the soaked garment falls to the concrete.

He bends to pick them up and then proceeds to shove them in the pocket of his slacks. Then resumes the hold on her wrist and pulls her with him into the front seat, placing her in his lap. "You're going to drive."

Her face pales.

"I- no... I haven't," she stammers. "This truck is huge and-"

"And you'll be fine. It's time you kick that bitch's words from your head." Ian says, soothing her from the passenger seat. "If you want to hunt down the son of a bitch that caused that wreck, we will, but you have to do this."

She stares at him for a moment, seeing the fight in his eyes that wills to enter her. Swallowing hard, she adjusts in the seat using Silas's legs to boost her enough to see. He starts the ignition, and the truck roars to life under us.

"Do you need some incentive?" Lyle asks, leaning up from the back next to me. She turns her head toward him, and he pins her against Silas's chest with a hold on her throat. He bites her neck, sucking it hard, his own hair brushing Silas's face.

Silas only looks to the vehicle's roof, and I struggle to stifle the laugh rumbling in my throat. She really does something to him.

Amelia groans as Lyle palms her breasts, showing each of them attention before quickly shoving his hand between her legs, grabbing her pussy.

"Easy," Silas growls, "my balls are down there too."

"What if I want to fondle you too?" Lyle kisses Silas on the cheek, and he hisses. "Now, pretty girl, you own this shit, so we can move on too much more fun lessons."

She smiles sweetly, and I know the thoughts in her head are far from matching the innocence on her angelic face.

"So what was the purpose of your pocket containing my panties?" She places her hands on the steering wheel, and Silas places his on her hips.

"So that when you are praised for completing what you were told to do, I can feel you soak me."

Silas would have no shame walking into the movie theater with this woman's cum clearly visible on his pants.

None of us would.

He fastens the seat belt around them, forcing their bodies tighter than before. The truck is shifted into drive, and Amelia's knuckles turn white as she pulls out of the parking lot and back onto the highway.

We lurch forward as she presses the gas to merge, and she gasps, her hands shaking. Lyle moves to reach for her, and I bar him across the chest with my arm, mouthing for him to wait.

Silas's hands run down her legs. "It's okay. Get a feel for her and take it slow." His hands move back up, her dress opening for him. "Be bigger than your fears."

Her grip loosens and I don't miss the way her legs open a little further for him.

"There you go, baby." He encourages her, the five of us reaping the benefits of her increasing performance as she moves through traffic beautifully, her confidence unfolding.

The truck glides between vehicles as she switches lanes, and despite the sweat beading on her forehead, her face tells me this wasn't nearly as difficult for her as she had convinced herself it would be.

As she follows Silas's next directions, I nod toward my twin, giving him the go-ahead to do whatever it is he does for her.

"It seems you need a more difficult challenge." Lyle says, and she smirks into the rearview mirror as an answer, so he continues. "Ian, do you know how it feels to have her on your tongue?"

Needing no further encouragement, Ian leans over the console and bunches the front of her dress before diving between her thighs, his hands braced on Silas's left thigh.

"Shit," Silas mumbles as he watches, fully trusting Amelia's eyes that seem to grow heavier with each moment she fights the urge to revel in the bliss firing through her nervous system.

She whimpers as Ian plays with her, his own sounds of pleasure mixing with hers. She's given instructions to take the exit, and Silas pulls her left thigh up, giving Ian more room to work.

"Ah!" she moans, and my dick pulses with the need.

"Do not cum." I tell her, not wanting to say the next words that come to mind, but she says them for me.

"Or I might kill us all?" she laughs, surprising us all, "Easy for you to say when you don't have a very skilled tongue begging you to do the opposite."

She completes the transition with shaky hands and ragged breaths, Ian relentless truly testing her mind's strength.

We pull into the parking lot, and she backs between two small cars, now just showing off. Silas reaches between her legs, spreading her open completely as she shifts into park. Her head falls back onto his shoulder, preparing to give herself what she wants, but Ian sits up, wiping his mouth with a smile before she can reach it.

She reaches down between her own legs, groaning in frustration, and Lyle stops her. He slips his arms around her and pulls her into the back. He opens the door, slides out, and throws her over his shoulder as she giggles.

We follow Lyle's slow run, Amelia's head bobbing and her hands patting his ass like bongo drums. He smacks her ass firmly as we pass through the front doors, and her yelp draws curious eyes from stragglers as we rush into our movie. We weave through the lightly lit room that holds rows of leather seats, each with its own reclining feature, almost all of them empty. Annoyed chatter sounds off lowly as we noisily find an empty row in the back and take our seats, passing Amelia back and forth between us, the next in line cussing as the previous tosses her body.

She lands in my lap one final time, turning to get comfortable, her feet in Silas's lap and Ian at her head.

"Guys, this movie is like halfway through," she whines, finally looking at the huge screen. A woman with short blonde hair turns around from the row in front of us, daggers for eyes as she cuts the lot of us. "Yeah, so how about you shut up so we can finish it in peace."

Amelia dramatically gasps, and then her face neutralizes. "My boyfriends will come down there and pummel your ass."

How to lose a guy in 10 days. Cute.

Boyfriends. She called us her boyfriends, and I feel like a thirteen-year-old girl that just got her first kiss.

Karen rolls her eyes after a long minute of us all staring at her, eventually getting the fucking hint that we will hit a woman when necessary.

"Bitch," Amelia mumbles, though I'm sure it was her intent to say it loud enough that Karen would hear it. The woman stands and abandons her seat for a new one.

"Now, we didn't come to watch the movie," Lyle says, pulling her into his lap. "We came to have some fun." He slowly pulls his buckle open, careful to minimize the jingling of the metal, watching for any indication she's not ready. She reaches between them, stroking him through his jeans in answer.

Under cover of darkness, Lyle pulls himself out of his pants and guides Mel down onto him, the smallest of whimpers the only sign of the act.

"Shh," Lyle whispers, "You are not going to move. You are going to listen and keep that perfect mouth fucking shut. Got it?"

She nods, and I watch as Lyle begins to move her hips back and forth in tiny motions, going unnoticed to those around us, though it's Ian who struggles to breathe sitting between us. He leans closer to her, his lips nearly pressed against her ear, and her head falls back as his whispered words hit their mark.

I nearly shit my pants as Ian kneels in front of them, checking around us for anyone that might have a clear view. Ian's tongue falls from his mouth only a second before his face disappears between their legs. Lyle pins her arms behind her as he continues to slowly fuck her with Ian's mouth only two inches from where they meet. She looks down, moaning at the sight, and Ian comes up, kissing her inner thigh.

"Stay quiet, baby. We'd rather not spill blood tonight," Ian warns.

Ian picks her feet up and sets them on the outside of Lyle's legs, instructing her to use them as leverage to lift up. Still baffled and thoroughly intrigued by his statement, she nearly loses her mind when Ian wraps his hand around Lyle's dick, pulling it from her, rubbing the glistening head back and forth from her clit to her opening.

Her hips rock, and Lyle sinks his teeth into her shoulder, both in enjoyment and warning. I hear Silas's heavy breathing behind me, leaving none of us watching the movie. Amelia's lips fold inward in an attempt to keep herself silent.

Ian allows my brother to re-enter her, though only halfway. He begins to swirl his hand around, matching the up and down motion Lyle creates with her body. His lips plant wet open kisses along every inch of exposed skin he can reach, Ian taking care of the ones he can't.

"You like that, don't you, baby?" Lyle whispers as her sight flicks between what is happening between her legs and the couple on the screen beginning to frantically tear their clothes off. I palm my dick through my pants, wanting to do the same thing so bad that my skin burns.

She hums in pleasure in response, and Ian's other hand finds her clit, rubbing firmly. Her climax builds; the little pinch of her eyebrows a clear sign. Ian's head tilts back, watching her every emotion as he works the both of them, the top of his fist pressed against her, giving her that extra contact.

Lyle grunts under his breath as Ian takes the top two fingers of his circled hand and glides them upwards along Lyle's dick, entering next to him and stretching her wider.

She cries out, and Lyle's hand clamps around her mouth, her own still pinned between their bodies. They don't pause; all of us now so transfixed on seeing this through that we would rather see our girl come than hesitate to see if anyone heard her. I can't say that putting someone in the hospital wouldn't add to the enjoyment of tonight.

Ian's face dips low again, his tongue replacing the fingers on her clit that now move to her left perky nipple pressing through the fabric of her dress. His head moves up and down, and although I don't have a perfect view, my mind can almost see his tongue nearing her filled hole. The fact of it being Lyle's dick is almost completely overridden by the sight of Amelia unraveling. Something I never see myself tiring of watching.

Amelia's body falls back into the one behind her, and her thighs clamp shut around Ian's head as she finally comes hard, her muffled cries only heard by us, her chest heaving from the adrenaline of being in public.

It would seem that more than two of us have a kink for putting on a show.

Amelia

We left the movie we didn't pay for and didn't watch, Silas driving us back to the lake house as Finn tried to undress me in the back seat.

Ian and Lyle were more than ready for another round, but Silas had slipped back into his usual bad mood and nipped that shit at the bud. A good time with him is always short-lived, though now that I have made it clear I'm not going anywhere, I guess I'm just going to have to label him as *my* brute and learn to love it. Loving the rose and its thorns, just as he has seemed to do for me.

Irritating him may just become my new favorite hobby.

Finn passes the blunt and slaps my leg playfully, clearly enjoying his high from the shit-eating grin on his face. "I am so fucking excited to see you walk right up to Jameson and shit on his perfectly shined shoes."

"I'm not sure shitting on his shoes is not something anyone wants to see, babe," I retort curling my legs under me.

"I would pay to see it," Lyle says with a shrug causing me to scrunch up my nose.

Both twins cackle, and as Silas comes to join us on the couch, he smacks them both upside the back of the head, only causing them to laugh harder.

"Nasty fucks." He sinks down next to me on the couch, and to my surprise, he casts an arm over the couch behind me. "However, I would like to know why you want to go so bad."

Silas looks at me curiously, but for the first time, I see a glimmer of something deeper in his expression. He looks at me like this is just another normal conversation between two people that have known each other their whole lives. Instead of dropping my gaze like my nerves tell me to, I hold it.

"Honestly, I just want to irritate him because he doesn't like me, and he doesn't deserve an easy life after the way he has treated Ian."

Ian smiles sweetly, having no qualms with my newly established mission to keep me occupied.

"So it has nothing to do with the fact that you want to dress up in a beautiful gown and feel like Princess Belle for a night?" Silas asks.

My heart stalls, and my head whips back to him.

Princess Belle.

She was always my favorite, and most people don't reference her first when talking about princesses.

His jaw twitches. "What? Cinderella is blonde."

"And who leaves behind a perfectly made heel?" I smirk as I carefully read his facial response, only being met with a mirrored half-smile. I take the blunt as it makes its way back to me. "I want to dress up, get drunk, break some shit, have the time of my life with my boys, and show Jameson just how much I *love* being the filthy trash he thinks I am." I take another hit and look off in an unfocused daze.

"I am so fucking done with people being able to hurt me and the people I care about." I look directly at Lyle. "If I'm an angel, I am the angel that will set the world on fucking fire, burning those who deserve it."

Lyle grins something out of the darkest nightmares. He stands, pulling me off the couch and up into his arms. I wrap my legs around him, laughing letting my head hang back as he swings us around in a circle, his own head buried in my neck.

He throws us onto the couch in a stagger and hovers above me.

"Tell me more!" he begs, and I oblige.

"I will not cower."

"More!" he teases, moaning exaggeratedly,

"I will fight, and God have mercy on those who do us wrong."

"Oh fuck!" he yells in a girly tone, throwing his head back and grinding into me, and I laugh uncontrollably.

He comes down to my stomach, raises my shirt, and kisses around all of my bare wounds. "No mercy. May they burn in hell."

Finn raises his fist in the air in agreement and then shoves Lyle onto the ground. "Beautiful speech. Now gimme. It's time to actually watch a movie, and I call her."

I raise a brow and peel his hands off of me. "You can both fuck off. My vagina needs a break."

Ian howls in laughter, and Silas cracks a smile. Ian pulls a lever on the side of the long couch, and another two rows come out, making a platform the size of a California king bed. I grab a pillow and stretch out on my stomach, scooting all the way up to the edge closest to the screen.

Lyle lies to my left and Finn on my right. Ian and Silas climb up and find their spots somewhere behind me.

"So what are we feeling? Horror, action, or comedy?" Ian asks, and I laugh, turning around to face him.

"Our whole lives have been a horror and action film. Let's go for comedy."

Silas laughs and throws a blanket to me. "Agreed."

"Thank you. It's freezing balls in here."

He gives me a nod and sits back, but I don't miss him scooting over just a few inches so he is touching my leg.

"Actually, the expression is '*hot as balls*.' Wanna feel to check my fact?" Lyle rolls to his side and wags his eyebrows at me.

I bite my lip and lower my hand between his thighs, gently feeling him through the outside of his pants. Then I squeeze tight, and he jerks upright with a high-pitched yelp. I squeeze harder, and he cries out, "Okay, okay! You win!"

Giving him a wink I release him, readjusting back into my place.

"Mean little thing," he teases, and I stick my tongue out at him as he stands and leaves to get snacks from the kitchen.

Ian chooses *Step Brothers* to watch, and Lyle returns with an assortment of candy, while the microwave still hums. The smell of popcorn fills the room, and my stomach growls. Finn holds out a few options of candy, and I take the Sour Patch Kids.

Lyle huffs. "Sweet *and* sour. Fitting, I think."

I look down at the –Whoppers he chose.

"Little balls. I could say the same."

His jaw drops open, and Finn snorts a loud laugh, turning his head away from me spewing drops of his drink onto Silas. Ian bursts into laughter and high-fives me. Silas slowly wipes his face, still chewing his Mike and Ikes, and laughs nervously, holding his palms in the air.

"Their fault, man." Silas looks at me, and we stare off for a solid ten seconds before I smile and shrug, "He wanted to play dirty. I can do that too."

The side of his lips tip upwards, and his eyes narrow. "Oh, can you?"

Before I can answer, he stops chewing and spits his wet, sticky candy on me. Luckily it missed my hair, but the few pieces that didn't land on my clothes stick to my face and arms.

"Ugh! Fuck's sake, Silas. That's disgusting."

He turns his focus back to the screen, leaving me to clean myself off.

Dick.

"Could have spit it in your mouth."

I pause, and the image flashes through my head. I see Silas pulling my head back, squeezing my mouth open, and bringing his mouth to mine to spit in it. I pick off the last piece of gummy candy from my skin and flick it at him, rolling to my stomach. Both twins staring at me with amusement as if they can read my thoughts.

I clear my throat as the microwave beeps and try to focus on the movie. Ian taps Lyle on the leg, letting him know that he's got it. He comes back with two large bowls filled with buttery goodness, passing one to me and keeping the other.

The next hour passes with laughter, us quoting the movie, and Silas telling us to shut up. I uncurl my legs from their current position and stretch them out between the boys. I feel a hand grab my foot from under the blanket and begin massaging it, pressing their thumbs into the skin and dragging them down. Fingertips tap a pattern on the top of my foot, and I smile to myself.

Ian.

Another hand moves up my thigh and wedges between my legs. The slight coldness of their touch makes me shutter and gives me tingles that start at the back of my neck and settle very close to where their hand now lays, no longer needing a break. I turn to each of the brothers finding they are no longer at my side. I try to turn further to find them, and a hand smacks my ass.

"Lay the fuck down, Amelia," Finn growls, and I plant my face in my pillow with a small laugh.

Soon, another hand brushes up the back of my opposite thigh, and I hold my breath, not taking my eyes off the screen. Another hand touches my lower back, and then another touches my hip.

Oh, shit.

I do the math in my head, trying to recognize left and right hands. Shoulders and arms adjust, rustling all the blankets, not letting me sense who is moving to figure out whose hand is where.

"Guys-"

"Shut up, Amelia," Ian says. "We're watching a movie."

Shocked but obedient, I lay there. My brain seems to be misfiring as it really sinks in that there are enough hands on me for each of them to be touching me now.

Their hands continue to move and shift, squeezing and caressing the skin from right above my knee all the way to the skin under the hem of the shorts I changed into.

I suck in a breath as someone's fingers trail up further and dip under my panties. Another hand rises higher, and I part my thighs just a little, allowing them more access. They slowly rub my pussy through my shorts, amplifying my heart rate and the wetness waiting for them. I stay as still and quiet as possible, trying to conceal just how much I want more.

The hand inside my panties runs a finger through my lips, coating their finger before pressing into me slowly. None of them give a hint as to who, and I'm unable to stop the gasp before it leaves me. The finger leaves me for a second before it is quickly replaced with two. His fingers move quicker, hitting that perfect spot. My head drops, and my hands grasp my pillow, squeezing it with everything I have.

Smack. A hand slaps across my ass, and I jump.

"Pay attention, Amelia," a voice growls, and it sounds like Lyle.

"Believe me, I am." I laugh out breathlessly.

Two hands grab my shorts and pull them down my legs and off. I feel movement behind me, but I can see nothing from my peripherals. Hands roughly rub up the back of my legs and up to my ass, squeezing firmly, making me groan in pleasure as it mixes with the ecstasy of the fingers still inside me. I try to turn over, but a strong hand pushes me back down.

"Don't even fucking try." a low voice rumbles, and my eyes go wide.

Silas.

I feel a body hover above me as whoever is still inside me continues a slow sensual movement, and I can see dark hair near my face.

"You are going to stay still and cum for us like a good little girl. The only movements or sounds coming from you are going to be ones of satisfaction. Do we make ourselves clear, Amelia?"

Ourselves.

I don't know where this is going but my stomach flutters at any possibility. I should protest for many reasons, but I don't. Not with them. I stop my effort and relax into their mercy. The body disappears behind me again, and my ass cheeks are spread open. The cold air hits my sensitive skin, and anxiety floods in as the blanket is pulled off me, baring me to four men at once.

Oh, Hell.

The hands that are just under my ass tighten, telling me to relax. I take a deep breath and exhale it slowly, letting my inhibitions leave with it.

"There you go, baby. You are doing so fucking good."

It's not like I haven't done ass play before, but for one, it hurts every time, and two, having four guys all back there at the same time is not something I am well acquainted with.

What if I didn't shave well enough? *Fuck*, I'm still living for it.

Kisses and nips meet my ass before a warm breath touches the hole. I feel a face line up, and then a tongue strokes me from the fingers inside me all the way to the top of my crack, then back down to the hole. He flattens his tongue and moves it back and forth ever so slowly. The fingers inside me fall in sync, and it is absolutely earth-shaking.

Another hand finds my clit, and together, the trio makes a symphony of my body, playing all the right cords and making me cry out in bliss. My muscles tighten around the fingers inside me, and my arousal drips to my clit, giving more lubrication for the fingers rubbing it.

"Faster. Please, faster," I beg.

After so much foreplay, something switches in my head, and I just want anything and everything - rougher, harder, faster. The pressure in my stomach builds higher, and my legs shake. I want so badly to curl them under me to give any kind of sense of stability because I feel like my head is going to explode.

A finger runs down the cum trailing down my legs then presses against my asshole. Someone rubs up my back, soothing me.

"Take a breath, Angel, and relax for us."

Then the finger presses into me.

Holy fuck. I was mistaken. *This* feels like my head is going to explode.

"God, yes. Right there." I say.

I feel my orgasm coming to a peak as everyone's fingers work together. Not being able to see them makes it all the more arousing. My heart races, and I'm damn near out of breath. It builds and builds and builds, none of them changing what they are doing as I moan and beg. I feel it near, and I attempt to pull my thighs together, but more than one of them holds my legs open. I come, screaming as everything in my body ignites.

"Oh, Yes!"

My body shakes with the aftershock, and my head falls into the pillow as I try to slow my burning lungs. My ears focus on the sounds around me, as the credits roll on the movie. I sit up, pulling a blanket over my waist and turning around. All four of them are now leaning against the back of the couch smiling, none giving anything away.

"What a great movie," Lyle says.

"Classic," Ian agrees.

"One that you could never get tired of watching if you ask me," Silas continues.

Finn lays his arms around the back of the couch. "Absofucking-lutely".

I suck my teeth and smile at them, then climb off the couch, dropping the blanket not bothering to reach for my shorts.

I stand, propping my hand on my hip, and tap my chin. "You know... it really was. If only I knew who to *properly* thank for my favorite parts."

Smiling to myself, I walk to my room my soul singing with happiness and something that feels like *home*.

Amelia

The weight of my bed tips and the air from my standing fan is blocked, partially bringing me from my deep sleep. Reality mixes with my dream as the warmth crowds around my body. A blanket of safety engulfs me, and the feeling is a place I never want to leave.

"Are you awake?" A husky voice asks.

"No," I mumble, unwilling to wake just to risk being irritated by whatever is bound to come out of Silas Steele's mouth.

He tugs the blanket back, and I groan irritated at the cold intrusion. "Come on, sit up, I want to show you something."

As I sit up, I can feel my frizzy and tousled hair falling in various ways of chaos. My tank top has ridden up and slid sideways, my breast nearly falling out of the side. Why I think sleeping in one will ever result in anything other than my own strangulation, I don't know.

Silas eyes me amusingly as I readjust, putting everything back in its rightful place. I pull my boy-short panties out of my ass crack before settling back in my warm spot, wrapping the blanket around my waist, then rubbing my eyes. "If the thing you woke me up to show me is your penis, I will cut it off."

"As charming as always," he smirks, turning his phone screen on and causing me to squint at the unwelcomed light. "Don't worry that pretty pink pussy. When I plan on showing you my dick, you will be begging for it along with my mercy."

I can't say that doesn't make my pussy throb. I bet his angry sex is unmatched.

In a flash, the side of his lips tilt, and in another, it's gone. As if his words weren't enough to add to the dream I was very much enjoying, every time he looks at me like that, I have the intense urge to sit on his face.

"I want to show you part of myself. A part that will show you the life you are so eager to join."

I raise a brow, but he beats me to my next thought before I can form the words. "The middle of the night is the only time I would be able to have a moment alone with you."

He wanted privacy. To lay himself bare without an audience. The least I can do is hear him out after he has fought so hard to keep me away. Knowing what he is so scared of might just help me to see past his walls.

"Carsyn is not the root of my fears with you being here. You are far different from her where it matters most. It's me that I fear you are more like." He scrolls through his phone, settling on a hidden album and turning it towards me. Flipping through multiple pictures of a body littered with bloody scrapes and bruises, he continues to talk. "This is me over the span of a decade."

I want to look away, but I can't. This is proof of his scars, and looking away would only serve to prove that I can't handle seeing it. That his history is too unbearable to witness, and no one deserves to feel like that.

You can't change what has happened to you, only where you choose to go from there.

He flips through over two dozen pictures that were likely taken by one of the twins. One's of him unconscious in various settings, others of him awake after being stitched back up but looking like he would rather be dead. His eyes are void of everything but misery. I recognize everything they say. He wanted this new life he had at his fingertips, but the guilt of bringing his pain to them was worse than enduring it first hand.

"It took me a long time to come to terms with the fact that I couldn't feel guilty for the pain someone inflicted and the pain others chose to help me carry. However, pain is a sign that things are changing, and we did. Though, the guilt that resulted from that change didn't last nearly as long."

He continues to scroll, the faces and bodies now belonging to others.

"These are pictures I keep to remind me what I have done and why. Each of them belongs to someone who has harmed one of us in one way or another. Some of them are dead, some of them only harmed and their lives destroyed, but all of them are our victims."

Things I already know are made more real. I see each body, the words written over the pictures of what was done.

"If you stay here with us, you will lose parts of yourself. Parts I can already see slipping away." He drops his phone to the plush comforter and takes my face in his hands. "You are perfect the way you are, Amelia. You will find traditional love with your soul unblackened . by our sins. You don't need us to survive."

"Do you regret your life?" I ask, trying to read everything he hasn't said.

He pauses.

His head sags, and upon instinct, I reach out to caress his cheek.

"Part of me wishes that I would have made different choices along the way, but no, I don't regret my life as a whole. I love the family I have created. Given who my parents are, if I didn't take this path, using my anger to lash out in the right ways, I may have only ended up dead or not knowing my own name by now."

"Then what is so wrong with me choosing the same path?"

He leans in, kissing my lips softly and stealing my breath as he retreats. "Is it so wrong for me to wish that you seek out better than we have found?"

I return a kiss to his lips just as sweetly. "Nothing you have shown me has scared me. This life is more than I could ever have dreamed for myself. So, If I told you that this is the life that would make me the happiest, would you accept me for the monster I want to be?"

"I will accept you in any form in any life. I may not be overly enthused that you continue to disobey my wishes, but a life with you in any shape is a life more than I could ever deserve."

"So, if you are done trying with your efforts to scare me away, can I go back to sleep now?"

He nods, his emotions seeming to be torn between two polar opposites as he climbs off of my bed. I watch as he nears the door, a light feeling forming in my stomach as the dynamic shifts between us.

"You can stay if you want," I say, part of me fearing the rejection that I half expect to come.

He turns in the doorway, surprising me as he makes his return. I watch every ripple of his muscles as he pulls his shirt over the back of his head. Then he climbs behind me and pulls me down onto the bed with him. His large form wraps around me, and that same feeling of familiar warmth consumes me whole. My heart's beating matches the pace of his I feel on my back.

"I'm not a nice person, little monster, but what I will always be, is yours."

Amelia's senior year...

I sink back in my truck seat, watching the students pour out of the high school, laughing and excited for the parties happening later tonight. It's homecoming weekend, and everyone is going down to Tipsy Turntop Lake. The tradition is well known, but the cops don't bother to break it up unless they get a call about it getting out of hand. Around here, minors drinking at the lake is not something they concern themselves with. Call it the fault of underpaid officers or overpaid white collars pulling strings so their kids don't tarnish their precious name.

Usually, she would have cheer practice before the game, but she quit the team a few weeks ago after falling behind, which everyone understood. I wish she wouldn't have. I prayed that it would help take her mind off all the bullshit. She genuinely enjoys the sport, but it seems that, like me, she likes to dwell on her pain.

Her long black hair flows behind her as she walks to her car with her head hung. She's been struggling for months with her dad gone. Since then, I have made time to see her at least two or three times a week. I usually watch her from the parking lot but prefer to catch her when she's home. Liking that I am the only one who gets to see her for who she really is.

No makeup to cover the dark circles under her eyes from lack of sleep, no smile plastered on so no one will ask if she is okay, no perfectly put-together outfit so she fits in. She doesn't hide her tears and frustrations. I get to see her pour her heart out in her journal while her head bobs to her favorite songs. I get to see her in her stained and baggy clothes, curled up on her bed with a book. I get to see her chest rise and fall steadily when she gets herself high enough to sleep uninterrupted.

Lance comes jogging up next to her, and I watch his lips move as he talks to her, trying to decipher what he is saying. She picks her head up, listening to him, but continues walking towards the exit of the parking lot. I crack my window and strain my ears, listening as they walk closer to my truck.

She shakes her head and Lance grabs her arm and jerks her around to face him. I lean closer to my window, their only a few feet from where I'm parked.

"Let go, Lance. I just want to go home," she begs, pulling her arm out of his grip.

"Let me take you home then," he says, taking her bag off her shoulder and grabbing her hands in his own.

She drops her head back and sighs. "Just go hang out with your friends before the game. I'll see you later."

He drops her hands and tosses her bag on the ground, the contents spilling onto the ground. "You are such a fucking bore. I don't know why I stay with you when so many other girls beg me for a good time."

My fists tighten on my steering wheel, and my knuckles turn white as I watch him leave her standing there tears falling from her eyes. She looks around nervously to see if anyone had seen or heard him. She takes a small breath of ease once she notices the parking lot is empty now.

But I'm here. I heard. I saw.

She slips her earbuds into her ears and begins her walk home. She could ask JJ, or someone else, for a ride home, but it would only lessen the time until she faces the second battle at home. Her mom started to take her pain out on Amelia recently, and I've had to slowly watch the girl I love decay from the inside out. Had to watch her spirit die and her soul cry out in agony.

I follow behind her, leaving enough distance that it doesn't look like I'm a creep trying to abduct her but stay close enough that I can see her around each block.

She doesn't notice me.

She never does, and that in itself is enough to make my blood boil.

I could be anyone with any motive, and she would never see me coming. She would be so wound up in her pain I bet she wouldn't even fight. Maybe that's what I love about her. She's not like me. Her pain didn't strip her of everything that made her human. She feels her pain so deeply, reminding her that she is alive. Maybe that's the worst part.

Empty or not, you would rather die than spend another minute in a world that feels broken.

Hours pass, and the sun starts sinking below the horizon as she slugs up the driveway and in through the front door. I park two blocks down, shut off my truck, and stick to the shadows as I sneak to the side of her house. I scale up, careful not to make myself known, and sit in my usual spot to the side of her window. I relax into the wall of the house and wait.

Minutes turn into an hour and a half, and I nearly doze off, but I jerk awake, hearing yelling coming from downstairs. I check her window and find it locked.

Fuck.

Well, at least she's not a complete idiot, but I don't like that it keeps me out. The argument gets louder as I assume she ascends the stairs.

"Just stop! You're drunk!" Amelia cries out, her voice sounding pained and tired.

"Sometimes I wish it was you. You know that? You just had to sneak out and get yourself into shit you couldn't handle! Stupid little bitch!"

My jaw tightens, and I flinch as I hear a hand crack across skin. My chest caves and bile rises to my throat.

Stop it. Stop it.

My head spins, but I shake it off, drawn-out seconds tick by as I wait for her to escape into her room.

"Failure, slut, embarrassment, murderer. I got it."

Her door opens and then clicks shut as if she used great effort to do it quietly in order to avoid any backlash from slamming it. I peer in, seeing her back to me as she rummages through the drawer of her nightstand. She pulls out an unlabeled orange bottle and gives it a little shake. No sound comes from it. Her shoulders slump, and her fist tightens around the empty pill bottle.

"Motherfucker," she groans, careful to keep her tone from rising too high. She throws the bottle across the room and it hits her makeup vanity crashing into a small perfume bottle, sending it plummeting to the ground. She startles at the commotion and then sinks to her knees. Her sobs start softly, barely a whimper leaving her lips, before she clamps a hand over her mouth as they turn more violent. Muffled screams leave her throat, and she hyperventilates, her other hand clutching her chest with each struggling breath.

I'm here, baby. Breathe. Just breathe.

I silently beg as I watch her, and my hands twitch with the urge to comfort her - to fight her demons for her.

Her head tilts up to the ceiling, and she wraps her arms around herself, trying to use the pressure to calm herself. She inhales deeply through her nose, holds it, then exhales slowly through her mouth. Repeating this a few times, her breathing slows, and her tears dry.

There you go, baby.

She climbs to her feet, her knees wobbling, and walks to her desk where she had set her bag. She pulls out a binder and flops down on her bed. I sink back further into the dark now that she is facing me. Scooting away from the window, I pull my phone out, and turn the brightness down. I click the side and see missed messages.

Finn:

Hey man, Carsyn has been asking about you

I roll my eyes. Why the fuck can't she take a hint. Blonde and perky is not my thing, but after seeing Lance fuck Amelia in the back of his truck last weekend, I needed to take my anger out on something, and my literal punching bag wasn't cutting it.

I don't respond to his text. Her drama is the least of my worries right now. The only girl I will ever truly want is just out of arm's reach.

Ian:
You good?

I haven't been home much recently other than to sleep and eat. Even though the other two leave me alone, Ian's observative ass won't. None of them know about this part of my life, and even though I know they wouldn't judge me for caring about her, there are things I don't want them digging into.

Silas:
Yep. Just needed to take care of some stuff. Be home late

Not a complete lie. I most certainly am not good for so many reasons, but this is as close as I'll ever be able to get.

Ian sends back a GIF of a girl blowing kisses, followed by a wink, and my chest shakes.

I hear something hitting the ground, and I slowly inch closer to the window again. Stopping as the latches on her window click.

She slides it open, and the sweet smell of her spilled perfume invades my nose. My nerves tingle, and my head spins as I savor it, saving it to my memory. I stay deathly still in the dark, listening to her sniff and sigh. I have watched her do this so many times I can picture her in my head. Her arms are braced on the windowsill, her head slightly tilted up as she searches for a certain cluster of lights above her.

In my head, this is our time. A moment that some nights we share, me only inches from her as her heart wishes on something that I gave her. A gift from a stranger that only wants to ease her pain, even if their love would never be felt from more than words on a half sheet of paper. I hear her soft voice whisper, and the hair on my arms stands up.

"You can come now."

Her tone doesn't show any of the pain I saw just a while ago like she has hidden it all just to talk to the person who promised to save her one day. She doesn't fake happiness or hide that she is unhappy with her life now, but she would not appear to be in misery.

When she speaks to him *at night, she has hope for a love that would be everything she has dreamed of. A love she only writes about. One that would be so perfect it would consume her in all the best ways. A love where two people only made each other better, stronger, and softer at the same time.*

I sit there, listening as she tells the stars about all the pain she wishes she could escape and everything she wishes she could change about herself.

My head falls back against the brick, and my eyes burn. Her voice muffles as my thoughts race with everything I wish I could say to her. Eventually I realize she has stopped talking and take the risk of being seen. I lean over, using my right hand for support to keep me from slipping, finding her head laid ever so softly on her crossed arms and her eyes closed. Her lips are slightly parted, and soft breaths leave them in a steady rhythm.

I pull my hood up and move closer. My heart racing faster with every inch I take, and then I'm there, sitting right next to her. I raise my hand and gently brush her hair behind her ear. She doesn't budge, and I smile. Only days of pure exhaustion does she sleep this hard.

I pull my legs underneath myself, crouching and pushing the large window open further before sliding one of my legs through it and stepping on the bench below. I turn and carefully pull the rest of my body through, making sure not to bump into her or knock anything off the bookshelf in the corner to my right.

I round her bed and see what hit the floor earlier. Her binder and pens lay scattered like she had swiped it all off in frustration. It seems her anger is there, but she lets her tears consume her, unable or perhaps too scared to let it loose. I clean up and set everything on her desk, closing her work and laying the pens in a line like she usually does. I turn to her bed and pull the covers back.

I turn the light off, leaving only a lamp on, and as carefully as possible, I scoop my arm around her stomach and pull her back into my arms. Her head nestles into my chest, and her arm wraps over my shoulder. I bring my knee up on the bed and lean forward, gently setting her down. I peel her arm off and move back, but she wraps her hand around my wrist, stopping me.

My heart drops.

Her eyes don't open, but she whispers to me in a hazy voice, "Stay a while?"

She must be dreaming, so I don't say anything, not wanting her to hear my voice and fully wake up. I scoot onto the bed and pull the blankets over us. She moves her head onto my chest, and my hand hovers in the air for a moment before I slowly lower it, placing it on her back.

I wait there, looking at the window, ready to make a break for it if this goes south. I shouldn't be doing this, but If I had pulled away, she might have woken up and seen me leaving anyway, so what the hell.

Her breathing slows, resuming its steady beat and I tilt my head into hers and breathe in the scent of her hair. I move my hand up, slowly stroking it and letting my heartbeat slow with every moment I spend holding her.

I have snuck in here many times, quieting her nightmares with gentle touches or reading her journal. I know that can seem like an invasion of privacy, but it always makes me smile to read the things that she writes because she usually titles her entries to "Not Him" or "Perseus" more recently.

However, I have never allowed myself to hold her like this. I always told myself I didn't deserve it, but right now, I can tell myself that I am doing it because she needs it, not because I want it.

I close my eyes. I'll lay here for just a little while longer.

Yeah, that will be alright.

I jerk awake some time later, hearing a buzzing sound. I snatch Amelia's phone off the nightstand and quickly mute the incoming call. Lance's name crosses the screen, and as the name disappears, her notifications show three unread messages. I check the time. 10 P.M.

He must be wanting to pick her up for the party. I look over at her sleeping peacefully, and grind my teeth. If she wakes up and answers his call, she won't be able to say no, and who the fuck knows what he might put her through tonight. I make sure to keep it on silent and set it back in its place. I push my arm deeper into the mattress and pull it from under her. Sliding off the bed, I take one last look at her, and my heart soars. A lifetime of this would never be enough, but for her, I would give anything.

I take a piece of paper from her binder, fold it, lick it, and tear it. Then use one of her pens to write her goodnight.

"Someday, I pray that you will find the lost piece of your soul in the eyes of someone who spent nearly their entire life loving you. But if the time never arises, I pray that you at least experience the feeling of loving someone that understands you.

You, my dear, deserve the world. Never settle for anything less.

-Not Him, but forever wishing to be your Perseus."

I climb out the window and shut it behind me, leaving the note wedged in it for her to find tomorrow.

***

Now...

I lay silently in the early morning light, Amelia sleeping softly in my arms, not far unlike one of my favorite memories of us. That time feels like a lifetime ago. Even after seeing proof of the lives we have taken and the ones we have ruined, she still demands that this is where she wants to be. She finds comfort in what this life can be for her.

I softly brush my hand over her hair, soaking in everything about her. I want her here just as badly. Here, she would never have to be more or less than she truly is. The worse she could ever be here is a murderer, and even that is acceptable to the people that love her. She would never have to feel guilty for what she likes, wants, or feels. Never have to apologize for her tears or anger. All that frustration that has always flooded her in the form of tears and panic attacks is now shifting and manifesting in vengeance, and she is not scared of it.

She craves it.

In my head, I had created this perfect life for her. One where she would graduate, work a nine-to-five job, have some kids with a good man, and could leave her past behind her. Including me, eventually. I had convinced myself that her being here would be a monumental mistake for us both, yet now I only feel the complete opposite.

Forcing her to leave would be just about as hard as convincing myself to make her leave.

She rolls towards me, nuzzling into my chest as her arm curls between us. I flinch at her nose's coldness, and she apologizes in a half-sleep mumble. I rub my hand down her back, and she moves into my touch. My teeth clench as she slides her own hand down my chest. My fist wraps around hers, stopping her path, and her head tilts up. She flashes me those big green eyes in an attempt to feign innocence, and my urge to protect it is absent, the need to taint it filling the empty spot.

"You don't want to play with me?" she whispers, lowering her eyelids before pressing her soft lips to my chest.

"I don't play nice," I warn.

"I don't need nice in here."

I pin her to the bed, hovering just above her face, dying to taste her lips. "As badly as I want to worship your naked body while you are bound and at my mercy, I also decide when you are ready for it."

She smiles sweetly, but her face lights up with mischief. Showing me she can play ugly is exactly what she is going to do, and I'm not sure which of us will enjoy seeing it more.

I lean down, breathing in her air as my next words pass between us. "I enjoy our chats but go find one of your other boyfriends to scratch that itch you have." I swipe my hand lower between us and press my lips to her forehead. "I can see how badly it's bothering you."

Giving her the space she needs to move from under me, she rolls to her stomach and slides back onto her knees, pushing her ass into the air. She crawls to the edge of the bed, giving me a perfect view as her hips purposefully sway slowly. She leaves her shorts where they lay on the floor and exits her room, casting a wink over her shoulder just before the door closes again.

I wait about twenty minutes, curious to see if she really would seek one of them out. I expect to hear her moaning exceedingly loud to spite me, knowing it would make me rage despite the decision being my own. When I hear nothing of that nature, my curiosity peaks.

As I creep out of her room, the light sound of her laughter beckons me closer to Ian's room. I tip my ear closer to the door, not wanting to disturb the sound.

Jealousy tightens around my heart like a noose at the sound of Ian's iPad playing a recorded acoustic song. A song that has echoed through our house many times, Ian's soft voice rearranging words over and over again to it, never satisfied with the results.

I strain my ears harder, needing to hear their conversation.

Does she even realize what he is doing?

She laughs as he playfully criticizes her in the form of a white lie for not knowing the words to the song. His angelic voice sings the familiar words, and her own fumbles along, catching onto the chorus more each time.

Finn's nearing presence has me spinning around, and his awe annoys me. He claps a hand on my shoulder and motions for me to follow him as he walks back towards the kitchen.

"I invited JJ and Tyler back up here. I think it would be good for her." He shoves half of a peeled orange into his mouth.

Narrowing my eyes, I take the other half from his hand and bite a piece of it off.

"Why do I have a feeling that the rest of this week will be a royal pain in my ass?"

"Because you are an uptight and overbearing douche that is allergic to fun."

I peg him in the center of the face with the remaining orange, his jokes long past old.

"And you're a sap scared she has enough pain to lose those soft parts of herself and that you won't be enough to stop it."

His eyes dart down to the table and then back up to mine.

Now who is reading who?

"Don't use her as ammo because you are too scared to rediscover those long-buried parts of yourself, Si."

Someday, I pray that you will find the lost piece of your soul in the eyes of someone who spent nearly their entire life loving you. But if the time never arises, I pray that you at least experience the feeling of loving someone that understands you. You, my dear, deserve the world. Never settle for anything less.

—Not Him, but
forever wishing to
be your Perseus

Amelia

Finn and I are elbows deep in bubbles when the doorbell rings. The door swings open, and an overly excited JJ emerges with a bag thrown over her shoulder.

"Surprise, Bitch!"

I run to her, slinging bubbles in my wake as I nearly tackle her to the floor. I hadn't realized how much had changed and how much I have needed her until I saw her face. I wrap my legs around her, and she squeals as my weight and damp clothes cling to her. She doesn't let me go as I explain our nightly dish washing turned into a foam party after we left the water running to have sex. The sink ran over from the clean side, spilling bubbles onto the counter and floor. Before the door sounded, we were throwing them across the room at each other, laughing until our lungs hurt.

Tyler walks in behind her, tossing his own bag onto the couch after giving Finn one of those nods that guys do. JJ pulls me to the back porch and closes the door behind us. Finn blows me a kiss before taking Tyler to the couch and out of sight. I adore him for always knowing what I need, even before I do.

"Girl, you have some major spilling to do," JJ says as she plants herself in a chair and tucks her feet to the side. I connect my phone to the Bluetooth speaker left sitting out here and light the remaining half of a blunt from its tray.

Fragile by *Tech N9ne* plays low, and I take a drag before I begin to unload everything since the night she was forced to leave. I can almost hear her heart beating out of her chest by the time I finish. Her clammy hands fist the arms of the chair, and she looks back through the glass door nervously.

"They would never hurt you or anyone else for no reason," I say.

"I am more concerned about you, babe."

Ian smiles at her, and I nearly laugh at how forced it is, the same constipated look he had given us the night we unofficially met. His true smile is one only a few people get the pleasure of seeing. Even fewer get to hear his laugh.

JJ waves back, her own nervous smile returning his.

I can trust JJ with anything of mine, but giving her the private details of the guy's history was not something I had the right to do. She doesn't trust them like I do. Love them like I do. Nothing would stop her from letting something slip and consequently putting them behind bars or worse. I don't know just how far their ties reach, and it isn't something I want to find out the hard way.

"They are not a danger to me. I chose to stay with them."

She looks at me curiously, and I realize I left a part out. Amusement tinges her stare as her cheeks turn pink.

"Yes. I'm with all of them."

"Oh. My. God," she says in the typically iconic JJ way.

"How's the sex?"

I roll my eyes, and she sighs exasperatedly. "Oh, come on!"

Chuckling, I decide to give her just enough to ease her imagination. "It's... unparalleled."

She doesn't need to know specifics of who or how many of them I've slept with at once. That is between us, but I can't say the thought hasn't crossed my mind multiple times.

She groans in a way that almost sounds sexual. "God, you are completely unhinged in the most envious ways. So what, you are some lawbreaking sexual deviant now?"

"You need to give that imagination of yours a break," I laugh, taking back the blunt that has rotated between us.

"So, do you plan on doing anything more with Lance?"

"Yes."

I would be doing something. Just how far I went would be decided the moment I saw his face again. It would be on my turf, on my time, and he would be at my mercy.

"I will ruin any chance he has at making a life for himself. Starting by taking back the money he earned for trying to ruin mine, then I will find out just how far Ian can reach." That, I would.

Lance will not have a penny to his name or a credible name at all. His crimes would be made public, and if time in prison was what I decided, it would only be the start of his punishment.

"Then what?" she asks. "How does this relationship work long term?"

I can't fault her for asking, but I honestly hadn't thought about it. I've always wanted that perfect life. A white picket fence and kids running around in the front yard.

"Honestly, I'm happy right now, and that's more on track for my dreams than I thought I would be at this point."

Her bottom lip pouts in sympathy, and I square my shoulders. I was never the girl that wanted pity, and I never will be. Pity is for the people too weak to do anything about their situation. I may have been scared and dependent, but I was never weak, and I damn sure am not now.

"A lot of what I thought I wanted months ago is nothing like what I know I want now. Dreams change."

She moves onto my lap and wraps her arms around me. "I'm sorry, Mel. I didn't mean... I know you have been through a lot, and I will always support you."

I pull her closer, and at this moment, I pray that losing her friendship is something I never have to endure.

Tough love comes with the kind of connection worth keeping. JJ's intention is never to hurt me, but to make sure I am not blinded, always looking out for me. The kind of genuine love we have for each other is something many people never find in a friend. It's more like the love of a sibling, perhaps sisters from another life, tying us together in an unbreakable bond.

The back door slides open, and a blonde cutie's face pokes through the crack, waiting for my cue before pushing it open the rest of the way. The rest of them follow out, and Ian shuffles a deck of cards.

Silas moves to my side resting his hand on the back of my chair. Tyler does the same to JJ, and I begin to suffocate in the testosterone around us.

Lyle leans into me and presses his lips to mine, stealing what little breath I had away. I grab the back of his neck, digging my nails into the skin as I speak.

"Where the hell have you been?"

He has been gone since last night without so much as an explanation.

"Did you miss me?" he purrs, bracing his hands on either side of me.

"You didn't answer my question," I say sharply.

The boys reassured me time and time again that he was fine and just running some errands, but it did nothing to ease the suspicion and worry.

I glare at him, and he scrunches his nose in the most adorable way. He knows by now I don't let shit go easily.

"Don't worry so much, Angel. If I was getting into trouble, I would make sure to have you tag along so I could see those hands get dirty."

Ian clears his throat, and the sound of cards colliding has Lyle backing up.

I can't go more than a few hours without wanting to rip one of their clothes off. Having to keep that in check for the rest of the week to be considerate of JJ and Tyler might be a difficult task.

"So, who is down for a drinking game?" Ian beams looking right at Silas, who audibly grinds his teeth.

We sit in a circle as the rules are explained. It's basically a distorted version of *Go Fish*. You ask a player for a number. If they have it, they have to give it up and take a drink. If they don't have it, the person that asked has to either answer a question truthfully or accept the dare to remove a piece of clothing.

"Additional rule. If you ogle something that's not yours, you get your shit rocked," Silas says before giving me a look that says I better answer any question I receive.

I wiggle in my spot with excitement while I wait for my hand of cards.

Finn goes first and asks me for any threes.

"Truth or strip, baby," I tease, unsure what answer I want to hear more.

"Truth."

"Do you jerk off to hearing me fuck one of them?" He grins a smile that nearly melts my panties right off. "Yes."

JJ's eyes widen.

The game continues for a few rounds, everyone drinking or answering truthfully. Tyler admits to trying hard drugs, giving us some very interesting stories. Lyle admits to initially wanting to steal me from Finn for fun, JJ admits to borrowing my favorite lingerie set, and I make a mental note to thoroughly sanitize it.

The turn falls to Silas, and he asks Tyler for nines. After collecting the cards, Tyler drinks, and Silas asks me for aces. I deny, and he accepts a truth.

"Why did you really not want me to stay?"

Without hesitating, he removes his shirt by pulling it from the back and over his head, refusing to answer. His muscles ripple, and my eyes linger for a beat before I take my turn and ask him for sevens.

None.

"Does it bother you that I haven't given you what you want yet?" His question is encrypted, but the four of us know what he is asking.

He wants to know how much I've read into him denying me.

The truth is that I have let that voice whisper to me, telling me I wasn't strong enough to be his partner or that part of him still didn't want me to be. I could tell him that because I have no desire to hide how I feel from any of them, but where is the fun in that?

He knows the bottom line is that he is denying me the ability to demand what I want, and it's thoroughly irritating me, so I might as well return the favor.

I grab the bottom of my shirt and begin lifting it keeping my eyes focused on him with an unspoken challenge. Silently he tells me to answer the question, and for a moment, I think he may even try giving me a different one. I slip off my shirt, and JJ whistles at my light pink bra left for everyone to see.

Tyler makes it very obvious that he's not looking at my breasts as he makes a show of studying his cards like his next play determines if he wins the lotto.

The game continues. JJ badgers them with variations of questions regarding me any chance she gets, and the boys bring out embarrassing truths about each other. Specific instances of regretful places they have put their dicks, dreams they have had, porn they watch, and even drunken bisexual curiosities.

We are all down at least one item of clothing and a sheet to the wind when my jaw nearly hits the floor as Ian admits he has been with a guy. It was a suspicion after our night at the movies, but I didn't want to assume.

My eyes subtly drift to Lyle only to find that his are already watching me. He winks, and my cheeks heat under his playful stare. You can never really tell when he is bullshitting you.

JJ giggles as Tyler kisses down her neck and chest, neither of them listening anymore unless it involves them. His hand snakes down her shorts, and although the motion draws their attention, none of the guys' stares linger, all of their eyes returning to me as now encouraged thoughts fill their minds.

I come up empty on my turn once again, and before Lyle can ask me another question about my sexual experiences at summer camps, I decide to speed the game up a little. I lift up on my knees and unbutton my shorts.

"I'll take the dare."

Shimmying them down mid-way, I move to my feet and stand between Lyle's thighs. I slip them off the rest of the way and kick the denim off into his lap. He sits below me with his head tilted back and his hands on the back of my calves, looking deliciously submissive.

Showing nothing more than most bikinis, I hold myself confident as I place one of my feet on the center of Lyle's chest. "And I raise you... night swimming."

"You are going to get someone killed one of these days, Amelia Mason." Ian's distinct softness in his voice has me looking over my shoulder, and I bet that behind me, Silas is watching Tyler for the smallest excuse to remove a few of his teeth.

But, I'm sure his face is buried inside JJ's mouth.

"Last one down gets sexually excluded!" I scream as I barrel down the lawn, then down the length of the dock and into the water.

I hear Finn's voice behind me, sounding closer than the trailing laughter as he reiterates that my offer excludes my best friend and her boyfriend.

Finn

I've spent a week watching Amelia smile and laugh. And I don't think I could possibly love her any more. The way her smile lights up a room makes it hard to believe she ever felt that no one appreciated it.

I watch as she laughs from deep in her belly, her eyes small slits as tears fall from them, and her hands wrap around her stomach. JJ snickers beside her on the large couch as they take each other down into the cushions. My stomach warms, but despite how much I want to be a part of the moment, I keep walking and leave her be.

Ian stands on the back porch looking down towards the dock, and I meet him, lighting a cigarette on my way. If the red of his eyes were any indication, I'd say he hasn't slept much.

"Whatever it is, stop letting it eat at you, man," I say, enjoying the sun warming my chest.

The only thing that's ever bothered him this much was his own head. If I had to guess, he's pissed we gave those scumbags the payoff they were looking for. And we hate nothing more than not finishing the job.

"We will finish the rest when she's ready."

"Something hasn't been sitting right with me," he confesses, fisting the wooden railing, waiting for me to indulge him.

I clear my lungs, blowing smoke into the air above us, watching as the wind whisks it away into nothing. Then turn and prop my back against the railing next to him, giving him my full attention.

"Why would Lance make a scene at the party knowing we would get our hands on him and demand answers?"

Ian nods, and I let his question bounce around in my mind.

"He had that paper in his pocket, ready for us," He scoffs.

Both valid points, though I doubt Lance would have the coherence for a strategy planned of that depth.

"Or maybe he's just another drug head, too stupid for his own good, and you are just overthinking this because you refuse to let yourself accept that she is good for all of us."

The money went through, and a portion of it was transferred to another account, most likely Lance's. Since then, we haven't heard a word from him.

There was nothing else on his phone that helped either. Code messages, short calls from a burner, and a shit ton of pictures of Amelia were the only things relating to his deal.

"Look, once we get home, we'll handle it, and then there will be nothing else threatening her."

He snorts a laugh, and pained amusement is cast my way before we turn to look back into the house.

His message is received loud and clear.

We always put ourselves in danger with the game we play, so now, she would be too. But he fails to realize she wasn't forced into our life.

She chose it, decided she wanted it. She was born for it. Even Silas could recognize that despite his same reluctance.

"I need my full setup to really dig deeper," he sighs. "Then I will let it go."

I chuckle to myself, letting him believe his lie.

He will unravel every sliver of data he can find until he's sure Lance is telling the truth. Even then, I'm not sure that he would let Lance live even if that was what Amelia decided. And taking that decision from her might just be more detrimental than anything that has been done to her.

"You have to let it be her decision, just as it was for each of us to determine if we could be that kind of person."

"And if she can't?"

She could choose to stay.

But would we let her if she had overestimated herself?

Watching someone experience pain so deep you can physically feel it yourself and watching the life leave someone's eyes are very different. It can be too much for those that don't have the right strength or control.

"She wouldn't turn us in," I state blandly. It wouldn't come to that. "She's not that stupid."

Ian lets out a ragged breath that steadies as he watches Mel hug her best friend goodbye. I give him a moment to compose himself, joining everyone inside to do the same.

JJ gives me one last hug whispering, "Keep her happy."

I say nothing and close the door behind her.

Lyle asks about our plans to wrap up our final few days before the gala as I slide my hand down the length of the kitchen counter moving towards Mel, having a few ideas of my own.

"I want to go tan," she says, standing abruptly.

Snatching a towel from the rack by the back door she leaves the door open as a clear invite, and I sigh frustratedly as I watch her walk away from us.

"She wasn't wearing a bathing suit," Ian points out.

It takes a minute, and then realization dawns.

We all rush to meet her down by the water, beer in hand. She is lying on her stomach with her head turned sideways, her bare ass clear as day for anyone to see.

"Are you fucking kidding me?" Silas booms.

She smirks and shields her eyes from the sun beating down.

"What's the problem? I'm avoiding tan lines."

Lyle and I sit to the side, seemingly both wanting the same view.

"Anyone could walk out here, and you are butt-ass-naked. Go put on a fucking swimsuit." Silas glares at her.

She lifts up, and the side of her small breasts makes an appearance.

"You know, I don't think I will. I like seeing you not get your way despite that big dick energy you have. It's adorable."

This push-and-pull kink they have, albeit toxic, is utterly amusing.

Silas is seething, his hands fisted at his sides, his nostrils flaring with each shaking breath he takes.

"Ian, would you be a doll and let me borrow your sunglasses?"

His eyes bounce from her to different locations as if he looks at her for too long, he might jizz in his pants. He hands her the glasses, but before he can stand back up, she grabs his wrist and pulls him closer.

She whispers something to him, and his eyes point upwards, searching for the strength to withstand whatever it is she said.

He reaches into the nearby bag he brought and pulls out sunscreen. Amelia rolls to her back and cups her breasts, as he pops the lid.

"You have *got* to be fucking kidding me," Silas grinds out, and Amelia turns her head toward us, casting a wink.

"Being part of this means we don't sugarcoat anything," Silas begins.

"Si, don't," Ian says through gritted teeth.

"No, let him say it," Amelia says, holding her breasts firmly as she looks at Silas through the tinted glasses.

"You see, my affection works differently than theirs." Silas points toward us, his eyes never leaving her. "I don't like my women to show off what is mine like trash."

"That's big talk for someone who has had a constant flow of trash because he didn't have the balls to go after the girl he really wanted."

Oh shit.

"The fuck did you just say?"

"I didn't stutter, and if you want a pet, you first have to prove that you can take care of one."

Don't do it, Si. Walk away.

Silas runs his tongue across his teeth.

"Take a walk, Si!" Ian shouts, and our heads snap to him.

Amelia running her mouth to Silas is one thing, but Ian has never spoken to him like that. Ever.

To my surprise, Silas leaves, taking a few beers with him down to the sandbar.

Ian exhales a long breath and starts rubbing his hands along the length of Mel's stomach, careful to avoid her bandages everywhere he goes. Her burns are still fresh, scattered on her thighs and torso.

I watch the motion with deep focus as his hands curl down her side and back up, making their way between her breasts, still covered by her hands.

"You know," she says, looking at Ian, who is focused on his own movements. "I've never seen you like that."

"He needs to watch his fucking mouth. Y'all's little tit-for-tat is cute, but he took that shit too far for no other reason than being unable to cope with how he really feels about you."

"His words don't hurt me. I see right through him now."

Ian's hands travel down her waist, massaging into the skin of her outer thighs.

"It doesn't make it right."

His hands smooth across her legs and onto her inner thighs. Her breath catches, and Ian falters, his hands jumping lower nervously, continuing at her shins.

She turns her head back towards us, and her steady breathing resumes.

We all lay on our towels, positioning around her, and I soak in everything around us. People laughing in the distance, boats creating waves that crash on the sand, the sun warming our skin, music humming out of our portable speaker. And the girl I am in love with lying next to me, appearing not to have a care in the world despite just how much her life has changed in only a few months.

And I do. I love her so fucking much it hurts.

I take in her small nose, the cupid's bow of her top lip and the pout of her lower one, the scattered freckles across her nose, and her long black lashes. She really is breathtaking.

As I take in her naked body as a whole. My chest tightens, and déjà vu washes over me.

Silas used to look just like that, only with stitches done by a kid and fractured bones. So many nights, I would lay awake as he slept on our floor, just making sure he was still breathing and the bleeding had slowed down enough. Many nights doing the same with Reina. Over time he got good at patching himself up, but the nightmares always came. They got worse after she died and never really stopped. Having to sneak out and go for a run or go down to the gym to wear himself out...

No.

I sit up and look around for Silas, finding him staring right at Amelia, a look of terror on his face I haven't seen in years. His eyes meet mine, and it seems we share the same thought. Standing up, I casually walk toward him. He stretches his stride wider, closing the few feet left between us.

"The cuts," I say, eyeing his chest's many scars. Small quick slices, the same as hers.

He says nothing as he holds up his phone to show me a picture JJ just sent him. A letter she found on her way out, the blue scribbled pen immediately recognizable.

I GAVE WHAT WAS NECESSARY YEARS AGO, BUT AN UNPAID DEBT STILL REMAINS. RUINING SOMEONE'S LIFE DOESN'T COME CHEAP.

-NS

Nickolas Steele.

This was never about Amelia's family money or Lance's personal fun. No, this was much bigger, and we were fools to not have seen it sooner.

Kacey and Jameson were both in on this, and we're back to playing in the big league again.

Blood will spill.

"Looks like we are attending that gala either way, and we need to pay Kacey Mason a visit." I say, controlling my tone just in case Mel can hear me.

Silas looks over my shoulder, then meets my eyes, fear shining in his own.

"You think she's fucked-up enough to knowingly get her daughter killed?" he asks, his brows pinched together, his fists wringing as his sides.

It had been a while since he really let loose. And the time was coming once again, and he was reveling in it. Holding it back with every minuscule amount of willpower to ensure it is released on the right person.

Persons.

"I think she's broken enough to not think past the haze of her own pain easing. You know that."

We had been here before with Lyle. Drugs blur the lines, making only one thing important.

Silas laughs painfully, and his eyes flare.

"Finn, I need you to understand that if that's the case, and her own mother knew what she was doing, I will fucking kill her." Silas stands firm, not a hint of a lie or exaggeration in his statement.

I try to fit the pieces together in my head, trying to decipher the lies and manipulations. He moves to walk back towards the house, but I grab his shoulder, stopping him.

"Something isn't adding up."

He turns back to face me but gives me nothing.

"If this is all Nickolas, why hurt a girl you have barely shown interest in other than to stir up old memories about Reina? It would be easier to go for us directly. Why go through all these people when he has an entire gang at his fingertips? This started months ago, years maybe, Before any of us were even in the picture."

His jaw tightens, and his nostrils flare, I struck a nerve.

"What aren't you telling us?"

His eyes fall to the ground, his chest rising and falling faster as he tightens and releases his fists.

"She plays a bigger part in my life than she knows... and I need it to stay that way, for now at least."

"And how long has she been a part of your life and you not hers?" I ask, risking pushing him more than he is comfortable with.

He kicks at the sand under his bare feet and walks in the opposite direction. Not getting a verbal thrashing or a fist to the face, I take that as my cue to follow.

"I first noticed her in high school. I was intrigued by her. 'Like calls to like' and all that bullshit, I guess." He kicks the sand again but doesn't look at me.

"I never acted on it because she was with that dickhole. I thought I would only damage her more. She didn't need someone like me, but I couldn't stay away. I watched her *all* the time, learned *everything* about her, and the more I did, the more..." He trails off, and I nod, realization dawning on me.

"The more you loved her." He sighs then squares his shoulders. "So, you can imagine my dismay when you two chose her and then moved her in right down the hall. Makes it a little difficult to shelter someone you love from the disaster of yourself."

The pieces start falling into place. The fights he got into.

The tension between them. The type of girls he slept with.

How could I be so blind?

"So why not tell her the truth now? Why are you still distancing yourself when she knows you love her?"

He looks over at me, his eyes glossy and red. "I'm scared, Finn. There are truths hidden in that story, things I have to take to the grave. If I let her trust me - love me - then that truth breaks her-" A tear slips free and falls down his cheek. "I would rather die."

My heart aches for him, he will carry whatever burden he has by himself, never letting anyone else shoulder the weight he feels entitled to bear.

"We all have to be completely honest with her, or we may lose everything."

He nods in understanding. We have to tell her that this isn't over and that it is because of us.

***

"I need a dress," Amelia grumbles, her face smashed in the towel after we tell her some of the new situation.

"I can't wait to see you in a formal dress." Ian beams. For someone who hates the richy lifestyle, he sure does love events like this.

"I'm not going if I can't find one that covers all of this," she says, gesturing to her scabbed cuts.

"I know a good shop in town. We will find something you feel sexy in," Ian says.

I think we can all agree that the bandages aren't going to make a difference to us, but she needs to feel good about herself, so that's what we will do.

"I think we need to take a little trip to the safe room too," Lyle mumbles, scratching his head and yawning.

"Do I even want to know what that is?" Mel raises a brow, looking at me.

"It's where we keep all of our favorite toys." I smirk.

The look on her face changes, and I know exactly where her mind goes.

"Non-sexual, babe. However, we do have a room for that too. It's called Silas's room."

"Enter at your own risk," Lyle mumbles, and she laughs nervously.

We know Silas likes to play games. Even if sometimes they aren't fun for everyone involved.

"We all have a few toys of our own," I say. "But his collection puts all of ours to shame. It's not *50 Shades* big, but it's enough to fill a wall of his closet. But we usually avoid asking to borrow any of his."

"Why?" she asks, her eyebrows shooting up, mischief written all over her face.

"He has a price. Typically you owe him a favor, or he gets to play, too, with a toy of his own choice."

Her eyes nearly bug out of her head as she looks at Silas, waist-deep in the water, still battling his thoughts, and I don't miss how she tucks her hand between her thighs. She is turned the fuck on by that idea.

Is it thinking about owing him a favor or him playing with her?

"That is if he catches you." Carlisle wags his brow, and I scoff. He always fucking does.

"Anyway, we thought we all needed some extra defenses for the gala." Lyle says.

Without knowing why Jameson is being extra slimy or who else might be working with them, we need to be prepared. And Mel needs to be able to defend herself if someone grabs her again. Her nerves get the best of her, and even though she told us she is done with allowing others to hurt her, emotional responses are not that easily rewired. Her fist and reactions are not likely to be fast enough, but a simple swing of a blade should do the trick.

"I'm good with a blade. Comfortable."

The air falls silent.

"God. Not like that. I took knife throwing and archery classes at summer camps."

We laugh it off, knowing her agreement to stop isn't written in stone. We find a way to cope with our pain and lean on it for so long it becomes second nature. It's a part of her just as music is to Ian or fighting is to Silas.

If only Silas had spoken to her back then, or we had found her sooner...

Maybe she could have saved all of us.

I gave what was necessary years ago, but an unpaid debt still remains. Ruining someone's life doesn't come cheap.

—NS

We take one last swim, shower, and pack our bags to leave. Locking up the house and getting into our cars, Amelia leads Finn to Lyle's car.

"It's only fair that I ride with y'all on the way back," she says sensually, and her tone does nothing to hide her intentions.

Lyle comes up behind her with a Cheshire grin, then yanks her ponytail downwards slowly, forcing her head up.

"How very considerate of you, Angel. However, Finn and Si are taking his truck back while Ian and I take my car. We'll stop at a few places on the way home to find you a dress."

She pouts, giving Finn a well-practiced puppy-dog look. He steps in front of her and kisses her pouting lips.

"Don't look at me like that, baby. Trust me, I would give anything to see you get undressed over and over again, but I lost rock-paper-scissors again."

She cocks her hip out to the side and raises an eyebrow at him.

"So what are you two going to go do? Gonna go beat up some kid for their lunch money?"

"Something like that," Silas mumbles, and I glare at him.

I am not thrilled about lying to Amelia, but I know it is a necessary evil. She's not ready to face everything. Not yet. If her mother decides to snap again, convincing Silas not to kill her might be near impossible.

Mel hums a sarcastic tone, wrapping her arms around Finn, squeezing him tightly. She looks up and his lips meet hers for another kiss. "Be careful. I'll see you at home later."

Home.

Silas's spine stiffens as she backs up from Finn and moves to him hesitantly. His eyes dart across the distance like one of us might have said something. In slow movements, she leans into him, reaching up to wrap her arms around his neck. He leans forward and slowly wraps his own around her waist, resting his chin on her head. Turning her head, she pecks a soft kiss on his cheek.

"You too," she says timidly, and for the first time, he smiles *at* her.

It's the first time she's showed she genuinely cares for him, despite his effort to push her away. And I can't help but smile at them both.

With that, they take off in Silas's truck, and Amelia climbs into the back seat of Lyle's car.

"Okay fuckers, where are they really going?"

Lyle snorts, and I shake my head as we pull onto the road.

"You can't freak or try to change plans," Lyle says, and she gives a look that says, '*Try me.*'

"After what Lance said about your mom, they want to see what they can figure out before the event tomorrow." He looks at her through the rearview mirror.

She slams her back into the seat, picking at her nails nervously, so I reach back and swat at them.

"Stop. Everything will be fine. They're only trying to help keep you safe."

A whisper of a smile plays on her lips, and she nods slowly. "I know, I can see that. I'm thankful. Really, I am."

I watch her for a few moments, seeing her eyes roaming around the floorboard of the car, her fingers picking at the loose strings of her blue jean shorts. I don't have to hear her say it to know what she's thinking.

She misses her mom.

But it doesn't change the fact that she knows nothing good will come from it, and although we claim to want nothing but the best for her, she's still having a hard time fully believing it.

"Hey, Lyle, don't kill us, would ya? Mel, climb up." I pat my lap, and she lifts her head, giving me that beautiful smile that makes me weak in the knees.

She unbuckles her belt and climbs over the console, sticking her ass right in Lyle's face. He bites her, and she yelps, collapsing into my lap.

"Don't you ever stick that thing in my face and expect me not to want to eat it until you are shaking and begging me to stop."

Her jaw slackens, and she looks at me, but I shrug. He has a valid point.

"Mr. Jones, you keep saying shit like that, and I might just suck you dry in this car."

He jerks the wheel, driving over the median a tad, and I wrap my arm around Amelia's waist as we jerk right then left.

Lyle clears his throat.

"I said don't kill us, asshole." I unfasten my seat belt and bring it over, Amelia, clicking it back in.

"Give me a break. She's over here taunting me with road head."

Amelia shakes with laughter, and she wiggles in my lap, getting comfortable.

Ah, shit.

I reach forward to turn the radio up, disguising myself as I readjust my hardening dick. Throwbacks from the 2000s rattle the car with the help of the system installed under the seats. My hands rest on Amelia's thighs, moving with the sway of her body as she dances to each song, singing to the windshield.

Ignoring the blood rushing to my dick, I try to focus on anything out the window. As the next song plays, she pulls slack into the seat belt and leans forward grinding her ass on me. Hovering just above my lap, each circular motion brushes over my cock, and there is no way I can ignore the hard-on now. I groan and grab her shoulders, pulling her back against my chest, wondering if she can feel how fast it's beating.

"If you don't stop grinding on my dick, I will bend you over this console and finger fuck you while you suck Lyle's dick. And I won't stop until you are shaking."

She wiggles again, and I slide my hand forward, grabbing her jaw, turning her head to the side. I growl into her hair, and more than ever before, I want to fuck her.

My muscles ache with the need to be on top of her, my dick buried inside her, the soft skin of her breasts marked by my mouth. My thumb brushes over her plump lips, and she parts them, sucking my finger into her mouth and drawing it out slowly.

Oh, God.

I yank the seat belt off us, throw her top half into Lyle's lap, and reach under her, unbuttoning her shorts and pulling them down to her knees. Amelia laughs and unfastens Lyle's jeans.

I pause briefly, the thought of Reina crossing my mind. Lyle looks at me giving me an encouraging nod.

I remember Amelia's words the other night. How understanding she was. We were still kids when Reina died. She was one of my best friends and I loved her, no doubt. She made me smile and welcomed me into their family with open arms. We needed each other, but I think she needed me more. That's why it hurts so much. I feel like I am letting her down.

But Amelia, she sets my soul on fire. She has a contagious smile and a laugh that makes you laugh. She's experienced pain like the rest of us, but deep down, she doesn't need rescuing. She just needs someone to stand beside her.

We thought that all of us caring for her would tear us apart, but I think she makes us stronger. She gives us a reason to fight again, out of love instead of anger. The love I felt for Reina is nothing like what I feel for Amelia, and I think that is what I need to remember. Reina will always hold a piece of my heart, but Amelia holds a piece of my soul.

Lyle grunts, bringing me out of my thoughts. He lifts up, letting Amelia shimmy his pants down over his ass, freeing his cock.

Rubbing my hands over Amelia's ass, I give it a tight squeeze, and she moans in approval. She licks up the side of Lyle's shaft, teasing, making him groan. I rub my thumb between her lips, spreading her open, her pink skin glistening. I play with her, running my fingers up and down, teasing her clit and raising her arousal. She opens her mouth, taking Lyle in and working her hand in a twisting motion.

"Ah, fuck," Lyle grinds out, fisting the steering wheel tighter, his knuckles turning white. She goes deeper, gagging before coming back up for air. Panting and raspy breathing melds with the sounds of the music still playing. I turn it down, wanting to hear every sweet sound she makes.

Lyle places a hand on her head. "Take all of me, baby girl. I know you can."

She opens her mouth wider, sinking down on him again and gently pushes her head further. "Relax your throat. Open it up real wide for me." He pushes again, as I push two fingers into her. Her tight pussy sucking them in greedily. She moans, and Lyle pushes her head down again, this time bottoming out.

"Fuck, Angel. Such a good girl."

She moans, and he pants at the vibrations he must feel on his cock. I put my left hand on the lower part of her stomach, pushing firmly. I rub my fingers against her walls, loving the feeling of her on my fingertips. My dick is rock hard and throbbing with the need to be inside her.

I use it as motivation, sweat forming on the nape of my neck as I push my fingers in as far as they will go, fucking her hard with them. I slam against her, causing her body to rock back and forth.

"Do you like the way Ian plays with your pussy?"

She mumbles and moans, her mouth still filled by my best friend. She works him faster, bobbing her head, meeting his small thrusts.

"You like the way I taste?"

She mumbles approvingly around him again.

"Good, because I'm about to come, and you are gonna swallow me down but not before you show me."

I keep my speed, feeling her tighten around me. Lyle grunts, fisting her hair and holding her still as he spills into her mouth, thrusting slowly.

She pants and groans, squeezing her thighs, coming hard. She pulses on my fingers, but I don't stop, her body jolting as I overwork her sensitive nerves.

I let her sit up, keeping my fingers inside her, slowing my pace. She sticks out her tongue, showing Carlisle his own product in her mouth. He glances between her and the road, then wipes her lip, pushing any remnants back into her mouth.

She whimpers, swallowing, her body trembling.

I pull her back into my lap, straddling me.

"You want to come again?" I ask, and she nods, her hair plastered to her sticky skin.

"Use your words, baby," Lyle encourages while righting his clothes.

"Yes. Please make me come again."

I tongue the inside of my cheek and push her back against the dash, sliding my seat back to give us more room. I spread her legs, and she stops me with a firm hand on my chest, then looks to Lyle.

"You want him, baby?" He grins wildly, and she nods, looking back at me.

"Yes."

Frustrated, he grunts. "I'll allow it if you promise to sleep with me tonight."

She leans over, licking up the side of his neck. "Deal, Hellcat."

"Are you sure?" I ask not wanting this to be for the wrong reasons.

"Yes. Are you?"

"Absolutely."

Sliding my pants down, I free my cock, and it bounces up standing at attention for her.

Her eyes widen, and Lyle chuckles. "Yeah, the man's hung."

Amelia licks her lips and wiggles the rest of the way out of her shorts.

Lyle smiles, eyes still on the road.

I lift her, lining my dick up to her entrance. Then drop my hand to her waist, allowing her to slide onto me at her own speed. She slides slowly, and we both groan.

Fuck, me.

She's like a damn drug, better than I could have ever imagined.

"This is all you, baby. Ride me hard and take what you want."

She doesn't need any more encouragement than that. She rocks back and forth on me, wincing slightly but not stopping.

"Oh, God. You feel so good," she whimpers, speeding up, her cum coating my dick and pubic area, allowing her to slip easily. Her clit rubs against me, and I reach forward, slipping my hands under her shirt, pinching her nipples.

She leans forward, readjusting to sit on her knees. Licking up the shell of my ear, her breath chills my skin sending shivers throughout my body. I groan, and she sinks her teeth into my lobe, bouncing her ass up and down on my dick as I place my hands on her cheeks lightly, feeling them shake.

"Shit, that's hot," Lyle says.

Her face buries in my neck while she bites and sucks between husky breaths.

"Come for me," I say.

She rides me harder and faster, chasing her orgasm.

"Yes, yes, yes!" she chants, throwing her head back, her pussy squeezing me. "I'm gonna come!"

"Hold on tight."

She grips the seat, and I grasp her hips, lifting her up, thrusting into her as fast and hard as possible. She shatters in my hands, screaming a stream of cuss words as I hold her immobile. The feeling of her throbbing around me throws me into my orgasm. I push into her one final time, my hot cum filling her.

I let her sink back down, and she moves on me slowly, and I savor every last moment as we come down from the high.

"Perfect timing," Carlisle says with a mischievous grin, shifting into park. "We're here,"

Amelia giggles, tossing herself into the backseat and sliding her shorts back up over her hips. She uses her fingers to comb out the tangles of her sweat-coated hair, and I hand her a napkin to clean off her skin. She dabs her damp skin then pushes her hand down between her legs to clean herself up.

"Where are we?" she asks, balling up the napkins and shoving them in her bag.

"There is a great shop in town; but this is my favorite." I rough up my own hair and use the dampness to put it back into place. Pulling the visor down, I inspect my neck, the delicious ache lingering. I run my fingers over the angry red marks on my skin, the perfect mold of her teeth imprinted on me, and part of me hopes it bruises.

"You're going to make me walk into my favorite shop looking like a common whore?"

"You are welcome to stay in the car. I'm sure Lyle can manage helping me in and out of my selections."

Over my dead body.

"There is no way that is happening. Gowns require a gentle touch, and *he* just doesn't have it."

"That may be true, but Amelia seems very fond of my *rough* touches." Lyle winks at her.

I raise a brow, smelling a pissing contest.

Amelia sits back in her seat, crossing her arms, looking rather amused. Despite her efforts, her skin is still flushed, a clear reminder that I was just inside her.

"That may be true," I say, turning my head back to Lyle, "but it's my cum that will be dripping out of her as we shop."

He smirks, having been bested in our child's play.

"I do recall it was you that once told us she wasn't a chew toy to fight over?" he says, opening his door and climbing out.

Little shit.

I climb out of the car and open the back door. She steps out and kisses me on the cheek.

"He only said that when he thought he had no interest in being part of our games," Mel says to Lyle, her eyes still on me.

The memory of the first time we all sat down together crosses my mind. She was on the table with her legs crossed, the first glimpse of her bravery clear to see. She talked about something so dark like it was just another day, and at that moment, my heart ached, the feeling all too familiar.

She slaps my ass and moves past me and into the shop.

I shake my head and smile.

Common whore.

"Good afternoon, Mr. Davis. Good to see you again," Jennifer welcomes. She is only a few years older than me but has been working here for a while. Her eyes land on Amelia then shoot back to me.

"I- Is there something I can help you find today?" she stammers, rounding the counter.

"Actually, yes. Amelia wants something black with a high neckline and matching gloves."

Jennifer stands a little straighter, her eyes trailing down the length of Amelia's body, where she stands looking through a rack of dresses. Eyes lingering a little too long on Amelia's bandaged wrists.

"About a size four, I presume. What event are we dressing for, sir?" Jennifer looks back to me.

I step closer to Amelia, seeing her eye a deep purple gown with mesh accent pieces.

"My father's event. I'm sure you are aware of it." I take the dress off the rack and fold it over my arm.

"I see," Jennifer says uncomfortably, shifting on her feet.

Amelia lifts up the bottom of the dress and holds it out slightly. "I love this fabric. Do you have anything we might like in it?"

"No, I don't have any full-length white dresses with a high neckline."

"Oh, no," Amelia says timidly, "I don't want white."

Jennifer moves in closer, setting her hand on Mel's shoulder, giving her a look of pity. "A woman's job is to compliment her escort, and Mr. Davis looks divine in light colors."

Amelia's face twists in discomfort, and rage boils through my veins. I snatch Jennifer's hand off Amelia and toss it back down to her side with force.

"If you wish to keep your job, I suggest you find dresses that fit *our* descriptions and keep your damn mouth shut. Amelia does not need you to tell her what she should and should not wear. That opinion is solely up to her and her escorts. Plural. Now, fuck off."

Jennifer's mouth gapes open and Lyle moves behind Amelia, stroking her arm as she wears a dismissive smile.

"Y-yes, of course. My apologies." Jennifer scurries off behind the desk making herself busy flipping through the catalog books.

I clear my throat, guiding Amelia with my hand on the small of her back. "Let's find you a few fits that you like. And we can see if it's available in the darkest shade of black possible."

I give her a wink and kiss the side of her head. Never again will she feel belittled or in debt to anyone.

We split up, meeting back at the dressing room where Jennifer has set a few of her choices, each of us holding a few of our own. Mel takes them all in the room with her requesting that we wait until she needs help with the zippers or clasps.

The first one she comes out in is clearly one of Lyle's choices. Sheer everywhere except her breasts and a small strip around her waist. I clasp the buttons in the back and help her onto the rise half surrounded by mirrors.

"Lyle," she says to him accusingly. "I'm basically nude."

He sits back in one of the waiting chairs. "Exactly why it's an excellent contender."

She scowls at him. "Next."

The next one she comes out in is a solid satin black ball gown with a halter top and a slit up to her hip. Again, I zip her up and help her to the mirrors. She does a little spin, taking herself in.

"It's beautiful, but I would like to cover these." She motions to the purple-red marks are higher on her arms.

They have almost healed. But the bruises still shine in all their glory. The dress covers the one on her chest nicely.

"No one would dare say anything with all four of us next to you," I say.

"I know. It's just wearing them for everyone to see at a formal event is slightly different from a casual day." She gives a half-smile, and I nod understanding.

Seeing those marks is a constant reminder of Lance and everything she has gone through, so I don't push it.

"We could always find a wrap or something of that nature."

I don't wait for her to answer or dwell on it, shooing her back to the dressing room to change into the next.

We place the dress to the side, starting a pile of her likes. We add a few more to the pile, all full-length gowns, some formfitting and some flowing, but none she has fallen in love with.

Then, she cracks the door open with a huge smile and requests my help.

Helping her into the gown, I can tell that this one is form fitting, but I can't tell much else about it. The stubborn woman demanded that I look as minimal as possible so she could present herself to us both outside.

I zip her up slowly, my knuckles brushing the small of her back, and I hear her suck in a breath. Moving to the buttons, I lean in close, purposely letting my breath hit the side of her neck. She tilts her head to the side, inviting me in, and I press my lips to the sensitive skin behind her ear taking in the sweet smell of her skin.

God, she's addictive.

I hear her let out a hushed whimper and can all but feel the desire swirling around us. I almost want to say fuck the dress, rip it off her, and fuck her against the wall, letting everyone hear her cry out for me.

But the smile I saw on her face said now is not the time, so I pull away from her with great effort, feeling an ache deep in my bones with every inch. I slip out of the fitting room and take my seat next to Lyle, who is now holding a pair of tall black gloves.

"Okay, close your eyes," she giggles, and I elbow Lyle, knowing he has to respond correctly to this one.

We do as told and I listen to her footsteps, walking in front of us and up onto the rise once more. The dress rustles as she works to situate it correctly.

She exhales slowly. "Okay, open."

All the breath leaves my lungs, like I've been punched in the gut.

Lyle rubs his chin, hunching over onto his knees.

"Fucking hell, baby. You look so Goddamn good it hurts," he says.

Her cheeks turn rosy, and she pulls her bottom lip between her teeth as she smiles big. "Yeah? You like it?"

It's off-the-shoulder and black as night. A solid fabric cuts straight across her chest falling tight on her body, splitting high on her thigh. The top layer is a thick designed lace that rises higher to her collarbone and trails down the sleeve a few inches, covering all of her scars nicely.

She turns in a half circle, showing us the back. It nearly matches the front except for the short train. She completes the circle, turning back to us.

Lyle hands her the gloves, and she slips them on, finishing the masterpiece.

"Abso-fucking-lutely." We both agree.

The other two are going to lose their fucking minds when they see her in this tomorrow night. I only hope that I'm the one that gets to take it off her. I would hate to see such a beautiful dress torn to shreds by the other three Neanderthals we live with.

"Lyle, help her out of that, and I'll check her out-. I mean, pay the bill."

Amelia scrunches her nose at me, and I turn, heading to the counter, tapping my fingers on my thigh.

Finn

We arrive at the Mason's two-story house, anxious to get what we need and make it back home. Although we know Lyle and Ian are fully capable of watching out for Mel, neither of us feels at ease about being away from her.

Silas knocks on the door, and Kacey Mason immediately answers. Looking at us confused, she glances side to side and then back to us, closing the door a few inches.

"Can I help you?" Her words slur slightly, her pupils dilated so much that the green pigment she shares with Amelia is barely visible. You can see their resemblance slightly, though Kacey's face is sunken in, with deep crescents under her eyes.

"Friends of your daughters. Can we talk for a minute?" I smile politely, trying to seem more welcoming than the brute standing beside me with his arms crossed and legs shoulder width apart.

"I don't have a daughter. You must be mistaken." She attempts to shut the door, but Silas jams his black steel toe boot in and shoves it back open, causing her to stumble.

"Wha- What the fuck are you doing?" she stammers, falling to her ass scooting backward across the hardwood floors.

"I'm here to get some fucking answers, and you are pissing me off," Silas says, walking towards her slowly.

She scrambles to her feet and turns, dashing for her room. Silas groans, following her but making no effort to run as if her effort is futile. Although we don't condone harassing women, I can't help the sliver of joy I feel right now.

Kacey meets us at her bedroom doorway, holding a bat over her shoulder, swinging it with a loud cry.

Silas catches it, yanking it from her, and sending her flying into his chest. He grips her around the neck, his hands shake, holding back with every ounce of willpower he has as his lip curls up in a snarl.

He walks her back slowly, anger rolling off him in huge dark waves, and I watch him, waiting for my cue to step in. She claws at his hand, her feet stepping rapidly to keep up with his long strides.

"You can give me answers, or I can take them." His voice is low and menacing..

Fear flashes in her eyes as she struggles to find her words. "Wh-what answers? Pl-please... don't hurt me."

Silas slams her against the wall, her head bouncing off it, missing a picture frame by barely an inch. I would have slammed her head into it solely for poetic justice.

He lets go, and she slides down the wall, sobbing as she claws at her neck. Silas sits next to me on the end of her bed and leans forward onto his knees, getting level with her face.

"I want you to tell me why the fuck you set Amelia up. Just a hint, there are no right answers."

She shakes her head, and Silas stands, causing her to cower and whimper incoherent nothings.

For fuck's sake.

This woman is all kinds of fucked in her head, and it is thoroughly pissing me off. She may be too fried to give us anything useful. I move closer, gripping her chin sternly forcing her to see all the anger I have inside of me begging to be released. Her bloodshot eyes narrow, and she jerks out of my grip.

"Jameson is an old work friend of Damian's." She sniffs, seeming to calm down, but her body continues to shake. "He only said he wanted to check on Mel; make sure she was dating a good guy, so I gave him Lance's name and number."

I grind my teeth, my patience wearing thin. "The money. Why would you say that Amelia had Damian's money?"

She stammers, her answer coming out jumbled up and making no sense. I take in her room, her sharply made bed, her family pictures still up, her messy vanity, and scattered pill bottles. It appears she's holding on to the way things were but fighting an internal battle on coping.

"Lance never asked you about the money, did he?" I ask.

She shakes her head furiously, her eyes darting around the room in a panic.

Silas's spine stiffens, bothered by her answer just as much as I am. We have no idea what they are after. Taking the pressure off Silas, I get her attention.

"You seem to also be confused about who is to blame for Damian's death because it sure as fuck isn't your daughter."

Kacey's eyes harden, and her lip curls in disgust as she lunges for me. "You don't get to speak on the matter. You know nothing!"

Silas quickly snatches her by the back of her hair, tossing her fragile body towards the door where she collapses and a pained groan fill the air. Pressing a foot on her chest, he pulls out his blade, pointing down at her.

"I know more than you do, bitch. I have seen all the fucked-up shit you put her through! She has spent her whole life only wanting to be good enough for you, just for you to toss her away like trash on some bullshit accusation that you try to make yourself believe to rationalize no official arrest for the crime." He leans in, just a little. "After all, she only went to the party to get plastered after you told her how much she was disappointing you. And Damian was already out driving because of a fight that you two had. Correct?"

She pants hard, fighting to get him off. Fear shines bright in her eyes once again as Silas places the tip of his blade to her throat. She stills, shutting her eyes forcefully like the coward she is.

"I should fucking kill you for everything you have done to her. I should rip your heart out the way you did to her time and time again. And her heart is so fucking big that she just keeps coming back for more, hoping that one day, Mommy will love her." He presses the blade a little deeper, just before it makes a cut. "So if and when your time comes, it will be her decision. You lost the daughter you once had. I hope you enjoy the monster we both have created."

He tilts his head to the side and gives the knife a small twist.

"Si."

"You wanna know why we are here? Because you set off the dominoes that had Lance raping and abusing your daughter and that's on you."

His tone grows louder, the anger inside him growing.

"Si."

"Guess who was there to pick up the pieces, time and time again." He pauses, and it just frightens her more. "Us! I should give you everything you have dished out to her, coming around tenfold."

He grins wickedly, bringing the blade to her arm.

"Si!"

"Seems like you were projecting. Does it not?"

He makes a quick move, slashing a shallow mark down her arm mirroring Amelia's.

Kacey howls in pain, grabbing her arm, thrashing it around. Silas lifts his foot, letting her scramble to her feet and I give him a look. He shrugs and I roll my eyes.

He's not wrong. It's only fair.

Kacey doesn't show any remorse for anything he just said, and his point is proven.

"If you leave right now, I won't call the cops," she says, her voice tired and irritated. She backs up slowly, and I cough on the laugh that forces itself out of my throat.

"Oh, honey. That doesn't scare us."

"Just leave... and take the rest of her shit when you go."

A fist wraps around my heart, hearing firsthand that her mother truly has no desire for Amelia to be a part of her life any longer.

Silas nods, moving to the kitchen and opening the medicine cabinet. He yanks every bottle out, dumping them down the garbage disposal. Kacey objects, moving to stop him, but I yank her back, wrapping my arms around her chest and pinning her arms down.

Finished, Silas comes back, getting an inch from her face, his blade pressed against her neck. "Lock yourself in your fucking room and detox. You make a big stink about this, and I swear, you will regret it," he sneers. "Consider this me showing you mercy, but don't think we won't be back when your daughter decides she is ready to settle the score."

He flashes an evil smile, and for the first time since we've been here, she sees Silas for himself, which alone proves to be more terrifying than her previous thoughts of him.

I shove her into her room without another word, slamming the door behind her and jamming a kitchen chair under the handle. Silas raises a brow at me, obviously not expecting such a cruel move from me.

"Sorry, are you the only one of us allowed to hate this woman? She can break down the door or smash a window when she's desperate."

He chuckles and shakes his head, taking out his phone. Dialing, he brings it to his ear. "Hi, I need to report someone that is a danger to herself and others at my current location... She's high on something, seeing things, and has a weapon. Please hurry."

He ends the call with a knowing smirk. Ian will have to file all the paperwork and make all the calls for involuntary commitment, but I know he'll be happy to help get this bitch out of Mel's life.

"I can finally do something about it," Silas says, walking up the stairs. "Now, if Mel wants to see her, it will be on her own terms and Kacey will finally be getting help."

Better than dead.

I follow him to Mel's room, not missing how he hesitates, once before opening the door and again before stepping inside.

We pack the remnants of her room in a few boxes, filling them with clothes, books, office supplies, and photos.

Silas sits on her bed, watching the sun dip down over the horizon, painting the sky in pink and orange. Sorrow and memories fill his eyes, his fingers brushing back and forth over the side of the mattress.

"Si."

He looks over at me, snapping out of whatever he was thinking about, and stands up as I walk over to the top of the mattress where a piece of paper sticks out. Lifting it, I pull out a stack of folded papers and flip through them.

Oh, Si.

"Perseus?" I raise my brows at him, and he drops his eyes to the letters, pulling them from my hands and looking them over himself. A small smile passes his lips before he places them safely on top of a box.

"You really do love her, don't you?"

"How could I not? Don't you?"

Amelia

Opening the bathroom door, I'm met with piercing green eyes.

"Are you ready for bed?" Lyle wraps me under his arm and leads me to my room.

He can pretend he wasn't snooping as much as he wants to, but I know better. I can feel them shadowing my every move just as easily as I felt him standing outside of the bathroom door I left unlocked.

They want to lurk, to try to catch me slipping back into my shell when they think I'm not looking.

Okay is a relative term, but for the first time in my life, I feel like I am exactly where I am meant to be. Hearing I've been used as a pawn in Nickolas's game only made me more determined to end this for all of us.

Finn darkens the doorway. His eyes light with hunger as he steps towards me.

"She made me a promise to sleep with me tonight, though I'm not opposed to sharing if she wants to," Lyle says, his eyes daring me with his proposal.

Did it just get hotter in here?

Finn keeps his eyes focused on me, leaving the question unanswered.

I glance between them and stutter, "I.. I've never done anything like that."

Finn grabs my waist and walks backward a few steps, Lyle slipping behind me. He trails his hands up my thighs and leans in; his hot breath hitting my lower neck before his tongue slides up behind my ear.

I stifle a whimper, but a shudder escapes, vibrating through my limbs.

"Does this turn you on?" Lyle whispers so close that his lips brush my ear when he speaks. "Seeing Finn in front of you while you hear me from behind you? Feeling two sets of hands on you?"

My knees quiver, and my breathing is fast. I know they see my body's response, leaving no need for me to answer, but I do anyway.

"Yes," I breathe out, enjoying this all too much.

"Are you imagining both of our mouths on you? Our cocks filling you at the same time?" Finn asks, and my breath catches.

"Y- yes." My voice cracks, and he chuckles at how much they're working me up.

"Finn?" Lyle asks, stopping his motions.

No. Please don't stop.

"What do you say, buddy?" Lyle slides his hands up the back of my towel and I relax into him.

Finn locks his eyes with mine running one a finger along the hem of the towel, teasing my still-warm skin. He pulls the towel from my body when I don't protest, leaving me fully naked between them. He cups my pussy, and my arms shoot out to grab his shoulders.

"Fuck," I choke out.

"You're soaked." Finn pulls his hand back, and his finger glistens in the light as Lyle gasps.

"Honestly, I don't think I've ever been harder in my entire life."

I look down and see his cock straining against his jeans, before my hand is on him, palming it. His head falls back, and he lets out a hungry growl. Then he drops to his knees in front of me.

Fuck yeah.

I look up at her from where I kneel, her body on full display above me, and my cock strains painfully against the fabric of my jeans. Sharing a woman isn't a first for me, but sharing with Lyle is, and for a moment I hesitate. But seeing Amelia unravel at the thought of both of us touching her makes me weak.

Lyle runs his fingers across her stomach, then up to cup her breasts.

"Your dick better stay far away from mine."

He laughs but doesn't look down at me, continuing his kisses along her neck. "Quit talking about your dick. You're making me soft."

I spread Mel's legs wider and sink lower to fit under her short frame. Positioning her on my face my open mouth splayed across her plush lips. Lyle pulls her arms back, pinning them behind her, as he continues to suck, lick, and nibble her skin anywhere he can reach. I lick and suck her, just enough to have her aching and trembling for more.

Standing, I draw her towards the bed and let her climb on as Lyle and I strip. She watches us with extreme focus as we climb further on the bed. Moving behind her, I turn her, pulling her back with me.

Lyle spins her back around to face him. He stretches out his legs and leans back on his hands. I loop one hand under her hips, gently pushing on her back with the other, bending her over into my brother's lap. I push a finger into her then two. She gasps, and my dick jolts at the sound.

Shit, I want her so bad, my dick throbbing, inches away from her pussy.

Lyle swipes his thumb over her bottom lip and pushes it into her mouth. He sucks in a breath sharply before speaking.

"Show me what that pretty mouth can do again, Angel."

I swipe the head of my dick along her pussy as she takes Lyle in her mouth. Gripping her hip with one hand, I guide myself into her slowly, taking my time. She moans around Lyle, and his head goes back.

I can't see past her shoulders, so Lyle's bottom half is hidden from view. With that small mercy, I get my rhythm going. I run my hand along the underneath of her belly and down further to her clit. Gently rubbing small circles as I pound into her, her body jutting forward with every thrust, her breasts swaying in tune.

She sits up, placing a hand on Lyle's chest.

"Oh, God. Fuck. Yes. Yes. Yes," she chants with a low feral growl, starving for more.

"My God, baby. You feel so fucking good," I groan.

She goes back down on Lyle, the slapping sound, saying she's working him with her hand too. I adjust my angle leaning over her to get deeper, then pound into her unyieldingly, placing my hand around her throat.

Three different voices pant loud and heavy. Lyle stiffens, releasing sharp grunts, shooting his cum down her throat. He waits a minute, letting her lick him clean as he tucks her hair behind her ear.

When she's finished I grab her by the arms, pulling her up against my chest, trapping her hands between us.

Lyle watches her intimately, and his eyes glisten like she just promised to show him all the world's wonders. He pushes a finger in and out of her mouth then starts rubbing her clit while tilting down to her chest, sucking and biting her perfectly pink nipples.

She wines with frustration, chasing her orgasm.

"Come for us, baby." We speak at the same time, and it's eerie how sinful it sounds.

Within seconds she is stiff, pushing back into me with all her weight.

"Fuck! Fuck! Fuck!" she screams as her orgasm tears through her, and her legs shake furiously. Her pussy grips my cock like a vice, my orgasm following hers.

Our bodies go slack and Lyle scoots back with a smug grin, appreciating that we gave her what she wanted.

I turn to grab my clothes from the floor, not wanting to be naked in front of my brother any longer than needed and find a shadow splayed across the floor.

Ian and Silas are standing there wearing opposite expressions.

Silas looks pained, and Ian looks thoroughly amused.

"Well... What. A. Show," Ian says, letting a laugh out and slowly clapping.

Amelia scrambles to cover up with a pillow, face crimson from exertion and embarrassment.

Lyle leans into her ear and whispers, "Nothing to be ashamed of, love. You own your shit, and we own you."

Her eyes darken as he removes the pillow relaxing and crossing her feet at the ankles.

"You were making a bit of a ruckus. We came to see what all the fuss was about." Ian teases mischievously, but you can feel the seriousness in his awkward statement.

"Just... praying," Lyle beams with his dick still on full display, and I toss a pillow in his lap.

"We know you two voyeurs just wanted a peep show. Next time all you have to do is ask." Mel stands, sauntering up to them, her hips swaying back and forth.

I would *die* seeing her go, but *fuck*, the view would be great.

"We should do this more often," she says, patting them on the chest as she pushes by them.

"Don't you dare shower again, Amelia Mason. We are not through," Lyle yells after her.

"Don't worry, Hellcat. Just going to get some water," she calls back from down the hall.

Silas's face stays in a state of panic.

"We are moving at her pace, Silas. She has chosen to move forward with each of us. It's time you make it possible for you to do the same." I tilt my head, hoping he finally lets her in.

His jaw twitches as he nods, and I silently pray to God that he doesn't fuck this up. I love my brothers, but I will not lose her.

She re-enters the room, scooping my shirt up off the floor and handing it to me.

"You look better in it," I smile. "Oh and we're playing a little game tomorrow evening, so don't wear yourself out too much."

I cast a wink over my shoulder and leave with the other two, giving her and Lyle some privacy.

***

I wake to a scream and barrel out of bed, nearly breaking my ankles to get downstairs. I grip my chest, begging my racing heart to slow, when I find Amelia trapped on the floor, Ian sitting on her feet, and Lyle sitting reverse cowgirl on her chest tickling her. Silas stands off to the side a smile on his face as he continues eating strips of bacon.

"Don't! Stop! I'm going to pee!" she cries out, laughing so hard that she looks like she's in pain.

"Don't stop? Oh Angel, I love hearing you beg for it."

Lyle grins at me, and I snort a laugh, seeing that joke coming from a mile away. He digs his fingers into her ribs, poking viciously. She squirms and jerks, trying to free herself.

"I swear. To God, I am going to beat. The shit. Out of you two!" Her words come out choppy as she fights to speak between every gasp of air she takes.

Silas stands, walks over to her, and hunches over her face. Her eyes widen with hope, and she raises a hand only for him to swat it back down. "No one is coming to save you from us, little monster. Figure your own way out."

He falls back onto the ground next to her, crossing his legs shoving the rest of the bacon into his mouth, chewing elaborately.

She cuts her eyes at him, and if looks could kill, his guts might be on the floor. She looks at me, and I wink, knowing that I have to play along, and this is far too amusing to end so soon. But if she pees, I will not be the one cleaning it up.

Lyle lifts up ever so slightly, moving lower to her hips, giving her the small opening she needs. She jerks her body, flipping over onto her stomach, freeing her feet. Kicking into the air, she nails Ian in the chest, knocking the breath out of him with a grunt. She pulls her knees under herself and bucks, pushing off the floor with everything she has, sending Lyle flying into Ian's lap.

She stands in victory, walks over to the puddle of men lying on the floor, and smacks them upside the head. Lyle laughs hysterically, still lying on top of Ian, still trying to suck in air. She raises her two middle fingers into the air and walks towards the kitchen. Her hand meets Silas's raised palm for a high-five, and then she follows it up with a slap on the back of his head, only making him chuckle.

She grabs the last slice of bacon and stalks toward me, pure evil in her eyes. I raise my hands in defense and back up slowly towards the front door.

"The only reason I am sparing you is because you just woke up, and I'm a good girl."

She motions two fingers from her eyes to mine, and I fake a large gulp. Plopping herself on the couch, we all follow, and I sit as far away as possible, leaving Silas to take the spot next to her.

"Everyone okay with going to load up soon?" I ask.

Agreement sounds off around the circle. I want to have time for everyone to get comfortable with their weapons of choice, primarily the only person with zero experience.

Ian gets antsy with these types of events, and none of us are happy to attend, given the circumstances. So it's best to not feel rushed and unprepared.

"Speaking of tonight, I need to pay y'all back for the dress."

I smile at her adoringly, absolutely loving that she hadn't pieced it together yet.

"It's on the house, babe," Ian grins, and she scrunches her face, still not getting it.

"No, I can pay it back-"

"Ian owns that shop, baby. Calm down." Silas' deep laughter forces the rest of us to grin.

Her mouth falls open, and then it clicks, probably replaying how everyone there probably kissed his ass.

"Consider it a gift." Ian nods at her, and she smiles nervously, obviously not comfortable with the situation from how she picks at the skin around her fingernails.

I can only imagine the dress she picked out. No doubt something black that is going to have me hiding my boner all night. Hell, I might let it rage just to add a little cherry on top of the statement we are going to make.

My mind drifts as I listen to her talk about her dancing skills, my eyes falling to the scar on her arm, and my mouth goes dry thinking about how she might react when she finds out about how it went with her mom. I'm not sure what part will upset her, but something will, and that thought alone has my stomach curdling.

"You aren't coming with us when we corner him, so one of us is going to stay back, and you can enjoy the party." Ian tells her, drawing me back to the present.

"Like hell!" she shouts, utterly pissed off and not accepting that order.

"We don't know how close my father and Lance are." Ian's eyes soften, cautiously insinuating the fucker might be there. A few broken bones might not have been enough.

"I don't give a rat's ass who's there. This is my fight more than any of yours, and I will play a part in making someone pay for making my life hell." Her face shows no sign of weakness, and I know Lyle is smiling like a moron at her comment. The rest of us make no move, unsure how to feel.

"She's right," Silas says, shocking me, and I narrow my eyes. "She is safer with all of us, and we all need to stick together. We have no idea how big this is now that Jameson is involved. He has all the same contacts we do."

I know he's right. Lance could have more people working with him and more orders than what pertains to her.

God, we really have no fucking clue what we might be walking into.

***

We arrive at my childhood home. The grass is a little overgrown, and the paint is chipping, but this little one-story house on the outskirts of town is where my family grew. I walk up the wooden steps, hearing the creek under our weight, and watch as Mel's head turns side to side, taking in a large part of our history. I place my hand on her lower back, needing to touch her in some way and guide her through the front door.

"Your armory is in your old house?" she asks in an amused and accusatory tone.

Lyle looks over his shoulder as he walks further into the house. "Where do you keep yours?"

"I don't have one."

Silas leans in as he passes her. "Maybe that's where you went wrong."

She jumps, his raspy tone right in her ear, and shoves him back.

"Sorry that I chose not to knife people that pissed me off. Though the thought suddenly seems appealing."

Lyle wags his eyebrows, getting hot at the thought of her sweaty, unleashing the hell he is constantly trying to lure out of her. I can't lie; the mental image is fucking gold.

"We'll meet you guys down there," I bellow at the crew, guiding Mel towards our old bedroom.

The room is empty except for some posters on the wall and our beds, perfectly made. It seemed silly, but when our uncle came home between trips, I didn't want an empty room to upset him. He spent half his life loving us like his own children when he never had to. It was the least I could do.

I look down at the hardwood floors, remembering all the shit that has been there. Playboy Bunny magazines shoved under the boards, soured beer seeping through the cracks, imprints from the various knife games we played. I move to the window where Amelia sits, rubbing her fingers over the carvings in the wood.

She smiles, tracing the three names dug into the wood, then moves to the corner. "Who did this one?"

I look at the light brown etchings of stars encasing the word *dreamer*.

"Si," I say in barely a whisper.

The stars.

Come on, baby, figure it out.

She hums. "This one is a lot deeper than the rest."

"Yeah, he used to sit here at night when he wanted to be alone and would trace over it."

I study her expression, seeing the emotion change a few times before she speaks. "Weird habit to have."

Dammit, I wish he would just tell her. I can't stand knowing something she doesn't. Especially when she is so close to figuring it out. All hell is going to break loose if she finds out that we all knew and said nothing. The way she kept her letters protected and hidden, she clearly adores her writer and the man responsible is downstairs staying quiet.

She deserves to know he had been keeping her hope alive long before she knew she needed it.

"I wanted to ask you a question," I say, breaking the silence.

"Oh, I thought you brought me in here because you wanted to have a quicky."

Damn, that idea isn't half bad. I adjust my dick, and she giggles, the sound a melody for my soul.

"Do you think anything one of us did would ever make you leave us as a whole?"

She pushes me onto my old bed and straddles my lap. "It would depend on what it was. I wouldn't want to, but you have made it perfectly clear that I can't choose between y'all."

"The idea of having you all to myself sounds like heaven, but there is something delicious in listening to my brothers make you orgasm so hard that the neighbors can hear. Even if it is hell."

"Yeah?" she teases, nibbling my ear.

"Mhm. I'm so hard right now thinking about all the sounds you might have made with Ian and Lyle yesterday. Tell me about it."

She slips her hand into my shorts wrapping it around my cock, wiping the pre-cum and sliding it around the head.

"I came twice on the way to the store. Once from Ian fingers, while I leaned across and sucked Lyle off. Then again when I rode Ian so hard I saw stars."

Fucking hell.

I groan, thrusting into her hand, feeling like I am going to blow my load any second like a teenager.

"I walked around that store, so sore but aching for more every time I felt him dripping out of me. And last night, Lyle fucked me so good. He fucked me so good that it left a bruise. Do you want to see?"

I bend her over the bed and yank her gym shorts down faster than the speed of light. The light purple blood bruise in the shape of half a handprint on her right cheek has me aching to do the same, and I place my hand on top. Pulling my dick out, I rub it up the length of her dripping pussy and push into her with a grunt.

"Ah fuck" she moans, and I slap my hand over her mouth.

"Shh. I am not sharing you right now."

I keep my hand on her mouth and fuck her hard, watching her ass as it slams back into me with every thrust. A view I could never get tired of. She reaches between her legs and helps herself along. I feel her tightening around me, and I know she's close already. I lick my thumb and press it to her ass, waiting for her to approve.

She bites into my fingers, and that's all I need. I shove my finger in, fucking her with it as I slam deeper into her. She detonates, pushing her ass into me as hard as she can, begging for everything I can give her. Her legs shake rapidly between mine, and I come hard, pulsing inside her. I empty everything I wanted to give her last night as I listened to her beg my brother for the filthiest of things.

I roll onto the bed next to her. "Fuck, I love you so much it hurts."

She flips her head over, her big green eyes staring at me. Scooping her up, I pull her on top of my chest, planting kisses all over her face, and she giggles.

"You don't have to say it out loud until you are ready, but I will shout it from the rooftops. I love you with my entire heart."

She rests her head on my chest, stroking her fingers through my hair.

"I love you too."

I push her up, my heart soaring like I never thought it could. And she grips my face, kissing it all over, copying me from our first night together. I wrap her in my arms, holding the woman I love in my old bed, as our house grows by one more once again.

***

I usher Mel down the steps, letting her go first but staying connected with interlocked fingers. Seeing the stained mats on the floor and all the workout equipment placed neatly on their racks sends me back to a time when a few teenagers toughened each other up and became something more.

Silas claps me on the shoulder, giving it a firm squeeze. We haven't been back here in a long time, having moved everything to our new house with Ian after high school. Amelia stands in front of the small wall lined with weapons and every type of strap or holster to conceal them.

"I'm not going to lie. This is equally awesome and disgusting." She takes a six-inch knife into her hands, flipping it over and inspecting the designs in the hilt.

"I could say the same about hearing you two bang," Lyle quips.

Fuck. I forgot how bad sound travels in this house.

"Are you planning on gutting someone?" Lyle teases, taking the knife from her, and her face pales.

"Are any of you?" she flicks her gaze to each of us like we are secretly mass murderers.

"Some are just for fun, baby," Lyle says. "Being real, the only ones we ever really keep on us are switchblades, brass knuckles, and a pistol."

She nods shortly, probably wondering how many times we have had to use them, and I want to know what she thinks of what we do.

Silas pulls his shirt over his head, showing off his tattooed muscles, and I roll my eyes. Amelia watches for a moment, and I can see the pulse in her neck and the light layer of sweat forming on her temple.

"Give me your hand," Silas demands.

"Wha- what?" she chokes out before shaking her head and giving him her back as she looks over the wall again. He reaches out, grabs her wrist, and jerks her to him. She slams into his body, catching herself with her hand on his chest.

"I'm serious. Close your eyes."

She hesitates a moment, her eyes locked on his. But she must see something that convinces her to trust him because her eyes flutter closed, and she exhales a deep breath.

He takes her hands, places her flat palm on his shoulder, and slowly guides it down the length of his arm. He repeats the same with the other arm then starts on his chest, taking both of her hands and placing them on his collarbone. Her breathing picks up as her hands skim over the tight skin of his pecs and abs until her hands hit the fabric of his shorts.

Her eyes open, and she stares at him, unmoving other than the heavy breaths that leave her soft lips.

"There are so many." Her voice cracks as her hands still rest under his on his lower stomach. "You hide them with your tattoos."

Silas nods, his heavy breathing matching her own. The sexual tension a suffocating cloud around them.

He's done so much to erase Nickolas, yet here we are.

"This is why." He tilts his head to the wall.

"Okay, so I may have had a little trouble grasping the necessity for all of this, but I get it now."

Most were left by his father using anything he could get his hands on. Silas covered them all so that people would stop asking questions, and he didn't have to see them daily. He has done so much to erase Nickolas, yet here we are.

Silas grabs his favorite gun, making sure it is empty, and motions for us to choose something. "Grab your weapons. Make it quick and let's go."

Mel grabs a knife that has two finger grips and swings open intricately. She flips it a few times, getting familiar with it. I reach for my switchblade, and Lyle grabs his trusty brass knuckles, flipping them around his finger. Ian takes a pistol from the wall, and we all meet Silas at the table piled high with ammo boxes to grab what we need.

"Alright bitches, we're ready to fuck shit up," Lyle states and promptly heads for the door.

Silas

Mel comes down the stairs wearing the most stunning dress I have ever seen in my life. And it has everything to do with her. I couldn't give a fuck about the dress Ian helped her get in.

Lucky bastard.

Her arm is threaded through his as he helps her descend in the red bottoms she's wearing. No doubt, a gift from Finn. I'm sure she's loving breaking the black-and-white dress code in the slightest way.

Her hair is in loose waves, and her makeup is dramatic. Winged eyeliner and bright lips with the perfect amount of dark eyeshadow above and below her eyes.

Lyle whistles and hollers his praise, dramatically fanning himself. She smiles, her bottom lip slightly tucked between her teeth.

She spins for us, revealing a butterfly pin securing the top half of her hair. A nod of symbolism.

Transformation.

"Dammit, baby." Finn coos.

As she reaches the bottom stair, I step forward.

"As stunning as ever," I whisper, pecking a kiss on her cheek.

She admires us dressed in matching all-black monkey suits, and her eyes sparkle with excitement as she turns back to me. "You all look very handsome. It's almost a shame we have to leave the house."

Did she just compliment me? Then sexualize me?

Am I blushing?

Finn grabs her blade and strap off the counter and kneels at her feet. She puts one leg out as he raises her dress to her hip in the most provocative way. The asshole knows what he is doing to all of us, yet I can't look away. The glimpse of her red lace panties makes me dig my nails into my palms in order to keep my composure.

Always with the red lace.

Red is *blood*. Red is *pain*. Red is *vengeance*.

Red is so fucking beautiful on her.

I told myself I could never let her love me or even like me, but her claws have dug in me so deep. She chose to stay, and I let her. She knows I love her... she just has no fucking clue how much.

Seeing how much she has pushed my letters to the back of her mind ripped my heart out and left it in a bloody heap on the floor. Especially when I, alone, was the one thing that kept her breathing. But she chose to stay, which means she feels something close to love for me too.

Maybe, just maybe, it will be enough for her to understand why I have been keeping it from her.

Tonight, I take the first steps and inch my way further into heaven or hell. Whichever fate she chooses for me, I will accept.

Finn secures the blade high on her thigh, opposite from the slit so she can access it easily. Personally, I think it would be hot as fuck being visible, but I was outnumbered. Apparently discretion outweighs means of necessity.

He drops her dress back to the ground, and I follow them out to the black limo waiting for us. Again I was outnumbered. We have to play the entire role tonight, and my truck wasn't suitable. I beg to disagree. She's a beauty.

The limo drops us off and we all take a deep breath as we walk through the large doors of Davis Mansion.

The bastard literally titled his own home. It's above the gate and everything.

Pretentious douche.

Everything is so white it's nearly blinding. Most men are in the typical black suit, while most women are in elegant white gowns. So we draw some attention, walking in looking like the four horsemen with a fallen angel at their center.

Amelia links arms with Ian and Finn while Lyle and I take up the outsides, almost forming a triangle with our girl at the point - our diamond. Our queen. Our everything. Should she choose to stay after everything has been brought to light, she wouldn't just be family.

She would own us.

We grab some refreshments from a circling waiter, and Jameson immediately spots us, his eyes widening as he politely finishes up a conversation with a middle-aged couple, who, by the looks of it, wipe their ass with hundred-dollar bills.

"Son, what a pleasant surprise. I wasn't expecting you and... your friends tonight."

Dickwad always thought we were so beneath him, but he wouldn't dare make a scene in front of all his wealthy friends and clients.

He gives a tight smile to Amelia. "Pleasure seeing you again. I admit it's even a bigger surprise to see you."

It seems none of us miss the underlying words left unspoken. *To see her whole and breathing happily.*

She is. Happy.

I would recognize her genuine smile anywhere. She feels in control, and the vibes radiate off her like a golden sun.

She pulls both men at her sides closer to her and rests her head on Ian's shoulder. "Well, I am so sorry that there was some miscommunication the first time we met. However, I have grown to love all four of these men dearly and plan to stick around for the long haul if they'll have me."

Love. All of us?

Ian kisses the top of her head. "We wouldn't have it any other way, and you know that."

She stumbles slightly and whimpers surprisingly. I look at her curiously, but none of the other guys move, except for the smirk playing on Finn's lips.

"Beautiful sentiments," Jameson forces through his porcelain white teeth. "Welcome to the family then. It's wonderful to see you all, but I know you must have other things to do than hang out with us old people."

Subtle, asshole.

"Actually, father. We were hoping to chat if you had the time. Seems we have a few things to catch up on."

Jameson's face pales, then he picks his chin up. "Of course. You enjoy yourselves, we can meet in my office in about an hour."

Ian gives him a tight nod, and he disappears into the crowd.

"I'll keep an eye on him until then," Finn says, giving Mel a light kiss, careful to not smear her lipstick. Then he casually moves about the room with charisma, his chameleon skills unmatched.

Ian outstretches his hand to Mel, her silk-gloved hand delicately falling in his as he leads her further into the ballroom. Partners pair up, and as the music lifts, they all sway in unison. Being part of the upper class growing up, Ian brings her in close for a dance. She fits in his frame perfectly as they effortlessly float around the room, and I am almost certain this was also a skill her mother instilled in her against her wishes. Although I cannot picture Amelia enjoying such a thing as a kid, her face tells a different story.

She smiles, her cherry red lips making it even more vibrant, and laughs a deep-belly sound of pure joy as she spins and twirls around Ian. It's contagious. I don't even realize I'm smiling with them until my cheeks start aching. Minutes pass, but I don't dare look away, wanting to forever remember this moment.

A moment where she loves all of us and is happier than ever. Just in case it ends.

Seeing the way Lyle watches them, too, the same smile on his face as he leans against a pillar, has me doubling down. I would break our vow if it came down to it.

I would have to. There is no way I could live with myself knowing my mistakes ruined their chance at a happy life with her.

I would do whatever it took, even if it means losing my brothers and disappearing forever. I would happily give them the life I always dreamed of for myself.

The song ends, and they come back to us panting, still floating on air. Maybe that's how life would always feel around her. She motions for Lyle to switch places with Ian and take her out there, and to my surprise, he does.

"You better be prepared to cause a scene," he says, and I chuckle, knowing exactly where this is going.

A violin plays a few soft notes, preparing for the next song, and Lyle centers them in the middle of the waltzing crowd. Just as the notes fade out, Amelia gasps, drawing everyone's attention, and her hands fall to her stomach.

"What the fuck is wrong with her?" I ask Ian, and he grins.

"Maybe just nervous jitters."

A mix of classical instruments plays a version of modern music, and it happens. The couples around them look appalled as Lyle starts waving his arms around like a lunatic, his bottom half thrusting and his feet squeaking against the waxed floor. Amelia doesn't miss a beat, hiking up her long gown and doing the same, completely off-beat, unnatural, and utterly fantastic.

Ian and I burst with laughter, and a few guests crack a smile, though no one seems more unamused than Jameson himself. I pull my phone out and record to document everything about this. Hell, we might even post it to every news outlet we can.

Amelia and Lyle begin grinding on each other, laughing and dry fucking for the whole room to see. Even though every part of me wants to keep those movements of her body private, I watch with pride as she helps cause the first stroke of tonight's chaos. I spot Finn out of the corner of my eye, perched on a wall, his hands adjusting in his pockets, as he talks to a young couple. Though, his attention is not focused on whatever it is that they seem to be discussing.

Amelia's hands grasp Lyle's shoulders, her body stilling as she pants, head upturned to the vaulted ceiling. Lyle grabs her face, kissing her hard, and I only wish I could hear the little humming noise that always leaves her plush lips when she's kissed like that.

The song ends, and she looks utterly exhausted as she fumbles ungracefully back to where we are. Her eyes land on mine, and for a moment, I am hopeful she'll ask me to dance next.

"He's not here," she whispers, still trying to catch her breath.

"That doesn't mean there isn't someone else here, and we just don't know who to look for," I say.

She says nothing, her fingers fiddling with the delicate designs of her dress, her eyes scanning the room. Before I can second guess it, I reach for her hand. She takes it, threading her covered fingers through mine.

"I'm scared," she admits.

"Good, that means you still have something worth losing. I'm scared too."

Her eyes soften, and her small body leans into mine. I press a kiss to her head and whisper, "Use your fear to fight for the thing you are scared to lose. No one takes anything from you ever again. Vow it."

I straighten back up, keeping our stance and outward appearance firm.

"I vow," she says, her little voice sounding bigger than she is.

Now. I have to do it now.

A slower song begins, and I swallow my pride. "Would you like to dance?"

"I'd love to."

I take her hand, guiding her through the crowd to the dance floor. She wraps one hand around my neck placing the other in my calloused hand, smiling nervously, but her eyes tell a different story. One of strength and determination.

Her body feels so good this close to mine. I can feel her warmth, and I don't think anything has ever felt so damn good.

I spin her, her body leaving mine and coming right back. "So, do you really love me, or were you saying that for show?"

"I think you are smart enough to have figured out that answer already."

"I know you would never throw that word around carelessly," I snap back.

I sway us side to side, taking only small steps to try to appear like I know what I'm doing. I spot Lyle giving me two thumbs off from the side of the dance floor, and I flip him off with the hand behind Amelia's back. His chest shakes with laughter as he throws back his glass of champagne.

Her eyes narrow, but I keep mine as soft as possible, hoping that's the way they truly look, with a nervous smile on my lips.

"You don't know anything of substance about me, Silas Steele. You haven't cared to." She sucks in a sharp breath, jerking her head around finding Lyle smirking like something is hilarious.

It's now or never. Either she will hate me, or she won't.

I pull her back towards me and continue our small sway.

"I know that in high school, you left sticky notes covering the entire mirror of the girl's bathroom with encouraging messages, and they were everything you wish someone had said to you. When you checked back the next class period, and they were all in the trash, you spent twenty minutes crying in that same bathroom."

Her movements falter, and I tug her gently keeping us in our little bubble.

"I know when you cry, your eyes turn a brighter shade of green. I know you hate when people look at your feet too long because someone once told you they were ugly. I know you drink coffee for the taste, not the energy. I know you sleep with a fan because the silence is uncomfortable. That you sleep even better when it rains."

Her eyes get lost as she soaks in my every word.

"I know you hate the feeling of cotton balls and microfiber towels. I know you love shopping, but hate the crowds because they're too loud and too close. Just like how you feel about being here."

I pull her in close, shielding her as much as I can.

"But you love concerts, big or small. That you listen to music while you clean so you can dance. I know you like the color red, not because it contrasts your black hair, but because it reminds you of blood."

Her eyes never leave mine, but as I go on, her brows pinch together, first in confusion and then in pain.

"I know when you have a panic attack, you wrap your arms around yourself and rock back and forth because you never had someone to do it for you."

The song ends before I'm finished and she pulls away, making a break for the bathroom. I raise my hand at Lyle, knowing he is about to follow her, but I do instead. I catch the door and lock it behind us.

"Silas-"

"I know that one morning you received a letter in your gym locker room after a particularly hard morning. I know that as those letters kept appearing in your lockers, binders, and then your window, you started smiling more."

I take a hesitant step closer.

"I know you stare at the stars when you are lost. I know your favorite constellation is Perseus because the person leaving you those letters told you the story, promising to always protect you the same way."

Another step.

A deep breath.

"I know I have been in love with you for a very long time, and I never told you because I was scared of bringing you more pain, but I am telling you now."

Hurt consumes her beautiful face, and her hand whips through the air, striking my cheek. Tears well in her eyes, and I clench my jaw, feeling her pain mix with my own. She stumbles back, bracing herself on the bathroom counter.

"If this is some fucked-up joke, I don't find it funny." Tears stream down her perfectly made-up face.

"I've never been more serious in my entire life."

We stand in silence as she stares at me like I am both a complete stranger and someone she has known her whole life.

"How fucking dare you," she finally says, stalking towards me, pure anger spilling from every pore.

"Do you know how many fucking years I poured my heart out to you? *You?*"

She spits that word like it is the foulest thing to ever leave her mouth.

"No. No way."

"Am I really that bad?"

She scoffs, realization written all over her face, now understanding all the comments I made to her.

"You left me!" she screams, slamming her palms into my chest.

That's it, baby. Get angry.

"You watched me for *years* Silas!"

She hits me again. Raging, letting the pain out. And it's beautiful.

"You saw me endure so much pain and did *nothing*. Because what? You thought your daddy issues would fuck me up worse than what I was going through?"

I open my mouth, and she slaps me again, busting my lip as it collides with my teeth.

"You invaded my space. My heart! And then you *left* me when I finally did what you begged me to do."

She takes a breath and I ready myself for another round of punches.

"But you didn't, did you? Not really. I just moved right down the fucking hall. Was that too much for you, huh?"

Yes.

"Because then you had to make me believe that you hated me in order to keep up this version of yourself."

She backs up, putting distance between us.

"You had to take away the only thing that kept me breathing for years - this sliver of hope that one day I would meet the only person who gave a fuck about me. Do you understand how fucked you are in the head for doing that?"

Her chest shakes with short, pained breaths, and I see the panic attack forming.

I put one foot in front of the other, slowly walking towards her, and place my hand on her cheek, hoping to ground her.

Please. Please look at me.

"You tricked me, Silas. Those letters were... everything to me, but only a joke to you."

Her voice shakes, and the pain underlining it shatters my heart into a million pieces.

"No. Everything I ever wrote to you was *me*. Baby, please look at me."

She tilts her face up, showing me the pain in her eyes and it kills me.

"You have it all wrong. I spent so long wanting nothing more than to hold you in my arms. I sat by your window and listened to you talk to me. I kept track of every part of your life and made it part of mine. You may not have even seen me, but I was always there. Always protecting you where I could. I would never hurt you,"

I close the distance between us, but she takes a step back.

"You already did."

I swallow the hard truth I knew would be there if this moment ever came.

"The night I was going to deliver my next letter, you were at our house. The night you met Finn. I saw all this happening before you even went to his bedroom, and I knew then our time was over. I couldn't keep writing to you when you were right in the middle of my world. Right where I fought for so long to protect you from. I was angry that my letters had taught you nothing."

She steps back again.

"Well, almost nothing. I taught you to be aware of your surroundings. To feel for me."

I take another step.

"I know you felt me. You would always look around in the most adorable way, not sure if you should be hopeful or fearful when you knew someone was lurking so close."

I step again, and so does she, her back bumping against the wall.

"But you never feared me, did you? You left your window open for me. You had no idea who I was, but you invited me in."

She sucks in a breath as I press my body to her, my dick hardening.

"On your hard nights, I would stay there all night, soothing the crease in your forehead when you had a nightmare."

I brush my thumb across the skin.

"Some nights, I let myself hold you, imagining the life we could have had. I know you knew I was there."

She closes her eyes, resting her head against the wall, her breathing deepening as she places my face in every fantasy she had about her anonymous lover.

I run my hand down her arm, enhancing her imagination with my touch.

"I know you smelled me. Felt my weight on the bed. Heard me whisper to you in the dark."

I push my knee between her legs, the slit in her dress separating perfectly for me, and she whimpers the smallest sound as I make contact with her middle.

"I know you dreamed about me because you would call out for me and grind your ass back on me. It took so much effort not to rip your panties off and sink into you while you dug your nails into me so hard it made me bleed."

She grinds on my leg, retrieving the friction she desperately desires.

Fuck me, it is so damn hot.

I lick up the side of her neck, and she pants, her warm breath caressing my ear.

"I dreamed about you too. I dreamed about you begging for me to own you in every way. I dreamed about our love, hate. Trauma. Intertwining in such an erotic way that sex always ended in blood, scratches, and brutal kisses."

Her eyes open, tears no longer threatening to spill over.

"I hate you, but I love him, and I want to make you both bleed," she says breathlessly, and my dick couldn't possibly get any harder.

"But I don't know if that is because of how much I hate that you lied to me or how much I hate that you never came for me when this is exactly where I would have wanted to be."

Moans and lust fill the air as we dry-hump each other against the wall, and I can't take it any longer.

"We can figure that part out later. Right now, I need to taste you. To fuck you."

She gasps as I slide my hands through the slit of her dress and sink down to my knees. Pulling her panties down, I hoist her leg up onto my shoulder. Her wet pussy, inches from my face, and my heart pounds in my ears.

She puts her hand out, stopping me. Then reaches between her legs and pulls out a familiar pink remote vibrator.

Those motherfuckers.

"Little monster, were you aware I have a rule about borrowing things from my room?"

She nods, looking down at me through her dark lashes, and a guttural growl rumbles inside me.

I grab the vibrator tucking it into my pocket, and shove my face into her, finally tasting her sweet cunt as she fists my hair, whimpering loudly.

"You have no idea how long I have dreamed of burying my face between your legs and never coming up for air."

"Silas."

Fuck.

Hearing her moan my name makes me feral. I eat her like I will never have another meal as long as I live. I grip her thighs, feeling her knife, and she fucks my face with wild abandon, chasing down her orgasm as I push my tongue inside.

"I'm going to come."

I smile, knowing damn well anyone passing by can hear her, and it turns me on even more. I would claim her in the middle of the fucking dance floor if she would let me.

I pull her off me, and she groans in protest.

"You are going to come on my dick. I am going to fuck you hard, and you are going to show me how much you hate me and hate yourself for loving me inside you."

I stand her on her feet, and we strip our clothes, neither of us moving fast enough. She leaves her weapon in place and seeing her wearing nothing but that is something I will definitely be jerking my dick to later, again and again.

I throw her onto the countertop, and without warning, pull her forward and thrust into her.

She cries out, begging me for more while cursing my name from betrayal and ecstasy. She digs her nails into my shoulder, and I groan, thrusting into her harder, wanting her aching for days when I am done with her.

"Fuck you feel so fucking good wrapped around my cock. Tell me why you hate me, baby." I dig my fingers into her scalp and yank her head back, biting her neck. She cries out again, and the sound is music to my ears.

"You are a liar."

She pants her insults with every harsh thrust, and I force her legs open wide, watching where we connect.

"You betrayed me."

I bite her neck, thrusting even harder.

"You hurt me."

Fuck. I'll let her hurt me again and again if this is my penance.

"You ruined everything."

I couldn't agree more.

I fist her breasts and crash my lips into hers for a bruising kiss, selfishly taking everything I want like I will never get to kiss her again. Our tongues fight for dominance, both of us starving for more. She bites my lip, breaking skin, making me taste copper.

"I hate you. I hate you," she pants, trying to catch her breath.

Yeah, baby. Give it to me.

She growls and pulls her blade out, pressing the steel to my chest, digging it in slightly.

"I should make you feel what it's like."

Oh, sweet girl. I already have.

Her eyes turn hard but not cold, like she wants to hate me, but she can't.

"Do it," I grunt, driving into her harder.

She presses the steel, breaking the surface of my skin, dragging it across my chest, matching her own scar.

We are one and the same baby.

"Harder," I grind out through closed teeth, and she hesitates a moment before digging the point of the knife into my pec a good half inch, watching my face instead of the blood pouring down my chest.

"I ruined you," I say, my dick throbbing and swelling at how much I love the pain.

"Yeah," she agrees, keeping the knife in her hand while moving the other to my head. In a swift move, she adjusts her grip on the handle and grabs a handful of my hair with it. She pulls so hard my scalp burns.

"You deserve better than me."

"Yeah," she says, moving her hands to my shoulders.

"But this feels so fucking right."

"Oh God. Yeah!" she screams, her pussy pulsing on my cock as she shatters, and the sight, mixed with the way she is digging her knife into me, makes me come undone.

"I lied," she leans forward, resting her head on my shoulder, careful to avoid the blood dripping down my skin. "I can't hate you, and you ruined nothing. Perseus meant too much to me."

I adjust slightly, my dick still in her. "Have you ever thought about how all the guys were lurking around in the dark after Finn called me on the dock?"

She shakes her head, keeping it pressed to my skin.

"The movie I said we would watch once we got inside. *Algol.*"

She lifts her head.

"It's the star in Perseus's constellation that represents the head of Medusa. We use it as a code word when we are in trouble."

Her eyes widen, and she places her hands on my chest, smearing the blood.

"I chose that because you were always a part of my life, and I always felt like the villain in your story. I always told you I wanted to be your Perseus… not that I was."

She places her hand on my face, and I lean into it, smelling the blood.

"I don't believe that."

She smears the blood across my lips and kisses me deeply, the wet color mixing with the matte red of her lipstick.

"Monsters are made, not born, and no one is past redemption," she whispers. "Two broken people may never fit together perfectly, but they may find the missing part of their soul in the shards of the other's."

"Or maybe they will only cut themselves and cause further damage trying to force it to fit," I whisper against her lips.

"You were the first person I ever really loved, Silas, only I didn't know it was you. You are cruel and crass because you think you don't deserve to be loved. But you have had my heart for just as long as you say that I have had yours. We fit."

I help her down and back into her dress, brushing her hair over her shoulder to zip her back up. She watches me as I get dressed, the black fabric covering the blood well since I refused to wash it off, at least for now.

"So, do you forgive me, Meda?" I ask, my outward appearance sturdy and confident, unlike the coward shaking within.

"Meda?"

"Short for Andromeda, saved by Perseus."

Her face lights up, and I fasten my tie back into place, watching as she combs out her long waves with her fingers, lost in thought for a minute.

"I like that," she whispers in the sweetest voice, completely contrasting the obscenities she was screaming at me minutes ago.

She double-checks that everything is back in its rightful place, including her blade and I step behind her, adjusting her butterfly pin.

Transformation.

"So?" I ask, after a comfortable silence.

She sighs. "I don't know how to feel right now. I love you, but that doesn't mean I forgive you. Don't think you are getting off easy."

I chuckle, following her to the door. "I wouldn't dream of it."

She mumbles as she opens it, the crowd's noise making her almost inaudible. "I just need to stab something."

Amelia

We find Lyle waiting for us around the corner, and I am instantly reminded of the cum slickening my thighs from the look on his too-sexy face.

"Hell, Mel. You look like a tornado threw you guys around a bit. Is everything okay?" Playfulness is in his tone, and a faked look of worry crawls across his face.

I love-tap his balls; not in the mood to deal with his smart ass.

"Mind your mouth."

"All fun and games," he squeaks out, cupping his jewels before searching for the strength to stand straight. He clears his throat. "They are heading to Jameson's office right now. And we spotted Emma here with a date."

Those two must still be bumping uglies. Good. Our leverage still stands.

I can almost see the dare on Lyle's lips as he speaks again. "She was eye fucking us, by the way." He spins on his heel, leaving me next to Silas, thoroughly pissed off.

I grind my teeth and push a mental note of cunt-punching her to the back of my mind before following Lyle. We walk down a long hall lined with professional artwork and not a single family photo showing Ian any older than maybe thirteen. Silas stays close, placing his hand on my ass. Feeling his possessiveness sends sparks through my body.

The sense of security and power I feel as I walk through the mansion confuses the affliction I feel about him hiding everything from me. He worked for so long to comfort me, always wanting to be the one to love me, but never once claimed me for his own. Worrying something in his past makes him unworthy. Could someone's love truly be so pure? So selfless? So wrong?

My mind aggressively passes over all the possibilities for his reasoning as we make our way to the office room, though I find nothing of substance. There's nothing that would make me love him any less, solely for the reason of how pure his intentions were.

Ian stands inside the room, looking constipated beyond belief, and Finn sits on the couch, sipping a golden liquid out of a short glass. I assume we are waiting for Jameson to make his grand, fashionably late entrance.

On cue, he stalks into the room, closing the door behind him. "I don't want to be rude to my guests, so excuse my bluntness, let's make this quick," he says taking a seat behind his desk.·

"We were thinking the same thing." Silas's voice sounds like thunder cracking through the night sky, and I shiver as he moves around me, leaving Lyle to move in closer, half shielding my body with his own. "We want to know why the fuck you wanted the name of Amelia's ex-boyfriend when we all know damn well you didn't give a single flying fuck about *how she was doing*?"

Jameson's face pales, knowing we've caught up to him and that he's about to get his shit kicked in if the wrong words come out of his mouth. Unfortunately for him, there are no right words.

"You are going to trust the words of a junky?" he spits, and my fists tighten into balls, as I let the rage trickle out of the little box I keep it in.

How fucking dare he talk about her like that? They were friends.

I step forward, and Lyle subtly squeezes my wrist.

"Not yet," he whispers, barely moving his lips.

"Are the words of your side-fuck intern more reliable?" Ian asks.

He barks a laugh, then Ian is moving, slamming his phone down on the desk, showing him the clip of security footage we have.

"Tell the fucking truth, or I swear to fucking God, I will ruin you and make sure mom leaves you with nothing but the shirt on your goddamn back."

I have never heard him so angry. So outspoken. Why is it so erotic?

Jameson stares off at his son, and Ian stares right back, moving an inch closer, daring him to call his bluff.

Striking a nerve, Jameson finally gives, leaning back in his chair, forfeiting his little charade. He pins his eyes on Silas.

"Nickolas Steele."

No one moves a muscle; the same thought going through all our heads, despite what we already know.

Mother-fucking fuck.

"Why?" The single word leaves Silas's throat, choking him on the way out. His fists ball at his sides, and I want to uncurl them and run my hand over the scars that lay across each knuckle.

I want him to know that he has me as an anchor. I know how it feels to hear the name or see the face of the person who has wrecked you. The least I could do for him is return the favor that he has done for me so many times before.

Still trying to keep his gall, Jameson crosses his arms on this chest, looking unamused. "He got word that his son was a weak little bitch, pawning over some cunt instead of running the family business. He wanted to know who and why, so I merely gave him the help he wanted. He has plans for his only son and needed pawns to get the ball rolling before he got out." Jameson stares Silas down, unflinching and unapologetic.

"Family business?" The question slips out before I can register that I want to ask it. I should have waited.

"Cocaine," Silas snips, not turning to look at me. "My dad dealt drugs with a local gang and tried to force me into it for years. Some of those *lessons* I got were targeted at that as I got older. My guess is that he was pissed to hear that I never stepped up, ruining his big game distributor plans and embarrassing him."

"Seems we can relate in the pathetic son department," James snorts, thinking this is all hilarious because he is untouchable.

For years I thought Jameson Davis was a well respected, trustworthy man, but I had completely misread him. He is just as crooked as the rest of the world.

"So you sell out the daughter of one of your employees because you are a skeezy bastard only concerned with self preservation?" I see red, hurting no longer for myself; but for those I love.

"Damian Mason was nothing more than my employee and a self-righteous do-gooder who couldn't see the bigger picture. You saw me as Daddy's best friend because you are just as naïve and blind as he was. Hopefully, it's not too late for you when you finally open your precious green eyes."

He smiles wickedly, and a fist flies through the air, connecting to his jaw, sending him backward over his chair shattering the huge glass window behind him. Silas jumps the desk, draws his gun, and crouches on top of him, pressing his pistol right between Jameson's eyes.

"I swear to God you better be telling the fucking truth, or I will dump your body at the bottom of the fucking lake, tied to him and Lance."

I rub my thighs together, and Lyle slips his hand around the back of my neck, digging his fingers in right below my ears.

"Are you getting wet for us watching this,

Angel?"

I say nothing, and he chuckles.

Jameson struggles to breathe as Silas presses his knee harder into his chest. "You're just as fucking crazy as he is!" he chokes out, looking like he's about to piss his pants.

That word. God, I hate that word.

Crazy. Crazy. Crazy.

This time, I don't fight it as my anger spills over. I storm over next to Silas, my heels clicking in the silent room, and I run my hand up Silas's neck, gently tugging as I pass, then squat down behind Jameson's head. My knee falls in the slit of my dress, giving all my men a clear view of my soaked red lace panties.

I slip my new favorite toy off my thigh and flip it open, pressing it to Jameson's jaw, forcing his eyes to mine. Silas allows me to take over, lowering his gun but keeping him pinned to the ground.

"Oh, you don't know the fucking half of it. We are all mad here." I dig in the same way I had done to Silas. The same thrill shooting through me giving me the best high I've ever had as I watch the bead of blood form. "What was promised to Lance?"

Jameson murmurs through his clenched teeth, and I dig in harder, causing the bead to grow until the weight of it drags it down his neck, staining the collar of his crisp white shirt. He grunts again, and I let up, allowing him to speak.

"An athlete deal. If he followed through, I had to get him an athlete deal and enough money to jump-start his career."

A chaotic laugh bubbles in my throat. For a split moment, I thought maybe this was about something more than something as shallow as a name for himself.

"And what do you get out of watching me suffer?" I ask, no longer assuming he may have been threatened. Lyle is at my back pulling my hand further to the side, placing the point of the knife on the side of Jameson's neck, and the warmth of his body soaks my skin deliciously.

"This is the carotid. Dead in seconds if you slash here."

I hum, twisting the knife, playing with the skin that separates this man from life and death.

Lyle runs his hand up my bare thigh and moves my wet panties to the side, my pussy now bare and hovering right behind Jameson's head. Silas growls low, barely audible, and I see Lyle's teeth shine out of the corner of my eye. "You never were good at sharing."

I lock eyes with Silas, pain and arousal written all over his face. Lyle dips a finger into me, then two. Silas's jaw flexes as he clenches his teeth. Lyle moves his fingers in me, hard but slow, ever so fucking slow. I moan, and my hand slips, nicking the skin it was pressed to.

I jerk my head, Lyle inside me, teasing my g-spot. "Oops. Sorry, I was thinking about how it might feel to fuck all my boyfriends at once. Lost focus."

"Nasty whore," Jameson spits, and I laugh, no shame in sight, though it's Ian who pries Jameson's tongue out of his mouth, holding his own knife against it.

"You speak to her like that again, and you will never speak again."

Oh, fuck me.

"Where were we?" I hum, patting him childlike on the cheek as Ian releases the gross organ.

"We made a deal," Jameson squeaks like a scared little bitch. "I keep him on the streets, and I get a cut of his profits as he takes over territories of other local gangs. A simple power move."

The wind blows through the broken window, cooling my sweaty skin, raising the hair on my arms as Lyle starts to fuck me again with his long fingers. I whimper, my knees shaking as I try to keep my stance in heels.

Jameson snarls but says nothing, fearing his son's threat and the weapons still aimed at him.

"Baby girl, don't you dare come yet," Finn says, licking his lips as he watches his brother work me over.

"I think I'll finish this up at home," I tell Jameson, flashing him a wink. He stays deathly still as I withdraw my knife. I look at Ian, silently asking him to wrap this up, and he smiles as I catch on to the power structure happening.

"You will keep your fucking mouth shut about this, or your little video will go viral. You will lose your wife, your job, and your credit. And if you aren't careful not to piss us off any further, you may find yourself... missing."

I can feel the wicked joy radiating off each of them at the reminder of all the times they have made someone go *missing*. I remember everyone always joking that our police force was a joke. Not that I ever got in enough trouble to know, but would murder really be hard to get away with if it looked like something else? It's not disgust that surges through me as I think about them taking fate into their own hands, but something far more... dangerous.

Excitement.

We pass Emma on the way to the door, my boys around me like I'm a fucking goddess with an army of vengeful demons, and I have never felt more loved in my entire life. They stay trained on our exit, not sparing her a glance, yet she stares lustfully at each of them.

She must not have gotten the hint.

I pause my steps, the guys stopping with me, and her face pales. She takes her date's hand and tries to lead him away, but I side-step, blocking her route before she even steps.

"Oh. Hi, Amelia. Nice to see you again," she says sweetly, trying to avoid a scene.

"Likewise." I smile, threading my hand through Silas's, feeling the others crowding my back.

Someone's hand squeezes my ass, and my money is on Finn, given how worked up he looked moments ago.

"However, I can see that you have your own date tonight, so between him and the other man you are fucking, I don't see why you continue to eye fuck mine."

I wouldn't doubt that her date is just a cover, so she isn't alone tonight. Her face pales, and her date looks appalled, jerking his hand away and storming out the front door with a string of muttered insults. Not the brightest crayon in the box and lacks simple observation skills.

"Green is an unflattering color on you, babe. Find someone else to bother and stay the fuck out of all aspects of my life, or your face might just match that ugly inside that you have."

Amelia

I'm jerked back into the limo seats closest to the door. Finn pulls me into his lap, prying my legs apart. My dress splits, and he tosses the fabric over my leg, revealing the mess Silas left. His dick straining against the tight fabric of his slacks. He forcefully rubs the palm of his hand along my wet panties, forcing a moan from my throat.

"Everyone realizes that we will have to maintain a low profile after that, right?" Silas asks with a grunt as he gets in last.

"Uh-huh," Finn mutters.

"Yeah," I breathe out.

Near murder at a public event. Bad. Got it.

Silas plops down between Ian and Lyle, sitting across from us and very quickly shuts the hell up.

The car begins moving, but we don't stop. I force my eyes to stay open, bouncing my gaze between the three of them as Finn's fingers slide beneath the clinging fabric. He plunges his fingers into me, curling them just right. And I hold back the whimper that wants to come out, watching as Ian's lips part with anticipation for it.

I manage a grin and Ian growls. The sound so unfamiliar coming from him. A daring look consumes his features, darker than any I've seen him wear before. "You evil little thing. Let me fucking hear it, baby."

"Oh, God."

The sound slips as Finn picks up pace, vigorously fingering me and taking my breath away with the intense sensation.

"That's a good fucking girl. I bet that feels so good, doesn't it?" Finn says.

"Yes. So fucking good."

I tighten around Finn's fingers and dig my nails into his arm, reaching around to press on my lower stomach. The pressure builds higher and higher. And I beg him to stay right there, my eyes locked on Lyle.

He reaches for the liquor at the mini-bar next to him and pours a drink.

"Who owns you?" Lyle asks, replacing the bottle.

"Lyle."

Fuck I'm so close.

"Finn."

God please don't stop.

"Ian."

Fuck!

"Silas."

Lyle moves to me, pulling my head back with a hand full of hair. "Who will kill any motherfucker that touches what is theirs?"

I repeat their names again.

So fucking close.

Lyle takes a sip of his drink, then his hand grips my jaw and pries my mouth open. His lips pucker, and the amber liquid spills from his mouth to mine. I hold it there, trying not to choke as my orgasm tears through me. The liquid burns going down.

"That's goddamn right," Lyle says with admiration.

He sets his glass into the cup holders next to us and slips the belt from around his waist, looping it intricately until it resembles handcuffs. He pulls me to my knees, my head spinning from my lingering climax. He binds my hands behind my back, then shoves me right at Silas's feet.

"Now, suck him, Angel."

I sink back onto my legs and peer up at the man in question. His gaze is firm but not cold. His dick is hard, but he doesn't move. Waiting for me.

"Ian, could you undo Silas's pants for me?" I ask my gaze never leaving Silas. I watch as Silas lets Ian unbutton, unzip, and slide his pants down just enough to free his dick. It springs up, standing proud for me.

"One more thing, love," I turn to Ian.

"Anything."

"I want you to give Lyle a hand job matching my pace. Let's see who comes first."

Ian's cheeks tinge pink, but he only hesitates for a moment. Carlisle moves and crouching behind me. His slacks are already undone when he sits on the other side of Ian. Ian's fingers dance on his thigh nervously and I give him a subtle nod of encouragement. He takes it, turning to Lyle, freeing his dick, and wrapping his hand around the base. Lyle groans, and then I have three sets of eyes on me.

Finn moves behind me grabbing onto the belt wrapped around my wrists. I lift on my knees, and he pushes me forward as I open my mouth, taking Silas in deep.

I work him slowly, getting his entire shaft wet with spit. I eye Ian, watching him match my slow pace. Two voices moan, groan, and cuss as we pick up pace.

Silas rests his hands at his sides, letting me do all the work. I work him faster, and Ian matches, glancing between me and what he's doing. Twisting and bobbing, I do the best I can without the use of my hands. I glance up at him a few times, and each time I see the same conflicted expression on Silas's face.

He groans when I swirl my tongue around the head of his cock. So I do it again every time I come back up. His expression changes - like he's holding back.

I sink down as far as I can take him. Spit gathers at the base of his shaft and strings from my mouth as I come up, gasping for air.

His hand finds the back of my head and shoves me back down before I've fully inhaled, something snapping in him. He forces me up and down as fast as he can, keeping me as low as possible, and I gag.

I hear a sharp grunt from Lyle and look over as cum spurts out, coating his dick and Ian's hand. He whimpers as Ian continues working him, still following my rhythm. I squeeze my eyes shut, gagging again as Silas holds me down and pours down my throat with the thrust of his hips. I swallow him down greedily then sit back on my heels with a content smile. The smell of cum and spit coating my face.

"So fucking beautiful," Silas praises, wiping my wet hair from my face. "You're our goddamn queen."

***

We used what we could to clean ourselves up and right our clothes before we made it home. Although, anyone with a pair of eyes and half a brain could see or *smell* what we just did.

Despite tonight's eventfulness, I'm racked with so much adrenaline there's no way I will be sleeping anytime soon. I make it through the front door behind Lyle, who collapses onto the couch in exhaustion. Riding the high, I bounce lightly on my toes and attempt to shake the tingling out of my hands.

"I think tonight is the perfect night for your gift. What do you think, boys?" Finn tests and gets positive responses.

After stripping off his jacket, Finn throws me over his shoulder, racing back toward the back of the house. I squeal using my hands against his ass to lift the upper half of my body up. The rest of them follow, stripping their outer layers as Finn scoops a set of keys from the table.

I like this surprise already.

"Are we leaving the house? I thought we had to lay low until we came up with a plan?" I ask.

"Hence the middle of the night," Finn says playfully pinching the inside of my thigh. "And where we're going, no one else will be around."

We slip out the back door, avoiding any of Jameson's or Nickolas's guys that might be watching the house, and out the back gate.

My many questions go unanswered, and just as I think I'm about to get answers, I get smacked on the ass.

"Shut up and enjoy the surprise." Lyle smirks.

Excuse me if I'm kind of over mysteries.

Finn sets me on my feet, and I begin walking in the middle of my human fortress, through a few backyards, and onto a dirt road overgrown with weeds.

Ian stoops at my feet and bends my knee, propping my foot on his thigh. He slides my shoe off, then does the same with the other, and kisses my calf before dropping my leg and standing back up. He holds my heels in one hand and intertwines our fingers with the other as we begin walking.

The fresh night air has a subtle hint of rain and moisture. I've always loved that smell. I inhale deeper, wanting to get more of it. The smell of wildflowers has my head turning toward a field. Dandelions and pink Buttercups litter the moonlit grass. Fireflies flicker throughout with a dim yellow glow.

I pull Ian with me as I walk closer and bend to pick one of the delicate balls of fluff from the ground, careful not to jostle it too much. I close my eyes, make my wish, and blow forcefully.

The flower bursts, the wind scattering the florets.

When I open my eyes, Lyle is bending to pick another. He twists it slowly between his pointer finger and thumb. His voice is soft and curious. "When you make a wish, do you make it for someone else or for yourself?"

"When you wish on flowers, you always make a wish for someone else." I smile.

He seems content with my answer. Then closes his eyes, hesitates, and blows the flower into the wind. "There. Now someone's made a wish for you."

I tilt my head back and my eyes search the starry black sky. The place that holds my many wishes.

Then my eyes fall to Silas, shifting uncomfortably, shoving his hands into the pockets of his slacks; the person those wishes were meant for.

"Thank you," I say softly. "Before tonight, I wasn't sure anyone had ever done such a thing for me."

I see Silas's lips part as if he is about to say something, then they promptly shut.

Ian gently pulls my hand. "Come on, we aren't too far from the spot."

We continue walking, and minutes pass before we stop.

Standing in the middle of nowhere, I look around at them like they have lost their damn minds.

They all look back at me with bright eyes, like they are waiting for me to do a trick.

"Can someone tell me what the fuck we are doing out here?"

Finn tosses me the set of keys he had grabbed and gives a little nod.

I roll them over in my hand, finding an older model key and an unfamiliar green tag that reads *1969 Chevrolet Chevelle*. I flip it over to reveal my scripted name on the back and my heart drops. My lips part, but nothing comes out. Still in awe, I watch as Lyle moves into the woods, and then I see it. A brown tarp draped over a car.

Oh my God. He really did it.

He pulls the fabric back, and although the dark of night looms over it, I can see the green paint.

"When did you do this?" I gush.

"Here and there, when one of us had *errands* to run," Lyle says proudly.

"We wanted it to be a surprise," Finn beams. "We didn't want to chance you seeing it at the house before we were ready, so I moved it here the day we came home from the lake."

Ian grabs my hand again and moves me to the driver's side. "We all took turns working on it, so you have a little bit of all of us no matter where you are. We each added a little something extra too."

I open the door. There is a small demon cat perched on the dash, a music note and star hanging from the rearview mirror. And a compass keychain sits in the driver's seat.

My heart cracks, and tears spill over in happiness as I giggle, turning the compass over in my hand.

"Just in case you ever need help finding your way home to us," Finn says, his eyes glistening.

Air is sucked from my lungs. "I love it," I praise through the tears. "I love it so much."

Sliding into the seat, I wrap my hands around the wheel. A sickness threatens to spoil the moment, but I shove it down with a deep breath, exhaling and stealing my spine.

You got this.

Joy, love, and excitement replace the fear of fault my mother instilled in my head. I turn the key, and the car purrs to life.

"What are y'all waiting for? Get the fuck in!"

They guys pile in, Ian taking the front seat, and I almost laugh at seeing the other three crammed in the back awkwardly.

"Where to?" I ask eagerly.

I follow their directions, slowly taking us through the back roads to avoid being seen or followed. We approach an iron fence surrounding the city track and roll to a stop. Before I can ask what we are supposed to do about the huge lock and no trespassing sign pinned to the front, Ian barrels out of the car with a pair of bolt cutters in hand.

Where the hell were those stashed?

He cuts the lock, and the chain falls to the ground. Then slides back into his seat and grins wide, as if nothing could bring him more joy.

"Now, floor it."

I look at him like he has lost his damn mind. Not only am I not doing that, but doing burnouts and skidding around the ends of the track is not exactly *lying low.*

His stare turns challenging like he would take almost as much joy in what would come after those words fell from my mouth. Looking into the back seat I find the other three are sitting in the same position. Leaned back, arms crossed, an indifferent expression plastered in place.

I exhale with a grumble and shift into drive. We bounce slightly as I pull onto the black tar not meant for vehicles. Rusted bleachers sit on each side of the old stadium, and a large post that used to hold a scoreboard stands at the far end.

Ian turns the music up, and all the windows get rolled down. I increase to twenty miles an hour as I get a feel for the turns and pulls off the track. Old classic rock plays, and the beat encourages my foot to lower on the gas pedal. I pull a hard left and increase a bit more on the straightaway before slowing again as I reach the next left. My heart pounds in my chest, and my throat constricts with a burn and I hope I don't throw up in my brand-new car.

"Stop pussy footing around and fuck this track up like it's your bitch!" Lyle yells from the back.

I press harder, still pulling back on the turns. My seat scooted far up to accommodate my short legs, and my face nearly pressed to the windshield like a grandma trying to do the speed limit on the interstate.

Silas slips his hand around the back of my neck "Loosen up. You control the power it has." I take another and steady my breath. "Now fucking floor it and show us how hard you can ride!"

I fight the urge to close my eyes of fear, forcing them to stay open as I slam my foot onto the petal and straighten the wheel. Within a second the curve comes, and I jerk the car hard left at full speed.

We skid, and my heart sinks as I slam my foot onto the brake pedal, fishtailing left and right as a scream rips from my lungs and I close my eyes. My right arm slams against Ian's chest as we spin off into the grass.

When my ears stop ringing, I hear laughter. And open my eyes, to see the guys hysterically laughing.

Psychopaths.

They are all psychopaths.

My heart pounds in my chest, but something feels lighter. I release my fist full of Ian's shirt and wipe the tear from my cheek.

"I'm sorry. I totally just soccer-mommed you."

A smile rips across my face, a huge, full teeth, pure joy smile. They chuckle as they resume their hollers of praise, shaking the seats and my body like lunatics.

"You fucking did that!" Finn praises.

"I almost killed us!"

"Maybe, but you let go! You took a risk. How do you feel?" he asks.

I assess my body and surroundings. The grass is torn with tire tracks, but other than that, everything is in perfect condition. I look inward. All I find is lightness and thrill. I was reckless, becoming more fearful than my fears themself. And I finally realize fear is your body telling you there is something you need to overcome in order to set yourself free.

And thanks to them, my only fear now is that this won't last forever.

I smile wide, without restraint, and I hope they can see the change I feel deep in my soul.

"I want to set the world on fire."

***

As quietly as possible, we creep back to the house and grab the necessary materials: gas can, matches, and weed.

We pile back into the car, and I drive without knowing where I'm taking us. But tonight is a turning point for me and someone will pay. I drive into the heart of our town. Streetlights and neon store signs shine on the road.

In the dead of night, it's almost peaceful, not a single car or person moving but us. As if this night has swallowed all the evil these streets have seen, clearing a path for me. For us.

Slowing, we pass through places the city has to offer our youth. I imagine kids running around, enjoying the pool, park, skating park, and drive-in movie and painfully remember how I never got to experience them.

My youth was stolen from me, just as it was from the boys. We may not have equally dreadful childhoods, but all of us were forced to grow up before we were ready. We were shoved into responsibilities and realizations at a young age, filling us with loss and emptiness before we had become legal adults.

And now Nickolas Steele is coming for our happiness.

The thought sting, but then it hits me, the only logical choice really.

"Where is your old house?" I ask, looking in the rearview mirror at Silas.

He gives me directions, taking us to a small blue house. The yard is overgrown, and the paint is chipped, revealing the weak and rotting wood beneath. Many windows are broken or boarded up, and the utter disgust and dismay that fills me only fuels the anger bubbling inside me.

Not wasting another moment, I throw all caution to the wind and take the gas can with me to the front door.

Fuck staying low-key.

Plan or no plan, Nickolas will get everything coming to him.

I stand at the front door that looks one solid kick away from collapsing. I would have thoroughly enjoyed watching one of them do that, but Silas pulls a key from his ring and unlocks it like it is just another day returning home. I swallow hard as I force my first step through the threshold.

Ian stops me with a solid hand on my shoulder, forcing me to let the others go first, with him taking the rear.

Silas scoped out the house when he found out his dad was returning. Though, I can't say I hope he isn't there because a large part of me wishes this could be as simple as him dying in the accidental house fire that is about to happen.

Silas immediately checks his father's bedroom, and I don't miss the slight drop of his shoulders. Cleared, I tilt the can and begin trailing it behind me as I take my own tour.

Ripped curtains, foul smells, torn couches, blood staining the dirty carpet in almost every room. It's likely been abandoned for years, but it's not hard to imagine this isn't far from the way it normally looked. Silas trails behind me, saying nothing, keeping his eyes focused on the liquid coating the ground.

I make it through each room. Silas's is the hardest to stomach, with a custom lock on the outside of the door and carvings littering every surface possible inside.

I return full circle to the front door and step back outside.

One by one, they follow me out before I toss the reaming contents of the can onto the porch.

Ian pulls the box of matches from his pocket and holds it out for me in the palm of his hand.

"Together," I say and pass each of them a match.

We each strike our own, and as one, we toss them into the house. Flames engulf the pitiful structure, and a large frame that feels a lot like a shadow wraps around my body. Silas's arms drape over my shoulders, his hands wrapping around mine at my chest.

"This is something I have dreamed about for a very long time," he says, and I love the way his voice always rumbles.

We stand there, time passing slowly as we watch the flames grow. I wish I could stay here until it is reduced to ashes, but we need to leave, and leave the past with it.

We turn and head back to the car, taking our first step towards a new life for us all.

Amelia

I park my car next to its almost identical twin and wait by the locked front door. My keys dangle in my hand, and Ian lifts it between us.

"You wouldn't have to wait for us if you would just use your key."

I inspect the keys again and notice an extra key I hadn't paid any attention to the first time. I push it into the hole and turn it with ease, sending my heart soaring with a feeling that is better than any high.

My home.

A home with people that love me, understand me, and accept me.

This one night has given me so much that I almost fear sleep. It would mean admitting this day is over. And there's no way tomorrow could possibly compare.

My hand runs along the chairs stopping on the jacket left the chair and I reach inside pulling out my favorite little toy from where Silas slipped it earlier for safekeeping.

"Ah, yes. Seems there is a debt to be paid," he says, stalking toward me. "Conniving acts don't go unpunished around here." His eyes darken as he peers at me through his lashes, casually stepping towards me with his hands in his pockets. "My choice of toys for our girl."

He gets nose to nose with me.

"Run."

I shriek, taking off running through the house and up the stairs. A stupid move, really. But I want to get caught.

Slipping into Ian's closet, because it has the most room to hide, I shut the door. Excitement and fear shooting through my veins like fire. My heart beats so loud in my ears I'm unable to hear footsteps approaching.

The door rips open, and Silas peers down at me his dark smile sending a shock through my body and warmth settling between my legs.

"Boo," he whisper-yells, jerking me forward and throwing me over his shoulder.

I squeal, wrapping my arms around his waist, head hanging down right over his ass.

"Come on, boys. Let's go have some fun."

I pick my head up, seeing the other three stalking behind me, never looking more enthused. All of them bulging in their tight suits. Silas throws me down on his bed and rips my dress straight down the center, jerking my body and forcing a startled breath to leave me.

"Oh, come on. Not the dress," Ian grumbles before closing the door, leaving only a lamp to light the room.

"You three can be in here until I say leave, and then you'll fuck off."

No one protests, but Finn rolls his eyes like it was expected, and jealousy fills me at the thought of this happening before with someone else.

Silas moves to his closet, flipping on a dim red light that glows warmly through the room as Ian climbs up on the bed, situating himself at the end like it is his rightful spot. But with the way he's looking at me, his rightful spot is with his dick in my mouth, bruising the back of my throat.

I hear clanging metal sounds coming from the closet and nervousness sinks deep in my stomach, making me suddenly feel like running again.

"Breathe, baby. It won't be all bad," Finn says, sliding between my legs, slowly peeling off my dress. My eyes follow it to the ground, lingering there, and I savor the feeling of his hands trailing over my shoulder and down to my bra. "Don't even think you are leaving this room without your pussy dripping with cum."

His fingers hook into the lace fabric.

"Leave it on," Silas growls, rounding the bed holding various items in his hands.

My mouth goes dry as I take them in.

He drops them on the bed and leans over me, nipping at my neck, and I raise my chin, offering more to him. "I get to choose what and how we play now, little monster. Decisions later. Are you ready?"

I whimper as his teeth dig in harder, nearly breaking the skin, but I can feel the restraint he's using to hold himself back. At least for now.

In one swift motion, Silas loops his hand under my bra, yanking me to him, as Lyle jumps behind me, yanking my head back by my hair, pressing his lips to my temple.

"He asked you a question, baby."

My pussy throbs, begging to be touched.

"Do your worst," I bite out teasingly, looking at Silas through my long lashes while reaching up to dig my nails into Lyle's arm.

Lyle chuckles, moving his lips to my ear. "You're gonna eat those words. I hope our little fun earlier was worth it."

Silas passes a piece of silk behind me to Finn, who drapes it over my eyes, blocking out all light. My body is pulled back into his, and my hands are pulled up and out to the side before cool metal pins them to the headboard. Someone shifts on the bed, and by the new dip of the mattress, my guess is Finn. My legs are pulled apart, and a weight sits on each of my feet.

I can't move.

A hand clamps down over my mouth before I can protest.

I can't talk.

Fear tears through me, and sweat trickles down the side of my face.

"Your punishment is to endure replacing what he did to hurt you with the same actions, only now by the hands of someone who truly loves you, re-branding the pain as pleasure," Silas says.

Wait.

My breathing picks up, and my throat tightens. The air feels thick, and the walls I can't see are closing in - caving in.

Lance's face appears in my head, and I am back at those parties, my emotional high suddenly crashing to the depths. I'm back in the tree-house and on the dock. I'm drug through every place he has ever made me feel less than I am, and it's the hands of the ones I love pulling the rope.

"Focus, baby," Finn whispers behind me, holding my shoulders tight to his body. "Focus on our touches. We are here. Can you figure out who is where?"

I breathe letting Finns game distract me, thinking back to a time I knew who's hands were on me.

The dock. Silas. Protecting me. He could have done more than roam my body with his calloused hands that felt all too good at the wrong moment.

I close my eyes, no longer trying to see through the dark, instead letting it guide me.

The hands around my mouth leave as shaky hands move over my breasts, pulling them out of my bra. The rough raised skin brushes over my nipples.

"Silas."

Long fingers trail down my stomach, teasing the lining of my panties.

"Ian."

More aggressive touches claim my thigh, kneading the skin close to my scars.

"Lyle."

The soft, yet purposeful, grip on my shoulders.

"Finn."

"Good girl," Finn praises, and pride swells within my heart.

I know their hands. I know where they like to touch me and how they like to do it.

Ian's fingers tap a little dance down my rips, and I smile, the feeling both tickling and comforting.

From the pace he taps, I can tell he is enjoying himself.

"Keep searching for us," he says, fingers gliding under my panties and pulling them off. Leaving me bare in front of them for the second time, but somehow, this time feels entirely different.

"What did he do next?" Silas asks, his tone angry but scared.

I swallow hard, forcing myself to recall but not return. "He forced himself inside me, and when I wouldn't pretend to like it, he flipped me over."

I hear the familiar sound of a belt being ripped through pants loops and pants being discarded onto the floor from multiple angles. And right now, wishing I could see them is the only thing going through my head. Finn's hand goes back to my mouth, holding me in place.

I feel the head of a dick touch my entrance, and in one thrust, he slams into me, causing me to suck in a sharp breath.

"Fuck, baby. You are taking my dick so good," Silas breathes out, his hands pinning my thighs apart. He slams into me harder, pounding me so hard it will leave a bruise. "Your pussy is begging for me to go deeper. I feel it sucking me in. I know you love this."

I stiffen as those last words echo, and I hear Lance's voice telling me the same thing.

Silas's hands move to my hips, and I tighten my hands on Finn's thighs, trying to steady my breathing. Silas pulls out of me, abruptly running his hands over my skin in short hard motions, soothing where they had been digging in.

"You will fucking say it," Silas growls, but Finn's hand stays plastered to my face, barely letting any air come and go through my nose. His other hand brushes the side of my cheek, and I lean into his touch, my limbs starting to tremble.

I have to say it. I have to comply, or it will only get worse. It always did.

No, this is different.

They are different. There is a purpose. And as I force myself to see through the fear, I get it. They are recreating the memory, finding the triggering words or touches, then soothing it.

I nod, letting them know I'm ready, and Silas slaps me across the face.

"Punishment isn't over yet, Meda," he grinds out, affection lacing his stern words. "Unhook her hands."

Someone frees me, the bed shifts again, and I'm flipped over to my stomach, feeling the warm empty spot where Finn was moments ago. A hand presses on the center of my back, and my face sinks further into the sheet that suddenly feels like wood.

"You are in the last position he left you," Lyle whispers next to me. "But now you are surrounded by four men that would burn the fucking world down for you."

Lips meet the opposite side of my neck, and Ian's soft voice caresses my ear. "He is nothing, and you are our everything. Let us show you."

My hips are jerked up, displaying my ass for them. A wet tongue slides down the length of my pussy then sinks in. His nose brushes my ass as he fucks me with his tongue, nipping and sucking the skin.

Silas.

"I-it feels so good, Si," I whimper, and he growls, pulling his face away from where he was biting my ass cheek.

"You don't know how fucking good it feels to know that you can recognize my tongue on your cunt."

"Let's see what else she can recognize," Ian says, and I imagine his beautiful blue eyes gleaming in excitement.

My chest is lifted off the bed, and a body settles underneath me, draping my thighs over each side of his. I attempt to reach my hands down, but my wrists are gathered and pulled behind me.

"No cheating," Silas whispers behind me, and I smile.

"Why start playing by rules of truth now?" I tease, trying to hit that soft spot.

"Because I said so and have no problem spanking that cute little ass raw."

Well, damn. Yes sir.

Silas tangles his hand in my hair turning my head to hover his lips over mine. "Now, guess who."

My body is lifted up and lowered back down slightly, suspended as someone slides into me.

"Oh, God," I moan, aching to free my hands so I can grab onto someone for stability.

He drives into me so fast my tits bounce and my cries come out jagged. A hand wraps around my neck, and I can hear his quiet whimpers and grunts as my head gets lighter. He sounds as though he is frustrated by the vulnerability in the sounds coming from him.

"Fuuuck. Just like that, Lyle."

My cries are silenced as he pulls me down and praises me with a bruising kiss, still fucking me good.

"I fucking love you," he growls into my ear, and my heart leaps straight into his hands.

My hands are released, and I place them on his chest as I grind back into him, slowing his rhythm and taking control for a moment. I dig my freshly manicured almond nails into his chest as I roll my hips, savoring the feeling of him so deep every time I rock back.

"I fucking love you too." I fist his hair, yanking it to the side, and suck his neck furiously hard as my love aggression takes hold of my arousal. He sucks in a breath, and the sound of it so close to my ear sends shivers down my back, and my pussy clenches around him, causing his dick to jump.

"Ah, don't do that again, or I might come in you before we've had any real fun."

I kiss him again, biting his lip and sucking it.

A hand comes down on my ass, and I yelp, unprepared but craving more of the burn it leaves. My ass spreads, and a cool liquid trails from my furthest hole down to my clit, making it tingle.

"This one is going to be tough," Lyle laughs out, and I am not sure if he is talking about my next guess or the dick that is likely about to be shoved into my ass.

A finger presses into my ass, and I groan, starting to ride Lyle again. The finger turns and pulls, stretching me, before another enters. The way his hand is positioned with his palm on the top of my ass says he's sitting in front of my by Lyle's head. He rocks with me, pressing back in with every backward stroke I make. I focus on the sounds around me, trying to ignore my building orgasm so I can figure this shit out.

I hear Lyle breathing heavily under me and Silas groaning behind me as he probably strokes himself. I train my ear harder, waiting for any sign of where the missing two are.

Lyle takes back control, holding my hips still and fucking me hard. The fingers in my ass follow, and it feels so goddamn good.

"Yes. I'm gonna come."

Then I hear it. The faintest sound of Ian's gasp that he always makes when I say that, like that sentence alone, is enough to get him off.

"Harder, Ian."

He rips my blindfold off, and I stare directly in his eyes so he can watch me fall apart. My brow bunches, and he mirrors me as my orgasm shoots through me, both holes convulsing tight around the objects inside.

Lyle comes with me, halting his movements as I scream and writhe. Ian continues to finger fuck my ass as hard as he can, watching my face as I ride it out.

Once I can see straight, I lean forward pulling Ian into my mouth, relaxing my throat and taking him fast and hard, knowing he's almost there just from watching. He grips my head, and I still, allowing him to thrust into me. He grunts, stills, and spills his cum down my throat.

"You are so loud. You know that?" he teases, collapsing back onto the bed, and I roll off Lyle, landing between them.

"So I have discovered," I smile.

I never was before, but I guess that had a lot to do with having to get myself off fast enough with Lance. I could never just enjoy it and let it build on its own.

Finn yanks me down the bed, and Silas grabs me, flipping me over on top of him.

"Didn't think we were done, did you?" Silas smirks.

Excitement sparks inside me, and I get my second wind. I lift up, and Silas pushes my shoulders, slamming me back down onto him. I situate on my knees and bounce slightly on his impressive size. He reaches up and pinches my nipples, rolling them between his fingers before palming my breasts.

Finn pushes me down, settling behind me, and lubes me up again. I give my ass a little wiggle, forcing a groan out of Silas, and he digs his fingers into my sides.

Finn lines himself up and slowly pushes in the first inch. My skin burns, and on instinct, my hand reaches back to stop him. He brushes his fingers over my hand and pushes in another inch the second my mind is distracted.

"Ah, fuck," I cry out, dropping my head to Silas's chest.

"Almost there, baby. You can do it."

I've seen his dick. Almost there, my ass.

Finn works himself in and out, sliding slightly further each time. He leans and presses his chest against my back, and the warm contact alone has me opening up more for him. His teeth sink into my shoulder, and the pain distracts me as he buries himself completely inside. He continues kissing and biting me even as Silas consumes my lips, both distracting me enough to get used to the new feeling.

They find their rhythm, rotating in and out of me, creating a delicious burn that hurts so good. I clench the sheets in my fist next to Silas's head as they work me over, then lift my head to see Lyle and Ian watching with hungry eyes and decide I need somewhere to put my hands.

"Come here."

They move like their lives depend on it each take a side, and I release the sheets, taking them in each hand instead. I rotate, licking and sucking each of them, mumbling and moaning with them in my mouth. Lyle reaches between Silas and me, pressing two fingers to my clit and rubbing firm little circles.

"She was fucking made for us," Ian praises.

I cry out inaudible pleasures, and my second orgasm sneaks up, sending perfect little shocks from my clit to my toes.

Lyle finishes next. He squeezes my jaw, instructing me to show him his presence left inside my mouth. His personal preference of marking me.

"Don't swallow until you have Ian's jizz in that pretty little mouth too."

God bless them.

I turn to Ian, and his eyes sparkle with delight as I open my mouth again, showing him Lyle's mess in my mouth before sucking him deep. I make a mess. Drool and cum run down my face and Ian's shaft as I continue sucking him with Finn and Silas still inside me.

Finn's breathing becomes more irregular, and I can feel his dick swell right before he slams into me and comes, emptying every last drop he has. I release Ian, look up at him, and continue stroking him.

I see his throat bob as he swallows, his orgasm on the edge. He takes Finn's place behind me and pushes his fingers into me again, spreading the cum leaking from me. Pushing the head of his dick in, he glides all the way in stretching me even further. He thrusts in and out of me. I look over my shoulder, loving the look on his face when he fucks me. He throws his head back, then pulls it back down, watching where we meet with a slack jaw.

The twins sit at the head of the bed while our grunts and groans fill the room. Silas is taking it easy, and I know he is just biding his time. Ian pulls out of me, yanking me back and turning my head to the side so he can make it to my mouth before he comes. I open my mouth, his cum adding to what is left of Lyle's, and I swallow them both, then lick the remnants from Ian's body.

"Fuck. That might be the hottest thing I've ever seen," Finn says, and I almost want to poke fun at the fact he is talking about his brother's cum, but I dare not ruin the chance of any future fun.

Before I can wipe my mouth, Silas throws me off him and stands at the end of the bed.

"Times up. Get the fuck out."

Amelia

M y eyes go wide at the darkness in his eyes, and though I know he would never hurt me, I am not sure just how far he would take it. A fraction of me is scared. The other large percent is bursting with excitement and curiosity to explore the pain part of pleasure I know is moments away. The guys each kiss me and leave, shutting the door behind them without a single objection.

"Why did they have to leave?"

"Because I am about to introduce you to a part of me that no one will ever get to see except for you, and they know that."

I snort, climbing up on my knees and bracing my hands on his shoulders. "I know you are tough with the girls you have sex with, and I can understand why you like that."

He takes my face in his hands, holding me like I might float away if he lets go.

"What you don't understand is that I have never let myself go for anyone because you were the one I dreamed that would one day hold that part of my soul. I prayed that you would accept the fucked-up part of me that fantasizes about the girl I love hurting me. The part of me that loved the idea of her wanting to see my pain in a physical way so she could understand." His face falls in shame, and I pick it back up.

"You tried to take my pain away for years in the only way you thought you could. I want to do the same for you."

He raises a brow, looking at me like I am a stupid child. "Do you not think that wanting to hurt the person you love is reason enough to not deserve them?"

I wrap my arms around his neck, leaning back and taking him with me. He braces himself above me, searching my face.

"I don't think you want to hurt me to see me in pain. I think you want someone to understand you, and this is the way your heart tells you to do that. To share the pain and blood. To turn it into something more than the experiences that caused your fascination with it."

Silas arches a brow at me, and I mirror it right back.

"Do you see me objecting?"

He has fought for so long, thinking something was wrong with him that he likes to inflict pain, but that is all he has known.

Pain is how he lost his family. Pain is how he gained a new family. Pain is what was gained after falling in love with someone who already had too much of it.

Pain is what shattered his soul when he thought he could never be selfish enough to have me, and pain is what he needs now to know that he can.

"Do you think I would let you?" he challenges darkly.

I reach down my thigh, pulling the knife that still lays sheathed there, and I hand it to him.

"Finish remarking my pain, and together we will be marked by the scars that prove we are alive and have someone that loves us enough to share it."

His eyes darken, and the sorrow lurking there is overtaken by lust and desire. Underlined with something vicious. He takes the blade from my hand and flips it open.

"If you want me to stop..."

"*Algol.*"

He smiles, gently kissing my lips. I part them, allowing his tongue to enter and ravage my mouth in slow, purposeful movements.

He places the tip of the knife where my scabbed wound across my chest starts on the left. I lock my eyes on him, focusing on every feature, curve, and slope of his face. His square jaw line and golden honey eyes. His high cheekbones, slender nose, and thick lips.

God, I love his lips.

Silas digs into my skin, and I wince but shove it down, willing myself to stand there and take what we both need to happen. Stronger than the night they were made, I don't shed a tear as the burning separation of my skin spreads to the right side. Blood drips down my chest and onto the bed.

His breathing is heavy as he meets my eyes again, searching for any notion to stop, but I don't miss the silent hope that he comes up empty.

I reach down and fist his impressive length, working him in my hand, feeling him quickly swell. With one hand, I pull down on his lower back, bringing him down to me, pushing him into me. My legs wrap around him, and he hands the knife to me, making slow strokes in and out of me with the tilt of his hips.

I take it into my hand and run my finger over the mark I left earlier tonight that matches mine. I didn't do that to share that scar, but the placement is uncanny. I look down at my right arm, seeing the nearly healed scar, and out of the corner of my eye, I see him nod before he moves my hand to his left arm. He moves in me faster, ripping moans from my lips, and the aggressive need fills me once again. I grit my teeth like I always do when anger surges, and he grips my jaw.

"Relax. You are holding back."

I release the strain on my jaw, letting it go slack, and it aches with the need to tighten again. But I use that urge to dig the tip of the blade into his skin, feeling it scratch that itch ever so slightly, and I smile. I slice in one quick motion, and his blood drips, falling down my arm.

He pins my thighs up, getting a better angle, and sinks into me again with a groan, using the pain as fuel for his arousal.

"Ah!" I cry out, and his voice gets so low that it makes my pussy ache with need.

"Fuck, I love when you scream for me."

I lay my other arm flat, showing him another mark. Placing my other hand between us to stop him, I split my fingers around him, feeling his dick. He thrusts in again and I move my hand to my clit, rubbing furiously, matching his aggressive pace watching every expression on his face. He hits a spot so deep I truly think he is fucking up my internal organs, but it feels so goddamn good. I need more.

"Harder, baby. Harder," I beg, and he slams into me, keeping his same pace.

His sweat drips down his face and chest. Our bodies sliding against each other. His face contorts into frustration. Pure hunger takes over as he slowly slides the blade down my left arm. I reach my climax, the burn slicing down my arm joining with the earth-shattering shock spreading throughout my body, making me let out a scream that sounds like a cry for help that Silas eats from my mouth savagely.

"Shiiiit!" I bellow, still rubbing my pussy as fast as I can while it's trying to force him out.

Wetness spreads under my ass, and I relax into the bed, exhausted and aching but still begging for more.

Silas reaches over on the bed and untangles a pair of clips connected by a chain. I lick my lips and cup my breasts, offering my hard nipples to him.

He clips them on, and I whimper as he tightens them. He stops just at the point where there is constant pain, but it isn't unbearable. The cold chain lies on my chest, and I shiver at the contrast of temperatures. He hooks a finger into it and gives it a tug, seemingly satisfied at my response of shock.

Forcing my mouth open, he slides a ribbed glass dildo in, and I suck it firmly, wetting it for him. He wastes no time, his composure long gone, flipping me over to my stomach and sliding the toy into my ass still covered in cum and lube. He moves it back and forth, my ass tightening around each bulb.

He lays flat on the bed and pushes it all the way in, leaving it there as he buries his face between my legs. He laps me up and sucks my clit so hard I think my soul attempts to leave my body multiple times.

"I still taste them inside you," he growls. "If I didn't know for certain that you would deny me, I would order that not another man on this fucking earth could touch any part of you without dying."

He dives back in, and I suck in a breath. His teeth graze my clit, and I force his head away, the overstimulation too much, but he slams my hands back to the bed.

"I never planned to share *you*. So, now that I have to, do me the smallest favor of behaving when I have you to myself. Deny me the pleasure of having you come so many times that my face is permanently etched on your heart, and I don't know what I might do."

It already is.

He looks up at me from between my legs. Only his eyes are visible, and I can't read him well enough to determine how much of his words are an exaggeration. I embrace the fire of him working my tired clit and force myself to relax into the bed. He pushes two fingers inside me, joining the pressure of the toy in my ass, and continues to massage my nerves with a flat tongue.

The newly familiar feeling builds in my stomach, and just the mental image of what is about to happen sends me spiraling into another orgasm. My pussy sprays aggressively.

He doesn't stop or back up even the slightest bit. Just opens his mouth wider, sucking me into his mouth whole, and swallows down every drop while I convulse like I'm having a damn seizure.

He slides up my body, grinding between my legs, his tattoos glistening in sweat, cum, and blood.

"Give me one more, baby. You can do it." he purrs, kissing up my bleeding chest to my neck then nipping my earlobe. He pants, nearly fully spent, but I can do this for him. I can give him one more.

He grabs the knife where we let it fall on the bed and places it in my slack hand. Wrapping his hand around my throat, he pulls me into his lap, sheathing himself inside me once more. He wiggles his way to the headboard and presses me into it, holding me there by my throat. His grip tightens as he uses the last of his energy to thrust into me unforgivingly. My vision gets spotty.

"Si," I choke out, barely able to breathe his whole hand pressing against my windpipe and no longer just the sides. I search his eyes, finding them darker than before, as if his mind is no longer with me.

"Do it. This time, you punish me."

Despite everything he thinks he has done to me, there is almost nothing that could sever the bond we have.

Not truly.

He presses harder, and my pelvis aches from his punishing blows.

"I lied to you. Do it," he barks, his tone sending a wave of fear through me.

My head races, trying to focus with the small bit of oxygen still circulating. I know I will pass out if he doesn't let go.

"I could have stopped your pain, Mel. Fucking do it!"

This time he spits it, anger and regret flashing deep in his eyes under the haze of absence that fogs them.

He needs this.

I turn my features to stone, and I let all my pain come to the surface. I think about everything he may have witnessed. Every time he was right there, watching me beg to the empty sky for someone to save me. Every night he came into my room and left without taking me with him.

Even the nights here that I laid unknowingly down the hall from *Him*.

I bore my eyes into him, and with one upwards stroke of my hand, I slash his right arm, the cut deeper than I intended. He releases me, his arm falling slack, and I shove him in the chest, pushing off the wall with everything I have. Seeing red, I come down on top of him, slamming my fist into his chest, and I chase my last orgasm. This time, I will be the one to take.

He grips my hip with his left hand, and without thinking, I slash at it, cutting across his knuckles.

"No."

His eyes widen as the smallest gasp leaves his lips, but he doesn't protest. He stays focused on my face, but I look away, focusing on the blood that covers us both instead. I press the blade to his neck like I had done to Jameson, and I ride him vigorously and angrily, channeling all my rage into retrieving my last orgasm.

Too rough of a move or a sudden jerk from him, and I could end his life. It's thrilling and terrifying - everything I need at this moment.

My clit rubs against his skin perfectly, and I climax once more, the release belittled by the tears streaming down my face. I drop the knife and grab onto his tattooed-covered shoulders, riding it out, then collapse on his chest. My head clears, and chills rack my rapidly cooling skin. My sobs fill the air, as his strong arms wrap around me, hesitantly at first and then securely, with a purpose.

"I know, baby. I fucking know. I am so goddamn sorry. I will spend my whole life trying to make it up to you if you will let me."

Amelia

Silas strips me bare and carries my worn body into the shower. The warm water cascades over us, burning the fresh cuts and turning the water an orangish pink. He sets me down on my feet, holding my sides firm to make sure I can stand. Then gently tilts my head back, letting the water soak my hair as one hand massages my scalp, while the other wraps around my waist holding me up and close to him. A headache builds behind my eyes as my head tries to wrap itself around whatever just happened.

My demon is quiet, but my heart is loud and confused. I want this so bad, but my heart's scars are all too visible to ignore the betrayal that swarms around it like smoke, waiting to lash out at the smallest sign of happiness.

"Get out of your head," Silas grumbles, his voice sounding exactly how I feel.

Opening my eyes, I realize I'm digging my nails into the palm of my hand.

"I am here *now*." He forces me to look at him.

But I needed you then.

"I have made mistakes, but I can't change who I am or what I've done. Only hope I measure up to everything you thought I'd be." He brushes his thumb over my lips, which feel swollen and bruised. "Did I scare you?"

"A little," I whisper, barely audible above the water hitting the tile floor.

"Was it too much for you?"

I remember the look of defeat and anguish that stared back at me as he begged me to hate him. It's the same look he gives me now.

He wants me to say he's too fucked in the head. His edges are too frayed, and what he has done proves he's undeserving of my forgiveness and love.

"If I say no, will you stay?" My voice shakes, all my emotions rising to my throat, making it nearly impossible to open my mouth from the ache in my jaw.

"If you say no, I will stay by your side, living with no other purpose than to protect you and worship you." He leans in close touching our foreheads together. "I will show you how I've wanted to love you since I first saw you."

I push into his body, wrapping my arms around his neck, feeling the burn on them as the skin stretches.

"The last time we were in this position, you called me spineless moments after you let me see through your exterior. Call me skeptical, but it's hard to believe this version of you will last. You can be cruel."

I don't look away as his face hardens.

"Believe me when I say there is no firmer truth than the fact that you own every part of my soul, but don't for a second think you'll change who I am or how things work around here. Both in my bed and out there, I worship the ground you walk on, but if you choose to stay, I own you. I don't tolerate weakness in my family, for the wellbeing of those I love because I've seen what it takes to survive in this world. Fight me on that, and there will be consequences." His hand smooths up my arm, and his finger digs into the shallow wound he reopened.

I hiss. "You're not the only one that owns me. You all fought hard to bring parts of me to light, so don't try to bury them now." I smile sweetly at him, slowly pressing my body closer to him. "I will fight where I see fit, and I will not allow what I want to be taken from me."

He growls, the sound vibrating off the walls. His lips smash into mine as he pins me to the wall, his hands ravaging my body just as harshly as his mouth does. I shove him away with great effort, our lips separating at the last possible second.

"You don't scare me, Silas. You have shown me a side of myself that I have spent a long time searching for. I enjoyed every minute of what we did, and although you have a shit ton of sucking up to do, this is where I want to be. I may belong to all of you, but I am just as much your equal."

He kisses me again softly, seeming to accept my response, and I dive into the high of his hands roaming up my back. A large part of me believes no matter what I did or demanded, he wouldn't have objected.

We finish washing each other, barely making it through without having sex again. He leads me back into his room through the dark hall, and I wonder if the guys have gone to sleep. Digging through his drawers, I find the softest shirt I can find, and gently pull it over my head as he remakes the bed with fresh sheets and discards the mattress cover that needs to be washed.

I climb on his bed the moment he lays the clean comforter down, and he shakes his head, wagging his finger at me.

"We need to take care of those. Again."

I groan but obey, moving to the side of the bed and letting him bandage me up. They aren't deep, so I won't be covering them once they stop bleeding. I want to see them every day - watch them heal with a new meaning. After taking notes, I cover Silas's wounds with the same method and care. I know he will be wearing them with pride the moment there isn't a risk of infection.

Silas puts the box of supplies away and climbs in next to me on the king bed, wrapping his arms around my waist pulling me closer to him.

"Why do you like to feel and inflict pain?" I ask.

"Aside from guilt, because something in my head tells me that if I am the one in control of giving and receiving it, then I am no longer that scared little boy."

My heart aches at the mental image of him cowering as his father unleashes undeserving rage, day after day. No innocent child deserves to feel like that. Worthless and never good enough.

"Why didn't you take control without asking me like you do to other women."

He hesitates, brushing his fingers through my hair. "More often than not, I needed the girls to resemble you to even get it up, and then I wanted to punish them like my father punished me. For not being good enough."

"And now that you have me?"

He kisses my head. "Now that I have you, I feel grounded. Of course, I don't need to punish you like I did them, but the desire for pain is never gone, so with you, I only want to feel that high. I like the look on your face when you enjoy me hurting you."

I turn on my back so I can see him.

"I need you to know that I would never take it too far with you. All I ever wanted was to take care of you in any way you needed. As fucked-up as it is, I used to watch you when you would hurt yourself, and wish that I could take over for the both of us... with my dick buried inside of you."

I chew on the side of my lip and smile at him before rolling back over. That is disturbingly romantic in the most fucked-up way.

"You know, Lyle is going to kill us."

He won't be thrilled that I'm cut up again.

"Lyle can lick my taint."

"He made me promise not to hurt myself anymore."

"You didn't. I did." He brushes his hand between my thighs, tracing the marks before grabbing tightly, making my pussy warm. "I agree with him, though. You will never hurt yourself again. If you need pain, I will be the one to deliver it. Are we clear?"

I nod, and he squeezes tighter, making me whimper.

"Sorry, I didn't hear you."

"Y-yes."

"Yes, what?" he growls, lifting his head, hovering over my ear.

"Yes, sir," I answer, almost questioning if that's what he wants.

"That's what I like to hear." He grinds his hard dick into my ass.

This man has stamina and apparently, a daddy kink. How appropriate for both of us.

"Get some rest. It's been a long day," he orders, turning off the remaining lights.

Although I wouldn't decline some lazy sex right now, I'm thankful he doesn't act on the need I know he feels right now.

I need some recovery time.

He settles in behind me, and his steady breathing brings me a kind of comfort I never thought possible.

This is what we were always meant to be, and without my past, I may not have turned out to be this person. Truthfully, I would have waited even longer if I knew this was my future.

He is finally here.

***

Someone beating on the bedroom door startles me awake. The sun peeks behind the blackout curtains and I turn on the lamp next to the bed. Looking over my shoulder, I find Silas still fast asleep and I can't help my smile, taking in the peaceful look on his beautiful face and tousled bedhead. I press a kiss to his cheek and slide out from under his arm.

Opening the door, I squint from the blinding light and see my three remaining men with the same worried look.

"What the fuck is y'all's problem?" I whisper, slightly pissed off that I was woken up from a great sleep.

"The blood trail down the hall is our problem," Finn snarls, trying to look past me through the opening.

Lyle pushes past Finn's shoulder and jerks my left arm up, inspecting the bandage then looks at me like he is envisioning all the ways he can kill someone and not get caught.

"I'm fine, so you can chill the hell out." I jerk my arm out of his grasp and cross them over my chest.

"What I can do is beat his fucking ass." Lyle tries to push past me, but I push them back and shut the door behind me, wanting to let Silas get some rest.

He probably hasn't gotten any since who the hell knows when.

"You will do nothing." I glare back. "I asked him to do this."

Ian looks at me like I'm a bleeding day-old puppy, while Finn looks at me like I've lost my goddamn mind.

I take a deep breath, trying to calm down, understanding their concern. "Look. Silas and I had a lot of shit to work through last night, and you three had no problem helping with the first fucked-up part of that. What we did after that is between him and me."

"Wrong," Ian says, his face turning to rage, "What happens with you concerns all of us."

Lyle sighs. "We just wanted to check on you, baby. Si can lose himself sometimes, so we were worried."

I smile softly, appreciating their concern and surprised they didn't just break down the door. "I can handle him."

I don't want to share details that Silas may choose to keep to himself. Although we are all in this together, the reasons why we enjoy hurting each other is something I think only the two of us will ever really understand.

These three only enjoy hurting someone else when necessary. Well, except for Lyle. I think he truly gets off on hurting other people, but not those he loves.

"I don't doubt that. If anyone can, it's you, Angel." Lyle pokes out his lip and pulls me in for a hug, resting his chin on the top of my head. "Breakfast is almost ready, when you are hungry."

"Pancakes?" I murmur into his chest.

"Nothing but the best for the only woman in the world I might let put something in my ass one day."

Jesus Christ.

I don't think I will ever get tired of hearing notions of such love from them.

After looking curiously at Lyle, I peer over the side of his arm, wanting to see Ian. I know he has a really hard time with situations like this, and I can only imagine how seeing the blood coming from his room must have triggered him.

"You wanna hang out later?" I ask locking eyes with Ian.

Lyle releases me, and I move closer to the blonde, ruffling his shaggy hair then pushing it away from his sapphire eyes. God, his eyes make drowning sound appealing.

"That sounds perfect." Ian leans in, holding the back of my neck, and kisses me so deep that I can feel the worry in his heart through every pass of his lips on mine.

They leave, stranding me with Finn, who still looks like he might strangle the both of us. I cock my hip out, waiting to hear the verbal lashing he needs to get out, but he doesn't give one.

"If you are happy, I'll be fine," he says. "But if he ever takes it too far, I might just have to kill him."

I chuckle, taking his hand in mine and interlocking our fingers.

"If he ever takes it too far, I might just do it myself." I give him a wink, letting him see the playfulness in my stature while reassuring him the scared little girl they met is long gone. "As weird as it is, we know each other on a very personal level. I trust him."

As soon as the words leave my lips, I question them.

I trust him with my life, but do I trust him with my heart?

I go back into the dark room and slip under the soft sheets, my spot now barely warm. Snuggling into Silas, nuzzling close, I inhale his scent. My brain almost tricks me into remembering having smelled him by my open window or passing through the school hallways.

"That went better than I thought," he grumbles, his voice raspy and vibrating my chest.

"How long have you been awake?"

"Since before you. They were raising hell five whole minutes before you even cracked an eye open."

I sit up and scowl at him. "You were awake and didn't handle that?"

"I was enjoying watching you sleep in my arms. It felt like old times." He pulls me on top of him, straddling his morning wood.

"You know, some people might find that sneaking into a girl's room while she is sleeping to be extremely sickening." I brace my hands on his chest, placing my fingers over the claw marks I left.

"You have always slept like the dead but still managed to feel me up time and time again." He presses up into me. "You have been begging for the cock of a man you'd never met. If I'm sick, baby, you're terminal."

My cheeks flush, sending heat to where I slowly grind on him. I remember having the best dreams some nights. Dreams that he had finally come for me, just out of reach but waiting for me to find him.

Circling back, I glare at him. "So you made me face them all on my own when you could have just told them to shut the fuck up?"

He chuckles, crossing his arms behind his head. "They needed to hear it from you, and so did I. I was wondering if you would hate me today once the adrenaline left."

"Who says I don't?" I scoot further up so the head of his dick rubs right at my entrance, a few layers of fabric stopping it from slipping in. He grabs my hips, pushing me harder into him, and I love how his fingers press into my back with such demand.

"You did."

"Breakfast is ready!" Lyle yells from downstairs, and I use it as my escape.

I scramble out of Silas's hold and jump from the bed before he can pull me back. Ignoring his statement, I fling the door open and sprint down the hallway.

"Sorry, pancakes are calling!"

I hear Silas shuffling behind me, and I force my legs to move faster. He makes it downstairs right after I do, and all eyes are on us and our uncovered lacerations longer bleeding.

"Well, I suddenly feel a lot better," Finn says after seeing that Silas looks just as rough as I do.

"You two are dangerous together," Lyle says without a hint of judgment.

Silas rounds the couch and winks at him. "You better believe it."

Finn pulls me into his lap, doing his best not to draw attention to him being wary of where he touches me.

I wrap his arms around me tighter and kick my feet into Ian's lap and he rubs my legs softly as we talk.

"No word from my dad running his mouth, so there's that."

"Do we think there are more people involved?" I ask, sipping the orange juice Lyle brought over.

"After last night, I'm sure he's on multiple payrolls, but there's no telling if he's paid off anyone else to secure his deal with Nickolas," Finn says.

"I'm going to be looking into that. I was able to download a copy of his files while you were... busy." Ian says, the corner of his lips tilting.

"Sex. We had sex."

"Oh, we know. We heard it multiple times last night. Quite a few ladies were waiting to pee at the gala and you made them blush with that filthy mouth of yours." Finn chuckles.

I can only imagine all of those uptight assholes grasping their pearls.

"No shame in my game when the dicks I get are just that good." I smile. "I hope they enjoyed the audible show."

"I know I did." Lyle wags his eyebrows, and I roll my eyes so hard they nearly get stuck in the back of my head. I wouldn't have put it past him to try to peek under the door to get the full effect.

"So now that we truly know Nickolas is the one that wanted to fuck with us, what the hell do we do now?" I ask.

"Well, we know why he's doing it..." Ian trails off, and the room grows silent.

"I think the fuck not!" I protest, reading the room. "You four are not leaving me."

"Mel, you have to think logically, at least unti-"

"I said no!" I yell cutting Ian off, fear causing my voice to shake. "Figure something else out because I am not losing you. Any of you. For any amount of time."

Silas's head falls. "You know what happened the last time we were in a similar situation," he whispers, unable to meet my eyes.

"Love is nothing but a weakness to him. The only thing he understands is control." Silas says, his eyes pleading with me. "Trying to convince him we don't care about you is our only chance of keeping you alive, at least until he's dealt with."

"Figure. Something. Else. Out." My tone is steady, venomous, daring them to fucking try me. I have lost so much. I refuse to let this happen to us.

"If you love me like you say you do, figure something else out. There is no difference between me and one of you. Any of us could get killed, and separating would only put an easier target on one of our heads."

"Okay, baby," Finn soothes, pulling me back into him, and I realize I was nearly standing up. "We will think on it. Until then, we need to stay out of the public eye. Low-key."

I inhale deeply.

"You and Ian, go have that date and relax. The three of us will work something out in the gym and blow off some steam." He kisses my forehead and I shift, narrowing my eyes.

I know damn well he is going to have a little too much fun with Silas in there.

Amelia

I lay on Ian's bed with him splayed across the end, both of us with a book in hand. I lower mine, peering around my bent knees. Soft music plays, and sunlight pours through the window, highlighting his light hair, making his eyes appear to glow. I watch as he taps the side of his book, his eyes scanning over the alternate world he holds rapidly.

Sensing me looking at him, his eyes find mine, and I jerk my book up, trying to hide my blush. He sets his book down and crawls over to me, wrapping his arms around my knees and resting his head atop.

"My love, we are supposed to be reading."

I keep my nose in my book, my smile growing wider.

"So why are you talking?" I whisper.

He bites my leg playfully. "Because you are *very* distracting."

He lowers my book before pulling it out of my hands and sitting it down on top of his. "Although reading about a sweet summer love may be appealing, the woman in my bed is giving all kinds of inspiration on her own."

"Is that so?" I tease, stretching out wider, my shirt riding up, revealing the small of my stomach.

Ian runs his finger along my hip and moves across my panties.

"I was thinking I would take you up on that offer of helping me write. I've had a melody stuck in my head for days, and I need to get it out."

I nearly tackle him, so excited to finally hear him play in person and not muffled through the walls.

He laughs and slides off the bed, then takes his white electric guitar off the stand and turns all of his recording equipment on. I watch him in adoration as he practically radiates pure happiness, staring down as he hums a few chords over and over again. He strums his thumb across the strings, and the vibration rattles through my body.

"You know, I didn't start by learning to read music. I did it by hearing it and repeating it." He adjusts a few things and strums again, this time playing a few cords together. "I later learned so I could write down what I was hearing in my head when my own ideas started coming to me."

A warmth bursts in my chest, watching someone so much like me enjoying something with their whole heart and feeling so ashamed about the journey they took.

He finds his rhythm, playing the chorus he had bouncing around in his head mixed with a few ideas he had already taken note of. It's a mix of solemn notes that pick up into something more passionate. Emotion lacing every note and hope underlining the ones to come.

He says so much with no words at all, so I use my own, inspired by the pain and longing in both of our hearts that I see clearly on his delicate face.

I give him words and phrases about searching for something you believe in so strongly. When you feel that the whole world is on your shoulders and you are always shoved to the ground, never feeling good enough. A smile teases his lips in approval, and the nerves slowly leave my body.

"I love that." He beams, swinging his guitar over his shoulder in the sexiest way. He hums, tapping his fingers along my thighs as he lays down next to me. "I want this song to portray everything you wish someone would have told you. The rainbow after the storm." He trails kisses up my thigh, and I hear the cap of a marker pop off.

He smiles at me before scribbling barely legible words onto my skin. "Why use paper when I have a perfect canvas right here?"

"And what about if you forget what you wrote?" I tease, sharing some common sense.

He pulls out his phone and takes a picture of my half-naked body.

"For documentation purposes, of course."

"Uh-huh," I murmur as he snaps another between my legs.

"That one is for personal use." He winks before pressing his lips to my panties, tugging the fabric with his teeth.

I dig my fingers into his hair, pushing his head back. "Well, if you can focus, I have a lot of things that were said to me that... are very special to me."

He looks up at me curiously, and realization flashes in his eyes. "Those are intimate. However, I'd love to include something real that meant so much to you if you wanted to share them."

I think it over, not particularly wanting to relive those times, but my heart still warms at the connection between now and then. Proof that timing may not be perfect, and the agony may feel never-ending, but eventually, you will find the life and love you have longed for, whatever that may entail. Finally, I nod, leaving to get my collection of letters from the box that the boys brought to my room.

I race down the stairs, skipping two at a time, and rush into the gym. The guys turn as the heavy door slams behind me.

"Sorry to interrupt, boys," I say rushing up to Silas, and leaping into his arms that wrap around me instinctively. I kiss him all over his sweaty face, tasting the salt as I work down his neck.

"Can I have what he's having?" Finn teases, and Lyle laughs, stripping his gloves and moving to the weights.

Silas growls into my ear in his territorial way, and I giggle, straightening my spine, loving the way his hands are gripping each of my ass cheeks.

"Why are you buttering me up, little monster?"

Busted.

"I'm writing music with Ian and wanted to know if you would be okay with me using some of your letters for inspiration."

He narrows his eyes, and then they soften before he takes my lips onto his before pulling back.

"I have no secrets in those letters. They are just as much yours to decide what to do with." He spins me around, pressing me to the wall's mirror. "However, you should know that Ian gets hot and bothered when he plays that deep. The same way I do when I see blood, and if I find you later with his cum dripping out of you, you will be in very big trouble."

I lean in, biting his earlobe but holding back the pleasure of drawing blood. "You don't get to tell me who I can't fuck within the four of you."

He wraps his hand in my hair, pulling my head back and biting my jaw. "I never said you couldn't fuck him. I said that I want to be the only one that comes inside you today. Maybe even the whole week." He sucks my neck bruisingly, and I groan, grinding my hips into him.

"I have lots of lost time to make up for before I want to share you completely, but if you want to piss me off, I can find enjoyment in that too." He winks at me, and I can almost see every filthy idea running through his head. I don't know which option turns me on more.

"I choose both."

He grins a look of pure sex, and I seek out a little punishment of my own.

I walk over to where Finn is benching and straddle his hips. Silas resumes his workout, but I don't miss his lingering glances and heavier punches smacking the bag. Teasing Silas more, I lean forward, placing my hands on Finn's chest and tilting my hips into his groin.

His eyes follow to the lyrics on my skin. "When do I get to mark you? Permanently," Finn says between heavy breaths.

I roll my hips as he starts a new set. "Whenever you want."

"You know," Finn grunts, thrusting the bar up and down, "they say this is a great way to boost testosterone for a better workout."

I hear Silas throwing everything he has into his punches, and now that I see his temper for what it is, I can't help but enjoy it a little too much. I pull my shirt over my head, leaving myself in nothing but my underwear.

Lyle laughs from the corner where he is curling weights in each arm, his veins popping out, almost making me drool all over myself. "You know, I think he has a point."

Finn chuckles, both of them enjoying this as much as I am. His movements seem to come easier, and I feel his bulge pressing into me.

"I wonder how much a blowjob could do," I ask out loud.

"Amelia," Silas growls.

"Okay, okay. Just having some fun," I tease, climbing off Finn and grabbing my shirt. I lean down and press my lips to Finn's neck, whispering in his ear, "I'm not joking, but Silas says I have to be a good girl for now."

Just as I stand back up, a sexually frustrated Lyle is undressing me with his eyes. Sauntering up to him, I grip his hard dick through his shorts, and he grunts while still pumping his weights. I stand on my tippy-toes and talk lowly. "What do you think, Hellcat? Should we piss off the lion?"

He smirks with a dark and breathy chuckle.

"Hmmmmm," I ponder out loud spinning around. I press my ass to Lyle's crotch and bend at the waist, wiggling my ass.

"What about coming in my ass? Is that breaking a rule, Si?"

"Amelia!" he booms, his angry tone ripping through the air like thunder as he punches the bag so hard I yelp.

I take off running out the door and back up the stairs, laughing so hard I almost pee myself. It's too easy.

Once I know he's not following me, I grab my letters and slip back into Ian's room, clutching my shirt to my chest.

"What happened to you?" Ian chuckles, strumming his guitar lightly.

I run my fingers through my hair, still trying to catch my breath.

"Oh, you know, just taunting the lion."

He laughs again, shaking his head in amusement as I join him on the bed.

I sprawl the letters out, covering nearly every inch around us. Dozens and dozens of letters written from Silas, dating back to freshman year of high school in the girls' locker room.

I find my favorites and lay them out in front of me, letting Ian read over them and scribble ideas on my skin. I know it would make more sense to just get paper at this point, but I'll indulge him for the sole reason of seeing his art on my body.

"I really like this one," he says with a soft smile, handing it to me.

The same smile finds my lips as I reread the smeared words from years ago.

THE REASON WE LIKE TO STAY UP ALL HOURS OF THE NIGHT IS BECAUSE, WITHIN THOSE HOURS, WE ARE ABLE TO JUST BE. NO EXPECTATIONS. NO CONSEQUENCES. NO BURDENS. FOR A SMALL AMOUNT OF TIME, WE CAN CLOSE OUR EYES AND BE ANYWHERE IN THE WORLD. FOR ME, IT'S IN YOUR ARMS. WHERE IS YOUR PLACE?

-NOT HIM

"My freshman year of college."

It was left on my car windshield. Not a likely place I would check, but after moving into the dorms, he could only get so far without getting noticed. Though I'm sure if it came down to it, Ian could have smoothed it over.

I remember my response. I had stopped begging for him to save me, realizing that, for whatever reason, he would keep his distance. I left the letter blank, only my signature at the bottom.

Anger filled me, but I suffered in silence rather than hurt the only person who seemed to care about who I was on the inside.

Teardrops have caused the ink to bleed here and there from nights of clinging it to my chest, but I can't remember the exact events that happened on those nights. Over time, they all started to blur into this one vast abyss with only a soft glow of *his* hope lingering in the distance to comfort me, begging me to hold on.

We play around for hours, stringing ideas and words together until the sun dips below the horizon and my legs are covered in ink. Ian takes pictures of our latest addition then begins to softly wash me clean. I take my phone, snapping a picture of the scattered music notes on my upper thigh, loving how it looks.

I yawn, laying back on the twenty-something pillows he has lined at the headboard.

"So when you finish that, what are you planning on doing with it?" I ask, pulling him down next to me and throwing my leg over his side.

He shrugs nuzzling his face into my chest. "Maybe record it. At some point, I have to prove my father wrong."

I hug him tighter, running my nails up and down his back. "You don't have to prove anything to that bastard. You being whoever you want to be is enough."

He relaxes into me, his fingers still and his mind at rest and peace overcomes me. This house.

This family.

My home.

This is where my heart is

"Do you want to stay in here tonight?" he asks, still half under me.

"We may have to put some beds together because I don't think Si is going to take no for an answer for a while."

Ian's chest shakes with laughter. "You may be right."

The reason we like to stay up all hours of the night is because, within those hours, we are able to just be. No expectations. No consequences. No burdens. For a small amount of time, we can close our eyes and be anywhere in the world. For me, it's in your arms. Where is your place?

-Not Him

-Amelia

Amelia

We lay in Silas's dark room, five deep on his California King. Me in the middle, Lyle and Silas on either side of me, and the other two on the outsides. Silas refused to move anything around, trying to make it difficult enough that they would cave and leave me all to him.

An arm reaches across, brushing mine, as Silas's voice vibrates my back. "That is my ass you are caressing, Lyle."

"I know," he responds in a sensual tone, making me giggle.

"This room smells like sex, blood, and testosterone," Ian murmurs from behind Lyle, and the mental picture I create in the dark of him spooning Lyle with his hand resting on my hip has my heart nearly leaping from my chest.

"If you don't like it, you are free to leave," Silas snips, the irritation clear in his voice.

"I didn't say that," Ian says, moving in closer.

The room quiets, and my heart calms as my head follows suit. Being with them is loud and chaotic. Messy and new. But it calms the wildness inside me - gives it purpose.

My head wanders less and less each week as I dive deeper into them, and soon I will be utterly consumed, arms outstretched and in full surrender, ready to die before I lose them. Most people see that as unhealthy, and maybe it is, but here I know my all-or-nothing qualities are what makes me belong. The four of them do nothing half-assed.

My eyes close, and I drift into sleep with the help of a symphony of soft sighs of breaths and snores.

***

I jolt awake from a dream, coated in a thin layer of sweat, so similar and yet different from the ones before. Sitting in nothingness again, except this time, I knew the warmness that protected me. My four boys were there, but so was the dark feeling that I was losing them. The message that pain was never far away was repeating on a loop.

It takes me a minute to separate the dream from reality. And I take in where I am.

My body is pinned in place by a heavy arm. I'm nose to nose with Lyle, Ian's fluffy hair in the curve of Lyle's neck. Lyle puckers his lips and kisses my lips so soft that they barely touch.

"Good morning," he says in a scratchy voice, and my cheeks turn warm enough to prove how much I'm in love with the sound that just came out of him and how embarrassed I am about my morning breath right in his face.

I cover my mouth and turn my head towards the ceiling as I mumble a distorted response. He pulls my chin back towards him and pushes his cold nose into the crevice of my warm neck, ensuring me nothing could repulse him or make him love me any less. My heart beats a little harder for him, but I still don't speak directly to his face, seriously worried I might kill him with my breath.

I slide out of bed and receive unhappy grumbles from all of them. I smile. Something I seem to be doing an increasing amount of the longer I live here. I head straight for the bathroom with the intent of getting a jump-start on the day.

Finn steps behind me, and I look at him in the mirror. His black, messy hair just as bad as mine was moments ago. He reaches over me to grab his own toothbrush smiling and begins brushing. I lean to spit, and he does the same, the white foam nearly landing in my hair.

My eyes widen in horror and I spin around and point my toothbrush at him like a weapon. He chuckles putting his toothbrush down before his hands are on my ass and his mouth is pressing against mine. The remnants of toothpaste mixed and smeared between our mouths.

There is something fascinatingly domestic about the act, and I want more. I want more of the comfort and how I sink effortlessly into my spot with them.

I push him back into the door and away from my body before wiping my lips and smearing it on the side of his face. His nose scrunches and I pat his chest with the cutest smile I can manage before stepping back into the hall and heading for my room.

I listen to their morning bickering as I dress. Then throw on a layer of my favorite dark purple lipstick with a touch of mascara, and by the time I am done and ready to go, they're all downstairs, ready to go.

Oh, the life of a man must be nice. Change your underwear and put some water in your hair. Then you are good to go for just about any occasion. At least they are smart enough to not complain dramatically about the time it takes me. I assume they learned that little tidbit from Ian. He is the only one that grew up with any sort of proper lessons on how to treat a lady. I haven't met the twins' uncle, but I assume he is the fun, crass type of man if their behavior is any indication.

Lyle meets me at the bottom of the stairs while the rest stay seated on the couch. "Mind if we push hanging with JJ back a little bit? I want to take you by the shop."

I look over my shoulder to the living room. Ian casts me a wink and resumes his conversation with Finn. With a smile, I accept Lyle's suggestion and take his hand, letting him lead me outside to my car.

Mel slides into the driver seat and we roll the windows down. Adjusting her mirrors, she pulls out of the drive, heading for the shop.

I need time with her, just us. Life is messy and hard, but she makes it just a little easier. A little more wonderful. And I want it, her, for the rest of my life. She takes a quick glance my way and the smile she gives me confirms it.

I need to talk to the guys about proposing.

I don't want to waste another second not having her officially bound to us.

She turns up the radio and when I reach for the knob, she slaps my hand, scrunching her nose at me. The wind whips her long hair around her face as classic rock plays softly through the speakers.

I watch her, unable to focus on anything but how breathtaking she is. Taking in the sight of her being everything I knew she could be as she drives comfortably and with confidence.

She sings to my addiction to people that are imperfect and complex. The people that are half-darkness, waiting to see if you stick around and pull them out of the shadows, before they show you their light.

The ones that can look death in the eyes because they have seen evil walk the earth. Yet they love deeper and softer, reading between the lines of every person they meet.

Broken, but not fragile.

"Milkshake?" she asks, finally lowering the music.

"Absolutely."

She pulls into the diner up ahead, parking in an empty stall, then presses the button to order and turns to me. "Flavor?"

"Chocolate, of course," I say, just as a voice comes over the speaker.

"Welcome to Dixie's Diner. What can I get for you?"

She leans out the window, getting closer. "A medium caramel milkshake and a medium chocolate milkshake. That's it."

I hand her the cash and she folds it up, holding it between her thighs while we wait.

"Do you ever want kids?" I ask, blurting out the question.

She looks at me curiously, chewing on her lip. "No."

Shocked, I turn further in my seat. "That's not the answer I expected."

"Are you disappointed?" she asks, a grin on her lips letting me know it wouldn't change her answer.

"No," I answer honestly. "But why?"

She leans against the door, bringing one of her legs up into the seat. "I wouldn't want to fuck them up like my mom did to me. The thought of having kids isn't unappealing, I just never saw it as a requirement for my happily ever after. Being loved is all I need. All I want."

"I can understand that." The lifestyle we have isn't exactly nurturing to innocent minds.

"Do you want kids?" she asks, a hint of nervousness hiding in her tone.

"No. With the vow to love the same woman, we agreed having biological kids wouldn't be wise with how jealous we can get." She nods, tension leaving her shoulders. "But maybe one day we'll find some older kids that have already been through hell. Take them in and show them how to set the world on fire."

She grins, her eyes sparkling with interest. Mother or not, Amelia will thrive when she can give all the love and advice she never got as a teen.

Our milkshakes come and were off, taking the back-roads so we're less likely to be seen.

She pulls the car around to back of the shop and kills it, running her hands along the steering wheel in appreciation. Taking in the interior, she smiles wide before looking at me.

"I love everything about this car."

I smile back, heart soaring that she is so in love with our gift. Creating it for her is a memory I will hold forever.

My heart leaped when she chose a paint color born from my eyes.

If she looked close enough, she would see herself in them, a pale blue, tethered by the black shadowed center.

A part of me forever.

Not sunshine, but rain.

Cloudy, storming skies. The promise of a new day with a touch of wear from living. Faded and tired, but unforgivingly certain of what she is.

Hope wrapped in darkness.

Amelia grounds my soul, gives it a home.

She is my everything, my little angel of death.

"So what are we doing here?" I ask, dropping into one of the bar stools by the front desk.

Lyle lights a joint and passes it to me.

"Honestly, I just haven't had any time with you where it was just us. We can hang out, talk, fuck. As long as it's just us for a little while, I don't care."

I hum in understanding and hit the joint again before passing it back. "How about you tell me why you like this place so much?"

He leans back against the old Chevy truck that looks like a new project in need of a lot of love.

"I built this place with Finn and my uncle. This was the first thing that was truly mine. Something sturdy and reliable that I had back then."

Something that was not going to leave.

He blows a smoke ring and shoots another through it. "My uncle Mark signed everything over to me when I turned eighteen. Finn helped build it, but he has never loved this place like I do. Soon after, Mark left to travel."

I nod and take in all the posters and pictures of their younger selves around the room.

"Do you still talk to him?"

"We hear from him often, but we try not to bother him. He put his whole life on hold to raise us. He never wanted kids and was still a better parent than we could have ever asked for."

I slide from my chair and inspect the family pictures of each of the boys. Younger versions of themselves that should shine with innocence but clearly had already seen more than most adults. A new question nags at my mind, but I roll it over in my mind a few times before I ask it.

"Does he know about y'all's... lifestyle?"

"We don't need to inform him of our every move, but we have had to call him in some sticky situations. He's someone you can trust."

I stop at a picture of Lyle somewhere around the age of eleven with long shaggy hair, covered in mud and oil. He's posing in a lunge next to a trophy nearly as tall as him.

He chuckles low behind me. "First place for a bike race. I ate shit but still won."

I continue walking around, enjoying the stories behind every display. I'm looking at what might be the first picture all four of them took when he speaks again.

"Can I tell you something, and it stays between us?"

My stomach sinks a little. "Yes."

"I recognized you. The first time Finn showed us a picture of you when he wanted to bring you home, I recognized your face."

I don't say anything.

"I couldn't place it until I saw how Silas started reacting towards you. Then it all started to fall into place, and I knew where I had seen you before. A couple years ago, I had been in Silas's room and found your picture with a letter you had written."

My heart beats heavily, and I search my erratic mind for the right words.

"Why- Why didn't you say something sooner?"

"Once you had me and Ian, I knew Silas would be the easy one to convince." He shrugs. "He already loved you. You weren't going anywhere. And if I had to call him out, I would have. But I wanted to see how it would play out first."

I shake my head with an incredulous laugh.

"You are such a shit starter. You could have helped avoid so much shit."

"Maybe. But everything worked out, right?"

"Yeah. I guess it did."

I keep walking around the room to a small wall dedicated to nothing but comic book villains.

"Of course, you support the villains and not the heroes." I snort.

"And you?"

I finish looking and return to him on the other side of the room.

"Hero or villain?"

I tilt my head to the side. "Am I supporting their choices or fucking them?"

"Hero or villain?" he repeats with a smirk.

I think it over for a minute.

"I'm gonna go with *villain*."

"Because?"

I climb up on the hood of the truck next to him, and he turns, wrapping his arms around my waist and resting his hands on my ass.

"Well, I think that a villain is dependent on perspective, and they usually have the better powers."

In any superhero movie I have ever watched, I always wondered what happened to the villain to make them the way they are. Monsters are made.

"I think you prefer the villain over the hero because the hero would put the many over his girl. Because you would adore the villain burning the world to the ground to protect you." He leans in close. "And now you have just that."

"We were talking about comic books, Hellcat. There was no need to make it so literal."

Lyle just shrugs, no apology for his comment. He passes me the remaining joint, and I finish it off.

"Doesn't change the fact that I'm right." He runs his hands up and down the tops of my thighs, the high making the contact feel so good. "You say the word, and I'll have their head on a stake for you."

Thrill shoots through me at his promise and settles low between my legs. I wrap my hands behind his neck, give him my best smile of pure mischief, digging my nails into the back of his neck, making him groan. He lifts me and pulls my shorts down my legs, tossing them behind him before pulling his underwear down over his ass. His hand wraps around my throat, and he pulls me close.

"You better come on my dick so fucking hard you black out."

He lifts me off the truck by my waist and lowers me onto him. And we both let out a sharp breath.

"Only if you keep your hand around my neck."

A lethal sound rumbles out of him in approval, and he presses my back against the truck for support. His hand squeezes tighter, and I tilt my head up, allowing the euphoria to consume me as my blood circulation is cut off. I place my hand on his chest as a blockade against his forceful thrusts.

"You feel so goddamn good. You can take me harder. I know you can." His fingers tighten on the sides of my throat.

"Drop that hand, Angel."

I move my hand to his arm and dig my fingernails in his skin as I allow him deeper. He pounds into me harder and faster. My eyes begin to grow heavy, my vision getting fuzzy.

"Don't you dare pass out before you scream my name."

"Oh fuck," I whine, tilting my hips forward to give my clit more friction. My arousal coats him, my pussy dripping all over him.

"Shit, baby." He squeezes harder again, and right as I begin to tighten on him, he releases his grip. Blood comes rushing back to my brain, and I come hard with his name on my lips. He follows right after me, then drops his head to my neck, sucking the skin bruisingly.

He looks up at me, panting. his dick still in me. "I'll give you another, but you have to beg for it." His voice dips, the word *beg* leaving his lips like sin.

I tangle my hands in his hair, pushing his face back into my neck, encouraging him to mark me again.

"Please."

"Please what?" he asks, gripping my ass and slamming me into him as he leaves blood bruises all along my neck.

"Please make me come again, baby."

He loses it. He stands up straight pulling my hips up at a slant, balancing me on the truck again and hitting me deeper. He reaches his hand between us and rubs my clit fast. Before I can process anything, my second orgasm tears through me with agonizing cries.

He smiles with accomplishment bracing his hands on either side of my head.

"You. Fucking. Own me," he says between struggling breaths.

"Bow down," I tease, but his face goes flat. He sits me back up on the hood and pulls out of me. Then bends down and bows between my spread legs.

He spends the next twenty minutes worshipping me to the point I can't tell where one orgasm ends and the next begins.

Amelia

Tyler's house is smaller than Ian's but not any less impressive. It's a beautiful one-story gray brick home with a circle drive. A classic southern look, and from the swimsuit that JJ greets us in, he also has a pool around the back to fully pull the look together.

I change into my swimsuit and JJ catches my arm before I can make it out the door, eyeing my healing cuts with a worried look.

I give her a soft smile, appreciating how much she cares. "Everyone has their own way of healing. I'm into it, and I'm happy."

She nods, accepting that answer.

I sit on the edge of the in-ground saltwater pool. The cool water splashes back and forth over my shins in waves as the boys rush around in a game of volleyball. JJ, Tyler, and Ian stand on one side of the net, opposing the other three in the deep end that sit on floats or hang to the side of the pool. I claimed the role of referee just to get my tan on.

Finn slides me down further towards him and braces himself between my legs. He kisses the top of my thigh, and the beach ball lands right behind him, followed by griping from Lyle and Silas.

"If you wanted me to spread my legs for you, all you had to do was ask."

He kisses my other thigh, and I move them farther apart, hoping he will head to the center next, right in front of everyone.

"Darling, I don't have to ask for anything."

I lean further into him, submitting my whole self to him, letting him see just how right he is. I would forever give everything to the four of them. He kisses closer and closer to where I really want him.

"I could spend forever between your legs, worshipping you."

"Can the two of you stop the foreplay so we can actually beat you fair and square?" JJ teases.

I lean back onto my hands and prop my feet on Finn's shoulders. "Go ahead. Go play your game."

He pulls me into the water with him and I hiss, the saltwater washing over my cuts. I wrap my legs around his waist, cross them behind his back, and lock my arms around his neck. He resumes his hold on the pool wall, and I stay in his lap as the game continues.

The ball is hit back and forth, and I am jolted around as Finn attempts to score with me attached to him like a leach. Many times he almost drowns me as he leaps from the wall and into the deep end. I sputter water for the nearly hundredth time and attempt to catch my breath as he swims us back to the wall.

Tyler and JJ fight over who gets to serve, purposely trying to drown each other. And while everyone's eyes are focused on them, Finn uses the opportunity to his advantage. My bottoms are pulled to the side, and the head of his dick presses into me. I stiffen but make no sudden moves. I feel his cheek lift against my own as he smiles. To everyone else, his smile appears to be because of JJ's actions. He stays focused on her, leaving us with a dirty little secret as I am fully seated on his dick.

I discreetly look down as everyone gets back into place, JJ having won her small battle for the ball. Finn has his swim trunks only lowered where I cover him with no indication he is completely sheathed inside of me.

The ball goes back and forth again, and Finn jolts me around again, though he seems to use his hips a little more than before. The small movements go unnoticed and drive me insane as my arousal increases and has me internally begging for more.

That irrational part of my brain lights up with filthy desires, no factor strong enough to stop it, as I wish Finn would take me against the side of the pool as everyone watches how angry and rough we get. I think about the other three joining us, leaving my body trembling in the wide open. I think about the act being so erotic that JJ and Tyler join separately, only feet away, and nothing but moans and skin smacking together to fill the silence.

Silas makes the winning score, and everyone except for us barrels out of the pool, heading to get drinks while still bickering about the score.

"She's biased; that's all I'm saying," JJ tells Ian with a shrug of her shoulders and a wink sent toward me as she trails the rest of them back inside.

Finn turns us and pins me against the rough wall, and the ledge digs into my neck as he pushes into me with force. I try to suppress the moan he literally forces out of me with a grunt.

"Are you biased, baby?" He keeps his eyes on the house as he talks. "I think you may have given me an unfair advantage and been a little distracted while calling shots." He draws out of me slowly, leaving only his tip inside for a long second. Then he slowly pushes back in until his hips are painfully pressing against me, and he's as deep as he could possibly get.

In and out.

In and out so fucking slowly that I feel like I becoming one with the water, only moving as a result of his motions and desires.

His eyes smile towards the house, and he runs his tongue over his teeth behind his lips. Someone is watching.

The back door opens, but he doesn't speed up.

"Pizza's here," Tyler says, and if I wasn't a horny mess, I might laugh at the fact that Finn continues to hold his stare as he grinds his hips.

"We're coming," Finn chimes in a perfectly flat tone,

"Right, baby?"

"Yes." I hear the word leave my lips, sounding more meant for Finn than Tyler, so I try again. "Yes, coming."

That was no better than the one before.

A lightning-fast orgasm comes and goes.

Tyler clears his throat and shuts the door.

Finn pulls out of me, and with a firm expression, he pushes me below the water and level with his dick that he's stroking. With one hand on my shoulder to keep me anchored, he shoves himself deep into my mouth and gives a few deep thrusts into the back of my throat. I grip his thighs, and he jerks as he spills into me. I immediately swallow the combination of his cum and the salty pool water before releasing him.

I resurface and gasp for air. His hands brush my wet hair back, and he kisses me deep in his perfect way that melts me to my core. His tongue leaves no part of my own untouched.

"I love the taste of me in your mouth."

***

I carry pizza into one of the two rooms designated for us to have some privacy. Ian sits on the bed with his iPad and notebook. I love watching him in his zone, so utterly consumed with focus and determination to find what he's looking for. His eyes break free from the screen when the bed tips beneath my weight.

I would ask him what he is doing, but I already know. Every minute of freedom he has, he is searching for the answers we need. Either way, it will happen, so I demanded that he not spend every waking moment driving himself insane with getting the jump on Nickolas.

I hand him his plate and tell him to take a break to eat. He holed himself up in here the minute he could take a shower after the game ended.

"Eat and work. I finally found a wall in my father's database." He shoves a bite of pizza in his mouth and wipes his fingers on his shorts before his fingers resume their swift movement across the glass.

I raise a brow that says *dumb that down for me.*

He groans frustratedly and more than a little annoyed, though I'm sure not entirely at me. "A wall means he's hiding something, so the faster I break through it, the faster I can determine if it is something we need to end this bullshit. There are likely other walls blocking each document behind this first, so this is pretty important."

Alrighty then.

I nod slowly and leave him to handle it. I'm starting to think Silas may not have been the only bear I was warned not to poke.

I spend the rest of the evening reading by the pool and sipping on my margarita with JJ in the chair beside mine, listening to her music. The guys really need a pool because this is a lifestyle I could very easily get used to. I wonder just how much they would do if I only asked.

Tyler's index finger drags my book down, and I cast him a death stare. He obviously never learned that you never, ever pull a book away from a woman reading romance unless you are prepared to sacrifice something of value.

Three margaritas in has me feeling extra feisty, as they usually do.

He holds his hands up in defense. "I just wanted to see if you wanted another drink on my way to fix another for JJ."

I give him a nod and shove my nose back in my book. A moment later, I tilt it back down to find him still standing in the same spot. I roll my eyes and thank him as unsarcastically as I can. It's not my fault he interrupted the tension break. He winks at me in combination with finger guns.

He returns with two fresh drinks, handing one to me and setting the other next to JJ's chair. He sits on the other side of her, and she blows him a kiss as she continues to slowly nod her head to the song busting her eardrums.

"Ian told me to tell you that the guys were all hanging in the room but for you to enjoy the last few hours here before y'all head home."

I lay my book in my lap and slurp down a few huge gulps. "Well, in that case, I better get drunk faster."

Whatever they are about to uncover, I already know I do not want to be sober to hear. Though I will be making my way up there to bitch about them trying to do any part of this without me.

"Can I ask you a personal question?"

It takes me a minute to realize Tyler is talking to me. I continue steadily sucking down the delicious strawberry poison but let him know that I am not declining.

"Is sharing multiple men something all women fantasize about?"

I nearly spew the melted contents in my mouth. I cup the bits that dribble from my lip. JJ has her eyes closed, so I assume she didn't hear any of that.

"I, uh-... no. I never did. It just kinda fell in my lap."

He scratches his scalp nervously. "Okay. I was wondering because I know she's a very sexually open person... I just don't think I could ever be with someone that wanted to be shared."

My jaw tightens, and I feel my face fall flat.

He tries to recover. "No, I just mean that I don't know how your boys learned to not feel like they aren't good enough or think that you wouldn't sleep with anyone when you get bored."

I don't care that Tyler doesn't find me dateable, but that was fucking rude, no matter how you look at it. Right about now, I'm wishing that a fist was in his mouth, and it may end up being mine.

"Tyler, I'm gonna stop you." I stand, and the alcohol hits me hard. I stumble, and my head spins but I catch myself on JJ's chair, causing it to shake slightly, but it doesn't startle her. My speech slurs, and I decide to wrap this up and make my way to the boys before this escalates. "You have the right to your opinion, but don't... don't..." I blink hard, trying to focus my spotty vision.

I attempt to walk past him but stumble right into him. He catches me by the arms on my way to my knees.

My eyes feel heavy in a familiarly wrong way. The twinkle lights hanging overhead seem too bright. His blonde hair and facial features look too wrong at this angle. His voice seems too loud.

"Don't speak on something that is none of my business? I would never."

His voice is the last thing I hear, before being lifted into his arms.

Then, only darkness.

Hours pass before I finally make it through the first block. The file opens, and many scattered files appear. I read through the labels. Bank statements, invoices, dates and locations, payroll, and people. I call for the boys, trying not to seem panicked, and pass the word for Mel to continue whatever she is doing. Anything we find here can be discussed after the four of us have a chance to process. She is just as much a part of this, but no matter what she demands, we will always be the ones to take the brunt of the fall.

They sit around the bed as I break through the next wall, deciding names are what we need first. We open the files individually, seeing what pictures and statements have been gathered for each person.

We sifted through the ones for each of us, including Amelia, JJ, Lance, and Emma, and found exactly what we expected. Images and videos of each of us and proof that both Lance and Emma were being compensated for their efforts.

My fist grips the side of my screen a little too hard when a video of Amelia is shown being sent from Lance to my father and then again to a burner phone. I don't have to click on it to know what it is. The inside of the tree-house is visible in the frozen preview image.

I push on, but three names on my shit list become written in blood. We pass through two names of the local gang's highest rankings - *Thomas Hennings* and *Dominique Rodrigeuz*.

Then we see *Damian Mason*.

I click on his file, needing to see why he could possibly be on this list if my father claimed that he was too clean to be any kind of dirty. There is a document inside titled with Nickolas's name, and my brows pinch even tighter. Then, my jaw turns slack. My brain nearly short circuits as I read a buried case overview.

Nickolas's case when we reported him years ago to get him locked up. The state prosecutor - *Damian Mason.*

"Fuck," Finn sighs.

Nickolas doesn't just want to hurt us. He wants an eye for an eye. Damian is dead, so the next best thing is his daughter. I keep searching. Finding the name, *Tyler Rutledge.*

I click on his next.

We decide there is too much unknown there to skip over it. Benefit of the doubt is not something we do well around here. I hit a passcode. It takes me only forty-five seconds to get in, and I mentally give my father the middle finger.

Moron.

Bank statements, hospital records, and a multitude of messages appear. I skim through them, and my heart nearly falls from my ass while the room falls deathly silent.

No. No fucking way.

"Holy shit," Lyle breathes, leaning back.

Tyler is... my half-brother.

I stare for minutes before I force my brain to compartmentalize until I can finish sifting through the rest. I speed through the messages from my father.

Today

Jameson:
Nickolas moving.

Tyler:
On it.

No. No. No.

Silas erupts from the bed, dashing out of the room and it takes everything in me not to follow.

My heart is pulverized into nothing, and my chest has a gaping hole where it used to be.

I keep reading, revealing everything about him. This whole time, Tyler knew who he was to me and was fucking playing us to try to gain my father's love.

The first correspondence was from Tyler, explaining that his mother had told him the truth. He wasn't sad or angry... he was pissed beyond belief. Threats and blackmail.

An illegitimate child conceived only a couple years after my parents were married would ruin my father's image. The business was built on their name together, and my poor mother has no idea how much shit he does under her name to help keep his own clean. And with Tyler older than me, the business should fall to him rightfully. My father refused and demanded that this never come to light, but to appease him, he had been sending large sums of money for years.

Tyler never truly let it go, and kept digging.

Without the family skills, he wasn't able to get the proof he needed, but the money he got allowed him to hire a private investigator. He was able to piece the connection between all of our fathers together before any of this was even in motion. He practically begged for the chance to prove he could be more useful than I am.

"Fuck!" I throw my iPad into my pack and race out of the room with the twins at my back. I call out for Amelia, keeping my voice as calm as possible and slowing as much as my frantic body will let me once I reach the common area.

Silas comes in from the back, his hair disheveled from pulling on it. "JJ's been drugged, and he took her. She's gone."

He paces back and forth and my gut churns as I try to think of a plan.

"No!" Silas bellows in anger, then once again in agony, "No!"

"Oh, God. I'm gonna be sick," Finn says in a pained tone, and Lyle's fists are balled at his side, fumes rolling off him in anger.

We fucked this up.

"God won't save any of us now," I grind out, my own voice sounding like darkness incarnate. My vision goes red and our hands will soon look the same.

We drive as fast as possible back to our house with JJ piled in our laps in the backseat of Silas's truck. We get her safely put in Amelia's bed with a scribbled note next to her, instructing her to stay here when she wakes. There is no telling how long she might be out.

And it's that thought that has me nearly clawing out of my skin, wishing we could get to Amelia faster than the hundred miles an hour we travel. We split into three vehicles to give us more possibilities as we try to come up with a plan. Tyler can't dodge us all at the same time.

I start tracking her phone, wishing like hell she has it on her. The ding of her location being found sends relief through my chest. In our fastest vehicle, we follow her moving signal. The locating dot moving towards the warehouse Nickolas's gang is known for working out of, where he is most likely waiting for them.

For her.

This whole fucking time, he wanted her.

Finn

Everything inside of me burns as my entire world crumbles around me more devastatingly than I have ever felt before. My life is tied to hers. If we lose Amelia, I won't live.

I can't.

I would never want to.

I love Amelia more than I ever thought possible. For me, she isn't the next one in line. She is the only one.

After our last attempt at this, I swore I would never let myself sink that deep again, but with Amelia, it doesn't feel like sinking. It's like flying. Free-falling into everything that was her. I didn't lose myself in her.

I found... everything, and now, Nickolas is once again trying to take that away.

I don't care how many bodies have to end up in the ground. He will not take her.

Ian's phone dings, notifying us the tracking stopped a mile from the warehouse. I slam my fist into the dash and slam my foot onto the gas. I try to focus on the memory of her smile and laugh, but suddenly, I can't manifest it. I have to see and hear her again.

I have to.

I take the turns sharp, and my wheels struggle to keep traction as I swerve around oncoming traffic about twenty minutes behind them. Twenty minutes too long. We were too comfortable. We left her with JJ to relax and didn't question the decision once.

The first time we leave her alone, we fuck it up. Never once hearing them leave. Never once checking on her as we did something she would have wanted to be a part of.

The drive feels impossible, but we finally make it to the gravel parking lot, the other two skidding in behind us. We barrel out and make no attempt to keep our arrival silent. It would have been smart, but none of our vehicles are quiet enough to go unnoticed.

We rush through the open metal doors. Blood stains everywhere, the smell of urine and drugs filling the air. It's empty to the naked eye, but we aren't stupid enough to think they aren't waiting for us.

Silas moves in front of us with his gun drawn as he quickly searches around the corners.

A large figure jumps from behind a row of crates. He's fast, but Lyle's reflexes are faster. Lyle swings his bat, connecting with the man's head, sending him to the ground. He swings again, and blood begins pooling around the man's head.

We keep moving, but I glance at Lyle. His hair has fallen in his eyes, and blood freckles his face curled in a snarl. The building is huge, with many hiding places, but we stick together.

Just as we round a corner, four meatheads turn our way.

"Fuck," Ian mumbles, speaking the thought we all had. He doesn't enjoy fighting like we do, but he did find a certain love for the power of wielding a gun.

Quickly, I move next to him passing him the second pistol I have holstered in my jeans. The sounds of one entering the chamber sound off throughout the room, and Ian lets off shots before any other man in the room can move. Within seconds, the four bodies are lying on the ground, and Ian bares a grin of nightmares.

Perfect shots.

A dozen more men enter the room. We gain feet one at a time.

Silas barrels into a mountain of a man after landing a shot into his shoulder, and the butt of his gun connects with the man's temple. I keep a cautious eye on him as I fight my next opponent off.

My gun is forced out of my hand and slides across the room and I reach for a crowbar sitting on top of a metal tabletop. My hand wraps around it just as I am thrown to the ground.

My face slams into the concrete floor, and I see stars. Flipping over, I slam my foot into the man's chest and flip back to my feet. I swing the crowbar, and he dodges it with a step back, his gun pointed directly at my head.

In one motion, I duck low and thrust the crowbar upwards and into his gut. His eyes bulge, and blood sputters from his mouth.

"Where is she?" I yell.

He spits in response and I shove the crowbar in further and twist it before tossing him to the ground.

I yank the tool back out and slam it in once more into his head. Then move for my gun. I turn just in time to fire a shot at the man coming for Lyle from behind. He spins as the body drops to the ground, and I nod at him.

We move together to end the last three men opposing us. Lyle lunges and swings his bat into one of their heads, disorienting him enough that his next kick puts him flat on his back. He raises the bat over his head, swings with every drop of force he has, and cracks the man's skull open.

Silas steps in front of Ian and lands a perfect shot between the second man's eyeballs. Spinning to the last man opposing us, Silas hits him, knocking him right into my body. I pull the crowbar in front of his neck, cutting off his airway until his body falls limp.

Once again, a small piece of this gang falls for taking something that belongs to us. Only this time, we won't be as generous.

I take in the carnage and the red river flowing like a calling sign.

We're coming.

As a unit and with no time to catch our breaths, we move through the room the men were in and search for her. It's quiet now, and my ears ring at the sudden contrast.

The sound of a car turning over has us busting through the side doors.

Amelia is conscious but dripping blood and being carried by two men. Thankfully, her clothes are still in place, but she looks like she is begging for death to take her. Her sad eyes roll to us, and I swear I see a spark of hope ignite within them.

Nickolas is crouched inside the open van door, five feet from her.

I run. I run so Goddamn fast.

Ian fires two shots, one in the chest and one in the head, taking down the man holding onto her feet, and it draws Nickolas's eyes to us.

He smiles. The bastard actually fucking smiles.

"Let's fucking end this!" Silas screams in guttural rage.

He aims.

He fires.

He misses, hitting the door as Nickolas slams it shut. The van peels out of the back lot just as we reach her, leaving his last man alone.

He drops Amelia to the ground and takes a few panicked steps away, and Silas rushes to her. With a one-track mind, he misses the fact that the stranded man fires a shot before any of us can. It lands in Silas's shoulder, missing his heart as he drops down next to our girl.

The man's curses get cut off as Lyle takes him to the ground. All his anger is unleashed onto the sorry bastard, slamming his fist again and again into his face. His blows are lethal, and it takes Ian and I both to pull him off once there is no doubt the man is dead.

Amelia wraps her arms around Silas's neck with a cringe, and he scoops her up in a bridal-style hold, carefully holding her head to his chest.

"Let's go!" he commands and we sprint back to the front.

Amelia groans as Silas places her as softly as possible into the passenger seat of my car to ride with Ian. Silas and I take his truck, and Lyle takes his own car.

"I'm okay," I say for the fifth time, going completely unheard as they talk on speaker-phone about having me checked out before finding Tyler, who has most likely run for daddy's protection. We are all covered in blood, though it appears I am the only one wearing my own. I'm not sure that any of them even have a scrape. They wear the blood like dark armor, proving that sometimes this world turns you into something darker when it spits you back out.

Despite my clear irritation, we race down the now empty road lit by streetlights and head back into town towards the hospital. I want to end this now, not once a doctor slaps some Band-Aids on me. I'm a little banged up, and the half-hour was enough to do a number on my head, but they are letting me make them softer and I tell them as much.

"Are you fucking kidding me?" Lyle says over the speakerphone call.

"Are you?!" I shout back, finding my strength again with the help of adrenaline.

He snorts an amused sound. "Not you. Look behind us."

Nickolas's van pulls out onto the road behind us. The fucking loser didn't dare fight them all at once. Running to wait and try to get the jump on us again. He didn't get very far with me between the time Tyler dropped me off and the boys showed up, but he promised it wouldn't be the last time he had some fun with me.

Fucking Tyler. Thankfully, Nickolas loves to brag about what he has achieved behind the scenes, Tyler being an amusing bullet point on that list to him. He may just be the one to pop my murder cherry.

How is that even a rational thought now?

JJ comes to mind, but I decide now is not the time to ask or panic, so, I compartmentalize that too. We turn left onto a highway and barrel away from town no destination in mind and barely a plan in place. I have no expectation of how this will end. Nickolas will never stop trying to kill me.

He stays hot on our trail, and we whip around corners in an attempt to lose him while the boys shout back and forth throwing a semblance of a plan together.

We come to a T in the road, us turning right, followed by Lyle and Silas and Finn turning left. I watch in the rearview mirror to see which way Nickolas follows.

My heart sinks as I see him drift the turn following behind us. The hope was for him to follow Silas.

"Fuck," Ian grumbles.

Lyle speeds up, getting closer to the back of our car. We speed up even more, my heart racing with adrenaline and fear as we turn corners, barely staying on the road. Lyle swerves back and forth on the road, Nickolas doing the same, trying to get around him.

I turn around in my seat and watch purposely as Lyle jerks his car from side to side, blocking him from passing.

"Hang on!" Ian yells before he slams on the brakes as soon as the other two cars are on the opposite side of the road. They shoot in front of us and my heart stops beating, a scream ripping through my throat. Nickolas clips the side of Lyle's car, sending it out of control and flipping his own.

Lyle's starts spinning, and my body goes ice cold, freezing my soul into glass and shattering it. My head screams, and bile rises as Lyle slams on his brakes, causing the wheels to lock up in black smoke and the car to flip.

It rolls again, and again, and again.

No. Oh, God. No.

We come to a stop, and I see Silas's truck coming down the road and slide to a stop next to us. Him and Finn throw themselves out of the vehicle.

Finn yells for his brother, but his voice is just an echo in my ringing ears. My chest rises and falls frantically as Silas and Finn sprint down the road, giving no regard to the van that skidded to a stop on the opposite side of the road. I peer through the windshield and see Nickolas unconscious, a large gash on his head.

I rip off my seat belt, yank the door open, and take off in a sprint toward Lyle's scraped and smashed car. Ian follows me out and reaches for my hand in an attempt to hold me in place, but I yank free.

"Mel, wait!" he yells after me, but again, I don't listen. I sprint at full speed, begging God it's not as bad as it looks.

All the windows are shattered, and the car landed top down.

My knees feel weak as I slow to a walk, mere feet away.

Ian must have chased after me, his arms now wrapping around me and pulling me back into his familiar chest.

Finn and Silas pull Lyle out of the driver-side window, carefully lifting his body through the shards of glass.

His eyes are cracked open, blood covering every inch of him. Flowing quickly from the large wounds on his stomach and the gashes on his head.

They drag him onto the pavement, and I rush to his side, placing my hands on his wound.

I look between the guys, and the emptiness that looks back at me shakes my soul.

Finn looks down at his brother as a tear rolls down his cheek and his hands shake.

Silas bows his head, shaking it slowly.

The streetlight shines directly on us.

"Do something!" I plead.

Ian kneels beside me, resting a hand on my thigh, tears falling rapidly as he reaches out to Lyle.

"Mel... I don't think there is anything we can do. He won't make it to the hospital."

I snap my head to the side and look at him with pained confusion, though I know he's right. I feel a wetness form under my knees and look down to see blood coating the asphalt.

"It's okay, Angel," Lyle chokes out, blood coating his lips.

My tears fall freely, and I panic.

"No," I cry, "It's not. I can't lose you!"

He forces a small smile, but I can see the pain he is trying not to show me. "You will be just fine without me, baby."

"You know that's not true! I can't do this without you," I beg, laying my head on his bloody chest.

"Look at me," he says softly.

I lift my head, peeling my eyes away from the quickly pooling blood, and he raises a shaky hand to my cheek.

"You can and you will. You will not let this break you." He pauses momentarily, sucking in a shaky breath with great effort.

"The world is a wicked place with pain always lurking around the corner. Happiness is something you fight for. Keep fighting."

I lean into his hand and nod softly at the familiar words. My throat constricts, preventing me from being able to speak.

I mentally hold on to the seconds we have left, wishing I could will them to last forever.

"I love you more than I have ever loved anything. My angel that will. Set the world on fire. It's been. A lovely view."

His sentences come out in choppy sections, each slower than the last. A pained cry leaves my throat in a hoarse moan. I place my hand atop his on my cheek, then feel it go slack.

My spine goes stiff, and I relax my hand, guiding his limp arm back to the ground.

"No! No! No! Don't go!"

His eyes close, and all his features relax.

I scream so loud my voice cracks. The tortured obliteration of my heart manifesting into one sound that could rattle Hell's gates.

"Mel," Silas chokes out painfully.

I scream again as I feel a part of my soul leave with his. I scream and scream, the pain unbearable as a man I love is torn from this world.

A smaller world.

Emptier.

Uglier.

I can't live in a world where Carlisle Jones doesn't exist.

Large arms wrap around me, and I'm hauled back from Carlisle's lifeless body.

"Let me go!" I beg. "I can't leave him like this!"

Finn lifts me to my feet and spins me to face him.

"Mel, look at me!" he says sternly, his own eyes pleading and pained.

I throw my fists into his chest over and over again, just wanting him to let go so I can hold Carlisle for a few more moments. My muscles tire, and my knees give out.

Finn wraps his arms around me, and we both fall to our knees. I burry my head into his chest digging my nails into his arms.

"Mel, you have to breathe!" he croaks his limbs shaking.

I can't. My heart feels like it was physically ripped out of my chest, and my lungs have collapsed. I wish they would so I could leave with the beautiful soul that has only ever wanted the best for me. I hate myself for ever fighting him on that. I will always regret every moment that I didn't give him everything.

Moments pass, an eternity of darkness, as Finn holds me in his embrace, and I sob uncontrollably. Ian takes my hand, placing a familiar pill in it. Finn looks at him, and Ian nods.

"You have to calm down. This isn't over yet," Finn whispers, rubbing his hand over my hair. I place the pill in my mouth and dry swallow it.

"Focus on my breathing and match yours to mine." Finn pulls me closer to his chest.

I do as he asks, unable to take my mind away from the pain but focusing enough on the movements and his pressure around me to slow my heart rate.

I hear laughter and Nickolas stumbles out of what's left of his holding his bleeding head.

The boys help me to my feet.

They all come to stand at my side, and we all turn to face him as an impenetrable wall, but I have never felt less solid in my life.

"You never learn, boy," he yells across the way. Silas's posture hardens, and I take his hand in mine. "You will always be weak! Don't you think your old man deserves justice?"

"Justice!?" I croak.

"Yes. Justice. Taking from those that have taken from you. Like how you'll want to kill my son once you finally learn the truth he's been hiding from you."

My head spins and whispers to me. I quickly glance to my left at Silas, who turns a shade of pale white that deeply contrasts his usual tan complexion.

"Don't," he orders his father, who plays with a gun hanging loosely at his side the smile of a psychopath plastered on his lips.

"I owe you nothing," Nickolas spits back. He mumbles as he taps the gun to his temple.

Silas steps forward, releasing my hand, and his father's gun aims at him.

"If you take one more fucking step before I've had my fun, I will kill you all just for shits and giggles." His eyes are void of any humanity, only sickness and ruin pouring out of him.

Silas stops, and his head lowers just an inch as he accepts whatever is about to come to light.

"You see, the big secret is that your poor old daddy wasn't hit by a drunk driver." Nickolas smiles even wider. "He was hit by my son on my orders."

My throat goes dry, and a single tear falls. I wasn't even sure that I had any left inside of me. I watch Silas out of the corner of my eye.

He looks... sad. Ashamed of what he has done and scared of what will happen now that I know.

Finn squeezes my right hand a little tighter.

It makes sense. There was always something more.

Something that I was missing, even after I found out who Silas truly is. There was still something about his guilt that was... more.

The voices gain volume in my mind, and my heart hardens and I pull my hand from Finn's.

The red out of the corner of my eye isn't a hallucination of anger; it's Carlisle's blood.

Tilting my head to the side, I walk that line of insanity as I stare at Nickolas.

"So, Damian was killed by your wishes. Carlisle was killed by your actions. Yet, you still think you deserve more than giving us a lifetime of pain?" I scoff a laugh. "You only got what you damn well deserved after beating your son his whole life and killing your own daughter. You are owed nothing, and you will take nothing more."

He steps forward, and I snatch the gun from Silas's waistband.

"You don't have the fucking guts," Nickolas laughs, standing firmly in place, completely unafraid of the gun directed at his face.

Anger and pain churn violently inside of me.

Then something snaps.

Any drop of uncertainty leaves my body, and my mind is deathly silent. Any dark, unaccepted part of myself has now become one with my soul.

"Wanna test that theory?" I step forward. "Move, I dare you."

I step again, and as he attempts to read me, I see him falter. The sound of guns loading behind me sends a sick excitement through me.

They have my back.

"You have broken this world more than any human has the right to."

I step again.

"You kill and destroy for no other reason than your own sick pleasure."

I pause but stand firm, and the three boys take my side like armor.

I step forward again, and no one stops me, as if they can feel the darkness swarming around me in determination.

"You are owed nothing," I repeat venomously, "Not from me and damn sure not from Silas. You broke him down to nothing. You are nothing."

I step.

"These boys picked him up and gave him a home."

Step.

"They became the family that you were too fucking weak to give him."

Step, now inches away from him.

Anger blares on his face, and he begins to speak, but I swiftly steal the words away from him, landing a right hook across his jaw, causing his head to jerk to the side.

"And me?" I breathe out, ducking under the hook that comes at me before landing another to his face.

This time he stumbles back taking a minute to regain composure.

"I am the one who taught him that it is okay to love. I brought out the man inside that is a hundred times the man you could ever dream of being because love is not a weakness. It's what makes a man truly great."

Nickolas spits blood at my feet and abruptly jumps towards me. "You stupid little bitch!"

I quickly raise the gun, take a step back, and shoot him in both knees. He collapses to the ground with a howl of pain and I soak in that sound and store it as a memory that I will forever hold dearly.

His pain is the sound of my own justice.

Finn steps forward and plants a boot in the center of his chest, kicking him backward and knocking his head so hard against the ground that it bounces a couple times.

I step over his knees and aim the gun once more.

Silas comes up behind me, but I don't take my eyes off Nickolas.

Finn and Ian stand on either side of his body. As his eyes roll around trying to focus, Finn gives the side of his head a firm kick, knocking him unconscious.

Silas reaches his arms around me placing his hands on mine. He feels like my shadow, like an extension. His firm stance solidifies my own, and his right hand pointer finger pushes mine to the trigger and rests on top.

"If you want to do this, we'll do it together. I won't let you carry this burden on your own."

I exhale a clipped breath and square my shoulders. Nothing will stop me from doing what I know I have to do, not even them.

Bang.

I flinch slightly at the sound, and Silas pulls the gun from my hand, passing it to Finn. He pulls me away from the second lifeless body that has been beneath me today. Pushing the hair out of my face he searches my eyes the way Carlisle always does.

Did.

"You did good. He's gone."

He's gone.

I turn, and the first face I see is the face of a broken brother. Silas and Ian lost a friend close enough to be a brother, but Finn lost his twin. Finn is without his brother for the first time in his entire life.

My heart cracks and I want to step toward him, but I can't force my feet to move.

Finn's angry eyes trail from Nickolas's still body to Carlisle's. Dark blood stains the road and our clothes. Finn looks down at his hands and wipes them off on his shirt. He wipes the tears that fall from his eyes and squares his shoulders.

"Make the calls."

Amelia

I refused to leave him. The boys begged me to see things rationally, explaining that leaving Carlisle in the street would make for an easier story and cleanup. But the thought of him being left on the asphalt for convenience made me physically sick. I fought like hell, vomiting the entire contents of my stomach between them after fighting them off me.

Finn was going through the motions, not allowing himself to grieve yet, and I lost it. They eventually caved, seeing me rave like a lunatic and promise them a life of hell if they could be so fucking cruel.

We placed Carlisle in Silas's truck and Ian drove us home. Now, I sit freshly showered as Finn inspects my body. My easily bruised skin is beginning to show evidence of Nickolas's short-lived torment. Finn is clear of any major damage, most of his discoloration coming from my own fists, most likely the same for the other two.

I listen as Ian makes calls to clean up the scene, but my mind stays on Lyle's wrapped body lying in the bed of Silas's truck, waiting to be taken away.

Nickolas's frantic escape from prison will be the cause of the accident. Any evidence of gunshot wounds will be erased, and the two deaths, once we find them, will be ruled as missing persons.

The sun is still hours from rising, giving us a few more hours to wreak havoc in the shadows before we have to revisit the highway and call like we just found him.

In the meantime, all calls in the city are jammed. The only downside is we can't call JJ. She left a message to Finn, saying she was safe and at her mom's house. With no reason for anyone to be after her, we have to trust that she is safe for now.

Silas cringes as he sits at the kitchen island and I know he can feel my eyes burning a hole into the side of his head.

I get up from the couch, and he stands.

"We need to leave."

Blocking his path, I reach for the hem of his shirt, and he swats at my hand. I tilt my head, daring him to do it again. I reach once more only to be met with the same thing. I swiftly slam my fist into his gut, and he grunts, gripping his left shoulder.

"Just let her see it, Si," Ian sighs.

Silas pulls his right arm out of his shirt, then pulls it over his head and off his left side, revealing a square bandage.

"Why the fuck didn't you tell me you got shot?" I say, shoving him down into a chair.

He continues his attempt to shrug me off like an overbearing mother.

"It's just a flesh wound."

Fuck this.

"I just lost one of you! What the fuck is the matter with you?" I slap him across the face with a heavy hand.

He takes it and his jaw ticks. I instantly regret it, but say nothing, inspecting the entrance and exit wounds.

The bleeding is slow, and I hate that he didn't see a problem with keeping it from me. I grab the aid kit from the cabinet and set out the needle and thread with slow movements.

"We will uh- meet you guys outside," Finn says, nodding to Ian to follow him out the front door.

I get into position, holding onto his warm shoulder pinching the skin together. I don't warn him before shoving the needle through the skin, but he doesn't flinch. My eyes drift over his tattooed skin counting the number of hidden scars I can find to keep me distracted from his stare I feel on the side of my face.

I lose count and cut the string then move behind him to close the exit.

"Penny for your thoughts?" he finally asks.

"I think," I sew the last stitch and cut it, "that this will heal just fine, and you are an asshole." I say patting him on the shoulder before I walk away to put shoes on.

He sighs. "That's not what I meant."

I know what he meant.

"Can I please-"

"No."

I exit the front door and shut it before he can say another word, exhaling once it separates us. I am not ready to talk about it.

Right now, I want to find the sorry son of a bitch that has death knocking on his door. My heart aches for JJ, but I know after what he has done, it won't be hard for her to believe he just left.

Amelia

Five days have passed since we found Tyler hiding in the basement of Davis Due Process and Emma cowering behind Jameson in his locked office.

The same building went up in flames that night, resulting in the *devastating* death of Jameson and his two interns, Tyler and Emma, who were working late.

The news ran with the story, an escaped convict's retaliation against the firm that incarcerated him, that ended with him taking the innocent life of Acadia Creek's Carlisle Jones in his attempt to flee the city.

Five days have passed since the last time I heard *his* voice and I've spent every moment possible curled up in his bed, clinging to the smell of *him* still lingering on his sheets. I have worn nothing but his hoodie, as if anything else would be a betrayal. I spent hours crying in hysteria until I finally fell asleep, only to be met with a nightmare matching my reality.

My head lies on his pillow in Ian's lap. Each time I lay here, I feel both, closer and farther away from *him*. Eventually, his bed will begin to smell like me and not him, and that day is a day that will wreck any progress I make all over again, just like today.

We buried *him* today. It was small and intimate, but seeing the black coffin and fresh dirt destroyed me. I met his uncle, and I know he would have loved that, but I knew he would have wanted to be here for it even more.

We decided he wouldn't have wanted a sappy funeral full of tears and sadness. Throwing a party in his honor would be more his style. Music, cars, and laughter. Telling stories and sharing memories we have to celebrate all the time we had with *him* instead of mourning all the time we lost.

But I will be doing both.

Ian strokes my hair softly, and silent tears fall down my eyes. The kind that fall freely without a sound. The kind that your soul weeps when the tears from your body fighting and bracing through the pain have come and gone.

"It's time," Ian whispers.

I stay staring at the open closet doors full of clothes that will never be worn by their rightful owner again and I softly shake my head.

"Mel, you have to let him know what's going on in your head."

I can't. How can I when that would mean I would have to redirect my thoughts away from *him* for even the smallest amount of time?

I barely eat or drink anything. Every move I make feels wrong and misplaced. I want to keep my promise to *him* that I won't let this break me, but how do you convince your heart of such a thing when it knows a piece of it has died?

Ian shifts and slides out from under me. My eyes follow him as leaves the room, passing Silas in the doorway. He leans against the frame, his arms hanging at his side. Looking like himself but not. He looks sad. Scared. Withering.

Not only has he lost *him*, but he fears he has lost me.

"Can I sit?" His voice is low- careful.

I nod but don't move from my spot in the center of the bed, and he slides in next to me.

"The psych hospital called. She's calmer now if you decide you want to visit."

I shake my head, sitting up. I have no intention of seeing her. I'm glad she's getting help, but I breathe a little easier with her gone.

He tilts my chin up. "I need you to talk to me, little monster. Tell me that you hate me."

A smile twitches in the corner of my mouth. "I hate you."

I hear a quick breath of air leave him in a half-laugh, still sounding nervous.

"More than before?"

More than before learning he lied to me.

To all of us.

Ian and Finn are still royally pissed. The fresh shiner under Silas's left eye, matching the one I gave him, a clear indicator of that. Though if I needed to do worse to come to terms with what he did, he would stand there and take whatever I dished out without a single word. He threw up the first night we came home and in the gym all hours of the night since then. He is punishing himself.

"No."

Silas is a difficult person to read and love. He can be cruel, but if there is one thing I am sure about in this world, it is that he would never intentionally hurt someone he loved. So, I give him that chance to explain. I talk to him, not as the man who belittled me and punished me when I first came to stay here, but as the man I have loved since I was fourteen.

"That night, I got a call from Nickolas. He was pissed that I wasn't stepping up." Silas shifts in his seat, his eyes low. "He told me I was being followed and if I didn't step up soon, he would eliminate the problem." I reach for his hand, and he swallows hard. "The accident... I thought he was someone working for my dad.... both of us were headed for your house, and I couldn't let him get to you."

His glossy eyes meet mine, a tear falling down his cheek. "I thought I was protecting the family I made." He shakes his head, stiffening his body. "But I ruined everything. Nickolas found out I was in love with you and to him, it was betrayal that couldn't stand."

It was the perfect trap, start his revenge journey and get his son on the path he wanted. With Jameson in his pocket, he had only one target left. Me.

Rather I fell for them or not, I was always going to be a part of this life. But it was all of their love that saved me.

He sniffs, his eyes meeting mine and his hands trembling. "You know, I was planning on revealing who I was that night. I was on my way to drop off the letter."

My heart stings at knowing just how close I was to having him. To being free of my torment.

Silas kept the truth, knowing at the time, it would destroy me. Nothing would overcome the storm that would have ripped through everything Finn and Lyle were trying to build, and it would have been the end before it even began. If I stayed, I had to love all of them. All or nothing.

Always, all or nothing.

I have always been all or nothing. I love entirely and without yield. I love too hard and too fast. I hate too hard and ache too hard. I feel everything, or I feel nothing.

Never in between.

I take Silas's hand in mine, running my thumb over his red and purple knuckles. I trace the scars and feel the cracks that never healed right, new and old. Tilting my head up I watch a tear fall down his cheek and onto his arm. I lean into him and swipe it away.

His golden eyes stay focused on mine, and for the first time, I can see everything. I can see every bit of his pain and every ounce of his love. I can feel him in a way he has never let me do so before. All the words written softly with love but never spoken in daylight were now everywhere around us.

Crawling into his lap I wrap my arms around his neck, breathing in his smell now instead of *his*.

It hurts, but I welcome it because he needs me.

"I don't blame you for his death." Tears tinge my voice, and this time, though my jaw aches, my tears are not from fighting or mourning but from love and acceptance.

Their deaths were not a result of Silas's actions, and I know that's what he fears. Their death is on the hands of a dead man, and now, Silas can finally breathe without the weight of his burdens pulling him down and restricting him.

He is free to be, no apologies or hesitation.

"You may be my monster, Silas, but you are not evil. And you are not guilty of anything more than loving with a heart bigger than this world is capable of appreciating."

His head falls into the crook of my neck.

And for the first time, Silas truly cries.

He lets everything out, letting me bare his pain once more. He guides me backward, and between soft whimpers, he kisses up my neck and across my jaw. I squeeze my eyes shut forcefully, and *his* scent fills my nose. I feel the ghost of *his* hands running across my skin everywhere that Silas touches me.

I'm sorry. I'm so sorry.

Silas's fingers dig deep into my sides, bruised by his father's beating. A tear slips, and rough fingers smooth it into my hairline.

"Look at me."

I do, and my lip trembles. I don't know how to continue doing this. I don't know how to feel not guilty every time one of them kisses me or tells me they love me.

He will never be a part of those things again. *He* will never be able to tell me those things again.

"Take the time you need, but don't you dare push us away out of guilt. He is always going to be with you, and he will kick your ass from beyond if he finds out that you stop living."

I smile. I smile wide and true for the first time in five days because I know he's right.

Silas slides down the length of my body and rests his head at the apex of my thighs. He plants a single kiss on my scars, reminding me of where we've been.

"There will never be enough words or enough time, but I will spend every day trying to repent for my mistakes and keep you from breaking your promises. This, right here, is where I will pray."

He keeps his face in my legs and wraps his arms under my body.

"I beg you, hold on. Forgive me. And remember the promises you made to each of us."

I run my fingers through the back of his hair, soothing both of our aching souls while sending a prayer of my own to wherever *he* is waiting for me.

I promise I will keep fighting for happiness.

One month later...

It's the last week of summer. She looks better. Her color has come back, and she's smiling more now. I still catch her drifting off into space sometimes and hear her crying in the shower most nights. She moved all of her things into Lyle's room and refuses to sleep anywhere else, but she asks us to sleep in there with her now. I admit that I like that, and though I do my best to seem solid for her, some nights in his room, I whisper up to him with tears in my eyes and my heart in my throat.

We're all still grieving and will be for a very long time.

I lost my brother – my other half.

Nothing will ever take that pain from my chest. Time doesn't heal wounds on the heart, but it eventually makes them easier to carry with you.

They aren't the wounds you want healed, they are wounds reminding you that what you lost means too much to you to forget. Remembering why it hurts is what gives you purpose as you continue living without it.

My brother's presence is everywhere in this house and at the shop, where she also spends a lot of time. She asked that we teach her so she can take over his spot there. I think she's scared that she'll forget parts of him over time, but I don't think she could if she tried.

He impacted her life the way the moon impacts the ocean. His pull will always have a hold on her, even now. Which makes missing him a little easier to carry.

I see him in her, and nothing but death will take her from us.

The small concert an hour away from Acadia Creek has her swaying side to side in an oversized maroon Alabama hoodie, wearing it as a dress with knee-high black boots and a matching cap. Her hair pulled back into a ponytail, showing the length of her neck and scattered freckles almost always hidden. She feels the music, really listening to every word with Silas holding onto her hips possessively.

She has been more suspicious of us crowding her now that there are no more names to cross off our list, for the time being, at least. So determined to keep herself busy that she doesn't even realize tomorrow is her birthday.

After Silas brought it to our attention last week and said that it was once her favorite day of the year, we were determined to make this one count. Especially since it marks a month since Lyle's death, so we knew that we had to do this right.

I'm not entirely sure she realizes that milestone, either.

Something grabs her attention through the crowd, and she taps my arm.

"I'll be right back," she says before weaving through the crowd.

Silas and I keep our distance but follow close behind. We stop when she does. She's only a few feet in front of us, separated by a few bodies, standing in front of a blond a few inches taller than her wearing little to no clothes.

"Rubie?" Amelia asks something dark in her expression.

Ah, fuck.

Amelia's eyes travel to the girl's torso and then back up to her face. "Glad to see you're not pregnant."

"Wha-" Rubie tries to ask something but is quickly knocked to her ass by Amelia's right hook.

"Oh shit," Silas chuckles.

The crowd parts and moves away with gasps and low comments. Some guy, assumingly Rubie's boyfriend, starts quickly moving towards our girl, dropping the drinks he appears to have just bought. The second he reaches for her, we are there. I drape my arms over Amelia's shoulders and look down at Rubie, still on her ass, and smirk.

"Don't be stupid," Silas warns holding the boyfriend by his neck.

You can see the regret in the poor dude's eyes as Silas releases him. He rubs his neck, picks Rubie up from the ground, and they scurry away.

"Have a good night!" Mel yells after them, and Silas chuckles.

"Atta girl," he praises with a wink.

The band clears the stage, and the lights dim. The crowd's chatter grows as the next performers set up.

I move next to Amelia, and she interlocks her fingers with mine without having to even look my way. I'm nervous. Butterflies fill my stomach, and I can feel the sweat forming between our hands. I meticulously watch the dark stage while listening to her talk to Silas.

She laughs as they banter playfully, and I smile that she is once again finding joy in irritating him. Silas calls her impossible and spins her around for a kiss, not letting go of my hand. She scrunches her nose in the adorable way she does when we are able to shut her up.

I check the time. Midnight on the dot.

The stage lights up the entire grass field, and a new vocalist yells an excited greeting into the microphone,

"Good evening, San Anderson!"

Amelia's eyes widen. She tries to turn, but Silas holds her in place with a grin enjoying the surprise and confusion on her face.

The vocalist strums his guitar as the drummer begins a low intro beat behind him. "I'd like to dedicate this song to the first and only woman I will ever love with every fiber of my being. Happy Birthday, Amelia Mason!"

Silas releases her, and she spins. Her hand jumps to her mouth, covering up the biggest smile as she lays eyes on Ian in center stage. He mirrors her smile and points directly at her through the crowd. Then plays.

He plays hard and with his whole body. He sings, pouring his entire soul into the song they wrote together.

A song that ties us all together.

Tears of happiness stream down her face, and she screams the lyrics back at him. She doesn't care that her voice is the only one coming from the crowd. She doesn't care that people turn and watch her. She sings her heart out with our hands in hers.

The song ends, and I kiss her head. She turns to us and swipes the tears that just keep coming. Her cheeks and nose are red and puffy, but her eyes are happy.

"*He* would have loved this." She's still smiling, but I can see the sting underneath.

"He did. Can't you feel him?" Silas asks, and she nods, slow at first and then faster. The tears come faster, and she cries a little harder.

"I do. I always do."

And she always will. We all will.

Because Lyle didn't just touch our hearts. He touched our souls.

A heart stops beating, but a soul is what makes you who you are, and Lyle will forever be intertwined in each of ours.

Amelia

"It was perfect." I can't find all the words I want to say because words will never be enough. There are some things so beautiful in the world that such simplicity will never do it justice.

My birthday was the last thing on my mind because I wasn't watching the months. I was watching the days - the hours.

Thirty days. And all I wanted to do was lay in *his* bed and eat *his* favorite snacks, but I had done enough of that. So I fought for my happiness, and allowed them to drag me to the rock concert I knew was no coincidence, falling on the day it did.

Ian and those strings.

"I'm glad you loved it, baby, but we do have one more surprise for you that we think will be very..." Ian trails off, grinning over at Silas.

"...Therapeutic," he finishes.

I take Finn's outstretched hand, and follow their guidance into our gym. Silas unlocks the new chain that loops through the door's handles and pushes them open then flips on the light.

The padded floors and walls are covered with tarps, and in the center of the room, a man dangles from where the punching bag usually hangs. I stare at the backside of the dangling man venturing closer.

I would know that head of hair body build anywhere.

"Lance," I purr, "You are very hard to track down when you're not making my life hell."

He dropped off the face of the earth, paying with cash and using burner phones.

"We found him holed up in a drug house," Ian says as I move around to the front of Lance.

He murmurs behind the gag in his mouth.

"Oh, I know. I'm so sorry I kept you waiting, but it looks like you were welcomed properly." I shoot an accusing look at the three guards standing behind him.

Silas shrugs without an ounce of shame for the bloody mess they left him in.

I grab the bloodied knife from the weight bench with my right hand and press the sharpened tip of it to my left index finger. Twirling it in circles, I pace in front of him, not minding the bead of blood it draws.

"I have no desire to waste any more of my time or breath on you, so I do hope you understand the sincerity in my voice when I tell you that although this will be quick, I do wish you an eternity in Hell."

He jerks his body frantically, futilely attempting to break from the chain holding him. And I move closer, truly loving how the tables have turned. I turn the knife in my fist, enjoying the fear in his eyes as he waits for my next move.

I keep my face void of emotion as I slice his pants open and his underwear off. The perfect opportunity to make a joke about the room being cold comes, but I let it pass.

I swiftly slice at his member and watch as it falls at an awkward angle, still attached but gushing blood. I bet I could have cut it clean off if it wasn't lying flaccidly against his balls.

The color in his face begins to drain. So I take the knife and jam it into his stomach, then using all my weight, I jerk it in a downward motion. He grunts, and blood spills from him, coating my legs and bare feet.

Silas moves to the wall and unravels the chain, dropping Lance's dying body to the tarped floor.

For good measure, I straddle his chest and slice through his neck. Watching as the deep crimson blood spills from his mouth, life draining from his eyes.

I feel absolutely no regret or fear. Only justice.

Standing, I huff a breath, feeling much lighter than before.

"You were right. I needed that." I hand the knife to Finn. "Make sure to wash this so it doesn't rust."

I raise my arms for Ian to lift me bridal-style and carry me to the bathroom without tracking blood through the house.

"Oh, yeah. I'm touching myself tonight," Silas says loudly.

Oh, no.

I'm fucking all three of them tonight.

Ian sets me on my feet inside the shower, and we both strip down now that he is wearing Lance's blood too. I tilt my head under the water, letting it wash the small amount of blood that made it into the long strands.

Ian's hands roam my skin, and the smell of coconut and almond fills the large shower as he washes me. His hands palm my breasts, and I hum an approving noise. He spins us around just as the door opens, and another body slides in behind me. Silas licks up the back side of my neck, and I shutter.

"Were you trying to have some more fun without us, Meda?"

I smile. "No, of course not. That would be inconsiderate."

"Damn right," Finn says, opening the door again, allowing the floor to get soaking wet just so he can watch.

Silas chuckles. His hands running up the length of my sides before he pulls me against his chest. He continues to lick and bite my neck and shoulder, driving me wild. I wrap my arms around his neck and Ian picks me up by my thighs and slides between my legs. He fists his hard length and rubs it up and down my center, teasing me.

"Do you see what you do to me?" he asks, holding my eyes intensely.

His head pushes into me slowly, then pulls out abruptly. He does this over and over again, pulling out every time I frustratedly buck my hips. He smiles wickedly, amused as his eyes see deep into mine.

"Baby, please!" I beg.

"Please, what?" he purrs.

"Fuck me. Please fuck me!"

He slams into me with one solid thrust and I cry out, digging my nails into the back of Silas's neck.

Silas groans pleasurably at the pain, his chest no doubt aching too. He squeezes me tighter and pulls my legs up higher like he is offering me to Ian with a prayer for him to ravage me.

Ian wraps one hand around the back of my neck and cups Silas's shoulder with the other, using us both to give me everything he has. Silas's body rocks with mine, his dick repeatedly tapping my ass.

I'm loud, crying from the pain I love, begging for more. I want everything he can give me until neither one of us can stand.

I hear the small grunts from Finn stroking himself as he watches. I hear Ian whimper only seconds before spilling into me, but he doesn't stop thrusting until his body is jumping from overstimulation.

Silas releases me, and I turn to meet his hand on top of my head. He guides me to my knees and I take him into my mouth, loving the sound he makes as he touches the back of my throat.

I wrap my hands around his thighs taking him as deep and fast as possible. Working him with everything I have.

I crave him. I want to please him. I want him to be begging to be inside of me.

I gurgle, slurp, and gag, finding the more sounds I make, the more it drives him wild. I move one of my hands between his legs and cup his balls squeezing lightly and roll them in my fist. They tighten and I'm jerked up to my feet.

Silas spins me, shoving me down once more with a firm hand in the center of my back, leveling me with Ian's dick standing at attention for me once again. I take him into my mouth, and he braces himself on the wall, giving Silas a little more room to move. Silas slams into me with a smack on my ass. And it stings so fucking good. I wiggle my ass on him, and he growls.

"You have no idea how fucking good you feel around me."

He slaps me so hard I gasp before moaning around Ian as tears run down my face. Silas fucks me with everything he has. He claws, chokes, and slaps me, pounding into me like he can't get deep enough. Like nothing will ever be close enough, like he has to brand himself inside of me.

My back and sides deliciously burn with his marks, and my pussy aches. Silas comes hard with a grunt, his hands soothing every inch of my sore skin, followed by kisses down my spine.

I look over to see Finn cleaning himself up, and in a blink, my heart calls out for *him*.

Finn holds a towel out for me once I finish washing again. He wraps me, and I giggle as he sprints from the bathroom with me in his arms, trying to steal me away. The other two yell obscenities at him from down the hall and chase after us, dicks flopping.

We topple onto the bed, laughing as they fight over me. I am yanked and pulled. Fist and feet flying.

My heart is full, and my soul is happy. For the first time in a long time, I am completely and utterly happy without a single fear haunting my dreams. There is nothing more I could want.

Then I hear the one thing that proves me wrong.

"Listen," I say.

We wait.

Then it comes again.

Boom.

Thunder sounds from outside, and rain tatters the glass. We all smile and relax into each other, just listening as we share this with *him*.

I hear you, Hellcat.

Silas

2 Years Later

"You know, I always wondered what you wished for that night y'all surprised me with the car," Amelia says from the bathroom getting ready for our date.

I smile, remembering that night like it was yesterday. "I wished selfishly that we could go back in time before the accident, and I could have you to myself."

I pull my shirt on, looking at myself in the mirror, picturing the broken man that stood in my place back then.

She pokes her head out, keeping the rest of her body hidden from me. "Really? Don't let the boys hear that."

"No, I wished for a bigger dick."

She rolls her eyes and disappears again.

"Meda, come on. We're gonna be late," I say, pleading with her as I smooth the sides of my hair back.

Finally the bathroom door swings open and Amelia steps through the frame wearing a strappy leather piece of lingerie. Garter straps around her thighs connect to the fabric around her waist, the right side holding a knife.

I raise a brow and she smirks.

I open my mouth the speak.

"Shh," she says, holding a finger to her red lips.

She tosses her long hair over her shoulder, sauntering up to me, lust clouding her eyes.

"Get on the bed," she says, walking me backward until my legs hit the bed, then pushes me onto my back.

Straddling my legs, her eyes fall to the bulge in my jeans. She brushes her hand over it softly and my head falls back with a groan.

"I wanna play," she says, teasing my lower stomach.

Fuck our dinner plans.

"You are playing a dangerous game, baby." I smirk.

Her hand rushes to my face, squeezing my cheeks with a tight grip, her nails digging in. "I said, shut. The fuck. Up."

My eyes go wide as she scoots further up, grinding on me. My hands move to her waist, only to be met with a slap.

"Don't touch. Don't move." She leans in close. "Don't make a sound."

My minds reels from such a new sensation, but I don't hate it.

She reaches to the side of the bed, grabbing a long strip of silk fabric and wraps it around my eyes, enhancing my senses.

Warm breath trails down my chest and my dick aches with need the lower she gets. She stops just above my pants, planting a small kiss there. I hear the flick of a lighter, then silence followed by a sensation of pain. My pec burns, and the rest of my chest follows as she drags it down to where her mouth stopped.

I suck in a breath and the pain turns sharp. The cold tip of her blade digs into my skin before she takes it away.

"You know, my fascination with fire started after one of your letters."

The lighter flicks again and the pause is longer.

She drags the hot blade down my chest and my mind struggles to think back all those years to remember what I wrote.

"Set the world on fire," she says, digging the cooled edge into my skin again, just enough to hurt.

"Those words came from you first. I don't know how I didn't put that together sooner."

Her blade hits the floor before her hands mess with the button of my jeans freeing my dick.

I do my best to play by her rules, fighting the urge to grab her hair and fuck her mouth, punishing her for the way she's talking to me.

Her warm breath trails down the side of my dick, her lips hovering teasingly. She repeats it on the other side and I ball my fists to keep my composure. She giggles softly, enjoying my suffering.

"I was so caught up in everything that I didn't see just how much you were begging for me to hate fuck you."

Her tongue flicks the head of my dick and I jolt, clamping my teeth so hard they almost crack.

She flicks her lighter, and the anticipation is agonizing. The flame runs along the outside of my thigh and over my hip, stopping at the base of my dick. Instantly thankful I decided to shave everything for her this week.

She flicks it again, dragging it up the length of my dick.

My mouth falls open and I pant.

Fuck.

I need her soon, or I'm gonna fucking lose it.

"Have you been a bad boy, baby? Do you need to be punished?"

Nearly bursting at the seams, I nod, obeying her order not to talk.

Fuck, yes. Hurt me baby.

"Yeah, you have been a very bad boy." She climbs back up my body and my body sings with anticipation. My dick brushes her pussy as her lips hover above mine.

She licks up the side of my neck, nipping my earlobe with her teeth.

"Think about this the next time you think about keeping a secret from me, Perseus."

It takes a moment for the brain fog to clear, her words not registering until my body goes cold from her absence and the bedroom door closes.

I rip off the blind fold, dick hard and temper flaring.

"Amelia!" I boom, only to be met with hysterical laughter.

Amelia

"Have you checked your messages from Ian today?" I ask, flicking the ashes off my blunt.

Silas grunts from under the truck he's working on. "No. Been tied up today, little monster." He grunts again, tightening something I can't see.

"You wanna get tied up? Is that what you said?" I ask playfully, hopping down off the tall toolbox and setting my blunt on top.

He slides out, just far enough to grab another tool and raises a brow at me. "What did Ian say?" He pushes back under, resuming his work.

"The new girl working at the hospital with JJ, is indeed a prostitute."

Silas hums a sound of acknowledgment. "Hand me that wrench."

I pass the tool under the truck. "She's really bad off. Beaten to hell most days. Ian wants us to help."

"So, are we just collecting strays now? First JJ and now a hooker?" Silas asks, a hint of annoyance in his tone.

"JJ is family." I prop my hand on my hip. "Are you seriously gonna say no because you haven't gotten to play with me by yourself this week?"

He slides out again and sits up, reaching for his grease rag. "Maybe."

Liar.

"Are you going to keep running your mouth until I put my dick in it?"

The bell rings as someone pushes through the shop door.

"Mel, someone's here to see you!," Ally, our receptionist, yells out.

"I'm coming," I say, motioning a dick going in my mouth, eyes rolling back, before I turn and start running to the front desk.

Silas quickly follows behind, pinching my ass.

I round the corner, out of breath with grease now on the ass of my shorts.

"Holy shit, what are you doing here?" I smile.

"Hey, darlin. I thought it was 'bout time I come see my boys." Mark says, meeting Silas for a hug with a smile across his face. He turns, wrapping an arm around me. planting a kiss on top of my head.

"And my favorite girl, of course." He releases me, looking me over with an adoring smile. "I ran into Ian at the house. Where's Finn?"

"He's playing doctor until six," I say with pride. "He'll be home all weekend though."

Mark nods and looks around the shop, taking in the changes we've made since he last saw it. He smiles at the neon sign reading 'Jones Automotive.'

"Y'all did good. He would have been so proud, honey."

My eyes sting as I hold back the tears, overwhelmed with love and pride.

"How long are you in town for?" I ask, grabbing a bottle of water from the mini fridge.

"Just a week or so. Passing through."

The joy on his face says he's living his life to the fullest.

"You wanna meet for dinner? We don't have plans tonight and ours got messed up the other night," I ask.

Silas grumbles from beside me, but I ignore him.

"I'd love to." Mark holds his hand up and my eyes land on the new gold band residing on his ring finger. "We have a lot of catching up to do."

I smile, glancing down at the emerald stone on my left hand.

"Yes we do."

Bonus Scene

1 year and 6 months after our hearts broke

Amelia

1 year and 6 months later...

My hair dances across my face in the wind and I close my eyes breathing in the crisp air. Digging my toes into the cool sand, the sound of the water brushing the shore calms my mind. This lake has become my favorite place.

A shadow falls over me before a warm body sits behind me. Finn wraps his body around mind, propping his chin on my shoulder. Tilting my head to his, I inhale deeply, a shaky exhale following.

"He loved this place almost as much as you do. Y'all were alike in so many ways," Finn says, making my heart crack in my chest. My jaw tightens as I hold back tears.

"I never thanked you," I say softly, watching the sun sink lower in the sky.

"For what?" He presses his lips to my temple.

"Bringing me into all of this. Putting such a perfect life in my hands when it was just out of reach." He pulls my hands from where they hold my legs and turns them over in his hands.

Finn huffs a laugh, "This is the perfect life you dreamed of?"

I smile, and for a second it fades for my missing piece. Memories bring *him* back, the lessons in strength I have learned firm it, and the love I have, for those living and dead, secure it. I smile again. "Something like that."

He hums, intertwining our hands. "You know, it never gets easier, living without my brother." His fingers brush over mine softly, his voice heavy and still so full of sorrow. "But it makes it hurt a little less knowing that he died for something bigger than himself. He died for love, and that's all he wanted out of life."

He sniffs and my heart aches, longing for just one more touch, though I know that would never be enough.

"Before he died, he ordered something for you. We've added to it and have been holding onto it, waiting for the right time," Finn says, getting to his feet. I look up at him curiously and take his outstretched hand. "Come on, I want to show you."

He leads me back to the house and my heart starts pounding in my chest with anticipation. He spins me toward him as we make it to the back porch, the curtains drawn, hiding something inside.

Finn's eyes sparkle with mischief and excitement. "Close your eyes."

Eyes closed, the sliding door opens. Soft music fills the room and I'm led inside.

"He knew you loved it here," Finn says.

"And he knew we couldn't live without you," Ian says, his voice coming from the left of Finn.

"And we all agreed with that," Silas says, coming from the right. "So if you want to open your eyes, we have a question for you."

Heart in my throat, I swallow hard, my eyes flittering open. The lights are low, and candles are scattered throughout the room. The three of them stand in front of me with nervous smiles on their faces, a picture of Carlisle sits on the bar to the left of Ian.

"From all of us." They sink to one knee and tears sting my eyes as I look down at them.

Finn pulls a little black box from his pocket, opening it to reveal a breathtaking emerald ring with intertwined diamond bands.

"Amelia Mason, will you marry us?" they ask in unison.

My tears fall and a sob rips from my chest, a smile spreading across my face as I nod frantically.

"Yes?" Silas asks enthusiastically.

"Yes!" I sink to my knees and kiss each of them again and again. "A million times, yes."

Finn takes the ring out of the box, and I hold out my hand, laughing through the tears as he slides the ring onto my hand. It's perfect.

"We got it in the mail months after he was gone," Finn says. "The three of us picked out the bands together once we knew there was no questioning the decision."

Silas takes my hand, rubbing his thumb over the large stone. "We chose to replace the center diamond with an emerald, so you'd always have a piece of him with you."

Ian grabs the picture frame from the bar and I take it from him, looking over every feature. "We knew without a doubt that this is what he wanted," Ian says and tears of happiness fall on the glass like rain, my ring shimmering green like *his* beautiful eyes.

Yes. This is the life I dreamed of.

Acknowledgments

Thank you to all the readers that took the time to read my first novel. I hope there is something in here that helps you find hope in this cruel world.

I have so much appreciation for my few friends that supported and encouraged me to go on this new and wild adventure of writing.

To the lovely Rachel and her golden pen that provides endless hours of wisdom. You have been my rock on so many occasions, and your beautiful words have truly impacted how this story was told.

To you, Kelsie, I could not love you enough for taking the time out of your busy life to help me edit my first draft. The endless hours we have spent laughing until we peed ourselves have been epic, and I will forever cherish your friendship.

Also, a huge fuck you/thank you to the boy that ruined a young girl but indirectly made her an even stronger woman. You gave me a shit ton of baggage and not a single orgasm. That takes talent.

Most importantly, thank you to my husband for always being my shelter in the storm and for showing me that when you find the right person, no amount of damage can mean you are unworthy of love or forgiveness. You love so fiercely, and if it came down to it, I know you would burn this whole world down for me.
You are my real-life book boyfriend.

Made in United States
Orlando, FL
12 December 2024